THE
SACRED
LAND

H. N. TURTELTAUB

TOR®

A TOM DOHERTY ASSOCIATES BOOK
NEW YORK

This is a work of fiction. All the characters and events portrayed in this book are either products of the author's imagination or are used fictitiously.

THE SACRED LAND

Copyright © 2003 by H. N. Turteltaub

Edited by Patrick Nielsen Hayden
Maps by Mark Stein Studios

A Tor Book
Published by Tom Doherty Associates, LLC
175 Fifth Avenue
New York, NY 10010

www.tor.com

Tor® is a registered trademark of Tom Doherty Associates, LLC.

ISBN 0-765-35072-6
EAN 978-0765-35072-5

First edition: December 2003
First mass market edition: March 2005

Printed in the United States of America

0 9 8 7 6 5 4 3 2 1

BATTLE IN A BACKWATER

Aristeidas peered out from a south-facing crevice between two good-sized stones. After perhaps a quarter of an hour had passed, he stiffened. "Here they come!"

"Oh, a pestilence!" Sostratos exclaimed. He'd been cautious, yes, but he hadn't really believed the Ioudaioi would come back and try to rob his companions and him. But when he peered south himself, he saw that Aristeidas was right. The Ioudaioi were loping across the fields toward the boulders among which the Rhodians sheltered.

"Shoot the gods-detested catamites!" Moskhion said.

Sostratos put an arrow in the bow and drew a bead on the closest Ioudaian. The fellow wasn't quite in range yet, but he would be soon. Sostratos drew the arrow back to his breast and then, in Persian fashion, back to his ear. The would-be robber ran straight at him—probably hadn't seen him there among the rocks.

Well, too bad for him, Sostratos thought, and let fly.

The Sacred Land *is dedicated to Patrick Nielsen Hayden, in friendship, with much appreciation for his enthusiasm about the adventures of Menedemos and Sostratos, and for being everything an editor should be.*

A NOTE ON
WEIGHTS, MEASURES, AND MONEY

I have, as best I could, used in this novel the weights, measures, and coinages my characters would have used and encountered in their journey. Here are some approximate equivalents (precise values would have varied from city to city, further complicating things):

1 digit = 3/4 inch	12 khalkoi = 1 obolos
4 digits = 1 palm	6 oboloi = 1 drakhma
6 palms = 1 cubit	100 drakhmai = 1 mina (about 1
1 cubit = 1½ feet	pound)
1 plethron = 100 feet	60 minai = 1 talent
1 stadion = 600 feet	

As noted, these are all approximate. As a measure of how widely they could vary, the talent in Athens was about 57 pounds, while that of Aigina, less than 30 miles away, was about 83 pounds.

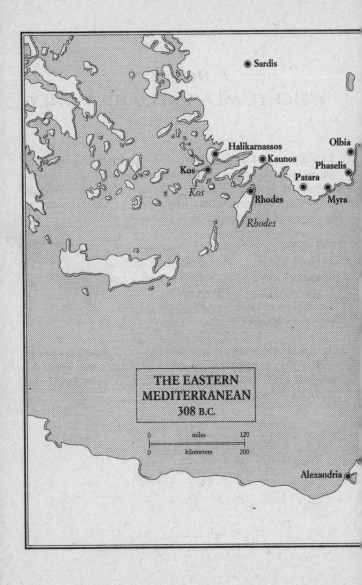

Sardis

Halikarnassos

Olbia

Kaunos

Phaselis

Kos

Patara

Kos

Myra

Rhodes

Rhodes

**THE EASTERN
MEDITERRANEAN
308 B.C.**

| 0 | miles | 120 |

| 0 | kilometers | 200 |

Alexandria

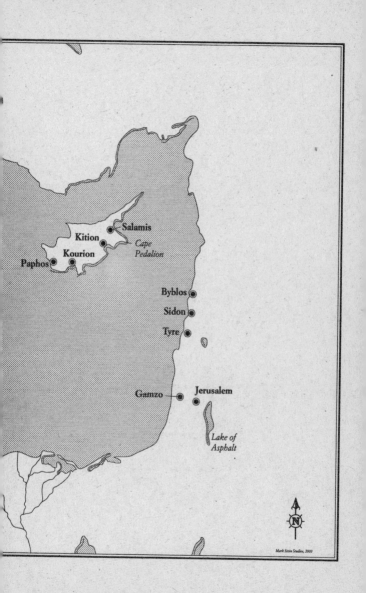

Salamis

Kition

Kourion

Paphos

*Cape
Pedalion*

Byblos

Sidon

Tyre

Gamzo

Jerusalem

*Lake of
Asphalt*

N

Mark Stein Studios, 2003

SOMETHING BETWEEN DRIZZLE AND LIGHT rain pattered down out of the sky onto the city of Rhodes. Every time a raindrop struck the flame of the torch Sostratos was carrying, the drop hissed out of existence. "Hymen! *Iô*, Hymen!" Sostratos called as he and his father led his sister's wedding procession through the streets toward the house of Damonax son of Polydoros, Erinna's new husband.

Lysistratos waved his torch, too. "Hymen!" he called, as Sostratos called. Then, in a lower voice, he grumbled, "Miserable weather for a wedding."

"Winter's the most auspicious time," Sostratos said, "but it's the rainy season, too. Chance we take." He was a tall, gangling fellow in his mid-twenties who, unlike most men of his generation, let his beard grow rather than shaving in imitation of Alexander the Great. He'd studied at the Lykeion in Athens and thought the beard lent him the appearance of a philosopher. On a good day, he was right.

Relatives and friends capered in the procession. There was his cousin, Menedemos, only a few cubits away, calling out to the god of marriage just as if he didn't enjoy adultery more. Menedemos was only a few months younger than Sostratos, the son of his father's older brother, Philodemos. Sostratos was most of a head taller than his cousin, but Menedemos was handsomer and more graceful.

And people like him, too, Sostratos thought with a mental sigh. He knew he perplexed people himself; he thought too much and felt too little. He read Herodotos and Thoukydides, and aspired to write history himself one day. Menedemos could quote long stretches of the *Iliad* and *Odyssey,* and of

Aristophanes' bawdy comedies. Sostratos sighed to himself again. *No wonder people like him. He entertains them.*

Menedemos, swaggering along with a wreath of ivy leaves and bright ribbons in his hair, blew a kiss to a slave girl carrying a jar of water up the street. She giggled and smiled back. Sostratos tried not to be jealous. He didn't have much luck. If he'd done that, odds were the girl would have laughed in his face.

"May the marriage bring you grandchildren, Uncle," Menedemos told Lysistratos.

"I thank you," Sostratos' father answered. He gave Menedemos more leeway than Sostratos was in the habit of doing. But then, Menedemos had been known to complain that his own father held Sostratos up to him as an example of good behavior. That made part of Sostratos—the philosophical part—proud. It embarrassed the rest of him.

He looked back over his shoulder. There was Uncle Philodemos, not far from the ox cart that carried Damonax and Erinna. Like the rest of the men in the wedding procession, Menedemos' father wore garlands in his hair and carried a torch. Somehow, though, he didn't look as if he was having a good time. He seldom did. *No wonder he and Menedemos have trouble getting along,* Sostratos thought.

Damonax dwelt in the southwestern part of the city, not far from the gymnasion. Since Erinna, after the death of her first husband, had been living in her father's house near the northern end of the city (and the northernmost tip of the island) of Rhodes, the parade went through most of the polis. Plenty of people had the chance to cheer and clap their hands and call lewd advice to the bride and groom. Knowing his sister, Sostratos was sure she blushed behind her veil.

With a final squeak from its ungreased axle, the ox cart stopped in front of Damonax's home. His mother should have received Erinna into the household, but she and his father were both dead, so an aunt did the honors instead. The men in the procession trooped into the courtyard. His slaves had wine and olives and fried squid and barley cakes and honey waiting in the andron, the men's chamber, where the rain couldn't spoil them.

The wine was fine Khian, and mixed no weaker than one-to-one with water. People would get drunk in short order. Sostratos took a long pull at his cup. The sweet wine slid down his throat and started fighting the chill of the day. He wondered if the *Aphrodite* or one of his family's other ships had brought it back to Rhodes.

Before long, someone out in the courtyard called, "Come on, everybody! They're going into the bedchamber!"

"So soon?" someone else said.

"Would you wait, on your wedding day?" a third man asked. "By the gods, *did* you wait on your wedding day?" Raucous laughter rose.

Chewing on a tender little fried squid and carrying his winecup, Sostratos left the andron. Sure enough, Damonax had opened a door and was urging Erinna through. When she went inside, her new groom turned back to the feasters and grinned. "And now, my dears, I'll see you later," he told them. "*Much* later."

People laughed some more and cheered and clapped their hands. Damonax closed the door. The bar thudded into place inside. Along with everyone else, Sostratos began to sing the epithalamion. Presently, he heard the bedframe creaking through the words of the wedding song. As was proper at such times, he shouted obscene advice.

When he turned to go back to the andron for more wine, he almost bumped into his father. "I hope she's happy," he said.

Lysistratos' smile was wide and a little silly; he'd already drunk a good deal. "If she's not happy now, when will she be?" he said. Sostratos dipped his head in agreement; he certainly didn't want to spoil the day by speaking words of ill omen.

Behind him, somebody said, "Will he show the bloody cloth?"

"No, fool," someone else answered. "It's her second marriage, so that'd be hard to do unless her first husband was no man at all."

Inside the bedchamber, the creaking grew louder and quicker, then suddenly stopped. A moment later, Damonax called, "That's one!" out through the door. Everyone whooped and applauded. Before too long, the noise of lovemaking started again. A couple of people made bets about how many rounds he'd manage.

All the numbers they argued about struck Sostratos as improbably high. He looked around for Menedemos, to say as much. Of course, his cousin was as likely as not to boast that such numbers were too low, not too high. And Menedemos was as likely as anyone to make such a boast good.

But Menedemos didn't seem to be in the courtyard. Sostratos wandered into the andron looking for him. His cousin wasn't there, either. Shrugging, Sostratos dipped out more wine and picked up another squid with the thumb and first two fingers of his right hand. Maybe that creaking bed had inspired Menedemos to go looking for some fun of his own.

As MENEDEMOS MADE his way up Rhodes' grid of streets, a ribbon on the garland he was wearing fell down in front of his face. It tickled his nose and made his eyes cross and reminded him he still had the garland on his head. He took it off and dropped it in a puddle.

His feet were muddy. He didn't care. Like any sailor, he went barefoot in all weather and never wore anything but a chiton. An older man with a big, thick wool himation wrapped around himself gave him an odd look as they passed each other on the street, as if to say, *Aren't you freezing?* Menedemos did feel the chill, but not enough to do anything about it.

He'd drunk enough wine at his cousin's wedding feast to want to get rid of it and paused to piss against the blank, whitewashed wall of a housefront. Then he hurried on. Daylight hours were short at this season of the year, while those of the nighttime stretched like tar on a hot day. He wouldn't have cared to be on the streets after sunset, not without the torch he'd carried in the wedding procession, and not without some friends along, too. Even in a peaceful, orderly polis like Rhodes, footpads prowled under cover of darkness.

He hoped Damonax would make a worthwhile addition to the family. He'd liked Erinna's first husband well enough, but the man had seemed old to him. *That's because I wasn't much more than a youth myself when she was wed then,* he realized in some surprise. *Her first husband would have been about thirty, the same age as Damonax is now.* Time did strange things. Half a dozen years had got behind him when he wasn't looking.

His father's house and Uncle Lysistratos' stood side by side, not far from the temple to Demeter at the north end of town. When he knocked on the door, one of the house slaves inside called, "Who is it?"

"Me—Menedemos."

The door opened almost at once. "Did the feast break up so soon, young master?" the slave asked in surprise. "We didn't expect you back for a while yet."

That almost certainly meant the slaves had grabbed the chance to sit around on their backsides and do as little as they could. Nothing was what slaves did whenever they got the chance. Menedemos answered, "I decided to come home a little early, that's all."

"You, sir? From a feast, sir?" The expression on the slave's face said everything that needed saying. "Where's your father, sir?"

"He's still back there," Menedemos said. The slave looked more astonished yet. Usually Menedemos' father was the one who came home early and he was the one who stayed out late.

He walked through the entry hall and into the courtyard. Angry shouts came from the kitchen. Menedemos sighed. His stepmother and Sikon the cook were wrangling again. Baukis, who wanted to be a good household manager, was convinced Sikon spent too much. The cook was equally convinced she wanted him to pass the rest of his life fixing nothing but barley porridge and salted fish.

Baukis stalked out of the kitchen with a thoroughly grim expression on her face. It crumbled into surprise when she saw Menedemos. "Oh. Hail," she said, and then, as the slave had, "I didn't expect you home so soon."

"Hail," he replied, and shrugged. When he looked at her, he had trouble thinking of his father's second wife as his step-mother. Baukis was ten or eleven years younger than he. She wasn't a striking beauty, but she had a very nice shape: a much nicer one now than she'd had when she came into the house a couple of years before at the age of fourteen. Menedemos went on, "I didn't feel like staying around, so I came back by myself while it was still light."

"All right," Baukis said. "Do you have any idea when Philodemos will be along?"

Menedemos tossed his head to show he didn't. "If I had to guess, though, I'd say he and Uncle Lysistratos and Sostratos will all come home together, with some linkbearers to light the way for them."

"That sounds sensible," Baukis agreed. "I really do want to talk to him about Sikon. The insolence that fellow has! You'd think he owned this place instead of being a slave here." She frowned so hard, a vertical line appeared between her eyebrows.

The expression fascinated Menedemos. All her expressions fascinated him. They were part of the same household, so she didn't veil herself against his eyes as respectable women usu-ally did around men. Watching her bare face was almost as ex-citing as seeing her naked.

He had to remind himself to pay attention to what she was saying, too. He'd given his father plenty of reasons to quarrel with him—and had also got plenty of reasons to quarrel with his father. He didn't want to put adultery with his father's wife on the list. That might be a killing matter, and he knew it very well.

Most of him, at any rate, didn't want to put adultery with Baukis on the list. One part did. That part stirred. He sternly willed it back to quiescence. He didn't want Baukis noticing such stirrings under his tunic.

"Sikon has his pride," he said. Talking about quarrels in the kitchen might help keep his mind off other things. "Maybe you would have done better right from the start if you'd asked him to be more careful what he spent than marching in there and giving him orders. That puts his back up, you know."

"He's a slave," Baukis repeated. "When his master's wife tells him what to do, he'd better pay attention, or he'll be sorry."

In theory, she was right. In practice, slaves with special skills and special talents—and Sikon had both—were almost as free to do as they pleased as were citizens. If Baukis didn't know that, she'd lived a sheltered life before she was married. Or maybe her parents were among the folk who treated slaves like beasts of burden that happened to be able to talk. There were some.

He said, "Sikon's been here a long time. We're still prosperous, and we eat as well as a lot of people who have more silver."

Baukis' frown got deeper. "That's not the point. The point is, if I tell him to do it the way I want, he should do it."

A philosophical discussion—that's what this is, Menedemos realized. *I might as well be Sostratos. I'm having a philosophical discussion with my father's wife, when what I want to do is bend her forward and . . .*

He tossed his head. Baukis glared, thinking he disagreed with her. In fact, he did, but at that moment he'd been disagreeing with himself. He said, "You ought to see you haven't got anywhere by charging straight at him. If you compromise, maybe he will, too."

"Maybe." But Philodemos' wife didn't sound as if she believed it. "I think he just thinks I'm some fool of a girl trying

to give him orders, and he doesn't like that at all. Well, too
bad for him."

She might well have a point. No Hellene would have
wanted to obey a woman's commands. Sikon wasn't a Hellene, but he was a man—and Hellenes and barbarians agreed
on some things.

"I've talked with him before," Menedemos said. "Would
you like me to do it again? With a little luck, I'll get him to see
reason. Or, if I can't do that, maybe I can frighten him."

"I haven't had much luck with that, but then I'm only a
woman," Baukis said sourly. After a moment, though, her
face lit up with hope. "Would you please try? I'd be ever so
grateful."

"Of course I will," Menedemos promised. "Nobody wants
to listen to quarrels all the time. I'll do the best I can." *Maybe
I can slip Sikon silver on the side, so we'll eat as well as always but Baukis won't see the money coming out of the household accounts. That might work.*

"Thank you so much, Menedemos!" Baukis exclaimed. Her
eyes glowing, she impulsively stepped forward and gave him
a hug.

For a moment, his arms tightened around her. He held her
just long enough for him to feel how sweet and ripe she was—
and, perhaps, for her to feel him stirring to life. Then they
sprang apart, as if each found the other too hot to bear. They
weren't alone. In a prosperous household like Philodemos',
no one could count on being alone. Slaves saw, or might see,
everything that went on. A brief, friendly embrace could be
innocent. Anything more? Menedemos tossed his head again.

Baukis said, "Do speak to him soon, please." Was that all
she'd had in mind when she hugged him? Or was she too making sure the slaves would have nothing to tell Philodemos?
Menedemos could hardly ask.

He said, "I will," and then deliberately turned away.
Baukis' footsteps went off toward the stairs that led up to the
women's quarters. Her sandals clacked on the planks of the
stairway. Menedemos didn't watch her go. Instead, he walked

off to the kitchen for what he knew would be one more futile talk with Sikon.

"GOOD DAY, MY master," Sostratos said in Aramaic. He was a free Hellene. He would never have called any man "master" in Greek. But the tongue spoken in Phoenicia and the nearby lands—and in broad stretches of what had been the Persian Empire before Alexander's great campaigns—was far more flowery, more formally polite.

"Good day to you," Himilkon the Byblian replied in the same tongue. The Phoenician merchant had run a harborside warehouse in Rhodes for as long as Sostratos could remember. Silver was just beginning to streak his curly black beard; gold hoops glittered in his ears. He went on, still in Aramaic, "Your accent is much better than it was when you started these lessons a few months ago. You know many more words, too."

"Your servant thanks you for your help," Sostratos said. Himilkon's dark eyes sparkled as he nodded approval. Sostratos grinned; he'd recalled the formula correctly.

"Sailing season comes soon," the Phoenician said.

"I know." Sostratos dipped his head; he had as much trouble making himself nod as Himilkon did with the Hellenic gesture. "Less than a month to go before the . . . vernal equinox." The last two words came out in Greek; he had no idea how to say them in Aramaic.

Himilkon didn't tell him, either. The merchant's lessons were purely practical. With a little luck, Sostratos would be able to make himself understood when the *Aphrodite* got to Phoenicia. He had more doubts about whether he would be able to understand anyone else. When he worried out loud, Himilkon laughed. "What do you say if you have trouble?"

"'Please speak slowly, my master.'" Sostratos had learned that phrase early on.

"Good. Very good." Himilkon nodded again. "My people will want to take your money. They will make sure you follow them so they can do it."

"I believe that," Sostratos said in Greek. He'd dealt with

Phoenician traders in a good many towns by the Aegean Sea. They were singleminded in the pursuit of profit. Since he was, too, he had less trouble with them than some Hellenes were wont to do. Sticking to Greek, he asked, "But what about the Ioudaioi?"

"Oh. Them." Himilkon's shrug was expressive. In gutturally accented Greek of his own, he continued, "I still think you're daft to want anything to do with them."

"Why?" Sostratos said. "The best balsam comes from Engedi, and you say Engedi is in their land. I'm sure I can get a better price from them than I'd get from Phoenician middlemen."

"You'll likely pay less money," Himilkon admitted. "But you'll have more aggravation—I promise you that."

Sostratos shrugged. "That's one of the things a merchant does—turns aggravation into silver, I mean."

"All right. Fair enough," Himilkon said. "I'll remember that and remind myself of it when I run into a Hellene who's particularly annoying—and there are plenty of them, by the gods."

"Are there?" Sostratos said, and the Phoenician nodded. *Isn't that interesting?* Sostratos thought. *We find barbarians annoying, but who would have imagined they might feel the same about us? Truly custom is king of all.* Herodotos had quoted Pindaros to that effect.

Himilkon said, "The gods keep you safe on your journey. May the winds be good, may the seas be calm, and may the Macedonian marshals not go to war anywhere too close to you and your ship."

"May it be so," Sostratos agreed. "By all the signs, Antigonos has a pretty solid grip on Phoenicia and its hinterland. I don't think Ptolemaios can hope to take it away from him. No matter what they do to each other elsewhere along the shores of the Inner Sea, that seems a good bet."

"For your sake, my master, I hope you are right," Himilkon said, falling back into Aramaic. "Whether the elephant tramples the lion or the lion pulls down the elephant, the mouse who gets caught in their battle always loses. Shall we go on with the lesson, or have you had enough?"

"May it please you, my master, I have had enough," Sostratos answered, also in Aramaic.

Himilkon smiled and clapped his hands. "That is perfect—pronunciation, accent, everything. If I had another half a year to work with you, I could turn you into a veritable man of Byblos, may a pestilence take me if I lie."

"I thank you," Sostratos said, knowing he meant it as a compliment. The Hellene tried to imagine himself a member of a folk that knew not philosophy. *What would I do? How would I keep from going mad? Or would I see what I was missing? A man blind from birth doesn't miss the beauty of a sunset.*

He got to his feet and left the Phoenician's ramshackle warehouse. Hyssaldomos, Himilkon's Karian slave, stood just outside, chewing on some brown bread. "Hail, O best one," he said in Greek.

"Hail," Sostratos answered. He switched to Aramaic: "Do you understand this language, Hyssaldomos?"

"Little bit," the slave said, also in Aramaic. "Himilkon use sometimes. Greek easier."

That probably meant Greek was more like Hyssaldomos' native Karian. Sostratos didn't know for certain, though. Rhodes lay off the coast of Karia, and Rhodians had been dealing with Karians for centuries. Even so, only a handful of Karian words had entered the local Greek dialect. Few Rhodians spoke the tongue of their nearest barbarian neighbors, and he wasn't one of them. But more and more Karians used Greek these days, either alongside their own language or instead of it.

Now that Alexander's conquered the Persian Empire, the whole world will have to learn Greek, Sostratos thought. In a few generations, wouldn't his language replace not only local tongues like Karian and Lykian but also more widely spoken ones like Aramaic and Persian? He couldn't see why not.

The *Aphrodite* lay drawn up on the beach perhaps a plethron from Himilkon's warehouse. The merchant galley's planking would be good and dry when she put to sea. Till it got waterlogged again, that would give her a better turn of speed.

A gull swooped down by the *Aphrodite* and flew away with a mouse struggling in its beak. *One little pest that won't make it on to the ship,* Sostratos thought as he walked toward the merchant galley. He was a neat man and didn't like dealing with vermin at sea. A couple of years before, he'd sailed with peafowl aboard the akatos. They'd done a fine job of eating roaches and centipedes and scorpions and mice—but they'd also proved that large pests aboard ship were worse than small ones.

Sostratos laid a more or less affectionate hand on the *Aphrodite*'s flank. Thin lead sheets nailed to the timbers below the waterline helped shield the vessel from shipworms and kept barnacles and seaweed from fouling her bottom. Rhodian carpenters had been over the repairs they'd had done in Kos the summer before, after a collision with a round ship that came wallowing out of a rainstorm. The workmen on Kos had also been repairing Ptolemaios' naval vessels at the time, so they should have known their business. Even so, Sostratos was glad the work met Rhodians' approval. His own polis, in his biased opinion, held the best and boldest sailors among the Hellenes these days.

One of the harborside loungers—a fellow who would do a little work now and then, when he needed a few oboloi for wine, or perhaps for bread—came up to Sostratos and said, "Hail. You sail aboard this one, don't you?"

"I've been know to, every now and again," Sostratos said dryly. "Why?"

"Oh, nothing," the other man replied. "I was just wondering what she might be carrying when she goes into the sea, that's all."

"She might be carrying almost anything. She's taken every-

thing from peafowl and lion skins and a gryphon's skull"—
Sostratos' heart still ached when he thought about losing the
gryphon's skull to pirates the summer before, when he was on
his way to show it off in Athens—"to something as ordinary
as sacks of wheat."

The lounger clucked reproachfully. He tried again: "What
will she have in her when she goes to sea?"

"This and that," Sostratos said, his voice bland. The lounger
gave him an exasperated look. His answering smile said as little as he had. His father and uncle's trading firm was far from
the only one in the city of Rhodes. Some of their rivals might
have paid a drakhma or two to find out what they'd be up to
this sailing season. Men who hung around the harbor could
make their money without getting calluses on their hands.
They could—with a little help from others. Sostratos had no
intention of giving that kind of help.

This fellow, if nothing else, was persistent. "You know
where you'll be sailing?" he asked.

"Oh, yes," Sostratos said. The lounger waited. Sostratos
said no more. The other man took longer than he should have
to realize he wasn't going to say any more. Muttering un-
pleasantries under his breath, he turned away.

I should have answered him in Aramaic, Sostratos thought.
I'd have got rid of him quicker. Then he shrugged. He'd done
what needed doing.

Another man called out to him: "Hail, Sostratos! How are
you?"

"Hail, Khremes." Sostratos had known the carpenter for
years and liked him. He wouldn't have to play games with him,
as he had with the lounger. "I'm fine, thanks. How are you?"

"Couldn't be better," Khremes told him. "Your cousin, he's
a pretty clever chap, isn't he?"

"Menedemos? I'm sure he'd be the first to agree with you,"
Sostratos said, a little more sharply than he'd intended.

A good-natured soul, Khremes missed the edge to Sostratos' voice. He was also in the grip of enthusiasm: "That no-

tion he had for the war galley made special to be a pirate
hunter—that was wonderful," he burbled. "A trihemiolia—a
ship that can fight like an ordinary trireme and stay up with a
pirate crew's hemiolia. Fabulous! Why didn't somebody think
of it years ago?"

Sostratos had hated pirates with a clear, cold loathing even
before they attacked the *Aphrodite* and stole the gryphon's
skull. Now . . . Now he wanted to see every sea robber ever
born nailed to a cross and dying slowly and horribly. If someone praised Menedemos for coming up with a ship type that
would make life harder for those whoresons, he wouldn't
complain.

He said, "When something matters to my cousin, he goes
after it." As often as not, Menedemos' ingenuity was aimed at
other men's wives. But he did hate pirates as much as Sostratos said. Sostratos had never heard of an honest sailor who
didn't hate them.

"Good for him," said Khremes, who didn't have to worry
about the results of some of Menedemos' escapades.

"Well, yes," said Sostratos, who did. He went on, "We're
really going to start building trihemioliai, are we?"

The carpenter dipped his head. "We sure are. The admirals
spent all winter talking about it"—he opened and closed his
thumb against his four bunched fingers to simulate a gabbling
mouth—"and now it's really going to happen. They'll make
three to begin with, and more if they turn out to be as good as
everybody hopes."

"May it be so," Sostratos said. Thinking of Menedemos as
someone who'd done something important for Rhodes didn't
come easy. More than a little bemusedly, Sostratos continued, "To tell you the truth, I wouldn't mind putting to sea in
one of those new trihemioliai instead of our akatos here.
We're going east this year, so we'll have to sail past the
Lykian coast, and the Lykians are pirates at sea and bandits
on land."

"Isn't that the truth? Miserable barbarians." Khremes

paused. "Do you suppose you *could* use a trihemiolia for a merchant galley?"

"No," Sostratos answered without hesitation, and tossed his head to emphasize the word. "However much I'd like to, there's not a chance it'd work."

"Why not?" the carpenter said. "You'd be the fastest trader on the sea."

"Yes, and also the most expensive," Sostratos pointed out. "The *Aphrodite* sails with forty rowers, plus enough extra men to handle the sail with all the rowing benches filled. They all make at least a drakhma a day; most of them make a drakhma and a half. That's two minai of silver every three days in wages, more or less. But a trihemiolia would carry more than three times as many men to pull the oars. That'd be—let me see—Zeus, that'd be about two minai every single day. We'd have to carry nothing but gold and rubies to have any chance of breaking even with expenses like that."

"Ah." Khremes dipped his head. "No doubt you're right, best one. I hadn't thought about costs, only about the ship."

Sostratos was toikharkhos aboard the *Aphrodite*. Everything that had to do with the cargo fell to him. He thought of costs first, last, and always. But, because he liked Khremes, he let him down easy: "Well, my dear fellow, I wouldn't know where to begin when it comes to putting a ship together."

"You begin at the beginning—where else?" the carpenter said. "You make your shell of planks, and you fasten them all together with mortises and tenons so the shell's good and strong, and then you nail some ribs to the inside for a little extra stiffness."

"Well, everyone knows that much," Sostratos agreed. "But knowing just how to do it—that's your mystery."

"No mystery to it at all," Khremes insisted. "Anybody who works around the harbor could make a proper job of it."

Sostratos didn't want to argue with him. As far as the carpenter could see, the harbor was the whole world. Khremes never thought about tanners and potters and farmers, for whom the shipwright's craft was altogether strange—and whose trades were as strange to him. His friends were other carpenters or men who worked in related trades. That all helped make him better at what he did, but did nothing to prove his judgment on matters unrelated to shipbuilding was particularly keen. Of course, he might not agree.

"When you do sail off to Phoenicia, I expect you'll slicker those barbarians right out of their sandals," Khremes said.

"I hope so," Sostratos said, and his opinion of the carpenter's judgment improved remarkably.

MENEDEMOS WAS FURIOUS and made only the slightest effort to hide it. "Olive oil?" He threw his hands in the air. "By the dog of Egypt, why are we taking olive oil to Phoenicia? They grow olives there, too, don't they?"

"Yes." Sostratos sounded embarrassed, which didn't happen very often. "We're taking olive oil because—"

"Don't tell me," Menedemos broke in. "Let me guess. We're taking it because it's what your new brother-in-law's family makes. Am I right, or am I wrong?"

"You're right," his cousin said unhappily. "Damonax used Erinna's dowry to get some of the crop out of hock, and—"

"And now he expects us to sell the oil and make him a nice profit," Menedemos interrupted once more. "We mght even do it if we were going to Alexandria, since they don't grow olives there. But that's *not* where we're going. Did you tell him as much?"

"Of course I did," Sostratos said. "He doesn't understand how these things work, though—not really, anyhow. He's no trading man. And . . . plague take it, he *is* my new brother-in-law, so I can't just tell him, 'To the crows with you,' the way I would with somebody who isn't part of the family. So we have to do our best, that's all."

"I'd like to do my best to boot him right into the harbor," Menedemos growled, but then, reluctantly, he subsided. "Family ties." He rolled his eyes. "My father's disgusted, too, but he didn't tell Damonax no, either. He has more trouble saying no to your brother-in-law than he ever did to me, I'll tell you that." The trouble his father had telling Damonax no rankled, like so many of the things his father did.

"Believe me, it could have been worse," Sostratos said. "When Damonax first came up with this scheme, he wanted to load the *Aphrodite* with oil to her gunwales, not leave a digit's worth of space for any other cargo. He had the oil, so why shouldn't we carry it?"

"Why?" Menedemos exclaimed. "I'll tell you—"

Now Sostratos cut him off: "My father and I have spent the past ten days arguing him down. We won't be drowning in oil, anyhow. Even if we do have trouble unloading it, we'll carry other things we know we can sell. Can't go far wrong with good Rhodian perfume."

"Well, no," Menedemos said. "And we still have some of the silk from Kos we got this past summer. All sorts of strange things come out of the east, but I think the Phoenicians will have a hard time matching that."

"I should say so." Sostratos dipped his head. "And who knows what we'll pick up along the way? We didn't expect the gryphon's skull last year, or the lion skins, or the tiger hide."

"And we got real money for the hides," Menedemos said. "The skull . . ." He'd twitted Sostratos about it ever since he spotted it in the market square in Kaunos. "I'll bet the pirate who stole it from the *Aphrodite* hasn't lived it down with his pals yet."

"Too bad," his cousin growled. "I still say we could have got something for it in Athens. After all, Damonax tried to buy it for six minai right here in Rhodes."

"And if that doesn't prove he has no idea what to do with his money, gods only know what would," Menedemos said.

"Oh, go howl." Sostratos eyed Menedemos. "Are you as eager to set sail as you were a year ago? You couldn't wait to get out of Rhodes then."

"I won't be sorry to see it drop below the horizon this sailing season, either," Menedemos allowed. He had tried to make that less obvious this past winter. Evidently, he'd succeeded.

His cousin frowned and scratched his head. "I never did understand why. You've got no outraged husbands sniffing after you here, or none I know of, anyway." He studied Menedemos as if Menedemos were the same sort of interesting specimen as the gryphon's skull. Sostratos had an itch to know, and he wouldn't be satisfied till he scratched it.

All Menedemos said was, "No, no outraged husbands here."

"What is it, then?" Sostratos picked at what puzzled him as if it were a scab.

"My, aren't we nosy today?" Menedemos murmured, and his cousin turned red. Menedemos brought the conversation back to the cargo the *Aphrodite* would be carrying. That was important to Sostratos, too, so he turned most of his formidable intelligence on the question. Most, but not all—Menedemos could see him casting about for a chance to start probing again.

Well, my dear, I'm not going to give you one, Menedemos thought. *Talk about outraged husbands—what would happen if I outraged my own father with my stepmother? I don't want to find out, and so I won't find out. But oh, by the gods, I fear she might want to go to bed with me, too.*

What *would* Philodemos do? No, Menedemos didn't want to find out. His father had never stopped mocking him, hounding him, for his love affairs. If the older man were to discover himself the butt of one . . . Sure enough, it might not stop at words. Menedemos feared it wouldn't. It was all too likely to end in blood.

And so I won't *sleep with Baukis, no matter how much I want to—and no matter how much she might want me to. And, O cousin of mine, I don't care how curious you are, either. Some secrets are going to stay secret, that's all.*

"Can we get more papyrus before we set sail?" Sostratos asked.

"Papyrus?" Menedemos echoed in some surprise. "I'm sure we can—the Egyptian grain ships that put in here often carry the stuff. But why should we bother? Phoenicia's a lot closer to Egypt than we are."

His cousin didn't say, *You thick-skull!* or anything of the sort. But the look he got made him wish Sostratos had come right out and called him an idiot. It wasn't that Sostratos was right so often, though he was. In fact, that made him very useful. But when he stared at you with pity in his eyes because you were too stupid to see what was obvious to him . . . *I haven't wrung his neck yet,* Menedemos thought. *I don't know why I haven't, but I haven't.*

"Ptolemaios and Antigonos are at war again," Sostratos said. "Ships from Egypt won't be going up to the Phoenician ports these days, not when Antigonos is holding those ports. If we can bring papyrus there, it ought to fetch a good price."

And he was right again. Menedemos couldn't have denied it if he tried. "All right. Fine," he said. "We'll get some papyrus, then. Might as well get some ink to take with it. We've done pretty well with ink before."

"I'll see to it," Sostratos said. "I'm not sure what the market will be, though. It's not like papyrus: the Phoenicians know how to make their own ink. They're clever about such things."

"They copy everything their neighbors do," Menedemos said with more than a little scorn. "They don't do anything of their own."

"Himilkon wouldn't care to hear you say such things," Sostratos remarked.

"So what?" Menedemos said. "Are you telling me I'm wrong?"

Sostratos tossed his head. "No. From what I've seen, I'd say you're right. But that doesn't mean Himilkon would."

Menedemos laughed. "Anyone hearing you would guess you've studied under the philosophers. No one who hasn't could split hairs so fine."

"Thank you so much, my dear," Sostratos said, and Menedemos laughed again. His cousin went on, "When do you plan on sailing?"

"If it were up to me—and if we had all our cargo aboard— we could leave tomorrow," Menedemos answered. "I don't think my father will let me take the *Aphrodite* out quite so early, though." He sniffed. "He went out right at the start of the sailing season when he was a captain—I've heard him talk about it. But he doesn't think I can do the same."

"Our grandfather probably complained that he was a reckless brat," Sostratos said.

"I suppose so." Menedemos grinned; he liked the idea of his father as a young man having to take orders instead of arrogantly snapping them out.

"I suppose it's been like that since the beginning of time," Sostratos said. "We'll be proper tyrants ourselves, too, when our beards go gray."

"*I* won't have a gray beard." Menedemos rubbed his shaven chin.

"And you accused me of splitting hairs—you do it literally," Sostratos said. Menedemos groaned. Sostratos continued more seriously: "I wonder how you'd find out about something like that."

"What? If old men were always the same?" Menedemos said. "I can tell you how—look at Nestor in the *Iliad*." He paused for a moment, then recited from the epic:

"'He, thinking well of them, spoke and addressed them:
"Come now—great mourning has reached Akhaian land.
Priamos and the sons of Priamos and the other Trojans
Would be delighted and would rejoice in spirit
If they learned of all this quarreling—
That you, best of the Danaoi in council, were fighting.
But hearken—you are both younger than I,
For I kept company with better men than you.
And never did they think little of me.
I don't see such men as I saw then:
Such as Perithoös and Dryas shepherd of the people
And Kaineus and Exadios and godlike Polyphemos
And Theseus son of Aigeus, like the immortals."'"

His cousin laughed and held up a hand. "All right, all right—you've persuaded me. Old men are old men, and they always have been."

"A good thing you stopped me," Menedemos said. "Nestor goes on blathering for a lot longer. He's a dear fellow . . . if he doesn't make you want to kick him. Most of the time, with me, he does."

"And why is that?" Sostratos asked. Menedemos didn't answer, but they both knew why: Menedemos' father put him in mind of Nestor. Sostratos said, "If you and Uncle Philodemos got on better, you'd like Nestor more."

"Maybe." Menedemos didn't want to admit more than he had to, so he tried a thrust of his own: "If you and Uncle Lysistratos didn't get on, you'd like Nestor less."

"Oh, I think Nestor blathers, too—don't get me wrong about that." Sostratos started to say something else, probably something that had to do with the *Iliad,* but then stopped and snapped his fingers. "By the gods, I know what else we can take to Phoenicia: books!"

"Books?" Menedemos echoed, and Sostratos dipped his head. Menedemos tossed his. "Are you witstruck all of a sudden? Most Phoenicians don't even speak Greek, let alone read it."

"I wasn't thinking about the Phoenicians," his cousin answered. "I was thinking about the garrisons of Hellenes in those towns. They ought to be good-sized; Antigonos builds most of his fleet along the coast there. And they won't be able to buy books from any of the local scribes, because you're right—those scribes don't write Greek. The ones who can read would probably pay plenty for some new scrolls to help them pass the time."

Menedemos rubbed his chin as he considered. "Do you know, that might not be a bad notion after all," he said at last. Then he gave Sostratos a suspicious look. "You weren't going to take along philosophy and history, were you?"

"No, no, no." Now Sostratos tossed his head. "*I* like such things, but how many soldiers are likely to? No, I was thinking of some of the more exciting books from the *Iliad* and the *Odyssey.* Anyone who has his alpha-beta can read those, so we'd have more people wanting to buy."

"It's a nice notion. It's a *clever* notion, by Zeus." Menedemos gave credit where it was due. "And books are light, and they don't take up much space, and we can get a good price for them." He dipped his head—in fact, he almost bowed to Sostratos. "We'll do it. Go talk to the scribes. Buy what they've got written out and see how much they can copy before we sail."

"I'll take care of it," Sostratos said.

Menedemos laughed. "I'll bet you will. If I sounded that eager, I'd be going off to visit a fancy hetaira, not some nearsighted fellow with ink stains on his fingers."

His cousin didn't even splutter, which proved his point. "I'm always glad for an excuse to visit the scribes," Sostratos said. "You never can tell when something new and interesting will have come into Rhodes."

"Happy hunting," Menedemos said. He wondered if Sostratos even heard him; his cousin's eyes were far away, as if he were thinking about his beloved.

EVEN A POLIS as large and prosperous as Rhodes boasted no more than a handful of men who made their living by copying out books. Sostratos knew them all. The best, without a doubt, was Glaukias son of Kallimedon. He was fast, accurate, and legible, all at the same time. None of the others came close. Naturally, Sostratos visited him first.

However good Glaukias was, he wasn't rich. His shop occupied a couple of downstairs rooms in a small house on a street near the Great Harbor; he and his family lived above them. The shop did face south, which gave Glaukias the best light for copying.

A skinny, angry-looking man was dictating a letter to him when Sostratos came up to the shop. The fellow sent him such a suspicious glare, he hastily withdrew out of earshot. Only after the man paid Glaukias and went on his way did Sostratos approach again.

"Hail, best one," Glaukias said. He was about forty, with big ears, buck teeth, and, sure enough, a nearsighted stare and inky fingers. "Thanks for withdrawing there," he went on. "Theokles, the fellow who was here, is certain a Samian merchant is cheating him, *and* that the Samian has hired people here in Rhodes to keep an eye on him and make sure he doesn't get what's his by right."

"By the dog of Egypt!" Sostratos exclaimed. "Is that true?"

Glaukias rolled his eyes. "Last year, he got into the same sort of mess with a trader from Ephesos, and the year before that with somebody from Halikarnassos. . . . I think it was Halikarnassos. He quarrels with people the way some men go to a cockfight. If he had his letters, he wouldn't have anything to do with me—half the time, he thinks I'm part of these schemes to defraud him."

"He sounds daft to me. Why do you keep writing letters for him?"

"Why?" Glaukias smiled a sweet, sad smile. "I'll tell you why: he pays me, and I need the silver. Speaking of which, what can I do for *you*?"

Sostratos explained his idea, finishing, "So I'll gladly buy whatever copies you've made of the quarrel of Akhilleus and Agamemnon, or of Akhilleus' fight with shining Hektor, or of Odysseus' adventure with the Cyclops, or of his return and his revenge on the suitors—that sort of thing."

"I see," Glaukias said. "You want all the high points from the epics."

"That's right," Sostratos said. "People don't have to buy books—I want the parts that would make them spend their money on Homer when they could be buying Khian wine or a night with a courtesan instead."

"People don't have to buy books," the scribe echoed mournfully. "Well, the gods know I've seen the truth of *that*. But you're right. When they do buy, that's usually the sort of thing they're after. And so, when I don't have someone's order in front of me, I copy out books like that from the epics. Let's see what I've got." He disappeared into a back room, returning a little later with ten or twelve rolls of papyrus.

"Oh, very good!" Sostratos exclaimed. "That's more than I'd hoped for."

"I do stay busy," Glaukias said. "I'd better stay busy. If I'm not busy, I'm starving. Personally, I wish I didn't have so many rolls to sell you. That would mean other people had bought 'em."

"What all have we got here?" Sostratos asked.

"The high spots, as you said," the scribe answered. "Most are the ones you talked about, but I also made a couple of copies of the next-to-last book of the *Iliad:* you know, Patroklos' funeral games."

"Oh, yes. That's a good one, too." Sostratos unrolled one of the books and eyed the writing in admiration. "I wish I could be so neat with a pen. Your script looks as though it ought to be carved in marble, not set down on papyrus."

"Believe me, it's only because I have so much practice." But Glaukias couldn't help sounding pleased.

"I'll buy them all," Sostratos said. The scribe's face broke into a delighted grin. Sostratos went on, "I'll buy them all if your price is anywhere near reasonable, that is."

"Well, best one, you know what these things cost," Glaukias answered. "If you were just walking in off the street to buy one book, I'd try to get eight or ten drakhmai out of you. People like that, a lot of the time they don't have any notion of what's what, and you want to make a little extra. But I'll sell you these for five drakhmai each—six for the two copies of those funeral games, because that's an especially long book and takes more time and more papyrus."

"You've got a bargain, my friend." Sostratos did indeed know what books were supposed to cost. He laughed. "I don't remember the last time I made a deal without haggling."

"It's been a while for me, too." Glaukias sounded almost giddy. What Sostratos paid him would keep him and his family eating for a couple of months. Sostratos wondered how long it had been since anyone last bought a book from him, and how desperate he was getting. When Glaukias went into the back room again, returning with a couple of cups of wine to celebrate, Sostratos suspected he wasn't getting desperate, but had got there some little while ago.

The wine was just this side of undrinkable. *The cheapest he could buy,* Sostratos thought. Aloud, he said, "I'm always glad to bring you business, Glaukias. Without the people who make books, what would we be? Nothing but savages, that's what."

"Thank you *so* much." The scribe's voice was thick with unshed tears. Muttering, he ran the back of his hand across his eyes. "That's a plain fact, you know. But does anybody think about it? Not likely! No, what I get is, 'You've got your nerve, asking so much to write things.' If I starve, if people like me starve, where do books come from? They don't grow on trees, you know."

"Of course not," Sostratos said. Glaukias talked right through him. Maybe that was the wine; maybe Sostratos' remark had struck a chord. Either way, Sostratos was glad to escape his shop.

But that didn't mean he was done with scribes. Nikandros son of Nikon had a place of business only a few blocks away from Glaukias'. Sostratos didn't like his work as well as the other scribe's. He wrote quickly; he could copy out a book faster than Glaukias could. With his speed, though, came sloppy handwriting and more mistakes than Glaukias would have made.

Sostratos didn't like Nikandros himself as well as he liked Glaukias, either. Nikandros had a face like a ferret's, a whining voice, and an exaggerated sense of his own worth. "I couldn't possibly part with a book for less than nine drakhmai," he said.

"Farewell." Sostratos turned to go. "If you come to your senses before we sail, send a messenger to the *Aphrodite.*"

He wondered if Nikandros would call him back. He'd almost decided the scribe wouldn't when Nikandros did say, "Wait," after all.

After some considerable haggling—Nikandros did not offer him wine—he got the books for the same price he'd paid

Glaukias. "This shouldn't have taken so long," he grumbled. "We both know what these are worth."

"What I know is, you're flaying me." Nikandros was not, however, too badly wounded to scoop up the silver coins and put them in his cash box.

"I'm not paying you any less than I paid Glaukias," Sostratos said, "but to the crows with me if I can see why I ought to pay you more."

"Oh. Glaukias." Nikandros sniffed. "I see. *I'm* paying the price because *he's* not a better bargainer. That's fair. It certainly is."

"Your ordinary book is five drakhmai in Athens," Sostratos said. "You know that as well as I do, O marvelous one. Why should it be any different here in Rhodes?"

"And the Athenian scribes are just as scrawny and starving as Glaukias is," Nikandros said. "I want something better for myself. I deserve more customers."

"I want all sorts of things. Just because I want them doesn't mean I'm going to get them, or even that I should have them," Sostratos said.

Nikandros sniffed again. "Good day," he said coldly. Now that the bargaining was done, he had trouble even staying polite. *How will you get those customers you think you deserve when you do your best to drive people away?*

Polykles son of Apollonios also copied books for a living, but when Sostratos went to his shop he found it closed. The carpenter next door looked up from a stool to which he was adding a leg. "If you want him," he told Sostratos, "you'll find him in the tavern down the street."

"Oh," Sostratos said. The word seemed to hang in the air. "Will he be worth anything when I do find him?"

"Never can tell," the carpenter answered, and picked up a small file.

The tavern smelled of stale wine and of the hot grease in which the proprietor would fry snacks customers bought elsewhere. The mug in front of Polykles was almost as deep as the sea. The scribe—a pale man with a withered left arm that probably made him unfit for any more strenuous trade—looked up so blearily, Sostratos was sure he'd already emptied it several times, too.

"Hail," Sostratos said.

"Hail t'you, too." Polykles' voice was thick and blurry. Sostratos could hardly understand him. The scribe blinked, trying to focus. "I sheen you shomewheresh before, haven't I?" He gulped from that formidable mug.

"Yes," Sostratos said without much hope. He gave his name. Polykles dipped his head and almost fell over. As he straightened up, he said, "Oh, yesh. I know you. You're that trader fellow—one of thoshe trader fellowsh. Watcha want?"

"Books," Sostratos answered. "Exciting books from the *Iliad* and the *Odyssey*. Have you got any copied out? I'll buy them if you do."

"Booksh?" Polykles might never have heard the word before. Then, slowly, he dipped his head again. This time, he managed to stay upright. "Oh, yesh," he said once more. "I 'member thoshe."

"Good. Congratulations." He was so fuddled, Sostratos was amazed he remembered anything. "Have you got any?"

"Have I got any what?"

"You'd do better to ask him questions when he's sobered up, pal," the taverner said.

"Does he *ever* sober up?" Sostratos asked. The man only shrugged. Sostratos gave his attention back to Polykles. "Come on. Let's go back to your house. If you've got the books I want, I'll give you money for them."

"Money?" That idea seemed to take the scribe by surprise, too.

"Money," Sostratos repeated, and then, as if speaking to an idiot, drunken child, he explained, "You can use it to buy more wine." He knew shame a moment later; wasn't he encouraging Polykles to ruin himself?

Whatever he was doing, it worked. The scribe drained the

mug and lurched toward him. "Let'sh go. Go back to the houshe. Don't . . . quite . . . know what I got there. We can shee."

He tried to walk through the wall instead of the doorway. Sostratos caught him and got him turned in the right direction just before he mashed his nose against the mud brick. "Come on, friend. We can get you there," Sostratos said, wondering if he told the truth.

Steering Polykles down the street was like steering a sailing ship through a choppy sea and shifting, contrary winds. The scribe jibbed and staggered and all but capsized in a fountain. *Maybe I should let him get good and soaked,* Sostratos thought as he grabbed him again. *It might sober him a little.* He tossed his head. *If he goes into the fountain, he's liable to drown.*

The carpenter who lived next door to Polykles looked up from that stool. *"Euge,"* he told Sostratos. "I never thought you'd pry him out of the wineshop."

"As a matter of fact, neither did I." Sostratos wasn't proud of how he'd done it. "Now let's see if it was worth doing."

Once they went inside, Polykles pawed through rolls of papyrus. "Here'sh one." He thrust it at Sostratos. "That what you want?"

Sostratos undid the ribbon holding the scroll closed. When he unrolled the scroll so he could read what was on it, he let out a long sigh of sorrow and pain. He turned the scroll so the scribe could see it. It was blank.

"Oh, a peshtilensh," Polykles said. "I'll find you another one. . . . Here!"

Without much hope, Sostratos took the new scroll. He opened it. It wasn't Homer, either. It was a poem of sorts, by a writer Sostratos had never heard of. It was also, as the first few lines showed him, one of the most remarkably obscene things he'd ever read. Aristophanes would have blushed.

He started to give it back to Polykles. Then he hesitated. *If I were a bored Hellenic soldier in Phoenicia, would I want to read this?* he asked himself. He dipped his head. That seemed true without a doubt. In fact, he read a few more lines himself. *Just to make sure it's all of the same sort,* he thought. And it was.

"I'll take this one," he told the scribe. "What else have you got?"

"*I* don't know," Polykles said, as if he hadn't the slightest idea of what he'd been doing lately. And, drunk as he was, maybe he didn't. He gave Sostratos yet another scroll. "Here. Thish one'sh new."

Sostratos began to read the book. It was part of Xenophon's treatise on horsemanship, something else a soldier might find interesting, or at least useful. It began very well, in a hand as neat and precise as Glaukias'. But Sostratos didn't have to go far before he found the quality sinking. *Poly-kles must have been working while he was drunk,* he thought sadly. The script grew scraggly. Lines wandered now one way, now another. Errors in grammar appeared, errors that would have earned a switching for a boy just learning his alpha-beta. Words were scratched out. Other inkblots seemed to be only that—blots. And, a little more than halfway through the scroll, words petered out altogether.

"I wish I could keep this one, but it won't do," he said.

"Why not, by the godsh?" Polykles demanded. Sostratos showed him the defects in the scroll. The scribe waved them away. "Who'll know? Who'll care?"

"The man who buys it from me?" Sostratos suggested dryly.

"Sho what?" Polykles said. "By the time he findsh that shtuff, you're long gone. Long gone," he repeated, and made flapping motions, as if he were a bird flying away. That struck him funny. He laughed hoarsely.

"Sorry, but no. I'm not a thief," Sostratos said.

"You fush about every little thing," Polykles told him.

Had the scribe sold a couple of books like the Xenophon? If he had, and especially if he'd sold them to Rhodians, he wouldn't get much business after that. If he didn't have much business, he'd worry more. If he worried more, he'd drink more. If he drank more, he'd turn out more books like the Xenophon . . . if he turned out anything at all.

More than a little sorrowfully, Sostratos held up the lewd poem and said, "I'll give you five drakhmai for this one." If anything, that was generous, for the scroll wasn't very long. Polykles just stared at him. "Five drakhmai. Do you hear me?"

"Yesh," the scribe said. "Five drakhmai. I'm shorry, besht one. I wish there were more. But . . ." Maybe he tried to explain. If he did, he had no words. But then, he didn't really need any, either.

Sostratos set the five silver coins where Polykles couldn't help but see them. "Farewell," he said, and walked—almost ran—out of the scribe's place of business. Would those five drakhmai make Polykles fare well? Would they even help him fare well? Or would he, as was much more likely, just use them to buy more wine to pour down his throat?

He would think that was faring well. But Sostratos tossed his head. How much did what Polykles drunkenly thought was faring well resemble what would in fact be well for him? Not much, Sostratos feared. And he'd helped the scribe continue on his drunken path.

He sighed and hurried away from Polykles', hurried back toward the comfortable life he led. He hurried away from what he'd just done, too. While Polykles didn't follow him—was, indeed, likely to be as grateful to him as his sodden state allowed—his own conscience did.

"FAREWELL!" MENEDEMOS' FATHER said, standing on the quay.

"Farewell!" Uncle Lysistratos echoed, adding, "Safe journey there, safe journey home."

"Thank you, Father. Thank you, Uncle," Menedemos called from the *Aphrodite*'s poop deck. She was ready to sail. Only a couple of ropes still bound her to Rhodes. Her cargo was aboard, her crew likewise. Soon she would nose out across the wine-dark sea to find out what profit, if any, lay in the east.

"Farewell!" Himilkon the Phoenician called. The bright spring sun glinted from the heavy gold rings he wore in his ears. A couple of the *Aphrodite*'s rowers, though Hellenes, wore their wealth the same way. Another had a torn, shrunken earlobe that said some of his portable wealth had been forcibly detached from him once upon a time.

Himilkon added something else, not in Greek but in a language full of hissing and gutturals. Sostratos, who stood only a couple of cubits from Menedemos, haltingly replied in the same tongue. "What did he say?" Menedemos asked. "What did you say?"

"He said almost the same thing Father did," his cousin answered. "He wished us good fortune on the journey. I thanked him."

"Ah." Menedemos dipped his head. "You really have learned some of that barbarous babbling, haven't you?"

"Some," Sostratos said. "I can count. I can haggle. I can get food or ask for a room in an inn. I can be polite."

"That should be plenty." Menedemos pointed to the base of the quay. "Here comes your brother-in-law."

"Farewell," Damonax called, panting a little. "Gods give you good weather and plenty of profit. You know you've got splendid oil there to sell."

"Yes, my dear," Sostratos said, proving he could be polite in Greek as well as Aramaic. Menedemos curtly dipped his head. He still wished they weren't carrying olive oil to Phoenicia.

He turned away from Damonax and toward Diokles. "Are we set to go?" he asked the keleustes.

"As soon as we cast off we are, skipper," Diokles answered. The oarmaster was getting close to forty-five, his short beard grizzled. He was the best sailor Menedemos had ever known. Whatever he couldn't get out of a crew and ship wasn't there to be had.

A couple of the men on the pier took care of the last detail, tossing into the *Aphrodite* the lines that moored her fore and aft. Sailors coiled the ropes and secured them. For the departure, rowers sat at all twenty benches on each side of the merchant galley. They looked expectantly back toward Diokles, who stood not far from Menedemos on the raised poop.

"Whenever you're ready," Menedemos murmured.

"Right," Diokles said. He took out a square of bronze hung from a chain and a little mallet he used to beat out the stroke. Raising his voice so it would carry all the way to the bow, he called, "All right, you lazy lugs, I know you haven't pulled on anything but your own pricks all winter long. But we've got people watching us, and I don't want us looking like a pack of idiots, eh? So even if you don't know what you're doing, pretend like you do, all right?"

"He'll make them sorry if they don't," Sostratos said.

"Of course he will," Menedemos answered. "That's his job."

Diokles poised the mallet. Menedemos settled his hands on the steering-oar tillers. They weren't so smooth as he would have liked, not polished by long, intimate contact with his callused flesh: the *Aphrodite* had lost both steering oars in separate accidents the year before, and the replacements still had a rough feel to them he didn't care for. *Time will fix it,* he thought.

Clang! Diokles smote the square. At the same time, he called out, "Rhyppa*pai!*" to help give the rowers the stroke. *Clang!* "Rhyppa*pai!*" *Clang!* "Rhyppa*pai!*"

The men at the oars did him proud. They pulled as if they were serving on a trireme or a five in the Rhodian navy. Indeed, a lot of them *had* pulled an oar in the Rhodian navy at one time or another. Slowly at first, then with building momentum, the *Aphrodite* glided away from the pier.

"Farewell!" Menedemos' father called one last time. Menedemos lifted a hand from the tiller to wave to him but didn't look back.

"Good luck!" Uncle Lysistratos said.

"Good fortune go with you!" Damonax added. With his olive oil aboard the akatos, he had reason to worry about good fortune.

Artificial moles protected the Great Harbor of Rhodes from wind and wave. The water inside the harbor was as smooth as the finest glazed pottery. A tower at the base of the eastern mole mounted dart- and stone-throwing catapults to hold enemy warships at bay. A soldier on the tower, tiny as a doll in the distance, waved toward the *Aphrodite*. Menedemos returned the greeting.

More soldiers in gleaming bronze corselets and helms marched along the mole toward the tip. The early-morning sun glinted from the iron heads of their spears. Thin across the water came the voice of the underofficer in charge of them: "Step it up, you sorry, sleepy bastards! You can sleep when you're dead."

"He sounds like Diokles," Sostratos said in a low voice.

"So he does," Menedemos agreed. "His job's not much different, is it?"

Little fishing boats were sculling out of the harbor, too. They couldn't move nearly so fast as the *Aphrodite* and made haste to get out of her way. None of their captains wanted the akatos' sea-greened bronze ram crunching into his boat's flank or stern. The fishermen and Menedemos waved to one another as the merchant galley slid toward the Great Harbor's narrow outlet.

Also making for the outlet was a big, beamy round ship, deeply laden with wheat or wine or some other bulk commodity. Like any round ship, this one was made to travel by sail. Her handful of crewmen strained at the sweeps, but the fat ship only waddled along. Expecting her to move aside for the *Aphrodite* would have been absurd. Menedemos pulled in on one steering-oar tiller and pushed the other one away from him. Graceful as a dancer, the merchant galley swung to port. As she passed the round ship, Menedemos called out to the other captain: "What's the name of your wallowing scow, the *Sea Snail?*"

"I'd sooner be aboard her than *Poseidon's Centipede* there," the other fellow retorted. They traded friendly insults till the *Aphrodite*'s greater speed took her out of hailing range.

Another round ship, this one with her enormous square sail lowered from the yard and full of the breeze from out of the north, was just entering the harbor as the *Aphrodite* left. Again, his ship being far more maneuverable than the other, Menedemos gave her as wide a berth as he could, though the harbor mouth was only a couple of plethra across.

As soon as the akatos got out onto the open sea, her motion changed. That breeze pushed swells ahead of it; the merchant galley began to pitch and roll. Menedemos kept his balance without conscious thought. Sostratos gripped the rail to help steady himself. He gripped it till his knuckles whitened, as a matter of fact, for he needed a while at the start of each trading run to regain his sea legs—and his sea stomach.

Some of the rowers also looked a trifle green. Maybe that meant they'd done too much drinking the night before. But maybe they also had trouble with the ship's motion. Most of them, like Sostratos, would soon master it. As for the ones who couldn't, what business did they have going to sea?

Menedemos said, "I think we can take most of the men off the oars now."

"Right you are, skipper," Diokles answered. He called out, *"Oöp!"* The rowers rested at their oars. Menedemos kept the merchant galley's bow pointing into the swells with the steering oars. Diokles asked him, "Eight men on a side suit you?"

"That should be fine." Menedemos dipped his head. "We don't want to wear them out." The akatos used its full complement of rowers for swank, as when setting out at the start of each new trading run, and for emergency speed, as when escaping from pirates or turning to fight them. Otherwise, the crewmen took turns at the oars.

While the sailors being relieved brought their oars inboard and stowed them, Menedemos peered north toward the Karian coast. *We're off again,* he thought, and the familiar excitement at being on his own coursed through him. *And I'm away from Rhodes, and from my father, and from Baukis.* That wasn't excitement, exactly, but it would do.

2

COMING INTO KAUNOS, ON THE KARIAN COAST,
Sostratos knew a certain surge of hope. So might a man coming back to a polis where he'd lived twenty years before have hoped a hetaira he'd kept company with then was still beautiful and still as glad to see him as she had been once upon a time. He'd been to Kaunos only the year before, but all the same. . . .

"Do you suppose . . . ?" he said to Menedemos.

Three words were plenty to let his cousin know what he was talking about. "No, my dear, I'm afraid I don't suppose," Menedemos answered. "What are the odds?"

Sostratos prided himself on being a rational man. He knew what the odds were—knew all too well, in fact. Yet, like someone hoping a long-dead love affair might miraculously revive, he did his best to look away from them rather than in their direction. "We found one gryphon's skull in the market square here," he said. "Why not another?"

"You'd do better to ask why we found one, wouldn't you, when none was ever seen in these parts before?" Menedemos said.

"I suppose I would." Sostratos heaved a melodramatic sigh. "After all the evils, hope came out of Pandora's box, and I'll cling to it as long as I can."

"However you like, of course," his cousin answered, guiding the *Aphrodite* alongside a quay with fussy precision and minute adjustments of the steering oars. Satisfied at last, Menedemos dipped his head. "That ought to do it."

"Back oars!" Diokles called to the rowers. After they'd used a couple of strokes to kill the merchant galley's forward motion, the oarmaster held up his hand and said, *"Oöp!"*

The rowers rested. Some of them rubbed olive oil into their palms. Their hands had softened over the winter, and the first couple of days aboard ship had left them sore and blistered. And they'd rowed all the way up from Rhodes. They'd had no other choice, not with the wind dead in their faces all the way north.

A couple of soldiers strode up the pier toward the *Aphrodite.* "*This* seems just like last year," Sostratos said.

"Are you trying to make an omen of it?" Menedemos asked. Suddenly shamefaced, Sostratos dipped his head. Menedemos laughed. "Omens are often where you find them, I admit, but do remember that last year the men who questioned us served Antigonos. Old One-Eye's hoplites are gone. Ptolemaios' men threw 'em out."

"I'm not likely to forget that," Sostratos said tartly. "Antigonos' soldiers almost caught us here in the harbor."

"Hush," Menedemos told him. "You don't want to say such things where these boys might hear you."

That, no doubt, was good advice. "What ship are you?" called the soldier with the fancier plume in his helmet. "Where are you from? What's your cargo?"

"We're the *Aphrodite,* best one, out of Rhodes," Sostratos answered. Rhodes tried to stay on good terms with all the squabbling Macedonian marshals, but was especially friendly to Ptolemaios of Egypt, who shipped enormous amounts of wheat through her harbor. "We've got perfume, fine oil, Koan silk, books—"

"Let me see a book," the soldier said.

"What would you like? We have some of the best parts of the *Iliad* and the *Odyssey,* or a poem that's as, ah, spicy as anything you've ever read."

Ptolemaios' trooper tossed his head. "I've never read anything at all, on account of I haven't got my letters." He seemed proud of his illiteracy, too. "But if you've really got books, I know you're traders and not some gods-detested spies."

Maybe that was logic. Maybe it was just stupidity. Sostratos couldn't quite decide which. Would spies be clever enough to bring books along in case some officious junior officer decided he wanted to have a look at them? Who could guess? Sostratos stooped under a rower's bench, opened an oiled-leather sack, and took out a roll of papyrus. He worked the wooden spindles to show the soldier the roll did indeed have words written on it.

"All right. All right. I believe you." The fellow motioned for him to stop. "Put the silly thing away. By Zeus, you are what you say you are." He turned on his heel and tramped back down the pier. The other soldier, who'd never said a word, followed him.

"That was easier than I've seen it a good many places," Menedemos remarked.

"I know." Sostratos looked up to the forts atop the hills west of Kaunos. Antigonos' soldiers had held out for a while in one of them, even after the city fell to Ptolemaios' men. "I wonder if the Rhodian proxenos ever came back here."

"If you really care, we can ask," Menedemos said with a shrug. A year before, the *Aphrodite* had taken the Kaunian who looked after Rhodian interests in his city to Rhodes itself; he'd feared arrest from Antigonos' men when word came that Ptolemaios' soldiers were sweeping west along the southern coast of Anatolia. He'd had reason to fear, too; soldiers who'd come to arrest him had got to his house just too late, and they'd come down to the harbor just too late to keep the *Aphrodite* from sailing.

Sostratos went back behind the steering oars, picked up the gangplank, and stretched it from the poop deck to the wharf. Normally, that was work for an ordinary seaman, not the merchant galley's toikharkhos. Sostratos didn't care. He was too eager to care. He gave Menedemos an inviting wave. "Come on, my dear. Let's see what there is to see."

"You're *not* going to find another gryphon's skull," his cousin told him.

"If I don't look for one, I certainly won't," Sostratos replied with dignity. "Are you coming?"

"Oh, yes," Menedemos said. "If you think I'll pass up a chance to see you act foolish, you can think again."

"I don't see how seeking something I want is foolish," Sostratos said, more dignified than ever. "When you seek what *you* want, it usually wears a transparent chiton and perfume."

"Well, I'd rather have a live girl than a dead gryphon. If that makes me a fool, I'll answer to the name."

Kaunos was an old town. Its streets ambled every which way instead of sticking to a neat rectangular grid like those of Rhodes. All the inscriptions used Greek letters, but not all were in Greek: a few were in the Karian tongue, for Kaunos had been a Karian town before Hellenes settled there, and it remained a place where folk of both bloods lived. Pointing to an inscription he couldn't read, Sostratos said, "I wonder what that means."

"Some barbarous blather or other," Menedemos said indifferently. "If it were anything important, they'd've written it in Greek."

"You say that, on your way to Phoenicia?" Sostratos said. "Hardly anyone knows Greek there. If more people did, would I have been wrestling with Aramaic all winter long?"

"If you want to wrestle, go to the palaistra," Menedemos answered, misunderstanding him on purpose. "As for the Phoenicians, well, there haven't been many Hellenes in their towns till lately. The Kaunians have no excuse."

"Always ready to see things to your own advantage, aren't you?" Sostratos said.

"To whose better?" his cousin returned.

Despite the town's twisting roads, Sostratos led both of them to the agora. "Here we are!" he said as the street opened out onto the market square.

"Yes, here we are." Menedemos scratched his head. "And how did you lead us here? Me, I'd've had to take an obolos out of my mouth and give it to somebody to get him to tell us the way."

"Why?" Sostratos said in surprise. "We were here last year. Don't you remember the way?"

"If I did, would I be saying I didn't?" Menedemos replied. "My dear, there are times when you forget ordinary mortals haven't got your memory. I'm not sure all-powerful Zeus has your memory."

"Of course not—he has his own," Sostratos said. Menedemos' praise displeased him not at all. Pointing across the agora, he went on, "The fellow who sold us the gryphon's skull had his stall there."

"Well, so he did." Menedemos started across the square, picking his way between a farmer hawking dried figs and a fellow who'd gathered a great basketload of mushrooms out in the meadows and woods in back of Kaunos. "Let's get this over with." He brightened a little. "Maybe he'll have more hides to sell us, anyhow."

Sostratos' heart pounded with excitement as he hurried after his cousin. For a moment, hope outran reason. There was the stall, there was the fellow who'd sold them the gryphon's skull, there was a lion skin on display. . . . No gryphon's skull. Sostratos sighed. He did his best to remind himself he really shouldn't have expected to see another one, not when the first had come from far to the east, beyond the edge of the known world.

His best wasn't good enough to mask disappointment.

"Why, it's the Rhodians!" the local exclaimed. "Hail, O best ones! Can we do business again? I hope we can."

"Of course he does," Menedemos muttered behind his hand. "He played us for fools once, unloading that skull on us."

"Oh, go howl," Sostratos told him. He asked the Kaunian, "Have you by any chance seen another gryphon's skull?"

"Sorry, my friend, but no." The fellow tossed his head, dashing Sostratos' hopes once and for all. Menedemos didn't say, *I told you so,* which was just as well. Sostratos thought he might have picked up a rock and brained his cousin for a crack like that right then.

Then Menedemos asked the Kaunian, "Have you seen another tiger's hide?"

The local tossed his head again. "No, not one of those, either. You fellows want all the strange things, don't you? I've got this fine lion skin here, you see." He pointed to it.

"Oh, yes," Menedemos said, though he sounded anything but impressed. "I suppose we'll buy it from you, but we'd make more money with the stranger things."

"Especially in Phoenicia," Sostratos added. "We're sailing east this year, and they have lions of their own there. How much would they care about one more hide in, say, Byblos?"

"I don't know about that, but if you're going to Phoenicia, you'll be going by way of Cyprus," the local merchant said. "They may have lions in Phoenicia, but they don't on the island. You could get a good price selling it there."

He was right. Neither Sostratos nor Menedemos had any intention of admitting as much; that would only have driven the price higher. Grudgingly, Menedemos said, "I suppose I might give you as much for this hide as I paid for the ones last year."

"Don't do me any favors, by the gods!" the Kaunian exclaimed. "This is a bigger hide than either of the ones I sold you then. And look at that mane! Herakles didn't fight a fiercer beast at Nemea."

"It's a lion skin," Menedemos said in dismissive tones. "I won't be able to charge any more for it, and you're mad if you think I'm going to pay any more for it."

"We wasted our time coming here," Sostratos said. "Let's go back to the ship."

Words like those were part of every dicker. More often than not, they were insincere. More often than not, both sides knew as much, too. Here, Sostratos meant what he said. When he saw the merchant had no gryphon's skull, he stopped caring about what the fellow did have. The sooner he got away from Kaunos and from the memory of what the local had had, the happier—or, at least, the less unhappy—he would be.

And the Kaunian heard that in his voice. "Don't get yourselves in an uproar, best ones," he said. "Don't do anything hasty that you'd regret later. You made a good bargain last year, and it would still be a good bargain at the same price this year, is it not so?"

"It might be tolerable at the same price," Sostratos said. "It might, mind you. But a moment ago you were talking about wanting more for this hide than you did for those. 'Look at that mane!'" He mimicked the Kaunian to wicked effect.

"All right!" The fellow threw his hands in the air. "You haggle your way, I haggle mine. When you do it, you're wonderful. When I do it, it's a crime. That's how you make it seem, anyhow."

Menedemos grinned at him. "That's our job, my friend, the same as your job is to sneer at every offer we make. But we do have a bargain here, don't we?"

"Yes." The Kaunian didn't sound delighted, but he dipped his head and stuck out his hand. Sostratos and Menedemos clasped it in turn.

Menedemos went back to the ship to get the money—and to bring along a couple of sailors to make sure he wasn't robbed of it before returning to the agora. Sostratos wandered through the market square till his cousin came back. He didn't think, *Maybe someone will have a gryphon's skull.* He knew how unlikely that was. Whenever the notion tried to climb up to the top part of his mind, he suppressed it. But he couldn't help hoping, just a little.

Whatever he hoped, he was disappointed. The agora held fewer interesting things of any note than it had the year before. He spent an obolos for a handful of dried figs and ate them as he walked around. Had they been especially good, he might have thought about getting more to put aboard the *Aphrodite.* But they were ordinary—Rhodes grew far better. He finished the ones he'd bought and didn't go back to the man who was selling them.

After Menedemos handed the Kaunian with the lion skin a sack of silver coins, Sostratos was glad to go back with him to the akatos. "This hide is better cured than the ones we got last year," he remarked. "You can't smell it halfway across a room."

"I know. I noticed that, too. It's one reason I wanted to pick it up." Menedemos cocked his head to one side. "I am sorry you didn't sniff out a gryphon's skull, my dear."

Sostratos sighed. "So am I, but I can't do anything about it. I'll keep looking, I suppose. Maybe, one of these days, I'll get lucky again." *Maybe,* he thought. *But maybe I won't, too.*

"RHYPPA*PAI*!" DIOKLES CALLED as the *Aphrodite* sailed east and south out of Kaunos. "Rhyppa*pai*!" The merchant galley's oars rose and fell, rose and fell. Before long, the keleustes stopped calling the stroke and contented himself with beating it out with his hammer and bronze square. That let him ask Menedemos, "Skipper, are you going to serve out weapons to the men?"

"I should hope so!" Menedemos exclaimed. "We'd look like fools, wouldn't we, going into Lykian waters without weapons to hand?"

The Lykian coast harbored pirates as a filthy man harbored lice. It was rocky and jagged, full of headlands and little inlets in which a pentekonter or a hemiolia might hide, and from which the pirate ship might rush out against a passing merchantman. And the Lykians themselves seemed to take the attitude that anyone not of their blood was fair game.

Not that Lykians are the only ones manning these pirate ships, Menedemos thought. Some of the sea raiders in these parts came from other Anatolian folk: Lydians, Karians, Pamphylians, Kappadokians, and the like. And some—too many—were Hellenes. Like Kaunos, the towns on the Lykian coast were half, maybe more than half, hellenized. But Greek pirates came to these parts no less than honest settlers.

Sailors passed out swords and hatchets and pikes and bronze helmets. Menedemos called, "Aristeidas!"

"Yes, skipper?" replied a young man at one of the oars.

"Get somebody to take your place there and go on up to the foredeck," Menedemos told him. "You've got the best eyes of anybody on this ship. I want you seeing where we're going, not where we've been."

"All right," Aristeidas said agreeably. "Come on, Moskhion, will you pull for me?"

A lot of sailors would have been angry to be bidden to hard work. Moskhion only dipped his head and sat down on the rower's bench as Aristeidas rose. "Why not?" he answered. "I'd sooner be doing this than diving for sponges any day."

Up on the foredeck, Aristeidas took hold of the stempost with one hand and shielded his eyes with the other as he peered first dead ahead, then to port, and then to starboard. Sostratos chuckled. "Not only are his eyes better than ours, he's showing us how much better they are. He ought to be a lookout in a play—say, in Aiskhylos' *Agamemnon.*"

"I don't care how showy he is," Menedemos said. "As long as he spots trouble soon enough for us to do something about it, that's what matters."

"Oh, certainly," his cousin said. "I wasn't complaining about the job he does, only saying he's got a fancier way of doing it than he did a couple of years ago."

"Not a thing wrong with that," Menedemos said again.

Sostratos looked at him. "Are we both speaking Greek?"

"Now what's that supposed to mean?" Menedemos asked. Sostratos didn't answer, annoying him further. He knew his cousin didn't think he was as bright as he might have been. More often than not, that amused him, for he thought Sostratos got less pleasure from life than he might have. Every so often, though, supercilious Sostratos struck a nerve, and this was one of those times. "What's that supposed to mean?" Menedemos repeated, more sharply than before.

"If you can't figure it out for yourself, I don't see much point to explaining it," Sostratos retorted.

Menedemos fumed. An ordinary sailor who spoke to him so insolently might have found himself paid off and let go at their next stop. He couldn't do that to his cousin, however tempting it was.

Before he could snarl at Sostratos, Aristeidas sang out: "Sail ho! Sail ho to starboard!"

Along with everyone else's, Menedemos' eyes swung to the
right. He needed a moment to spy the little pale rectangle;
Aristeidas *did* have sharper eyes than the usual run of men.
Having spotted it, Menedemos struggled to make out the hull
to which it was attached. Did it belong to a plodding round
ship or to a wolf of the sea on the prowl for prey?

Sostratos said, "I don't think that's a pirate."

"Oh? How can you be so sure?" Menedemos snapped.
"Your eyes aren't even as good as mine."

"I know that, but I also pay attention to what I see," his
cousin replied. "Most pirates dye their sails and paint their
hulls to look like sky and sea, so they're as hard to spot as
possible. That ship has a sail of plain, undyed linen, and so
she probably isn't a pirate."

He spoke as if to a halfwitted child. What really stung was
that he was right. Menedemos hadn't thought of that, and it
was true. *Furies take me if I'll admit it, though,* he thought.

A couple of minutes later, Aristeidas said, "Looks like she's
turning away—maybe she thinks *we're* pirates and doesn't
want any part of us."

"We see that every year," Menedemos said.

"We see it every year even though we're still close to
Rhodes," Sostratos said. "That's what really makes me sad,
because our navy does everything it can to put pirates down."

"Ptolemaios' captains seem to go after them pretty hard,
too," Menedemos said. "That's one reason to like him better
than Antigonos: they say old One-Eye *hires* pirates to eke
out his own warships. To the crows with that, as far as I'm
concerned."

Sostratos dipped his head. There the two cousins agreed
completely. "It's all one to Antigonos," Sostratos said. "To
him, pirate fleets on the sea are the same as mercenary regiments on land."

Menedemos shuddered. Any trader would have done the
same. "Mercenary regiments can turn bandit—everybody
knows that's so. But pirates *are* bandits, right from the begin-

ning. They live by robbery and plunder and kidnapping for ransom."

"Robbery. Plunder." Sostratos spoke the words as if they were even viler than was in fact the case. A heartbeat later, he explained why: "The gryphon's skull."

"Yes, the gryphon's skull," Menedemos said impatiently. "But you seem to forget: if those gods-detested, polluted whoresons had had their way, they wouldn't just have taken your precious skull. They'd have gone off with everything the *Aphrodite* carried, and they've have murdered us or held us for a ransom that would have ruined the family, or else sold us into slavery."

"That's true," Sostratos said in thoughtful tones. "You're right—I don't usually remember it as well as I ought to." More readily than anyone else Menedemos knew, his cousin was willing to admit he was wrong. He went on, "All the more reason to crucify every pirate ever born. I'd nail 'em to the cross myself." That carried more weight from him than it would have from another man, for he normally had little taste for blood.

Diokles said, "Begging your pardon, young sir, but I'd have to ask you to wait your turn there. I've been going to sea longer than you have, and so I've got first claim."

Sostratos bowed. "Just as you say, most noble one. I yield to you as the heroes of the *Iliad* yielded to ancient Nestor."

"Now wait a bit!" Diokles exclaimed. "I'm not so old as that."

"Are you sure?" Menedemos asked slyly. The keleustes, who was graying—but no more than graying—gave him a sour look. The rowers close enough to the stern to hear the chatter grinned back toward Diokles.

"You're making for Patara?" Sostratos asked as the *Aphrodite* sailed southeast.

"That's right," Menedemos said. "I don't want to put in anywhere along this coast except at a town. That'd be asking for trouble. I'd sooner spend a night at sea. We were talking about bandits a little while ago. This hill country swarms with 'em, and there might be bands big enough to beat our whole crew. Why take chances with the ship?"

"No reason at all," his cousin said. "If you were as careful with your own life as you are with the akatos here . . ."

Menedemos glowered. "We've been over this ground before, you know. It does grow tedious."

"Very well, best one; I'll not say another word," Sostratos replied. Then, of course, he said several more words: "Helping to keep you out of harm's way after you debauch some other man's wife grows tedious, too."

"Not to me," Menedemos retorted. "And I don't usually need help."

This time, Sostratos said nothing. His silence proved more embarrassing to Menedemos than speech might have, for his own comment wasn't strictly true. Sometimes he got away with his adulteries as smoothly as Odysseus had escaped from Kirke in the *Odyssey*. In Taras a couple of years before, though, he had needed help, and in Halikarnassos the year before that. . . .

He didn't want to think about Halikarnassos. He still couldn't set foot there for fear of his life, and he'd been lucky to escape with that life. Some husbands had no sense of humor at all.

Gulls and terns wheeled overhead. A black-capped tern plunged into the sea only a few cubits from the *Aphrodite*'s hull. It emerged with a fine fat fish in its beak. But it didn't enjoy its dainty for long. A gull started chasing it and buffeting it with its wings and pecking at it. At last, the tern had to drop the fish and flee. The gull caught the food before it fell back into the water. A gulp and it was gone.

Sostratos had watched the tern and gull. "As with people, so with birds," he said. "The uninvited guest gets the choice morsel."

"Funny," Menedemos said, grinning.

But his cousin tossed his head. "I don't think so, and neither did the tern."

"Haven't you ever got drunk at one symposion and then gone on to another one?" Menedemos asked. "Talking your way in—sometimes shouting your way in—is half the fun. The other half is seeing what sort of wine and treats the other fellow has once you do get inside."

"If you say so. I seldom do such things," Sostratos answered primly.

Thinking back on it, Menedemos realized his cousin was telling the truth. Sostratos always had been a bit of a prig. Menedemos said, "You miss a good deal of the fun in life, you know."

"You may call it that," Sostratos said. "What about the fellow whose drinking party you invade?"

"Why would he throw a symposion in the first place if he didn't want to have fun?" Menedemos said. "Besides, I've been to some that turned out jollier on account of people who came in, already garlanded, off the street."

He suspected he sounded like Bad Logic in Aristophanes' *Clouds,* and he waited for Sostratos to say as much. Menedemos liked Aristophanes' bawdy foolery much more than his cousin did, but Sostratos knew—and disapproved of—the *Clouds* because it lampooned Sokrates. To his surprise, though, Sostratos brought up the Athenian in a different way: "You may be right. You know Platon's *Symposion,* don't you, or know about it? That's the one where Alkibiades comes in off the street, as you say, and talks about the times when he tried to seduce Sokrates."

"Wasn't Sokrates supposed to be ugly as a satyr?" Menedemos asked. "And wasn't Alkibiades the handsomest fellow in Athens back whenever that was?"

"About a hundred years ago," Sostratos said. "Yes, Sokrates was ugly, and yes, Alkibiades was anything but."

"Why did Alkibiades try to seduce him, then?" Menedemos asked. "If he was as handsome as that, he could have had anybody he chose. That's how things work."

"I know," Sostratos said, a certain edge to his voice. Menedemos feared he'd stuck his foot in it. He'd been an exceptionally handsome youth and enjoyed the luxury of picking and choosing among his suitors. Nobody'd paid court to Sostratos, who'd been—and who still was—tall and gawky and plain. After a moment, Sostratos went on, "If Alkibiades could have chosen anyone he wanted but set out to seduce Sokrates, what does that tell you?"

"That he was very nearsighted?" Menedemos suggested.

"Oh, go howl!" Sostratos exclaimed. Diokles laughed out loud. He wasn't beating out the stroke now; with a good breeze from out of the north, the *Aphrodite* made for Patara by sail alone. Sostratos visibly gathered himself. "He knew Sokrates was ugly. Everybody knew Sokrates was ugly. So what did he see in him, if not the beauty of his soul?"

"But it wasn't his soul Alkibiades was after," Menedemos pointed out. "It was his—"

"Go howl," his cousin said again. "That's the point of the *Symposion:* how love of the beautiful body leads to love of the beautiful soul, and how love of the soul is a higher thing, a better thing, than love of the body."

Menedemos lifted a hand from a steering-oar tiller to scratch his head. "Love of the beautiful body, yes. But you just got done admitting Sokrates' body wasn't beautiful, or anything close to it."

"You're being difficult on purpose, aren't you?" Sostratos said.

"Not this time." Menedemos tossed his head.

"A likely story," Sostratos said darkly. "Well, look at it like this: Sokrates' soul was so beautiful, Alkibiades wanted to take him to bed even though his body was ugly. That's quite something, don't you think?"

"I suppose so," Menedemos said. Sostratos looked as if he would have brained him with an amphora of olive oil had he said anything else. *Of course he looks that way,* Menedemos thought. *If somebody handsome could fall in love with ugly Sokrates for the sake of his beautiful soul, why couldn't someone do the same with plain Sostratos for the sake of* his *soul? No wonder he takes that story to heart.*

He wasn't used to such insights. It was as if, for a moment, a god had let him look out from Sostratos' eyes instead of into them. He also realized he couldn't say anything to his cousin about what he'd seen, or thought he'd seen.

The sun set. Sailors ate barley bread and olives and onions and cheese. Menedemos washed his frugal supper down with a rough red Rhodian wine: good enough to drink, but not to sell anywhere off the island. He stepped to the rail and pissed into the sea. Some of the sailors settled down on rower's benches and went straight to sleep. Menedemos couldn't. He sat down on the planks of the poop deck—he'd been standing all day—and watched the stars come out.

The moon, a waxing crescent, hung low in the west. It wasn't big enough to shed much light, though its reflection danced on the sea behind the *Aphrodite*. Ares' wandering star, red as blood but not so bright as it sometimes got, stood high in the southeast.

Sostratos pointed east. "There's Zeus' wandering star, just coming up over the horizon."

"Yes, I see it," Menedemos said. "Brightest star in the sky, with Ares' fading and Aphrodite's too close to the sun to spy for a while."

"I wonder why a few stars wander like the moon but most of them stay in one place in the sky forever," Sostratos said.

"How can you hope to know that?" Menedemos said. "They do what they do, that's all, and there's an end to it."

"Oh, I can *hope* to know why," his cousin answered. "I don't *expect* to, mind you, but I can hope. Knowing why something happens is even more important than knowing what happens. If you know *why*, you really understand. Sokrates and Herodotos and Thoukydides all say the same thing there."

"And that must make it so." Menedemos gave his voice a fine sardonic edge.

But Sostratos refused to rise to the bait. All he said was, "Homer says the same thing, too, you know."

"What?" Menedemos sat up straighter, so abruptly that something in his back crackled. Unlike his cousin, he had no great use for philosophers and historians. They breathed too rarefied an atmosphere for him. Homer was another matter. Like most Hellenes, he looked to the *Iliad* and *Odyssey* first, everywhere else only afterwards. "How do you mean?" he demanded.

"Think about how the *Iliad* starts," Sostratos said. The *Aphrodite* bobbed up and down in light chop, the motion just enough to remind men they weren't on land any more. Sostratos went on, "What's the poet talking about there? Why, the anger of Akhilleus. That's what causes the Akhaioi so much trouble. Homer's not just talking about the siege of Troy, don't you see? He's talking about why it turned out the way it did."

Menedemos *did* think about that famous opening. After a moment, he dipped his head. "Well, my dear, when you're right, you're right, and you're right this time. Do try not to let it go to your head."

"Why don't you go to the crows?" Sostratos said, but he was laughing.

"I've got a better idea: I'm going to bed." Menedemos got to his feet, pulled his chiton off over his head, wadded up the tunic, and laid it on the planks for a pillow. Then he wrapped himself in his himation. Like most sailors, he made do with chiton alone in almost any weather. But the thick wool mantle, though he didn't wear it over his tunic, made a perfect blanket. "Good night."

Sostratos lay down beside him, also snug in his himation. "See you in the morning," he said around a yawn.

"Yes." Menedemos' voice was blurry, too. He stretched, wriggled . . . slept.

PATARA STOOD NEAR the mouth of the Xanthos River. The hills above the city put Sostratos in mind of those above Kaunos, which the *Aphrodite* had just left. Red and yellow pine, cedar, and storax grew in those hills. "Plenty of good timber there," Sostratos remarked.

"Hurrah," Menedemos said sourly. "More for the polluted Lykians to turn into pirate ships."

A couple of fives patrolled outside Patara's harbor. The big war galleys had two rowers on each oar on the thranite and zeugite banks; only the bottom, or thalamite, oars were pulled by a single man. All those rowers made the ships speedy despite their heavy decking and the planks of the oarbox that protected the rowers from flying arrows. One of them, displaying Ptolemaios' eagle on mainsail and small foresail, made for the *Aphrodite*.

"I don't mind Ptolemaios drawing timber from this country," Sostratos said.

"Better him than the Lykians, that's for sure," Menedemos agreed. "And the trees he turns into triremes and fours and fives, they can't use for hemioliai and pentekonters."

"Ahoy!" The call from Ptolemaios' war galley wafted across the water. "What ship are you?"

Menedemos' chuckle had barbs in it. "Sometimes it's funny when round ships and fishing boats think we're a pirate. It's not so funny when a five does: this bastard can sink us by mistake."

"Let's make sure she doesn't, eh?" Sostratos cupped his hands in front of his mouth and shouted back: "We're the *Aphrodite,* out of Rhodes."

"A Rhodian, are you?" the officer at the bow of the war galley said. "You don't sound like a Rhodian to me."

Sostratos cursed under his breath. He'd grown up using the same Doric drawl as anyone else from Rhodes. But he'd cultivated an Attic accent ever since studying at the Lykeion. More often than not, that marked him as an educated sophisticate. Every once in a while, though, it proved a nuisance. "Well, I *am* a Rhodian, by Athana," he said, deliberately pronouncing the goddess' name in the Doric style, "and this is a Rhodian merchant galley."

"What's your cargo?" the officer demanded. His ship came up alongside the *Aphrodite*. He scowled down at Sostratos; the five had twice as much freeboard as the akatos, and its deck had to rise six or seven cubits above the water.

"We've got fine olive oil, the best Rhodian perfume, silk from Kos, books, and a lion skin we just picked up in Kaunos," Sostratos answered.

"Books, is it?" Ptolemaios' officer said. "Can you read 'em?"

"I should hope so." Sostratos drew himself up very straight, the picture of affronted dignity. "Shall I start?"

The man on the war galley laughed and tossed his head. The crimson horsehair plume on his bronze helm nodded above him. "Never mind. Pass on to Patara. No pirate would get so pissy when I asked him a question like that." The five went back to its patrol, big oars smoothly rising and falling as it glided away.

"Pissy?" Sostratos said indignantly. He turned to Menedemos and spread his hands. "I'm not pissy, am I?" Once the words were out of his mouth, he realized he'd asked the wrong man.

Menedemos smiled his sweetest smile. "Of course not, O marvelous one, not after you stood by the rail just a little while ago." He could have done worse. Having expected him to do worse, Sostratos took that with hardly a wince.

Patara had two harbors, an outer and an inner. Menedemos took the *Aphrodite* into the inner harbor, but clucked distressfully when he saw how shallow the water was. He ordered a man up to the bow to cast the lead to make sure the merchant galley didn't run aground on the way to a quay.

"Here we are," he said with a sigh of relief as sailors tossed lines to longshoremen standing on the wharf. Some of the longshoremen were Hellenes, others Lykians who wore hats with bright feathers sticking up from them and goatskin capes over their shoulders. Most of the Hellenes were clean-shaven; the Lykians wore beards.

"This is a good harbor—now," Sostratos said, looking around the lagoon. "I wonder how long before it silts up too much to use, though."

"Well, it won't be before we sail out of here," Menedemos answered. "Nothing else matters right now."

"You have no curiosity," Sostratos said reproachfully.

"I wonder why not," Menedemos said—curiously. Sostratos started to reply, then gave his cousin a sharp look. Menedemos favored him with another of those sweet smiles he would sooner not have had.

One of Ptolemaios' officers came up the quay to ask questions of the new arrival. Patience fraying, Sostratos said, "I just told an officer aboard one of your fives everything you're asking now."

The soldier shrugged. "Maybe you're lying. Maybe he won't bother telling what you said in any report he makes. Maybe he won't come back here for a day or two, or maybe his ship will get called away. You never can tell, eh? And so . . ." He went right on with the same old questions. Sostratos sighed and gave the same old answers. When the grilling ended, the officer dipped his head. "All right, I'd say you are what you claim to be. That's what I needed to know. I hope the trading is good for you." Without waiting for a reply, he turned and went back down the quay.

"What can we get here?" Menedemos said as he and Sostratos headed into Patara.

"Lykian hams are supposed to be very good," Sostratos said.

"Yes, I've heard that, too," his cousin replied. "Maybe we can take a few to Phoenicia."

"Why not?" Sostratos agreed. A moment later, he snapped his fingers.

"What is it?" Menedemos said.

"We can take hams to Phoenicia, yes," Sostratos answered, "but not inland, to the country of the Ioudaioi. Their religion doesn't let them eat pork, Himilkon told me. Good thing I remembered."

"So it is," Menedemos said. "Why can't they eat it?"

"I don't know—Himilkon didn't explain it." Sostratos wagged a finger at his cousin. "You see, my dear? *Why?* is always the interesting question."

"Maybe," Menedemos said, and then, "Maybe it's for the same sort of reason that Pythagoreans can't eat beans."

"I've never heard that ham makes you windy," Sostratos said.

"You're already windy, seems to me," Menedemos said. "You're ready to quibble about almost anything, too, but that isn't news."

"To the crows with you," Sostratos said, but he and his cousin both laughed. And he knew Menedemos hadn't been wrong, either. *Me, ready to quibble about anything? Now why would he say that?*

Lykian houses looked little different from their equivalents back in Hellas. They presented blank fronts to the street. Some were whitewashed, some of unadorned mud brick, some of stone. They all had red tile roofs. Whatever beauty and valuables they held lay on the inside, behind tiny windows and stout doors. They gave robbers no clues about who had money and who didn't.

Patara's streets also seemed much like those of an older polis back in Hellas. That is to say, they were narrow and smelly and wandered every which way, more often than not at random. Dogs and pigs chased rooks and jackdaws away from piles of garbage. The stench was overwhelming.

"You forget how bad a city smells till you get out to sea for a while," Sostratos said.

"You're right." Menedemos looked more nearly green than he ever did on the ocean.

Here in town, Sostratos couldn't always tell whether the people walking along the streets were Hellenes or Lykians. A fair number of Lykians affected Hellenic styles, wearing chiton and himation, shaving their faces, and even speaking Greek. Their tongues betrayed them more readily than their outward seeming, though. They couldn't shed the accent of their native tongue—and Lykian, to Sostratos' ear, sounded like a series of sneezes strung together into a language.

Menedemos noticed something else. "Look how many women are out and about—and not just slaves and poor ones who can't help coming out, either. That lady who just passed us had gold earrings and a gold necklace that had to be worth plenty, but she didn't even bother wearing a veil. She was pretty, too."

"Yes, she was." Sostratos wasn't blind to a good-looking woman, either. He went on, "I'm not surprised the Lykians give their women more leave to go out and about than we do."

"Why? Because they're barbarians who don't know any better, do you mean?"

"No. Because they reckon their descent through the female line. If you ask a Hellene who he is, he'll give you his name, his father's name, his father's father's, and so on. But if you ask a Lykian, he'll tell you his name, his mother's, *her* mother's. . . ."

"Why do they do that?" Menedemos asked.

"I don't know," Sostratos answered. He poked his cousin in the ribs with an elbow. "You see? Another *why* question."

"All right. Another *why* question. I'd like to know."

"So would I," Sostratos said. "Just as a guess: a man's always sure who his mother is. There's room for doubt about his father."

"Ah, I see. You're saying the Lykians figure that way because they know their women are sluts."

"I don't *think* that's what I said," Sostratos answered. "And I don't know for a fact whether Lykian women are sluts or not. I've never had anything to do with them."

By the gleam in Menedemos' eye, he was about to impart much more information on that topic than Sostratos wanted to hear. But he fell silent when a couple of squads of soldiers tramped by on a cross street, holding up traffic on the way to the market square. Some of the men were Hellenes, with pikes in their hands and shortswords on their hips. The rest were Lykians, many of them in their feathered hats and goatskin cloaks. In place of spears, some carried iron ripping-hooks; others were archers, with bows bigger than Hellenes usually used and with long, unfletched arrows in their quivers.

Once the soldiers had turned a corner, Sostratos remarked, "Well, best one, you were probably wise not to talk about their women where they could hear you." His cousin gave him a re-proachful look, but kept quiet.

The street Sostratos had hoped would lead to the agora abruptly ended in a blank wall. He and Menedemos went back to the nearest intersection. As soon as he found someone who spoke Greek, he took an obolos from his cheek and gave the little silver coin in exchange for directions that would work. The Lykian turned out not to speak *much* Greek, and Sostratos made him repeat himself several times before letting him go.

Even then, he wasn't sure he was heading the right way till he walked into the market square. By Menedemos' pleased murmur, he was taken aback, too. "I only understood about one word in three from that barbarian," he said.

"I had the advantage of you, then," Sostratos said, doing his best not to show how relieved he was. "I'm sure I understood one word in two. Now let's see if that obolos was silver well spent." It wasn't much silver, but he hated wasting money.

Menedemos pointed. "There's a fellow with hams for sale. Shall we go over and see what he wants for them?"

"Why not?" Sostratos said again. He and his cousin pushed their way through the crowded market square. He heard both Greek and Lykian, sometimes in the same sentence from the same man. A fellow shoved a tray of plucked songbirds to-ward him, urging him to buy. "No, thank you," he said. "I can't cook them up properly." The vendor gave back a spate of incomprehensible Lykian. Sostratos tossed his head and went on. The fellow understood that.

One of Ptolemaios' soldiers was haggling with the man who sold hams. "Come on," Menedemos said out of the side of his mouth. "Let's look at something else for a little while."

"Right you are," Sostratos agreed. If they started bidding for a ham, too, the bearded Lykian could use them and the sol-dier against each other and bump up the price.

"Here." Menedemos took a Lykian-style hat and set it on his own head. "How do I look?"

"Like an idiot," Sostratos told him.

His cousin bowed. "Thank you so very much, my dear. The Lykians who wear our clothes don't look idiotic."

"That's because we don't wear such funny-looking things," Sostratos said.

"I should hope not." Menedemos put back the hat. "And all those goatskin cloaks look like they've got the mange."

"They sure do." But then, instead of going on and mocking the Lykians even more, Sostratos checked himself, feeling foolish. "It's only custom that makes our clothes seem right to us and theirs seem strange. But custom is king of all."

"That last bit sounds like poetry," Menedemos said. "Who said it first?"

"What, you don't think I could have?" Sostratos said. His cousin impatiently tossed his head. Sostratos laughed. "Well, you're right. It's from Pindaros, quoted by Herodotos in his history."

"I might have known you would have found it in a history— and I *did* know it was too good for you." Menedemos peered around the agora. "Do you see anything else you want around here?"

"One of the women who was buying dried figs, but I don't suppose she'd be for sale," Sostratos answered.

Menedemos snorted. "That's the sort of thing I'm supposed to say, and you're supposed to roll your eyes and look at me as if I were a comic actor who's just shit himself on stage. My only question is, how do you know she's not for sale unless you try to find out?"

"I'm not going to worry about it," Sostratos said. "Unlike some people I could name, I know there are other things in the world."

"Oh, I know that, too," Menedemos replied. "But none of the others is half as much fun." He checked himself. "Well, I suppose boys are half as much fun. They'd be just as much fun if they enjoyed it the way women do."

"I won't quarrel with you," Sostratos said. "A lot of men don't care whether boys enjoy it or not, though."

"They're the same sort of men who don't care if their women take pleasure, either." Menedemos' lip curled in contempt. "And, when a man like that beds a woman, she *doesn't* take pleasure. You wonder why they even bother."

"That soldier's gone," Sostratos said. "Let's go find out what the Lykian wants for his hams."

The merchant's price for one ham didn't seem too high. Menedemos asked him, "How many have you got?"

"Twenty-eight. No, twenty-seven. I just sell one."

In a low voice, Menedemos asked, "How much is twenty times his price, my dear?" Sostratos stood there in a lip-moving trance of concentration. Part of him resented being used as an animate abacus. Much more of him, though, enjoyed showing off. He gave Menedemos the answer. Menedemos gave it back to the Lykian, saying, "We'll give you that for all of them together."

"All?" The fellow stared.

"Yes, all. We'll take them east. For that. Not an obolos more. Yes? No?"

"All," the Lykian said dazedly. He wasn't used to doing business on that scale. He made mental calculations of his own, wondering whether a low price for one ham was worth getting a big sack of silver for the lot of them and not having to worry about when or whether they'd sell. Suddenly, he thrust out a hand. "All!"

Menedemos clasped it. Sostratos said, "Let's head back to the ship. We'll see how lost we get."

He didn't expect to; he'd made it from the *Aphrodite* to the agora, and, with his good head for directions, thought he'd be able to retrace his steps without much trouble. But he'd reckoned without Patara's streets, which doubled back on each other even more enthusiastically than those of a Hellenic polis built before Hippodamos popularized the idea of a rectangular grid.

He came upon a carved stone column, inscribed in Lykian, planted in front of a potter's shop. "Give the potter an obolos," Menedemos said. "He'll tell us how to get out of this maze."

"Wait," Sostratos said. He found a word on the column he recognized. "Mithradata put this up, I think."

"Who's Mithradata?" Menedemos asked.

"He was satrap here about the time our grandfather was born," Sostratos replied. "He was one of the very first people to use his own portrait on his coins."

"Everybody does that nowadays," Menedemos said. "All the Macedonian marshals do, anyhow."

"No, not all of them," Sostratos said, precise as usual. "Antigonos' silver still has Alexander's head on it."

"Fine." Menedemos sounded exasperated. "So old One-Eye puts somebody else's portrait on his money. It's still a portrait."

"I wonder how much the portraits on coins and statues really look like Alexander." Sostratos remained relentlessly curious. "He's fifteen years dead, after all. They aren't images of him any more: they're copies of copies of copies of images of him."

"You could have asked that of Ptolemaios when we were in Kos last year," his cousin said. "You could ask any Macedonian veteran, as a matter of fact, or any Hellene who went east with the Macedonians."

"You're right. I could. Thanks, best one. Next time I think of it, I will." Sostratos beamed. "Nice to run across a question that has an answer."

"Ah, but has it got one answer or many?"

"What do you mean?"

"Well, if you ask one veteran, he'll give you *an* answer. But if you ask ten veterans, will they all give you the same answer? Or will some say the coins look like Alexander while others tell you they don't?"

"I don't know." Sostratos plucked at his beard. "Finding out would be interesting, though."

Once past the potter's, they turned a corner and saw blue water ahead. "There's the gods-cursed harbor," Menedemos said. He threw his arms wide. *"Thalassa! Thalassa!"* he called, and burst out laughing.

Sostratos laughed, too. "You didn't march through all of Asia to find the sea, the way Xenophon's men did."

"No, but I came through all of Patara—through some of it two or three times, too—and that seems even farther," Menedemos retorted. "And I tell you something else, too: after I go back with some men to get the hams and pay off that Lykian, I'll be just about as glad to get on the sea again as Xenophon's men were. Have you ever found a place that's harder to get around in than this?"

"Not lately," Sostratos said. "I hope some of the other Lykian towns will be better."

"They could hardly be worse," Menedemos said.

'OÖp!' DIOKLES CALLED, and the *Aphrodite*'s rowers rested at their oars. The keleustes went on, "Bring 'em inboard, boys. We're running nicely before the wind."

The rowers did ship their oars and stow them. As the oarmaster had said, a brisk wind from out of the north filled the merchant galley's sails. The *Aphrodite* sped southward, bounding over the waves as nimbly as a dolphin.

"No sailing better than this," Menedemos said. Before long, he would swing the akatos east to follow the Lykian coastline. For now, though, he just stood at the steering oars and let her run.

Even Sostratos dipped his head. He was getting his sea legs faster this year than he had on the ship's last couple of trading runs; its pitching didn't seem to bother him at all. He said, "A pirate ship would have trouble catching us today."

"Don't count on it," Menedemos said. "They sail at least as fast as we do, and when they sprint with all their rowers going flat out there's nothing in anybody's navy can keep up with 'em."

The wind continued to rise. It thrummed in the merchant galley's rigging. The akatos' creamy white wake streamed out behind it. Menedemos turned to look back over his shoulder, trying to gauge just how fast they were going.

"Skipper, I think maybe you ought to—" Diokles began.

"Take in some canvas?" Menedemos finished, and the oar-master dipped his head. Menedemos raised his voice to call out to the sailors: "Come on, boys—brail it up a couple of squares' worth. We don't want anything to tear loose."

Strengthening lines crossed the sail horizontally. The brails ran vertically, giving it a pattern of squares. Hauling on the brails, the sailors could, if they chose, shorten part of the sail and leave the rest fully lowered from the yard, so as to take best advantage of the wind. Now, with that wind blowing out of the north, at their backs, they shortened the whole sail evenly.

"That's better," Menedemos said, but it still wasn't good enough to suit him. He ordered the yard lowered on the mast. Again, that helped. Again, it didn't seem quite enough.

Quietly, Diokles said, "Don't mean to bother you, skipper, but—" He pointed toward the north.

Menedemos looked back over his shoulder again. "Oh, a pestilence," he said, also quietly. "Well, that spills the perfume into the soup, doesn't it?" The line of dark, angry clouds hadn't come over the horizon the last time he'd looked. They swelled rapidly. No matter how fast the *Aphrodite* was going, they outpaced her with ease.

"Squall," Sostratos said.

Menedemos started to spit into the bosom of his tunic to turn aside the omen, but didn't bother completing the gesture. Sostratos hadn't really made a prediction. He'd simply stated a fact.

"Brail up the sail the rest of the way," Menedemos ordered, and the men leaped to obey. He had to call louder than he had only a few minutes before: the wind was rising fast and starting to howl. "Rowers to the oars," he added, and swung one steering-oar tiller in and the other away from him. "I'm going to put her into the wind. A storm like this one usually blows out as fast as it blows up. We can get through it quicker heading into it than running away."

Oars bit into the sea. The *Aphrodite*'s steady pitching motion changed to a roll as she turned and presented her flank to the waves. Sostratos gulped and turned green as a leek; he didn't like that so well. The rowers handled it with untroubled aplomb. In one ship or another, they'd done such things before.

Diokles began calling out the stroke as well as using his bronze square and little mallet. "Rhyppa*pai!*" he boomed. "Rhyppa*pai!* Steady, boys. You can do it. Rhyppa*pai!*"

Pushed on by the wind blowing the squall line toward the ship, the waves got bigger. They crashed against the *Aphrodite*'s ram, throwing up plumes of spray. As the akatos turned into the wind, she began pitching again, but harder; Menedemos felt as if he were aboard a half-broken horse that was doing its best to throw him off.

The ship groaned as she rode up over one of those waves. Being long and lean helped her slide swiftly across the sea. But, in a storm like this, it left her vulnerable. In heavy waves, part of her was supported by nothing but air for long heart-beats, till she rode down into the next trough. If she broke her back, everyone aboard would drown in short order.

One of those waves threw water into her bow. Everyone aboard her might drown even if she held together.

"Here comes the squall!" Sostratos shouted, as if Menedemos couldn't see that only too well for himself.

Black, roiling clouds blotted out blue sky overhead. The sun vanished. Rain poured down in buckets. Zeus hurled a thunderbolt, not far away. The noise, even through the pound-ing of the rain and the wind's shrill, furious shriek, seemed like the end of the world. If one of those thunderbolts struck the *Aphrodite,* that would take her down to the bottom of Po-seidon's watery realm, too, and all the men aboard her down to the house of Hades.

Howling like a bloodthirsty wild beast, the wind tore at Menedemos. He clung to the steering-oar tillers with all his strength, to keep from being picked up and flung into the Aegean. The steering oars fought in his hands, the ferocious sea giving them a life of their own.

A stay parted with a twang like that of an enormous lyre string. The mast sagged. If another stay went, the mast would

likely go with it. In its fall, it might capsize the merchant galley. "Fix that line!" Menedemos screamed. He didn't think
the sailors could hear him. He could hardly hear himself. But
they knew what needed doing without being told. They
rushed to seize the flapping stay, to bind it to another line,
and to secure it to a belaying pin. More men stood by with
hatchets, ready to try to chop the mast and yard free if they
did come down.

And then, as suddenly as the squall line had engulfed the
Aphrodite, it was past. The wind eased. The rain slackened,
then stopped. The sea remained high, but the waves became
less furious without that gale to drive them. A few minutes
later, as the clouds roared off toward the south, the sun came
out again.

Water dripped from Sostratos' beard. It was dripping from
the end of Menedemos' nose, too, and from the point of his
chin. Now he wiped his face with his forearm; he'd seen no
point in bothering before.

"Just another day," Sostratos remarked, just as if that were
true.

Menedemos tried on a grin. It felt good. Being alive felt
good. Knowing he'd probably stay alive a while longer felt
best of all. He dipped his head, admiring his cousin's cool-
ness and doing his best to match it. "Yes," he said. "Just another day."

A sailor at an oar near the stern grinned, too. He took a
hand off the oar to wave to Menedemos. "One thing about a
storm like that," he said. "If you piss yourself, who'll know?"

"Not a soul." Menedemos laughed out loud. The harried little men who filled Aristophanes' comedies might have said
something like that.

"Came through pretty well," Diokles said.

"Is everyone hale?" Sostratos asked.

One of the men at the oars was groaning and clutching his
left shoulder. "Did you break it, Naukrates?" Menedemos
called.

"I don't know, skipper," the man answered through

clenched teeth. "When the sea started going crazy there, it gave my oar a wrench I wasn't expecting, and I got yanked pretty good."

"I'll have a look at it, if you like." Sostratos sounded eager. He wasn't a physician, but he'd read something about the art of medicine. Sometimes that made him useful. Sometimes, as far as Menedemos was concerned, it made him a menace. But then, sometimes physicians were menaces, too.

Naukrates dipped his head. "Sure, come on. If you can do anything at all, I won't be sorry."

You hope you won't be sorry, Menedemos thought as his cousin made his way forward. Sostratos felt of the rower's shoulder. "It's not broken," he said. "It's out of its socket. I can put it back in, I think, but it will hurt."

"Go ahead," Naukrates told him. "It hurts now."

Before beginning, Sostratos had the sense to get a couple of other men to hold on to Naukrates. Then he took hold of the injured man's arm and twisted it at an angle that made Menedemos queasy to see. Naukrates howled like a wolf. Menedemos started to ask his cousin if he was sure he knew what he was doing; it seemed more like torture than therapy. But then the joint went back into place with a click Menedemos heard all the way back at the poop.

Naukrates let out a sigh of relief. "Thank you kindly, young sir. It's easier now."

"Good." Sostratos sounded relieved, too. How much confidence *had* he had in what he was doing? Less than he'd shown, Menedemos suspected. "Here, leave it like this," his cousin said to Naukrates, setting his left hand on his right shoulder. "I'm going to put it in a sling for a while, to make sure it stays where it belongs and heals."

He haggled off some sailcloth with a knife and bound up the rower's arm. Like everything else aboard the *Aphrodite,* the cloth was soaking wet. Naukrates didn't seem to care. "That *is* better," he said. "It still hurts, but I can bear it now."

"I've got some Egyptian poppy juice mixed into wine,"

Sostratos said. "I'll give you a draught of it. It will do you some good—I don't know how much."

"I'll try it," Naukrates said without hesitation. Now that Sostratos had helped him once, he seemed to think Menedemos' cousin could do no wrong. Menedemos had a different opinion, but kept it to himself. When Naukrates drank the poppy juice, he made a horrible face. "By the gods, that's nasty stuff!" he exclaimed. Before long, though, a dreamy smile spread across his face. He murmured, "It does help."

"Good." Sostratos started to slap him on the back, then visibly thought better of it. He came back up onto the poop deck.

"Nice job," Menedemos said.

"Thanks." Sostratos looked pleased with himself. "First time I ever actually tried that."

"Well, don't tell Naukrates. He thinks it was skill, not luck."

"There was *some* skill involved, you know."

"Oh, don't get stuffy with me, my dear," Menedemos said. "There was some luck involved, too, and you know *that*." He looked a challenge at his cousin. "Or are you going to try to tell me otherwise?"

He was ready to call Sostratos a liar if his cousin tried any such thing. But Sostratos only gave him a sheepish smile. "By no means, O best one. And I suppose you're right—I won't tell Naukrates."

"Won't tell me what?" Naukrates had sharp ears.

But his voice was as blurry as if he'd drunk too much wine. "Never mind," Menedemos and Sostratos said together. Normally, that would have made the sailor want to dig more, as it would have with anyone. Now, though, Naukrates just dipped his head and smiled that drugged smile. "How much poppy juice did you give him?" Menedemos asked.

"Enough to take away his pain, I hope," Sostratos answered. "I wouldn't be surprised if he goes to sleep in a while."

"*I* wouldn't be surprised if he sleeps for the next ten days."

Menedemos paused to pull his soaked chiton off over his head and stand naked in the sunshine that had returned. After a moment, Sostratos followed his example. Most ordinary sailors went naked all the time at sea. The few who usually wore loincloths had already shed them.

"That reminds me—when we get to Phoenicia, we'll make people upset if we take off our clothes whenever we happen to feel like it," Sostratos said.

"Catering to the foolish prejudices of barbarians goes against my grain," Menedemos said.

"Does making a profit go against your grain?" Sostratos asked. "If we offend our customers, will they want to trade with us?"

Menedemos grunted. That made more sense than he wanted to admit. Himilkon always wore long, flowing robes, no matter how hot the weather got. The same held true for other Phoenician merchants he'd seen in Hellenic poleis. "Very well," he said. "As long as I don't have to put on shoes."

"Himilkon didn't say anything about bare feet," Sostratos told him. "I don't want to wear shoes, either." Sailors always went barefoot aboard ship, and they kept up the habit on land, too.

Peering south, Menedemos clicked his tongue between his teeth. "That squall line's already out of sight. It could have been a lot worse for us. A ship that isn't quick or lucky could go to the bottom."

"Let's hope a couple of pirates did," Sostratos said.

"Yes!" Menedemos dipped his head. "If navies don't care about keeping pirates down, maybe the gods will take care of it for us."

"Maybe." But Sostratos didn't sound convinced. "I wish the gods had done a better job up till now."

"Oh, go howl," Menedemos said. "You always have reasons not to believe in anything."

"That's not true, and it's not fair, either," his cousin answered. "I'm trying to find the truth and to live by it. If you want to follow the first story you happen to hear, go right ahead. I can't stop you."

They glared at each other. Their own squall seemed as bad as the one that had blown out to sea. For the next couple of hours, they said not a word to each other. Sostratos watched birds and flying fish and leaping dolphins. Menedemos steered the *Aphrodite* toward Myra, where he'd been heading before the storm hit.

There were plenty of other places to anchor if he didn't make Myra by nightfall. The Lykian coastline might have had fewer long, projecting fingers of land than did that of Karia, but it was full of little inlets and harbors and coastal villages. The only trouble with them was, Menedemos wanted nothing to do with them. Every other village kept a pirate ship or two ready to sally forth against any quarry that looked catchable. Menedemos was usually sad and sorry when fishing boats fled from the akatos. In these waters, he was just as well pleased the *Aphrodite* so closely resembled a pirate ship herself.

When Myra came into sight, Diokles let out a sigh of relief. "This place is big enough for Ptolemaios' men to garrison, same as Patara was," he said. "They wouldn't bother with all those little hamlets in between Patara and here. The Lykians in them have got to be as wild as they were in Sarpedon's day."

"Sarpedon was the son of Zeus, or that's what the *Iliad* says," Menedemos answered. "If you ask me, the Lykians nowadays are mostly sons of whores."

The oarmaster laughed. "If you think I'm going to quarrel with you, skipper, you'd better think again."

Myra itself lay about twenty stadia inland—*far enough*, Menedemos thought uneasily, *to make an attack from the sea harder than it would be if the place were right there by the shore.* A couple of war galleys flying Ptolemaios' eagle and several round ships lay at anchor in the bay in front of the town. They all hailed the *Aphrodite* when she came into the harbor. Her sleek lines once more created some alarm, but Menedemos did manage to convince the officers aboard the triremes he was a Rhodian, not a pirate with more nerve than was good for him.

He was eating barley rolls for sitos with an uninspiring opson of salt fish when a coughing roar came from the mainland. Even though his ship bobbed a couple of plethra offshore, his hand froze halfway to his mouth. The hair at the back of his neck tried to stand up. "What's that?" he said, his voice high and shrill. He felt foolish as soon as he spoke; he knew what that was, all right.

"A lion," Sostratos answered. "It is an awe-inspiring noise, isn't it?"

"I should say so!" Only then did Menedemos remember he'd quarreled with his cousin. He shrugged. How could a mere quarrel survive in the face of . . . that?

Sostratos might have been thinking along with him. "Well, my dear," he said, "we aren't eaten yet, by lions or by sea jackals."

"No, not yet," Menedemos agreed. "Do you suppose Myra has anything worth buying, or shall we press on?"

"I'd go on," Sostratos said. "How many lion skins can we carry?"

Menedemos thought it over, then dipped his head.

MYRA HAD STRVCK SOSTRATOS AS NOTHING OVT of the ordinary. Phaselis, on the other hand—the last Lykian city to the east—impressed him a good deal more. It was large enough to boast three harbors. The locals fished not only on the sea but also in a nearby lake. The population was a mixture of Lykians and Hellenes.

As the *Aphrodite* tied up at a quay, Menedemos said, "I wish we had a letter or a friendship token from that Euxenides we carried last year. He was about the best carpenter I've ever seen—and if he still has kin here in Phaselis, they'd probably feast us for taking him out of danger."

"Well, they might," Sostratos answered. "But even if they did, would we want them to? Euxenides was one of Antigonos' officers, remember, and Ptolemaios is lord of Phaselis—for the time being, anyhow."

His cousin grunted. "I hadn't thought of that, but you're right, no doubt about it. If Euxenides' relatives are all for old One-Eye, Ptolemaios' men won't be very happy about them . . . or about us for dealing with them."

"That's what I meant," Sostratos said. "This whole business of trading is hard enough without getting soldiers angry at you. And speaking of trading, what do they sell here? Hides, I suppose, and timber, which we've got no real use for."

Menedemos' smile was almost a leer. It said, *I know something you don't know.* Sostratos hated being on the receiving end of a smile like that. He hated having other people know things he didn't, too. Menedemos, who knew him as well as anyone, undoubtedly also knew that. "You were studying Phoenicia and Aramaic so hard, you forgot to pay attention to how we would get there."

Sostratos said something in Aramaic. Not only was it splendidly vulgar in its own right, it sounded like a man ripping a thick piece of cloth in half. Best of all, Menedemos didn't understand a word of it. Returning to Greek, Sostratos said, "What *do* they have here, then?"

"Why, smoked fish," Menedemos answered. The fearsome noises Sostratos had just made kept him from rubbing it in. "This place is supposed to have some of the best smoked fish in the world."

"Papai!" Sostratos said.

"What's the matter?" his cousin asked.

"I actually knew that, but it had gone clean out of my head."

"I'm not surprised, my dear. You've got so many useless facts jostling and crowding each other in there, it's no wonder some of then fall out now and again."

"But they shouldn't." Sostratos hated forgetting things. A man who prided himself on his wits naturally worried about any failure. He changed the subject, as much for his own sake as for Menedemos'. "If it's good enough, we can carry smoked fish to Phoenicia."

"Better than the dried and salted stuff that usually travels." The horrible face Menedemos made showed his opinion of that, though the *Aphrodite* carried some to feed its crew. "We ought to be able to charge enough to make it profitable, too. That's your job, of course."

"Of course," Sostratos agreed. It wasn't that his cousin was wrong—Menedemos was right. But if they couldn't make a profit on smoked fish, Menedemos wouldn't get the blame. Sostratos would. That was what being toikharkhos meant. With a small sigh, Sostratos said, "Let's go into town and see what they've got."

One thing Phaselis had—as Patara had had, and Myra, too—was plenty of soldiers. Some were Hellenes and swaggering Macedonians: Ptolemaios' garrison troops. Others were Lykians, who sounded as if they were sneezing whenever they opened their mouths.

"Looks like Ptolemaios thinks his men are on this coast to stay," Sostratos remarked. "He's training up plenty of local barbarians to give them a hand."

"If he does, he's liable to be an optimist," Menedemos answered. "Antigonos is going to have more than a little to say about who rules Lykia."

"I know. I'm not saying you're wrong. I'm just telling you what it looks like to me," Sostratos said.

They walked past a statue whose base had an inscription written in Greek letters that spelled out nonsense words. "Must be Lykian, like that stele in Patara," Menedemos said.

"No doubt, though it could be anything at all for the sense it makes to me," Sostratos said. "Karian and Lykian both, even if I did figure out a name on the stele."

"If they want anybody to care about what they say, they'd better use Greek," Menedemos said.

"Well, yes, of course," Sostratos agreed.

Phaselis stood on a long spine of land projecting out into the sea. The market square lay in the center of town, not far from the theater. Pointing to the bowl scooped out of the gray local stone, Menedemos said, "*That* looks Hellenic enough."

"So it does," Sostratos said. "There *are* Hellenes here. There have been for hundreds of years. Lakios of Argos paid Kylabras the shepherd a tribute of smoked fish in exchange for the land on which to build the city, and that was back in the days we know only from myth and legend."

"I think I'd heard that once, but I'd forgotten it," Menedemos said. Unlike Sostratos, he didn't seem worried about forgetting something. He went on with his own thought: "They've been smoking fish here for a long time, too, then."

"I've heard they still offer it to Kylabras," Sostratos said. "They reckon him a hero."

"If I were a hero, I'd want a fat bullock, or maybe a boar," Menedemos said. "Fish is for ordinary mortals and their opson."

"Custom," Sostratos said, as he had not long before.

"Smoked tunny!" shouted a fellow in the agora. Another chimed in with, "Smoked eels! Who wants some fine smoked eels, nice and fat?"

"Smoked tunny? Smoked *eels*?" Menedemos' ears seemed to prick up like a fox's. "I thought they'd smoke any old thing. But those are some of the best fish there are. I wonder how they taste smoked."

"Shall we go find out?" Sostratos said. "If they won't give us samples, we've got no reason to buy, do we?"

"Not a bit," Menedemos said. "Not a bit, by Herakles—and he'd have a taste, too, if he were here." Sostratos dipped his head. If there was food around, food of any sort, Herakles would eat it.

The fellow crying his eels was a bald Hellene with a freckled scalp and startling green eyes. "Hail, my friends," he said as Sostratos and Menedemos came up. "You're new in Phaselis, aren't you?"

"That's right," Sostratos answered. "We're from the *Aphrodite,* an akatos out of Rhodes. Smoked eels, eh?" He gave his name and his cousin's.

"Pleased to meet you both. I'm Epianax son of Kleito-menes. Yes, smoked eels. We give 'em to the gods, and you can't say that about fish very often."

"We've heard stories about that," Sostratos said. "Your hero's name is Kylabras, isn't it?"

Epianax dipped his head. "That's right. I wouldn't have expected a man from as far away as Rhodes to know it, but that's just right. And what's good enough for Kylabras is more than good enough for mortal men."

Menedemos grinned at him. "I hope you're going to give us a chance to eat your words, O best one."

"Give *you* a chance to eat my . . ." Epianax frowned, then laughed when he got it. "Say, you're a clever fellow, aren't you? That's a neat way to put things, to the crows with me if it isn't. I'll use it myself, if you don't mind."

"Be my guest," Menedemos told him. "After all, we'll only hear it the once." That made the eel-seller laugh again. Sostratos and Menedemos shared a look. The people in Phaselis' agora were liable to be hearing the same line thirty years from now, if Epianax lived so long. Menedemos went on, "You will let us try a sample, won't you?"

"Oh, yes." Epianax had a formidable knife on his hip: another few digits and it could have been a hoplite's shortsword. He used it to hack off a couple of lengths of smoked eel, then handed one to each Rhodian. "Here you are, most noble ones. Take a taste, and then we'll talk."

Sostratos popped his piece of eel into his mouth with the thumb and forefinger of his right hand: it wasn't sitos, which he would have eaten with his left, and it wasn't fresh fish, for which he would have used two fingers and his thumb, not just one. He chewed, savoring both the smoke and the fatty richness of the eel. He had to work hard not to show how delicious he thought it was.

"Not bad," Menedemos said after swallowing. A certain

tension in his expression said he was having the same problem as Sostratos. Maybe Epianax, who didn't know him, wouldn't notice. His voice sounded casual enough: "What do you want for it? If the price is decent, we might take some along with us—we're bound for the east, and it could do well there."

"You talking about cash, or do you want to trade for it?" Epianax asked. "What are you carrying?"

"We've got prime olive oil, fine Rhodian perfume, Koan silk, hams from Patara, papyrus and ink, and some books," Sostratos said.

"Didn't expect you'd have oil," Epianax remarked. "Most places can make that for themselves."

This time, Sostratos didn't meet Menedemos' eye. His cousin muttered something he couldn't make out, which was probably just as well. *Damonax,* he thought unkindly. He hadn't imagined that acquiring a brother-in-law would hurt his business, but it had. As loyally as he could, he said, "It's excellent oil, from the very first of the harvest."

"Must be," Epianax said, and let it go at that. Menedemos' snicker wasn't very loud, but a snicker it unquestionably was. Sostratos wished the vulture that tore at Prometheus' liver would give the Titan a holiday and torment Menedemos for a while. But then Epianax surprised him by asking, "What sort of books have you got?"

"You know your letters?" Sostratos said, blinking.

"Wouldn't be much point to the question if I didn't, would there?" the eel-seller answered. "Yes, I know 'em. Don't have a whole lot of cause to use 'em, but I can fight my way through Homer, say."

"We have some of the most exciting books of the *Iliad* and the *Odyssey* with us," Menedemos said. The look he gave Sostratos added that it was only because of him that they had those books, which wasn't true at all. Sostratos felt hampered, constricted; he didn't want to start an argument in front of a stranger.

To help remind his cousin he'd been the one who actually

bought the books from the scribes who'd copied them, he said, "And we also have a, ah, spicy poem from a modern writer, a fellow named Periandros of Knidos."

"Spicy, eh?" Epianax's eyes lit up. He knew what that meant, or hoped he did. "What's it about?"

"You know the statue of Aphrodite that Praxiteles put up at Knidos, the one that shows the goddess bare?" Sostratos said.

"I should hope I do," Epianax answered. "Everybody knows about that statue."

He was right, of course. The image of Aphrodite had roused enormous interest and excitement when it went into her shrine a generation before. *Roused* and *excitement* were words literally true, too. Hellas was a land where respectable women veiled themselves on the rare occasions when they appeared in public. Not long after the astonishing, shocking statue went up, a man ejaculated on its marble crotch. For him, Aphrodite proved truly the goddess of love.

Sostratos said, "It's about that fellow—you'll have heard the story about him." Menedemos would have given the details. Sostratos didn't, and didn't need to; the eel-seller dipped his head. Sostratos continued, "It's about what would have happened if the statue turned to flesh and blood just then."

"And?" Epianax asked hoarsely.

"And you'll have to buy the poem to find out what Periandros has to say about that," Sostratos told him.

"Well, what do you want for it?" Epianax demanded.

How often does anyone sell books in Phaselis? Sostratos wondered. *Not very, unless I miss my guess. In which case . . .* "Normally, I'd ask twenty drakhmai, but I'll make it eighteen for you," he said, and waited to see if the eel-seller would go right through the cloth roof of his stall.

When Epianax didn't, Sostratos knew he would make a good profit. "You mean eighteen drakhmai's worth of my eels, right?" Epianax asked.

"Yes, certainly," Sostratos said. "I suppose you sell them

for a drakhma apiece, the same as they do in Rhodes?" Nobody in Rhodes sold smoked eels like these, but Epianax didn't need to know that, either.

He dipped his head now. "I'd've asked a little more if you didn't know what you were doing, but a drakhma's fair. Still and all, I think eighteen drakhmai's a little on the steep side for a book. What do you say to fourteen?"

They settled on sixteen after a short haggle that left Sostratos feeling happy at his profit and vaguely guilty at the same time. He and Menedemos chose their eels; Epianax threw in a beat-up leather sack in which they could carry the smoked fish back to the *Aphrodite*. Sostratos got the book of poetry from the ship and gave it to the eel-seller.

"Thanks, best one." Epianax looked as if he could hardly keep from unrolling the scroll and plunging right in. "I'll read this myself and I'll read it to my pals in taverns and such—a book's always better in company."

Sostratos didn't think so, but knew he held a minority opinion. Until only a few generations before, hardly anyone had owned books of his own, and they were always read in public. With a shrug, the Rhodian said, "However you like, of course."

"I'll do you a good turn, if I can," Epianax said. "Do you know the place called 'Dinos'?"

"'Whirlpool'?" Sostratos echoed. "No. Where is it? To a sailor, a whirlpool's a good thing to stay away from. Do you fish for your eels as well as smoke them? Is that how you know about the place?"

"No, no, not at all," the eel-seller said. "You misunderstand. It's an oracle—a grove sacred to Apollo by the sea, a few stadia north of here. There's one particular pool that's always full of eddies. The person who wants to know the god's mind takes two skewers, each with ten pieces of roasted meat on it. Some say you can use boiled, too, but I think they're wrong."

"An oracle," Sostratos murmured. He prided himself on his

rationality, but how could you deny there were ways of knowing the future? Intrigued in spite of himself, he asked, "How does the priest divine the god's will?"

"He sits at the edge of the grove, while the man offering the sacrifice looks into the pool and tells him what kinds of fish come and eat the different pieces of meat," Epianax answered.

"That would be a fine oracle for fishermen," Sostratos said. "But suppose a farmer who eats cheese and olives for his opson every day comes to the sacred grove. How would he know what to tell the priest if he can't figure out which fish is a mackerel and which one's a shark?"

The eel-seller scratched his head. "Good question, my friend. I don't know the answer, but I suppose the priest does, and I'm sure the god does. An oracle wouldn't hardly be an oracle if just anybody could see how it worked, now would it?"

In a way, that made sense. In another way, it annoyed Sostratos. He had a restless itch to know, to find an explanation. Epianax had a point: divine things didn't lend themselves to explanation. But weren't things that didn't lend themselves to explanation likely to be unreal? Part of Sostratos was tempted to think so. The rest resisted the impulse.

"If you're going that way, you can see for yourself," Epianax said.

They *would* be going up the Lykian coast toward Pamphylia, then east to Kilikia and the shortest crossing to Cyprus. Sostratos hedged: "I don't know whether we'll stop or not. My cousin's the skipper. It'll depend on how much of a hurry he's in to get to Phoenicia."

"Is *that* where you're headed?" The eel-seller started to giggle.

"What's so funny?" Sostratos asked.

"Only that you may have a harder time selling those smoked eels than you think," Epianax answered. "A lot of Syrians and other folk like that don't eat fish. Their gods won't let 'em, or some such."

"*Oimoi!*" Sostratos clapped a hand to his forehead. "I knew the Ioudaioi won't eat pork, but I'd never heard that any of those people wouldn't eat fish. What do they do for opson?"

"Not my worry," Epianax said.

"No, it's mine," Sostratos agreed. *Why didn't Himilkon tell me? Did he think I already knew? Or has he lived among Hellenes long enough to get over his silly superstition?* No way to tell, not without sailing back to Rhodes to ask the Phoenician. After a moment, Sostratos brightened. "Well, there'll be plenty of Hellenes in the coastal towns. If the barbarians don't catch fish, the men who serve Antigonos will be all the gladder to see us."

"Mm, that's so." Epianax looked down at the roll of papyrus in his hands. "I still think I got the better of the bargain. When those eels are gone, they're gone for good, but I'll be reading this book twenty years from now if I can keep the mice from nibbling at it."

"The best sort of bargain is one where both sides go away happy," Sostratos said diplomatically. "I'm heading back to the harbor now. Farewell, and enjoy the poem."

"If it's got Aphrodite in it without her clothes, I expect I'll like it just fine." Epianax sounded very sure of himself.

When Sostratos came aboard the merchant galley, he told Menedemos what he'd learned from Epianax. His cousin shrugged. "I'd thought we'd sell the eels to the Hellenes in Antigonos' army anyhow," he said. "I know we're all opsophagoi when we get the chance. Who wouldn't rather stuff himself with turbot or tunny or cuttlefish or lobster than with barley cakes or wheat bread?"

"Sokrates wouldn't, for one. Opson is fine, he'd say, but it's the relish—it's what you eat *with* the staple, *with* the sitos. If you do it the other way round, then your bread turns into the relish, doesn't it?"

"So what?" Menedemos said cheerfully, and smacked his lips. "If I had the silver for it, I'd eat fish till I grew fins."

"Gods be praised you don't, then," Sostratos said. But how could you argue with somebody who not only admitted he was an opsophagos but sounded proud of it? Seeing no way,

Sostratos didn't try. Instead, he passed on what Epianax had said about the oracle at Dinos.

"That *is* interesting," Menedemos said. "But what did he tell you? It's only a few stadia north of Phaselis? I don't see much point in stopping."

"You surprise me," Sostratos said. "Don't you want to learn what the god has to say about our voyage?"

Menedemos tossed his head. "Not me, my dear. I'll know in a few months any which way. Why? Are you that curious?" He answered his own question: "Of course you are. You always are. Do you really care about what the god says, or are you interested in watching how this particular oracle works?"

Sostratos' ears heated. "You know me too well," he mumbled.

"Only your mother and father have known you longer," Menedemos said. "And they have to love you, for they bore you. Me, I see you as you are—and, somehow or other, I put up with you anyway."

"Thank you so much," Sostratos told him.

His cousin ignored the sarcasm. "My pleasure—most of the time, anyhow. But listen—I've got news. While you were talking with the eel-seller, I chatted up some of the sailors here in port. Things are stirring, sure enough."

"What sorts of things?" Now Sostratos sounded interested. If anything could distract him from his own gloom, it was news of the outside world.

"Well, do you know Kleopatra, Philip of Macedon's daughter and Alexander's sister?"

"Personally?" Sostratos said. "No."

Menedemos gave him the exasperated stare he'd hoped for. "No, not personally, you thick-head. Do you know of her?"

"Who doesn't?" Sostratos replied. "When she married Alexandros of Epeiros, Philip was murdered at their wedding feast. That put Alexander the Great on the throne. It made him Great, in fact, because who knows what he would have been if Philip ruled another twenty-five years, as he could have? After Alexandros died, she married Alexander's marshal Perdikkas, and after *he* died some other officer—I forget whom. She's in one of Antigonos' Anatolian towns these days, isn't she?"

"Yes, in Sardis—for the moment," Menedemos said portentously.

"Ah?" Sostratos said. "'For the moment,' is it? Tell me more."

"Well, what one of my chattering friends told me was that she doesn't want to stay in Sardis or under old One-Eye's muscular thumb any more," Menedemos replied. "The story is, she wants to go over to Ptolemaios."

"He's got that base over there on Kos, right across from the Anatolian mainland," Sostratos said, and Menedemos dipped his head. Sostratos thought quickly. The conclusion he reached didn't take much in the way of complicated calculation. "Kleopatra will never get to his men alive."

"You sound sure of that," Menedemos said.

"I'll bet a mina of silver on it, if you're in the mood," Sostratos told him.

"A hundred drakhmai? By the dog of Egypt, you *are* sure, aren't you?"

"Will you take the bet?"

Now Menedemos thought it over. He didn't need long, either. "No, thanks. Antigonos can't afford to let her get to Ptolemaios; he'd lose too much face. And he's ruthless enough to kill her if she tries. In other words, you're likely right."

"Whether I am or I'm not, we're both reasoning the same way, anyhow," Sostratos said. "All right, then, we won't bet. And we won't stop at the oracle, either?" He did his best to sound woefully disappointed.

"Not if it's that close to Phaselis," Menedemos answered. "Don't you want to get to Phoenicia and Ioudaia and practice your Aramaic?"

The question was good enough to keep Sostratos from complaining as the *Aphrodite*'s rowers took her out of the harbor of Phaselis. He wondered whether Kleopatra had already fled Sardis. *Poor woman,* he thought. *If she's tried it, she's probably already dead. Who's left from Philip's dynasty, then? No one. No one at all.*

AS THE *APHRODITE* slid past the sacred grove at Dinos, Menedemos eyed the pines and oaks. The grove looked like any other unhallowed Anatolian forest to him. As Epianax the eel-seller had told Sostratos, though, it did come right down to the sea. Its holiness had let it survive in the lowlands where most timber had been cut away to make room for farms. The only trees close by were cultivated groves of olives and almonds. But the hills rose steeply from the sea. A man wouldn't have to go many stadia inland to find himself in the woods once more.

"Rhyppa*pai*!" Diokles called. "Rhyppa*pai*!" The breeze was fitful. When it did blow, it came mostly from the north. If the akatos was going to get anywhere, it had to travel by oar power.

Dolphins leaped and frolicked alongside the ship. "They're a good omen," Menedemos remarked to his cousin.

Sostratos dipped his head. "So says the part of me that goes to sea every sailing season. The part of me that went to the Lykeion in Athens has its doubts."

"Why take chances?" Menedemos asked. "If you take omens but they aren't real, you don't hurt yourself, but if you ignore them and they are, you can end up in all sorts of trouble."

"You can end up in trouble following omens that aren't real," Sostratos said. "Suppose you believe some lying fool of a soothsayer and do what he tells you, and it turns out to be the worst thing you could have done? Or what about the prophecy the Pythia at Delphi gave to King Kroisos of Lydia:

'If Kroisos o'er the Halys River go
He will a mighty kingdom overthrow'?

What about that?"

"Oh, no, my dear." Menedemos tossed his head. "You won't get me with that one. That's not the oracle's fault. It's

Kroisos' fault, for not asking whether he'd overthrow the Persian kingdom—or his own."

Sostratos gave him an impudent grin. "I can't fault your logic. I doubt whether Sokrates himself could fault your logic. But logic, remember, lies at the heart of philosophy. And you're a man who sneers at philosophy. So where, O marvelous one, is the logic in that?"

"In your *proktos*," Menedemos suggested.

"Aristophanes and his jokes are funny in their place. When they get out of their place . . ." Sostratos sniffed.

Menedemos started to point out that Aristophanes had had a good deal to say about philosophy and especially about philosophers. At the last instant, he held his tongue. He knew what would happen if he sailed down that channel. He and Sostratos would get into a row about how big a role Aristophanes and *Clouds* had played in Sokrates' death. How many times had they had that argument? Too many for Menedemos to want to go through it again. By now, the steps were almost as formal as a dance.

"Sail ho!" Aristeidas shouted as Menedemos was casting about for something different to say. "Sail ho off the starboard bow!"

A sail was more important than any argument. Menedemos peered out to sea. After a moment, he spotted the sail, too. "Looks like a round ship. And . . . isn't that another sail behind it?"

"Yes, skipper, it is—more than one, in fact," the lookout answered.

"By the gods, you're right," Menedemos said after another look. "Three, four, five, six . . . I make it eight sail altogether. Is that right?"

Aristeidas shaded his eyes with his hand. "I see . . . ten, skipper, I think. A couple of them are well out to sea there. And look! To the crows with me if the lead ship hasn't got Ptolemaios' eagle on its sail."

"They must be grain ships, keeping his garrisons in Lykia supplied," Sostratos said.

"He's got nerve, sending round ships along this coast without any war galleys escorting them," Menedemos said. "Two or three pirates could put paid to that whole fleet."

"Ptolemaios has garrisons in all the good-sized towns around here," Sostratos reminded him. "That has to make a difference."

"*Some* difference," Menedemos allowed. "How much, I don't know. Most pirate ships don't operate out of those towns. They skulk behind headlands or at the mouths of little streams, and then leap out at whatever passes by."

"You make them sound like ferrets, or other little vicious animals," Sostratos said.

"That's how I feel about them," Menedemos replied. "Don't you?"

"I feel that way about pirates, not about pirate ships," Sostratos said. "Ships are just—ships. It's the whoresons inside 'em who make the trouble."

"You're too subtle for me. If I see a pentekonter or a hemiolia, I want to sink it right there on the spot," Menedemos said. "I don't care who's in it. Whoever's in a ship like that is bound to be up to no good, because you can't do good in a ship like that. If it weren't for pirates, there wouldn't *be* ships like that."

"That's why they're going to build that trihemiolia you were talking about last fall," Sostratos said. "She'll be a pirate-hunter's dream ship, if she sails the way everybody thinks she will."

"And that's why you build a new ship: to see if she sails the way everybody thinks she will, I mean," Menedemos answered. "I wouldn't mind being her skipper, though—I'll tell you that."

"If anyone's earned the right, you have," his cousin said. "If not for you, there wouldn't be a trihemiolia."

Menedemos shrugged. "That's true. But I'll tell you something else every bit as true, my dear: I'm out here on the Inner Sea, bound for Phoenicia to make a living for my family, and there are plenty of captains back in Rhodes who want to command a trihemiolia every bit as much as I do."

"That's not fair," Sostratos said.

"The world's not fair," Menedemos replied with another shrug. "Anybody who goes out in it a little bit will tell you the same. Sooner or later, I expect I'll get a chance. And when I do, I'll show people what kind of officer I am." That seemed enough of that. He pointed toward Ptolemaios' approaching merchantmen. "Those are big ships, aren't they?"

"I think they're bigger than the ones that brought grain into Syracuse for Agathokles sailing season before last." Sostratos plucked at his beard. "It makes sense they should be, I suppose. Agathokles had to take what he could get. Ptolemaios can pick and choose."

"And Ptolemaios has more money than Agathokles ever dreamt of," Menedemos added.

"I said something about Kroisos a little while ago. Ptolemaios has more money than Kroisos ever dreamt of," Sostratos said. "Ptolemaios has more money than *anybody* ever dreamt of, except maybe the Great Kings of Persia—and they held Egypt, too."

"Egypt's the richest country in the world. It's so rich, it hardly seems fair," Menedemos said. Not only was the land rich in gold (and emeralds, as he had reason to know), but the Nile floods renewed the soil every year. They let the peasants raise enormous crops (some small part of which lay in the holds of those approaching round ships), and let whoever ruled Egypt collect even more enormous amounts of taxes.

"Ahoy!" The shout came thin across the sea from a sailor at the bow of the leading merchantman. "Ahoy, the galley! What ship are you?"

Are you a pirate? If you are a pirate, will you admit it? That was what the fellow meant. Menedemos shouted back: "We're the *Aphrodite,* out of Rhodes."

"Out of Rhodes, eh?" The sailor on the round ship sounded suspicious. He had reason to; with Rhodes a leading trading partner for Egypt, a pirate would do well to disguise himself as coming from that island. "What trading house are you from?"

"Philodemos and Lysistratos'," Menedemos replied. "Philodemos is my father; Lysistratos is my toikharkhos' father." Maybe Ptolemaios' man knew a bit about Rhodes, or maybe he was just seeing if pirates would stumble trying to invent something plausible. Either way, Menedemos was not the sort of man to let him get by with cheek unchallenged. He shouted a question of his own: "What ship are *you?*"

And he got an answer. "This is the *Isidora,* out of Alexandria," answered the sailor on the round ship. Then the fellow realized he didn't have to tell Menedemos anything. He shook his fist at the *Aphrodite.* "It's none of your business who we are and what we're doing."

"No, eh? But it's *your* business who we are and what we're up to?" Menedemos returned. "Well, you can go howl, pal! We're free Hellenes just the same as you are, and we've got as much right to ask you questions as you do with us."

"Euge!" Sostratos and Diokles said together. A couple of sailors clapped their hands. Menedemos grinned at the praise. The arrogance of the soldiers and sailors who served under Macedonian marshals could surpass belief.

The man on the *Isidora* had it in full measure, too. He threw back his head and laughed as the two ships passed closest to each other. "Go ahead and bark, little dog," he said. "When a big dog decides he wants your house, you'll run away yelping with your tail between your legs."

Rage ripped through Menedemos. "I ought to sink that son of a whore. Who does he think he is, to talk to me that way?"

Again, Sostratos and Diokles spoke together. This time, they both said, "No!" Menedemos knew they were right, but he still steamed like a sealed pot forgotten in a fire. He felt as if he could burst and scatter shards everywhere.

One after another, the grain ships glided past the *Aphrodite.* The men aboard them no doubt thought them majestic. To Menedemos, *wallowing* seemed a better word. They sailed well enough with the wind right behind them, as it was now.

Trying to tack against it, though, they were so slow as to be nearly helpless.

A sailor on the *Aphrodite* shouted, "I hope real pirates get you, you fig-suckers!"

That went too far. "By the dog, Teleutas, keep quiet!" Menedemos hissed. "They aren't our enemies."

"No, but they're acting like a bunch of wide-arsed little pricks," Teleutas answered. Menedemos snorted out an exasperated breath. He'd had Teleutas aboard for three sailing seasons in a row now, and he kept wondering why. The man did as little as he could to get by. He wasn't particularly brave. He wasn't even an entertaining sort, to make up for his other lacks. *If he keeps on like this, I'd do better to leave him behind next year,* Menedemos thought. *Let him drive some other captain crazy.*

He'd certainly hit a nerve aboard Ptolemaios' transports. Mention of pirates did, with honest sailors. The sailors who heard him screamed abuse at the *Aphrodite.* They made obscene gestures. They shook their fists. One of them even threw something at the merchant galley. Whatever it was, it splashed into the Inner Sea far short of its goal. Teleutas laughed a mocking laugh, which only inflamed the men from Alexandria more.

"They know who we are," Sostratos said unhappily. "They won't forget. They'll blacken our name in every port Ptolemaios holds—and he holds a lot of them."

"I know," Menedemos said. "What can I do about it now, except maybe pitch Teleutas over the side?"

"Nothing." His cousin scuffed a bare foot across the planks of the poop deck. "I'm the one who took him on a couple of years ago, there right before we sailed. I've been sorry at least half a dozen times since."

"I had the same thought," Menedemos answered. "He doesn't really pull his weight, and he does get into trouble—and get us into trouble. But he's never made me quite angry enough at him to sail off without him . . . and I did bark at the Alexandrians before he did, curse it. I guess I'm likely not the first captain he's aggravated, that's all."

"Well, there goes the last grain ship," Sostratos said. "Many goodbyes to them—but I wouldn't wish pirates on anybody."

"No, neither would I," Menedemos said, and then, "Well, hardly anybody."

He couldn't tell by the coastline where Lykia stopped and Pamphylia began—the difference lay in the people, not the landscape. But Olbia, a strong fortress on the far side of the Kataraktes River, unquestionably belonged to Pamphylia. The Kataraktes lived up to its name, rushing down from the mountains in back of Olbia toward the sea and booming over the rocks as it came.

Menedemos, used to the little Rhodian streams that dried up in the summertime, eyed the river with no small wonder. Sostratos smiled at him and asked, "If you think this is such a marvel, what will you make of the Nile if we go to Alexandria one day?"

"I haven't the faintest idea, my dear," Menedemos replied. "But the Nile, I'm sure, doesn't make such a racket as it flows into the Inner Sea."

"No, indeed. You're right about that," his cousin agreed. "The cataracts of the Nile are thousands of stadia up the stream. Herodotos talks about them."

"Herodotos talks about everything, doesn't he?"

"He was curious. He traveled all over the known world to find out what really happened, and how it happened, and, most important of all, *why* it happened. If it weren't for him, there might not be any such thing as history today."

"And would we be any worse off if there weren't?" Menedemos murmured. That horrified Sostratos no less than Teleutas had horrified Ptolemaios' sailors. Menedemos had hoped it would.

But then Sostratos gave him a sour smile. "You're trying to poke me again. I'm sorry, best one, but I don't feel like being poked."

"No, eh?" Menedemos used a finger to poke his cousin in the ribs. Sostratos yelped. Then he snapped at the finger as if he were a dog. Menedemos jerked it back in a hurry. They both laughed. Menedemos said, "If you think I look tasty, you haven't been taking enough opson with your sitos. You need to eat better."

"If I wanted to eat well all the time, I wouldn't go to sea," Sostratos answered. "Stale bread, cheese, olives, dried fish . . . Not your opsophagos' feast. And what you can get in a port-side tavern isn't much better. You can't catch enough fish from an akatos to make for much in the way of fancy opson, and, even if you could, you couldn't cook it in any particularly interesting ways."

"Nothing wrong with grilling a fish on a brazier," Menedemos said. "These fancy chefs who want to smother everything in cheese aren't half so smart as they think they are."

"Don't let your Sikon hear that," Sostratos warned him. "He'll throw you out of his kitchen on your ear."

"Oh, no." Menedemos tossed his head. "Sikon's a good cook, but that doesn't mean he's always fancy. He says sometimes cooks use those complicated, spicy sauces because they don't want you to know they've botched the cooking of the fish itself."

"I wouldn't want to argue with him."

"Neither would I, by Zeus!" Menedemos said. "Nobody in his right mind would want to pick a quarrel with Sikon. He's one of those slaves who've been there forever and think the place is really theirs. And that's part of the trouble he's having with Baukis."

"She thinks he has to watch every obolos?"

"Partly that. And partly she's my father's second wife, so she doesn't think she gets the respect she deserves." Menedemos laughed. He could talk about, even think about, Baukis as long as he did so impersonally. He went on, "And, of course, Sikon doesn't give anybody any more respect than he has to, and not as much as he should. That's why they squabble all the time."

"What does your father say?"

"As little as he can. He doesn't want to make Baukis angry, but he doesn't want to make Sikon angry, either." Menedemos rolled his eyes. "If he were as mild with me as he is with them, we'd get along a lot better."

"If he won't do anything to end the bickering, isn't ending the bickering your place?" Sostratos asked.

"Well, it might be, if I weren't at sea half the year. And I don't want to get stuck in the middle of the quarrel, either. Sikon's a jewel. I don't want him mad at me. And I don't want to get my stepmother"—he chuckled at that; the idea still struck him as absurd—"upset, either. That might make my father give me an even harder time than he does already."

What he wanted to do with Baukis, to Baukis, would make his father give him something worse than a hard time. So far, here as in few other places, his will had ruled his desires. That was what a man was supposed to do. Having desires was one thing, acting on them when they were foolish something else again. In the *Iliad*, both Agamemnon and Akhilleus had put their individual desires above what was good for the strong-greaved Akhaioi, and both had suffered because of it.

"You do make sense," Sostratos said. "You make more sense than usual, as a matter of fact." He reached out and set a hand on Menedemos' forehead. "Are you feeling all right, my dear?"

"I *was,* till you started bothering me." Menedemos shook the hand away.

His cousin laughed. "That sounds more like you. Are you enough like yourself to answer a question?"

"Depends on what it is," Menedemos replied. More than once, Sostratos had asked why he seemed quieter and gloomier than usual. He'd given either evasive replies or none. He didn't intend to tell Sostratos or anyone else what he thought about his father's second wife, what he wanted to do with her.

But Sostratos had something else in mind: "From where along the coast do you want to sail for Cyprus?"

"Ah." Menedemos beamed at his cousin. That was a completely legitimate question, and one he'd been thinking about himself. "I'd like to go a good deal farther east before I swing the ship south across the Inner Sea. The shortest passage between the mainland and the island, I think, is about four hundred stadia."

"Yes, I believe that's about right," Sostratos agreed. "My only reservation is, this whole southern coast of Anatolia—Lykia, Pamphylia, Kilikia—crawls with pirates. I was just wondering if you'd weighed the risk of a longer voyage over the open sea against that of an attack as we make our way east."

"Not easy to do," Menedemos said slowly. "There are always risks when you cross the open sea. You can't avoid them. That's why you stay within sight of land whenever you can—unless you're going somewhere downhill, so to speak, the way Alexandria is from Cyprus, where you can really count on the wind wafting you along during the sailing season. Pirates, now, pirates are different. They might not bother us at all, and there's no risk to sailing east if they don't."

"Of course there's a risk," Sostratos said. "They *might* attack. That's what makes a risk. If we knew they *would* attack, it wouldn't be a risk any more. It would be a certainty."

"Have it your way, then. I think we're saying the same thing in different words. But I don't know how to weigh the one risk against the other. Since it's easier to gauge the risk of sailing across the open sea, that's the one I want to cut out as far as I can."

"All right," Sostratos said. "I'm not sure I agree with you, but I'm not sure I don't, either. You're the captain."

"Would it make you happier if I talk to Diokles before I finally make up my mind?" Menedemos asked.

Sostratos dipped his head. "I'm always happy when you talk to Dio-kles. He's forgotten more in the way of seamanship than most people ever learn."

"I'm not interested in what he's forgotten. I'm interested in what he remembers."

But the oarmaster proved less helpful than Menedemos had

hoped. He scratched his chin as he thought it over. At last, he said, "I've seen skippers do both, matter of fact. Six oboloi to the drakhma either way."

"Well, in that case, I'm going to keep sailing along the coast here, as I'd planned," Menedemos said. "Even if a pirate does look us over, we aren't likely to have to fight him. Most of them want easy pickings—a round ship with only a few sailors aboard that's too slow to run away and too weak to fight back. They can see that we'd give 'em a good battle even if they did manage to catch us."

"Most of them can," Diokles agreed. "Of course, there's always the odd bastard you can't count on, like that fellow in the strait between Andros and Euboia last season."

Menedemos relayed most of Diokles' opinion to Sostratos. He didn't mention the pirate who'd attacked them the previous sailing season. He knew what his cousin would do on hearing about that pirate and his crew: he would start cursing them for stealing the gryphon's skull. Menedemos had heard those curses too many times to want to listen to them again.

Sostratos said, "It's your choice to make. I hope it turns out well."

"You're not going to make doleful comments like that till we get to Cyprus, are you?" Menedemos asked. "They don't make the crew very happy, you know."

"Oh, yes. I'll keep my mouth shut. I do know the difference between what I can say to you and what I can say when the sailors are listening, believe me."

"I hope so." But Menedemos didn't press it. His cousin had always been good about keeping his opinions to himself when they might damage morale. To change the subject, Menedemos asked, "Shall we find the market square here? You never can tell what they might have."

"Yes, we might as well, because you never can." By Sostratos' expression, he hoped for another gryphon's skull. But he also remembered the practical side a merchant needed, for he went on, "And I'll bring some perfume along. You never can tell what we might sell, either."

"No, indeed," Menedemos said. "If we sold a book in Phaselis, by the gods, we can sell anything anywhere."

But Olbia's agora, close by the harbor, proved a disappointment. It wasn't that the market square had nothing for sale, only that it had nothing to warm the heart of an akatos' captain. The Olbians bought and sold grain and olives and local wine and dried and fresh fish and plain pots—all useful stuff, but none of it worth Menedemos' while. There was also a separate timber market next to the main agora, but that didn't interest him, either.

"Round ships would do splendid business here," he said. "As for us . . ." He put a hand in front of his mouth, as if hiding a yawn.

"I know." Sostratos sounded gloomy, too. "You couldn't imagine a more ordinary place if you tried for a year." He raised his voice nevertheless: "Perfume! Fine perfume from Rhodian roses!"

People walked by without even looking. "I wonder if they have noses here," Menedemos grumbled. "By the way some of them smell, I doubt it."

"Fine Rhodian perfume!" Sostratos called again, before going on in a lower voice, "You never can tell. That hetaira in Miletos last summer—"

"Oh, you lucky dog!" Menedemos said. "That she wanted silk was one thing. That she wanted you, too . . ." Such things happened to him now and again. He hadn't expected them to happen to his staid cousin.

Thinking along with him, Sostratos answered, "You can't have all the luck all the time, you know. Some of it has to stick to other people, too."

"Oh? Why?" Menedemos asked.

"That's an argument for another day, my dear," Sostratos said as he held out a jar of perfume to a passerby. "From Rhodes. The finest . . ." The passerby kept walking. Sostratos' shoulders slumped. "This is the hardest part of the business for me: telling strangers they ought to buy something from me, I mean."

"Well, how will they know if you don't tell them?" Menedemos asked reasonably.

"I keep telling myself the same thing," Sostratos said. "It helps, but only so much. Then I remember how it annoys me when I'm walking through the agora at Rhodes to have some loudmouthed, quick-talking fellow from another polis stick something under my nose and tell me I can't hope to live another day without it, whatever it is."

"But you buy every once in a while, don't you?" Menedemos said. "I know I do."

"Yes, but I always feel like a fool afterwards," Sostratos said.

"That's not the point," Menedemos said. "The point is, every so often somebody *will* part with his silver. And who cares how he feels afterwards?"

As if to prove the point, they did make some sales. The first was to a Hellene a few years older than they were, who said, "I just got married a couple of months ago. I think my wife would like this, don't you?"

"Would you expect us to say no?" Sostratos asked.

"Pay no attention to him, best one," Menedemos told the prospective customer. "He's too honest for his own good." He laughed.

So did the newly wed Hellene. After a moment, halfheartedly, so did Sostratos. The local himself smelled powerfully of fish. Fish scales glinted on his arms and legs and on his chiton. *Probably in the dried-fish trade,* Menedemos judged. Whatever trade he was in, he made good money at it, for he paid the Rhodians' price with little haggling.

Menedemos didn't doubt the trade of the next fellow who stopped before them. The sword on his belt and the scars on his face and right arm proclaimed him a soldier. So did his Macedonian accent, which was so thick as to be almost unintelligible. Little by little, Menedemos gathered that he wanted the perfume for a hetaira named Gnathaina.

"Ah, she calls herself after her jaw, eh?" Menedemos had to tap his own jaw—*gnathos* in Greek—to get the Macedonian to understand what he meant.

"Aye, so she do," the soldier said at last.

"Well, friend, is she good with that jaw of hers?" Menedemos asked with a wink. The Macedonian didn't follow that at all. He did buy the perfume, though, which was what really mattered.

They made their biggest sale of the day as the sun sank in the direction of Lykia. The fellow who bought several jars was plump and prosperous, as smoothly shaven a man as Menedemos had ever seen. He couldn't decide if the local was Hellene or Pamphylian; most of the people hereabouts spoke Greek with the same slightly nasal accent. Whatever he was, the Olbian already smelled sweet.

He also haggled with great enthusiasm and persistence, and he got a better price for his perfume than either the newlywed or the Macedonian. After he'd clasped hands on the bargain, he said, "My girls will be happy to daub this stuff on."

"Your girls?" A lamp went on in Menedemos' head. "You keep a brothel?"

"That's right," the sleek fellow answered. "I'll do plenty of extra business on account of this, too. Men want their girls smelling good, not all sweaty and nasty." He hesitated. A moment later, when he asked, "You and your friend here feel like one on the house?" Menedemos understood why: generosity warring with a brothelkeeper's usual stinginess. For a wonder, generosity won.

"What do you think?" Menedemos asked, expecting his cousin to toss his head.

But Sostratos said, "Why not? Been a while since I had a little fun." He turned to the brothelkeeper. "The sun will probably have set by the time we have to go back to the harbor. Will you give us a torchbearer to light the way?"

"Certainly, best one," the man said. "You'll be a paying customer if you come for another go tomorrow, or I may want to buy something else from you. Either way, I can't afford to have you knocked over the head."

He sounded perfectly serious, as if he wouldn't have cared what happened to the Rhodians if it weren't for the off chance he might do business with them again one day. And he probably wouldn't. Traveling all over the Inner Sea, Menedemos had got to know a fair number of brothelkeepers. Their trade made them hard and remorselessly practical.

"Well, come on," the fellow said now. He sounded resigned; he might be regretting his impulse of a moment before but without any good way to go back on it.

"No point to bringing more than a drakhma or so along," Menedemos said pointedly. Sostratos got the hint and dipped his head. They both took leather pouches from their belts and stowed them on the *Aphrodite*. The brothelkeeper watched attentively. Menedemos wanted him to; this way, he wouldn't decide robbery made good business.

The brothel lay only a few blocks from the harbor and the agora. Menedemos thought he could have found his way back on his own. Still, though, a torchbearer who knew Olbia would be welcome. Navigating in a strange town by moon- and starlight wasn't something Menedemos wanted to try unless he had to, and that would be all the light there was if he and Sostratos came back by themselves. No one wasted torches or lamp oil to light the streets after sunset.

Inside the brothel, some of the dozen or so women were spinning wool into thread, which made the brothelkeeper money even when they weren't lying with men. Three or four others played dice for khalkoi or oboloi. A couple of others ate bread and olive oil and drank watered wine. They weren't naked—they hadn't been expecting business. But none of them veiled her face, as a respectable woman or even (perhaps, or especially) a high-class hetaira would have done. As far as Menedemos was concerned, that was exciting enough by itself.

"Take your pick, friends," the brothelkeeper told the Rhodians. He held up the perfume jars to the women. "I got this essence of roses for you from these fellows. I want whichever of you they pick to give 'em a good time."

Menedemos pointed to one of the women playing knuckle-bones. "Come on, sweetheart. Yes, you."

"All right. I come," she answered resignedly in accented Greek. She was about his age, swarthy, with a prominent nose and hair so black it was almost blue. She wasn't beautiful—as well hope to find a ruby the size of a man's thumb as a beautiful girl in a harborside whorehouse—but she wasn't ugly, either. As she got to her feet, Sostratos picked a woman, too: one of those who'd been spinning. Menedemos hadn't given her a second glance and had other things on his mind now.

The whore he'd chosen took him to a little room that held a bed, a stool, and not much else. As Menedemos shut the door behind them, he asked, "What do I call you?"

She looked at him in surprise. "Most men do not bother to ask. You can call me Armene. It is not my name, but Hellenes cannot say my name."

"That means you're from Armenia, doesn't it?" he said. He had a vague idea where the place was: somewhere in eastern Anatolia or the Caucasus. He didn't think he'd ever met anyone from that land before.

Armene nodded, which by itself would have proved her no Hellene. "Yes. My valley had no rain two years in a row. My father sold me to a slave trader to keep me alive and let him and my mother buy food so they could live, too. The slave trader sold me to Kritias here, and so. . . ." She shrugged once, and then, shrugging again, pulled her long chiton off over her head.

Her body was stocky but still curved, her breasts large and heavy and tipped with dark nipples. Though a barbarian, she'd taken up the Hellenic custom of singeing away the hair between her legs. Menedemos took off his tunic, too, and sat down on the edge of the bed.

"I am a gift for you, yes?" Armene said. "Tell me what you want, then." She couldn't keep a certain apprehension from her voice. He'd heard that in other brothels. The women had no choice and knew it too well.

Menedemos stretched out on the bed. "Come here. Lie down beside me." She did. The bed was narrow for two side by side. Her breasts brushed his chest; her legs bumped his.

She gave him a worried look. "I am sorry."

"It's all right." He squeezed her breasts, then lowered his head to them. Surprisingly often, even a slave in a brothel would take pleasure if a man worked a little to give it to her. Menedemos caressed her. He stroked her between her legs, as a Rhodian hetaira had taught him to do a long time before.

After a while, though, Armene set her hand on his. "You are a kind man," she said, "but I do not kindle. I do this, but I do not enjoy it."

"All right. I thought I'd try," he said, and she nodded again. He rolled onto his back. "Why don't you ride me like a race-horse?" If the brothelkeeper—Kritias, Armene had called him—was going to give him a present, he'd take the most expensive one he could get. If he were paying for it, having the girl climb on top would have cost him more than bending her forward or bending her back.

She nodded as she swung herself over him. "I thought you would ask this."

"Why?"

"Because I am doing the work," she answered. She took him in hand and guided him into her, then slowly began to move. Her breasts hung just above his face, like sweet, ripe fruit. He leaned up a little and teased her nipples with his tongue. She kept methodically moving up and down, up and down.

Before long, Menedemos was moving, too, driving his spear home with every thrust. His hands clutched her meaty buttocks. The bed squeaked under the two of them. As his delight peaked, he went into her as deeply as he could, holding her against him till the spasm of pleasure passed.

Then, laughing, he said, "You see? You didn't do all the work."

"No, not all," Armene agreed as she slid off him. Some of his seed dribbled down onto his hipbone. "Good," she said. "The more out, the less in to make a baby." That wasn't Menedemos' worry. He rubbed the stuff off of him and onto the mattress cover while Armene squatted over a chamber pot she pulled out from under the bed. He'd seen more than a few women, whores and bored wives alike, assume that position after making love. He'd heard more than a few of them say the same thing, too.

He and Armene both dressed. With a conspiratorial grin, he gave her a couple of oboloi, whispering, "Don't tell Kritias." She popped the little silver coins into her mouth. She and Menedemos went out into the waiting room.

Sostratos and the woman he'd chosen emerged from her chamber a few minutes later. Menedemos still thought her plain. By the way she smiled now, though, Sostratos had made her enjoy their time together. Menedemos laughed to himself. He tried to please women because, when they took pleasure, it added to his own. Sostratos, he suspected, did it for its own sake. He hadn't asked his cousin about that, but Sostratos also looked pretty contented now.

The whores had lit lamps in the waiting room. "Boy!" Kritias the brothelkeeper shouted. No one appeared. Kritias muttered to himself. "Boy!" he shouted again. "Get your lazy, worthless carcass in here, before I sell you to a silver miner I know!"

That brought the slave—a scrawny youth of about fourteen—on the run. Maybe Kritias was joking. The boy didn't care to take the chance. Slaves sent to the mines seldom lasted long. "What you need, boss?" he asked.

"Light a torch and take these fellows back to the harbor. Then hurry back here. I know how long you need to get there and back. If you don't hurry, I'll make you sorry."

"I'll hurry. I'll hurry." Under his breath, the slave added something that wasn't Greek. The torch hissed and popped and crackled as it caught from a lamp. The boy nodded to Menedemos and Sostratos. "Let's go."

"Have a good time?" Diokles asked when they got back to the *Aphrodite*.

"Hard to have a bad time with a woman, wouldn't you say?" Sostratos answered. He handed the slave an obolos. The youth stuck the coin in his cheek and went back into Olbia. Sostratos continued, "She said her mother sold her into slavery to keep them both from starving."

"Did she?" Menedemos said. "The girl I was with said her father sold her for the same reason." He shrugged. "They both might have been telling the truth."

"Yes, but they both might have been lying to make us feel sorry for them and give them a little something," Sostratos said. "You have to be foolish to believe much of what you hear from a whore in a brothel, I suppose, but from now on I'll believe even less."

Menedemos took off his chiton, crumpled it into a ball, and laid it on the poop deck. He wrapped himself in his mantle and lay down for the night. Sostratos imitated him. The timbers were hard, but Menedemos didn't mind. He slept aboard the merchant galley often enough during the sailing season to be used to the way they felt. He yawned, twisted a couple of times, said, "Good night," to his cousin, and slept.

THE *APHRODITE CRAWLED EAST* along the southern coast of Anatolia from Pamphylia into Kilikia. Every so often, when she went farther from shore than usual, Sostratos got glimpses of Cyprus, lying low on the southern horizon. He'd never come so far east, but the island didn't excite him as it would have had it been the merchant galley's destination. As things were, he looked forward to visiting it for a little while and then pressing on toward Phoenicia.

"Some of the towns on Cyprus are Phoenician, you know," Menedemos reminded him. "They planted colonies there at the same time we Hellenes did."

"Yes, yes, of course," Sostratos said impatiently—everyone

knew that. "But we probably won't stop at any of them before we go farther east, will we?"

Menedemos tossed his head. "I hadn't planned to, no. I was going to round that eastern peninsula the island has and then sail down to Salamis, and that's a Hellenic city. From Salamis, you go straight across the Inner Sea to Phoenicia."

"All right." Sostratos sighed. "I'd have liked a chance to practice my Aramaic before we got there, though."

"Well, when you were picking a girl in that brothel in Olbia, you should have asked if any of them could make those funny noises," Menedemos said.

Sostratos stared at his cousin in astonishment. "By the dog of Egypt, you're right. I should have. Slaves come from all over the place. One of them probably did speak it. I never would have thought of that."

"To be fair, my dear, you didn't go there to talk," Menedemos said.

Diokles laughed. He sent Menedemos a reproachful look. "Confound it, skipper, you made me mess up the rowers' stroke."

"Too bad," Menedemos said with a grin.

"Why didn't that occur to me, though?" Sostratos asked himself, ignoring both of them. "We could have screwed *and* talked."

"And talked, and talked," Menedemos said. "If you'd found a woman who spoke Aramaic, you probably wouldn't have bothered getting her clothes off."

"Not likely!" Sostratos said what he had to say, though Menedemos might have been right. Would he have been too interested in talking with a woman to bother bedding her? It wasn't certain, but he knew it wasn't impossible, either.

While Sostratos pondered that, his cousin pulled one of the *Aphrodite*'s steering-oar tillers in toward him and pushed the other away. The akatos swung toward the south, away from the Kilikian coast and toward the island ahead. The yard had run from the port bow back toward the stern on the starboard side, to take best advantage of the northerly breeze as the *Aphrodite* sailed east. Now, with the ship running before the wind, the sailors hurried to straighten the yard even before Menedemos gave orders.

We have a good crew, Sostratos thought. *They know their business.*

He looked back past the akatos' sternpost. The stretch of sea between the ship and the mainland grew wider and wider. In most circumstances, that would have filled him with foreboding. Not here, not when every stadion farther from Kilikia meant a stadion closer to Cyprus.

The sun shone brightly from a blue sky dotted by only a handful of puffy white clouds. A storm seemed unimaginable. Sostratos resolutely refused to imagine one and tried not to remember the squall off the Lykian coast. Instead, he turned to Menedemos and said, "We ought to make the island by nightfall tomorrow."

"Yes, that seems about right," his cousin said. "If I'd turned south earlier today, I'd sail on after nightfall tonight, steering by the stars. But we'll be at sea all night either way, so I don't see much point to it."

"One night at sea shouldn't be bad." Sostratos pointed down to the blue, blue water. "Look! Isn't that a turtle?"

"I didn't see it," Menedemos answered. "But I've heard they lay eggs on that eastern promontory. Hardly anybody lives there, though, so I don't know for sure. Here—take the tillers for a minute, will you? I've got to piss."

When Sostratos did take hold of the tillers, he felt rather like Herakles taking the weight of the world so Atlas could go after the golden apples of the Hesperides. Menedemos handled the steering oars from dawn till dusk every day. The only difference was, Atlas had intended to walk away from the job for good. Menedemos would take it back in a moment.

Sostratos felt the *Aphrodite*'s motion much more intimately through the tillers than he did with the soles of his feet. The slightest swing of the steering oars made the ship change direction; they were strong enough to control the akatos' course despite the best efforts of the rowers. She could have got along perfectly well with only one, though the second did make her easier to handle.

"No rain today," Sostratos said to Menedemos' back as his cousin eased himself over the side. "No gods-detested round ships coming out of the rain, either."

"There'd better not be," Menedemos said with a laugh.

"That wasn't my fault!" Sostratos exclaimed. He'd been steering a year before when a merchantman loomed out of the rain and struck the *Aphrodite* a glancing blow, carrying away one steering oar and staving in some portside timbers. She'd had to limp back to Kos and wait for repairs, which took much longer than anyone had expected.

Menedemos shook himself off and let his chiton fall. "Well, so it wasn't," he said. Had he tried to say anything else, Sostratos would have given him all the argument he wanted and then a little more besides.

As things were, Sostratos just said, "May I steer a little while longer?" He scanned the sea. "There's nothing for me to run into—I don't even see any dolphins right now."

"All right, go ahead." Menedemos made as if to bow. "I'll stand around being useless."

"If you're saying that's what I do when I'm not steering, I'll have something to say to you, too," Sostratos replied. Menedemos only laughed.

A tern flew out from the direction of the mainland and perched on the yard. The black-capped bird cocked its head now this way, now that, as it peered down into the sea. Laughing still, Menedemos said, "All right, O best of toikharkhoi—what fare do we charge for taking him to Cyprus?"

"If he pays us a sprat, we're ahead of the game," Sostratos answered. "If he shits in a sailor's hair, we're behind, and we tell him we'll never take him anywhere else."

After perhaps a quarter of an hour, the tern took off and

plunged headfirst into the water of the Inner Sea. It emerged a moment later with a fish just above sprat size in its beak. Instead of returning to the yard, it flew over the *Aphrodite* and away. It must have clamped down on the still-wiggling fish, for the last couple of digits' width of the tail fell at Sostratos' feet.

"There, you see?" he told Menedemos. "I wish some of the people we deal with would pay us so promptly."

"Well, that's the truth, and I can't tell you otherwise," his cousin said.

Menedemos let him steer for about an hour, then took back the tillers. As Sostratos stepped away from them, he did feel useless. *Most of what you do on a trading run, you do ashore,* he reminded himself. He knew that was true, but it made him feel no more useful at this moment. He looked back past the stern again, back past the ship's boat that followed the *Aphrodite* almost as the Great Dog and the Little Dog followed Orion through the night sky of winter.

Not long after Menedemos took the tillers, Aristeidas spotted a sail off to starboard. Sostratos peered east himself. He might have got a glimpse of a pale sail right at the edge of the horizon, or he might have imagined it. He couldn't tell. Did he really see it, or did he imagine he saw it because sharp-sighted Aristeidas said it was there? Plenty of men believed things for no better reason than that someone they respected—whether rightly or wrongly—said it was so. *Am I one of the herd? Maybe I am.*

Then the lynx-eyed lookout said, "Gone now—under the horizon. Must have seen us and not wanted to find out what we were."

"If we were pirates, they wouldn't get free of us so easy," Menedemos said. "We'd be after them like a hound after a hare. And we'd catch them, too. No place to hide on the sea— they couldn't duck into a hole or under a thorn bush, the way a hare can."

Cyprus was visibly closer than the Anatolian mainland when, with the setting of the sun, the *Aphrodite*'s anchors splashed into the Inner Sea. Sostratos washed down barley rolls, cheese, onions, and briny olives with watered wine. "I should have kept the fish tail the tern dropped," he said. "It would be the fanciest opson I've got."

"An opsophagos who goes to sea for the fish is going to be disappointed most of the time," Menedemos answered. "Yes, he's right above all those beauties, but how often does he ever see them?"

"Somebody caught a lovely mullet last year—remember?" Sostratos said.

"Yes—one mullet, for one sailor out of the whole crew," Menedemos said. "Those aren't good odds, you know."

"Too true," Sostratos agreed. "But I do wonder what sort of interesting fish they catch off Cyprus and Phoenicia."

"We found out some of the people thereabouts don't eat fish at all—and you say your Ioudaioi won't eat pork, isn't that right?" Menedemos said. Sostratos dipped his head. His cousin laughed. "Who can guess why barbarians have the strange customs they do? If they didn't, they'd be Hellenes."

Once more, Sostratos quoted Herodotos quoting Pindaros: "'Custom is king of all.' That's true wherever one goes, I'm sure, with Hellenes as well as barbarians."

By the next afternoon, he could clearly see the forested hills of Cyprus' eastern spike of land. Hawks wheeled above the woods. Now and then one would swoop down after prey it could see and Sostratos couldn't. A gull that was resting contentedly on the masthead took off all at once with a harsh squawk of fear and a mad flapping of wings. The falcon that flew past paid it no heed but went on its way straight and swift as an arrow.

"Splendid bird," Sostratos murmured.

"The gull didn't think so," Menedemos said.

"Yes, the gull hared out of there," Sostratos replied, and his cousin made a face at the pun on *laros* and *lagos*. Sostratos smiled. As far as he was concerned, that pun welcomed him to Cyprus.

4

MENEDEMOS LOOKED AHEAD TO THE PORT AP-
proaching on his right hand. Thanks to favorable winds,
they'd reached it on the second afternoon after coming to
Cyprus. He pointed toward the narrow mouth of the harbor.
"There's a place with a famous name."

"Salamis?" Sostratos answered. "Yes, my dear, I should
hope so. It's a name that means liberty for all Hellenes, a
name that means Xerxes the Persian king watching from the
shore as his ships were beaten." He laughed. "The only trouble is, it's the *wrong* Salamis for that."

"Yes, I know," Menedemos said, wondering if his cousin
thought him so ignorant as not to know. "I wonder how a town
in Cyprus got the same name as an island off the coast of Attica." Then he snapped his fingers. "No, I don't wonder. I
know."

"Tell me," Sostratos said.

"Teukros founded this Salamis, didn't he?" Menedemos
said.

"So they say," Sostratos answered.

"Well, then, Teukros was Telamon's bastard, right?"
Menedemos waited for his cousin to dip his head, then continued, "And who's Telamon's legitimate son?"

"You're the one who knows the *Iliad* backwards and for-
wards," Sostratos said.

"Oh, come on!" Menedemos said. "Everybody knows this
one. Telamon's son is—"

"Aias." Sostratos supplied the right answer. Menedemos
clapped his hands. Sostratos went on, "I see. I have it now. Be-

cause there are two Hellenic heroes named Aias in the *Iliad,* there must be two places named Salamis by the sea."

"No, no, no!" Menedemos exclaimed. Only then did he notice the wicked gleam in his cousin's eye. "You—you cacodaemon!" he burst out. Sostratos laughed out loud. Menedemos glared at him. "Now you're going to hear the right answer, curse it, you scoffer, you." Sostratos bowed, as if at a compliment. Menedemos doggedly plowed ahead: "Teukros founded this Salamis—and Aias, his half brother, was lord of the Salamis in Attica." He quoted the *Iliad:*

"'And Aias from Salamis led two-and-ten ships
And, having led them, placed them where the Athenians'
   formations stood.'

So you see, this Salamis is named for the other one—in spite of your dreadful jokes."

"Some people say the Athenians put those two lines into the Catalogue of Ships themselves, to justify their claim to the island of Salamis," Sostratos said. That rocked Menedemos. To him, Homer's poems were perfect and unchanging as they passed from one generation to the next. Adding lines for political reasons seemed as vile as adulterating barley for the sake of profit. But if people did the latter—and they did—why not the former, too? His cousin added, "Can't fault your argument, though. If Aias was lord of Salamis and if Teukros founded this Salamis, this one is named after the other. You *can* think logically when you want to. If only you'd want to more often."

Menedemos hardly noticed the gibe. He was thinking about the rest of the *Iliad.* Aias wasn't associated with Menestheus of Athens anywhere but in the Catalogue of Ships, as best he could remember. His ships were sometimes mentioned as lying alongside those Protesilaos—first to land at Troy, and first to die there—had brought from Phylake, up in Thessalia. He sometimes fought in the company of the other, smaller, Aias.

Except in that one passage, he had nothing to do with the Athenians.

"Filthy," Menedemos muttered.

"What's that?" Sostratos asked.

"Perverting the *Iliad* for the sake of politics."

Sostratos' smile looked anything but pleasant. "Shall I really disgust you?"

"How?" Menedemos asked. "Do I want to know?"

"I don't know. Do you?" Sostratos returned. "Here's how: there are a couple of lines in place of the ones you quoted, lines that tie Salamis to Megara, which also claimed it in the old days. But those lines don't say how many ships Aias led to Troy, the way the Catalogue of Ships does for all the other places and heroes, so *they* probably aren't genuine, either."

"Well, what did Homer truly say, then?" Menedemos asked. "He can't have left Aias out of the picture altogether—Aias is too great a warrior. He's the only one among the strong-greaved Akhaioi who keeps fighting back when Hektor goes on his rampage. The poet wouldn't—couldn't—have just forgotten him in the Catalogue of Ships."

His cousin shrugged. "I agree with you. That doesn't seem likely, and both the Athenian lines and the ones from Megara are suspect. I don't think there's any way now to find out what Homer first sang."

That bothered Menedemos, too. He wanted to think Homer's words had passed inviolate from generation to generation. So much of what being a Hellene meant was contained in the *Iliad* and *Odyssey*. Of course, one of the things being a Hellene meant was carefully examining the world in which you lived. Homer's poems were part of the world in which all Hellenes lived, and so. . . . Menedemos still wished people had kept their hands and minds off them.

Musing thus, he almost took the *Aphrodite* right past the opening to Salamis' harbor. It was even narrower than that leading into the Great Harbor at Rhodes, with room for no more than ten or twelve ships abreast. If he'd daydreamed any longer, he would have had to double back to go in. In the

akatos, that would have drawn jeers from Sostratos and silent
scorn—which might have hurt more—from Diokles. In a
round ship that had to beat back against the wind, it would
have been worse than merely embarrassing.

When the *Aphrodite* did enter the harbor, it was full of
ships: big war galleys displaying Ptolemaios' eagle, a few on
lowered sails, all on banners at stern and bow; little fishing
boats, some of them no more than one-man rowboats; and
everything in between. "Same sort of jumble as we saw at Kos
last year," Diokles remarked.

"Even worse, I do believe," Sostratos said. "About one merchantman in three looks like a Phoenician. I've never seen so
many foreign-looking ships all in one place."

"I think you're right," Menedemos said. Telling Phoenician
ships from those sailed by Hellenes wasn't usually a matter of
lines; both folk built their vessels in much the same way. But a
thousand things, from the choice of paints to the shape of the
eyes the ships carried at their prows to the way the lines were
coiled to the fact that Phoenician sailors stayed fully clothed
even in warm weather, shouted that those vessels belonged to
barbarians.

"I wonder if we seem as strange to them as they do to us,"
Sostratos said.

"If we do, too bad, by the gods," Menedemos said. "They
fought for the Great King against Alexander and they lost, and
they'd better get used to it."

Diokles pointed. "There's a mooring space, skipper."

Menedemos wished a Phoenician ship were making for it,
too. He could get there first and score his own triumph over
the barbarians. As things were, he had no competition. The
Aphrodite slid into the space. The rowers backed oars for a
few strokes to stop her in the water, then rested on the oars and
shipped them, bringing them inboard.

Sailors tossed lines to longshoremen, who made the merchant galley fast to the quay. One of the Salaminians asked,
"What ship have we here? Whence come ye?"

Smiling a little at the old-fashioned Cypriot dialect,

Menedemos answered, "We're the *Aphrodite*, out of Rhodes." He named himself and Sostratos.

"Gods give ye good day, O best ones," the local said. "And what cargo bring ye hither?"

Sostratos spoke up: "We have ink and papyrus, Koan silk, Rhodian perfume, the finest olive oil from our native land, books to make the time pass by, Lykian hams, and smoked eels from Phaselis—they melt in your mouth."

"And melt silver from you, too, I doubt not," the Salaminian said with a longing sigh. He glanced down toward the base of the quay. "And now, meseems, you shall answer these same questions over again, and more besides."

Sure enough, a soldier strode importantly toward the *Aphrodite*. At almost every port the past couple of years, Menedemos thought sourly, soldiers had had questions for him and Sostratos. Sometimes they belonged to Antigonos; sometimes, as now, to Ptolemaios. Who paid them didn't matter (with so many of them mercenaries, it often didn't matter even to them). Their attitude was always the same: that a mere merchant skipper ought to go to the closest temple to offer sacrifice in thanks that they didn't take everything he had.

This one was an exceptionally big man, with fair skin weathered bronze and with piercing gray eyes. When he barked, "Who are you?" he proved to have his own accent, very different from that of the longshoreman. If he wasn't a Macedonian, Menedemos had never heard one.

"We're the *Aphrodite*, out of Rhodes," Menedemos answered, as he had before. Then, because he couldn't resist, he added, "And who are you?"

"I'm Kleob—" The Macedonian, probably Kleoboulos, caught himself. "I ask the questions!" he roared. "Have you got that? It's none of your gods-detested business who I am. Have you got *that*?"

Sostratos clucked reproachfully, as Menedemos had been sure he would. He had a point, too. Getting smart with Macedonians wasn't the wisest thing Menedemos might have done.

"*Have you got that?*" the officer shouted again.

"Yes, O marvelous one," Menedemos said.

Sostratos clucked again. But the Macedonian, as Menedemos had hoped, took irony for frightened politeness. "That's better," he growled. "Now tell me your cargo, and no more back talk." Menedemos let Sostratos do that. After his cousin had gone down the list, the officer ran a hand through his gray-streaked auburn hair. "Books? Who's going to buy books?"

"People who like to read?" Sostratos suggested.

The Macedonian tossed his head. Plainly, the idea was alien to him. He shrugged and found another question: "Where are you bound?"

"Phoenicia," Menedemos answered unwillingly. "We're going to trade for scarlet dye and balsam and whatever else we can find."

"Are you?" Those gray eyes went hard and predatory. "Or are you here spying for Antigonos the Cyclops?"

"By the gods!" Menedemos exclaimed. "Last year we did a service for Ptolemaios, and now his servant calls us spies. I like that!"

"A service? What sort of service? His laundry? Did you fetch him a clean chiton or two?" the officer jeered. "Or did you bend over and give him a different kind of service? You're pretty enough; he might've enjoyed that. And so might you."

Accusing a free adult male Hellene of playing the boy for another man was one of the nastier insults someone could hurl. Menedemos steamed. His hands balled into fists. "Easy," Sostratos murmured.

"Easy? I'll tell him to—" But Menedemos caught himself. In Rhodes, he could have told the Macedonian anything he pleased. Not here. Cyprian Salamis was Ptolemaios' city. One of the lord of Egypt's officers carried far more weight than a merchant skipper from a distant polis. Mastering himself wasn't easy, but Menedemos did it. "No, sir," he told the Macedonian in the iciest tones he could summon. "Last year, he brought Polemaios son of Polemaios from Khalkis on the island of Euboia to Ptolemaios, who was then staying at the city of Kos, on the island of the same name."

The officer gaped. Whatever answer he'd expected, that wasn't it. He tried to rally: "A likely story. What did he pay you for it?"

"One talent of silver, of his own weight," Sostratos answered. "I have it listed in the accounts here. Would you care to examine them?"

"No," the Macedonian growled. He spun on his heel and clumped back up the pier, scarlet cape billowing around him.

"Euge!" Menedemos said. "But tell me, why on earth have you brought last year's accounts along?" His cousin was mad for keeping every little detail straight, but that seemed excessive even for him.

Sostratos grinned. "Oh, I haven't. But, by the way he laughed at the idea that anyone might want to buy a book, I guessed he probably didn't have his letters. And that turned out to be right."

"That's sly, young sir," Diokles said admiringly. "That's mighty sly."

"It seemed reasonable," Sostratos answered, shrugging. "But I want to say *euge* to my cousin. When that Macedonian oaf reviled him, he didn't lose his temper. He stayed calm, and the Macedonian ended up playing the fool."

Menedemos wasn't—emphatically wasn't—used to praise from Sostratos. His cousin was more apt to call him things like a thick-skulled bonehead who thought with his prick. He was used to that. This, though . . . "Thank you very much, my dear," he said. "Are you sure you're well?"

"Quite sure, thanks," Sostratos answered. "And I think— though I can't be so sure—you may be starting to grow up at last."

"Me?" Menedemos tossed his head. "It's not likely, let me tell you."

"I don't know," Sostratos said. "My guess is, a couple of years ago you would have called him something filthy you got out of Aristophanes, and that would have spilled the perfume into the soup."

Menedemos thought it over. Much as he would have liked to, he couldn't deny it. Now he shrugged. "I didn't, and that's all there is to it. Now maybe these cistern-arsed titty-gropers will leave us alone and let us get some business done."

"Er—yes," Sostratos said. "More Aristophanes?"

"Of course, my dear," Menedemos answered. "Only the best."

WHEN SOSTRATOS AND Menedemos walked into Salamis' market square the next morning, Sostratos stopped, stared in delight, and pointed. "Look!" he exclaimed. "Phoenicians! Lots of Phoenicians!" Sure enough, many of the men in the agora were swarthy and hook-nosed, and wore long robes despite what promised to be a warm day. The harsh gutturals of their language mixed with the rhythmic rise and fall of Greek.

Sostratos' cousin laughed at him. "Well, of course there are lots of Phoenicians here, my dear," Menedemos said. "We're close to the Phoenician coast, there are Phoenician towns on Cyprus, and all those Phoenician ships in the harbor didn't get here without sailors and merchants in 'em."

"No, of course not," Sostratos said. "But now I get to find out if they understand my Aramaic—and I understand theirs. I thought we'd run into more of them in Lykia and Pamphylia and Kilikia, but"—he shrugged—"we didn't."

"It's the war," Menedemos said. "Antigonos rules Phoenicia, but Ptolemaios just took the southern coast of Anatolia away from him. The Phoenicians are probably nervous about going there."

"Maybe—but maybe not, too," Sostratos said. "Ptolemaios also holds Cyprus, so why don't the Phoenicians stay away from Salamis?"

"For one thing, like I said, Kition and some other Phoenician cities are here on Cyprus, and Ptolemaios holds them, too," Menedemos answered. "For another, he's held Cyprus longer, so things here have settled down. And, for a third, if Phoenicians don't come *here,* they don't come anywhere."

Since he was manifestly right, Sostratos didn't argue with
him. Instead, he went up to the closest Phoenician merchant,
a fellow who'd set up a stand with jars of crimson dye.
"Good day, my master," Sostratos said in Aramaic, his heart
thumping nervously. "Would you tell your servant what city
you are from?" Speaking Greek, he wouldn't have cared to
sound so submissive even to a Macedonian marshal. But Aramaic, as he'd discovered to his frequent dismay, did things
differently.

The Phoenician blinked, then showed white, white teeth in
an enormous grin. "An Ionian who speaks my language!" he
said; in Aramaic, all Hellenes were Ionians. "And may I go
through the fire if you didn't learn it from a man of Byblos.
Am I right, my master, or am I wrong?"

"From a man of Byblos, yes." Sostratos had all he could do
not to dance with delight. This fellow had followed his Aramaic, and he'd understood the reply.

That grin got wider yet. "Your servant is from Sidon," the
Phoenician said, bowing. "I am called Abibaal son of Esh-
munhillek. And how does my master call himself?"

Sostratos gave his own name, and that of his father. He also
introduced Menedemos, adding, "He speaks no Aramaic."

"That is only a small thing," Abibaal replied. He bowed to
Menedemos as he had to Sostratos and said, "Hail, my master," in good Greek.

"Hail," Menedemos replied. He chuckled and poked Sostratos in the ribs with an elbow. "See? He knows Greek."

"Yes, *he* does," Sostratos said patiently. "But before long
we'll be getting to places where people don't."

"Would you rather go on in Greek?" Abibaal asked in that
language.

"No," Sostratos said in Aramaic, and tossed his head. "I
want to use your speech, please."

Abibaal gave him another bow. "It shall be as you desire in
all ways, of course. Would your heart be gladdened to think
on the many fine qualities of the crimson dye I have here?" He
patted one of the jars on his little display.

"I do not know," Sostratos answered: a useful phrase. He paused to think, then went on, "How much more charge you here than in Sidon?"

That made Abibaal blink and then laugh. "Eshmun smite me if my master is not a merchant himself."

"Yes." Sostratos dipped his head. Then he remembered to nod instead. It felt most unnatural. "Please answer your servant's question, if you would be so generous."

"Surely, sir, you know a man must make a profit to live, and—"

"Yes, yes," Sostratos said impatiently. "You must make a profit, but I must make a profit, too." He pointed first to the Sidonian, then to himself, to make sure he was understood.

Some of Abibaal's patience began to wear thin. "I charge only a twelfth part more here in Salamis than in my own city."

Sostratos returned to Greek to speak to Menedemos: "Come on. Let's go."

"What's the matter?" his cousin asked. "You sounded like you had something stuck in your throat and couldn't get it out."

As the two Rhodians started on their way, Abibaal called after them in Greek: "What is the trouble, best ones? Whatever it is, I can make it right."

"No. You lied to me," Sostratos told him, sticking to Greek himself now. "No man would take such a small extra charge after shipping his goods across the sea. How can I trust you when you will not tell me the truth?"

"You will find no finer dye anywhere in Phoenicia," Abibaal said.

"That may be, or it may not. Because you lied to me before, I have a harder time believing you now," Sostratos answered. "But whether it's so or not, I'm sure I can find cheaper dye there, and I intend to."

"You told him," Menedemos said as the dye merchant from Sidon stared after them.

"I don't like being taken for a fool." Sostratos could, in fact, think of few things he liked less. After muttering darkly to himself, he went on, "Actually, my dear, you'll be the one buying dye and such in the coastal cities. I aim to go to that Engedi place and buy balsam straight from the source."

"I know what you aim to do." Menedemos didn't sound happy. "One Hellene wandering through a country full of barbarians where he barely speaks the language—"

"I did well enough with Abibaal."

"And maybe you would again. But maybe you wouldn't, too," his cousin said. "Besides, a lone traveler is asking to be robbed and murdered. I would like to see you again."

"Would you? I didn't know you cared." Sostratos batted his eyelashes. Menedemos laughed. But Sostratos wasn't about to be deflected from his purpose. "We've been talking about this since the end of last summer. You knew I was going to do it."

"Yes, but the more I think about what it means, the less I like it," Menedemos replied. Sostratos started to get angry. Before he could say anything, though, Menedemos continued, "Why don't you take four or five sailors with you? Bandits would think twice before they bothered a band of armed men."

"I don't want—" Sostratos checked himself. It wasn't the worst idea he'd ever heard. He still saw difficulties with it, though. "They speak nothing but Greek. I'd have to translate for them all the time. And, sailors being what they are ashore, they'd want to spend their time pouring down wine and bedding women, not traveling and bargaining."

"Oh, I think that, if one of them found a pretty girl, he'd want to dicker," Menedemos said innocently. Sostratos made a horrible face. Grinning, his cousin went on, "I'd sooner see you come back safe, even if you did have to keep an eye on your guards while you were away."

"We'd need to pay them a bonus, too, to tempt them away from the taverns and brothels of whatever cities we go through," Sostratos said.

"Maybe we could make it payable afterwards, for good behavior," Menedemos said.

"Maybe." Sostratos wasn't convinced. "And maybe none of them would want to go for the sake of a bonus he might not earn. Besides, who says I want to play nursemaid to a squad of men who don't want to be with me? And how could I learn anything about the countryside and its history if I am playing nursemaid?"

Menedemos pointed an accusing finger at him. "There's your real reason!" he exclaimed. "You're not making this jaunt just for the sake of the balsam. You want to spy out these Ioudaioi and see what you can find out about their funny customs."

"Well, what if I do?" Sostratos said. Herodotos had managed to travel for the sake of travel, or so it seemed from his history. Sostratos wished he could do the same, but no such luck. "As long as I bring back the balsam, how can you complain about what else I do?"

"How? Easy as you please. You never miss a chance to complain when I find some bored, pretty wife whose husband's not giving her enough of what she craves."

The unfairness of that almost choked Sostratos. "Lying with other men's wives—especially with our customers' wives—is bad for business, and it's liable to get you killed. Remember Halikarnassos. Remember Taras."

"Getting robbed and murdered because you're stupid enough to travel by yourself is bad for business, too," Menedemos retorted. "And it's also liable to get you killed. *And* it's not nearly so much fun as getting laid. Either you take an escort or you don't go to Engedi."

Sostratos glared. "I'll make a bargain with you. I'll take an escort along if you swear not to commit adultery this sailing season. If your spear gets too stiff to bear, go to a brothel and buy your relief."

"It's not the same at a brothel, and you know it," Menedemos said. "The girls there have to give you what you ask for, whether they want to or not—and mostly they don't. But there's nothing randier than a wife who's done without for too long, and you know it's more fun when the woman enjoys herself, too."

"I'd have more fun going to Engedi alone," Sostratos answered.

"Till the first arrow got you in the ribs, you would."

"That's the chance you take in your games, too. You ask me to give up something, but you won't do the same. Where's the justice in that?"

"By Zeus, I'm the captain," Menedemos said.

"But you're not Zeus yourself, even if you swear by him, and you're not a tyrant, either," Sostratos replied. "Have we got a bargain, or haven't we? Maybe I'll just stay along the coast myself, and to the crows with getting the best price for the balsam at Engedi."

"What? That's mutiny!" Menedemos squawked. "We set off to the east to buy balsam. You learned that horrible language they speak so we could buy balsam. And now you say you won't go where they have it?"

"Not with a squad of clumping, gallumphing sailors, not unless you give me something in return," Sostratos said. "That's not mutiny, my dear—that's haggling. Are you saying you *can't* keep away from other men's wives till I get back from Engedi? What kind of weakling are you, if that's so?"

"Oh, all right!" Menedemos kicked at the ground, sending a pebble spinning. "All right. You'll go with guards, and I'll fight shy of adultery till you're back. What oath would you have me swear?" He held up a hand. "Wait! I know! We need some wine first, though." In Salamis' bustling agora, buying some was a matter of a moment. "All right. Here: 'These things fulfilling, may I drink from this source.'" He sipped the wine and passed it to Sostratos, who did likewise. Menedemos finished, "'But if I should break it, may the cup be full of water.' Now you repeat it after me."

Sostratos did. Then he said, "That's a good oath. But why did you use a feminine participle there?—'these things fulfilling,' I mean."

His cousin grinned. "That's the end of the oath Lysistrate and the other women swore in Aristophanes' comedy—the oath not to let their husbands have them till they ended the Peloponnesian War. It fits here, doesn't it?"

Laughing, Sostratos dipped his head. "It could hardly fit better, my dear. Shall we finish that wine now?" They did and gave the cup back to the skinny little Hellene who'd sold the wine to them.

By the time they'd gone through the market square, Sostratos had got a lot of practice saying, "No thank you, not today," and other such phrases in Aramaic. The Phoenicians—and the Hellenes—in the agora were slaveringly eager to sell to the Rhodians. Sostratos could easily have spent every obolos he had. Whether he could sell what he bought for enough to turn a profit was a different question, though he had a hard time convincing the merchants at Salamis of that.

He also discovered that Damonax's olive oil was going to be even harder to move than he'd feared. Whenever he mentioned it to a trader, whether a Hellene or a Phoenician, the fellow would roll his eyes and say something like, "We make plenty at home."

Wearily, Sostratos would offer a protest: "But this is the finest oil, from the very first picking, from the very first pressing. The gods couldn't make better oil than this."

"Let it be as you say, my master," a Phoenician told him. "Let everything be just as you say. I will pay a premium for fine oil, certainly. But I will not pay a big premium, because the difference between the finest oil and an ordinary oil is so much less than the difference between the finest wine and an ordinary wine. It is there. You will find a few people who seek it out. But you will find only a few. My heart is full of grief to have to tell you this, my master, but it is so."

Sostratos would have been more irate had he not heard variations on the theme from merchants along the southern coast of Anatolia. He went on his way, wondering if urging his father to let Damonax marry into the family had been such a good idea after all.

"What *are* we going to do with that oil?" Menedemos said morosely after he'd translated.

"Burn it in lamps, for all I care," Sostratos answered. "Rub it all over yourself. If my brother-in-law were here, I'd give him an enema with it, as much as he could hold."

Menedemos let out a startled laugh. "And I thought I was the one who liked Aristophanes."

"I won't say anything about Aristophanes one way or the other," Sostratos told him. "What I will say is, I don't much like my brother-in-law right now."

"We could have carried quite a few things we'd have had an easier time selling," Menedemos agreed. "We'd probably have made more money from them, too."

"I know. I know." Sostratos had been thinking about that even before Damonax's slaves stowed amphora after amphora of olive oil aboard the *Aphrodite*. "At least we have *some* room for other cargo. He wanted us to fill her to the gunwales, remember. I did manage to talk my father out of letting him get away with that."

"A good thing, too," Menedemos said. "Otherwise, we'd have come home from our trading run without having sold anything. That'd be a first. And I'll tell you something else, too: one way or another, my father would manage to blame me for everything that went wrong."

He often complained about his father. Sostratos had never had any particular trouble with Uncle Philodemos, but he wasn't Philodemos' son, either. And, from everything he'd seen, Menedemos had cause for his complaints, too. "What is it between the two of you, anyhow?" Sostratos asked. "Whatever it is, can't you find some way to cure it?"

"I don't know. I doubt it." Menedemos sounded surprisingly bleak. He also sounded as if he was lying, or at least not telling all of the truth.

Sostratos thought about calling him on it. Menedemos had frozen up a couple of times before when Sostratos asked him questions like that. It was as if he knew the answer but didn't want to air it to anyone, perhaps even—perhaps especially—to himself. *What could it be?* Sostratos' ever-lively curiosity sniffed at that like a Molossian hound sniffing for the scent of a hare, but found nothing.

That being so, changing the subject looked like a good idea. Sostratos said, "The king of Salamis and all these little Cypriot kings have to pay tribute to Ptolemaios nowadays. I wonder how they like it."

"Not much, unless I miss my guess, and I don't think I do," Menedemos answered. Sostratos dipped his head in agreement. His cousin went on in musing tones: "I wonder why towns full of Hellenes here on Cyprus have kings, where most poleis back in Hellas itself and over in Great Hellas are democracies or oligarchies or what have you."

"There's Sparta," Sostratos said.

"I said most poleis. I didn't say all poleis. And Macedonia isn't a polis, but it's got a king, too."

"At the moment, it *hasn't* got a king, which is why all the marshals are hitting one another over the head with anything they can lay their hands on," Sostratos pointed out. He thought for a little while. "That's an interesting question, you know."

"Give me an interesting answer, then," Menedemos said.

"Hmm. One thing Cyprus and Macedonia have in common is that they're right at the edge of the Hellenic world. Old-fashioned things stick around in places like this. Listen to the dialect the Cypriots use. And Macedonian's even worse."

"I should say so," Menedemos agreed. "I'm not even sure it's properly Greek at all. But tell me, then, O best one: are kings old-fashioned? What about Alexander?"

"Certainly not," Sostratos said, as if he were responding to a question from Sokrates in a Platonic dialogue. In those dialogues, though, Sokrates got all the best lines. Here, Sostratos had some hope of having some himself. He went on, "But even if Alexander was something special, kingship isn't. It *is* archaic in most of Hellas. Sparta's the most conservative polis around. Add that to kings hanging on in backwoods places like this and Macedonia, and to other evidence—"

"What other evidence?" Menedemos broke in.

"Look at Athens, for instance," Sostratos said. "Athens hasn't had a king since the days of myth and legend, since King Kodros went out to fight knowing he would get killed, but would bring his city victory doing it."

"Why talk about Athens, then?"

"If you'll *let* me talk, my dear, I'll tell you. Athens doesn't have a king—hasn't had one for ages. But it still has an arkhon *called* the king, who takes the place of the king it used to have in some religious ceremonies. So Athens is a place that once had a king, that shows it once had a king by keeping an official with the name but none of the power, but that doesn't need him any more than a bird needs the eggshell it hatched out of. You see? Evidence."

"Well, if you went to trial with it, I don't know if you'd convince enough jurors to win a conviction, but you've convinced me; I will say that." Menedemos clapped his hands together. Sostratos grinned. He didn't win an argument with Menedemos—or rather, Menedemos didn't admit he'd won one—every day. But his cousin added, "No matter how old-fashioned kinging it is, the Macedonian marshals have all of the job except for the name, and they seem to like it pretty well."

"Of course they do," Sostratos said. "They're all rich as you please—Ptolemaios especially—and nobody dares tell them no. How can you not like that? But do the people in their realms like it? That's liable to be a different question."

"Except in Macedonia itself, most of those people are just barbarians. They don't know what freedom is—they lived under the Great Kings of Persia before the Macedonians came," Menedemos answered. "And, from everything I've ever heard, Egyptians don't like anything foreign."

"Yes, I've heard the same," Sostratos agreed. "From what Himilkon says, it sounds as if the Ioudaioi don't fancy foreigners, either."

"All the more reason for you to have some guards along, then," Menedemos said. "If the people you're going to do business with want to kill you because you're foreign—"

"Nobody said they wanted to kill me," Sostratos broke in. "And I've agreed to bring along some sailors, remember? You'd better remember—and you'd better remember what you agreed to, too. Do you?"

"Yes, O best one," Menedemos answered glumly.

MENEDEMOS WAS IN a sulky mood as he and Sostratos made their way back to the harbor from Salamis' market square. No adultery, no chance for adultery, for the rest of the sailing season? He came close to wishing he'd let his fool of a cousin go off alone and get himself killed. It would serve him right, wouldn't it?

After contemplating that, Menedemos reluctantly—very reluctantly—tossed his head. He did like Sostratos, in an almost avuncular way, and they would be able to make a lot of money on Engedi balsam if they could bring it back to Hellas without having to pay any Phoenician middlemen.

All the same . . . "The sacrifices I make," he muttered.

"What's that?" Sostratos asked.

"Never mind," Menedemos told him. "I'd have to explain to my father—and to yours—how I happened to lose you to bandits, and that's more trouble than it's worth. Just as well, then, you're going with guards." *And if I happen to have to pay a price for it, I pay a price for it, that's all.*

Then Sostratos pointed to a peculiar structure off to the left and asked, "What's that?" in an altogether different tone of voice.

"Why are you asking me?" Menedemos asked in turn. "I don't know. It's sure funny-looking, though, whatever it's supposed to be, isn't it?" The more he looked at it, the stranger it seemed, too. "Some sort of shrine?"

"Beats me." Sostratos was staring, too. The base of the structure was of mud brick, with a mound of what looked like charcoal raised above it. Statues of a man, a woman, and three children surrounded the strange erection. Sostratos was normally a shy man, but curiosity could make him bold. He stepped in front of a passing Salaminian and asked, "I beg your pardon, but could you tell me what this building is?"

"Know you not?" the local said in surprise. But when Menedemos and Sostratos both tossed their heads, he said, "Why, 'tis the cenotaph of King Nikokreon, of course."

"Oh, a pestilence!" Menedemos snapped his fingers, annoyed at himself. "I should have thought of that. Ptolemaios made him kill himself when he took over Cyprus, didn't he? So there isn't any king of Salamis any more, Sostratos. Two or three years ago, it would have been. I heard about it in Rhodes."

"Aye, you have't," the Salaminian said. "'Twas not Nikokreon alone made to slay himself, but wife and offspring as well. The monument you see here raised commemorates them all. Farewell." He walked on.

"Ptolemaios doesn't like murdering people," Menedemos remarked. "Maybe, to his way of thinking, there's no blood guilt if he makes them kill themselves. Polemaios last year in Kos, and Nikokreon here, too. I daresay Polemaios had it coming, though. I never would have trusted him at my back, anyhow."

"By the dog of Egypt, Nikokreon had it coming, too," Sostratos said, his voice suddenly savage. "I'd forgotten what Ptolemaios made him do, but it wasn't half what he deserved."

"Why?" Menedemos asked. "I'd never even heard of him till word got to Rhodes that he'd slain himself. Life's too short to keep track of every little Cypriot kinglet who comes along."

"Life's never too short to keep track of anything," Sostratos said.

Menedemos would have bet his cousin would come out with something like that. He retorted, "You're the one who forgot Nikokreon's dead, back there earlier today."

Sostratos turned red. "Well, I shouldn't have. What he did deserves remembering, whether you usually keep track of such things or not."

"Now you've got me curious," Menedemos said. "What *did* he do, my dear?"

"He's the abandoned rogue who tortured Anaxarkhos of Abdera to death," Sostratos answered. Menedemos must have looked blank, for Sostratos continued, "Anaxarkhos was a philosopher from the school of Demokritos."

"Oh, I've heard of *him*," Menedemos replied with some relief. "The fellow who says everything's made up of tiny particles too small to cut up any more—atoms, right?" To his relief, Sostratos dipped his head. Menedemos said, "All right, Anaxarkhos followed him. What then?"

"He was a man who spoke his mind, Anaxarkhos was. Once when Alexander got hurt, Anaxarkhos pointed to the wound and said, 'That is the blood of a man, not a god.' But Alexander liked him, and didn't take offense. Nikokreon was different."

"You're a tease, do you know that? If you were a hetaira, you'd have more customers than you knew what to do with, the way you promise and promise without actually giving very much." Menedemos poked his cousin in the ribs.

"If I were a hetaira, all the men would run screaming, and I don't mean on account of my beard," Sostratos replied. "I know what my looks are."

Menedemos had been a much-courted youth before his beard sprouted. No one had paid the least attention to his tall, gawky, horse-faced cousin. At the time and since, Sostratos had made a good game show of not caring. But, down deep, it must have rankled. Here, ten years later, Menedemos saw it coming out. He made a point of not overtly noticing. "Nikokreon was different, you say? How? What did this— Anaxagoras?—do?"

"Anaxarkhos," Sostratos corrected. "Anaxagoras was a philosopher, too, but a long time ago, in the days of Perikles."

"All right, Anaxarkhos," Menedemos said agreeably, glad he'd steered his cousin away from thinking about himself. "What did he do to get dear Nikokreon angry at him?"

"That I don't know, not exactly, but it must have been something special, because Nikokreon thought up a special death for him," Sostratos replied. "He threw him into a big stone mortar and had him pounded to death with iron hammers."

"Pheu!" Menedemos said. "That's a nasty way to go. Did the philosopher die well?"

"Anaxarkhos? I should say so," Sostratos said. "He told the Salaminian, 'Go ahead and pound my body, for you can't pound my soul.' That made Nikokreon so furious, he ordered Anaxarkhos' tongue torn out, but Anaxarkhos bit it off before the torturer could get to him, and he spat it in Nikokreon's face. And so you see, my dear, Nikokreon might have got off better than he deserved when Ptolemaios told him to slay himself. If *I'd* been the one giving the orders . . ."

"You sound as bloodthirsty as any of the Macedonians," Menedemos said, eyeing Sostratos with unwonted wariness. "More often than not, you're as gentle as any man I've ever known. Every once in a while, though . . ." He tossed his head.

"Someone who tries to kill knowledge, to kill wisdom, deserves whatever happens to him," Sostratos said. "That polluted whoreson pirate who stole the gryphon's skull, for instance. If I got my hands on him, I'd send for a torturer from Persia and another one from Carthage, and let them see who could do worse to him. I'd pay them both, and gladly."

Menedemos started to laugh, but stopped before the sound escaped. When he looked at Sostratos, his cousin's expression said he hadn't been joking. That pirate was lucky he'd managed to get off the *Aphrodite*. And he'd stay lucky if he never complained in a tavern about the old bones he'd taken in lieu of other loot more worth having. If word of such grumbling ever got back to Sostratos, that pirate would have to look to his life.

When they returned to the merchant galley, Diokles proved to have done some scouting of his own. The oarmaster said, "They've got a fine kitharist from Corinth playing at one of the inns here. They say he's the first kitharist to play in Salamis since Nikokreon flung the one named Stratonikos into the sea. Now that the king's dead, they dare show their faces here again."

"Oh, by Zeus!" Menedemos exclaimed. "Another one Nikokreon put to death?"

"Another one?" Diokles asked.

Together, Menedemos and Sostratos told him about Anaxarkhos. Then Menedemos asked, "What happened to Stratonikos?"

"Why, he spoke freer about Nikokreon's family than he should have," the keleustes answered. "That's why the king drowned him."

"This has a familiar ring, doesn't it?" Sostratos said, and Menedemos dipped his head. Sostratos went on, "I believe it about Stratonikos, too. I saw him in Athens, years ago. Marvelous kitharist, but he *would* say the first thing that popped into his mind, and he didn't care where he was or to whom he said it."

"Tell me more," Menedemos urged.

"He was the fellow who called Byzantion the armpit of Hellas," Sostratos said, and Menedemos guffawed. His cousin added, "When he was coming out of Herakleia, he looked around carefully, this way and that. Somebody asked him why. 'I'm ashamed of being seen,' he answered. 'It's like coming out of a brothel.'"

"Oh, dear," Menedemos said. "No, I don't think he'd have got on well with Nikokreon."

"He didn't get on well with anybody," Sostratos said. "When he was playing in Corinth, an old woman kept staring and staring at him. Finally, he asked her why. She said, 'It's a wonder your mother bore you for ten months when we can't bear you for even a day.' But by Apollo, Menedemos, he played the kithara like no man since Orpheus."

"He must have, or somebody would have drowned him sooner." Menedemos turned to Diokles. "How did he fall foul of the king of Salamis?"

"I know he insulted Nikokreon's two sons, but I don't know how," the oarmaster answered. "But once when the king's wife—Axiothea, her name was—came in for supper, she hap-

pened to fart. And then later on she stepped on an almond
while she was wearing a slipper from Sikyon—and Stratonikos sang out, 'That's not the same sound!"

"*Oimoi!*" Menedemos exclaimed. "If he said that to anyone
from my family, I'd probably pop him in the chops myself."

"Ah, but would you kill him?" Sostratos asked. "That's
what's wrong with what Nikokreon did—nobody could stop
him if he set his mind on killing or torturing someone. That's
what's wrong with kings generally, if you ask me."

"I'm as good a democrat as you are, my dear," Menedemos
answered. "But you have to remember, too, it wasn't a king
who killed Sokrates."

"Democracy isn't perfect, either—the gods know that's so,"
Sostratos said. "If we didn't live in a democracy, we wouldn't
have to listen to Xanthos blather on and on whenever the Assembly meets, for instance."

"You're right," Menedemos said. "One more reason to be
glad we can get out of Rhodes half the year on trading runs."

"Pity we can't hear Stratonikos, though," Sostratos said.
"Who's the kitharist who is in town, Diokles?"

"Areios, his name is," the keleustes answered.

Menedemos nudged Sostratos. "What did old Stratonikos
have to say about him, eh, best one?"

"He told him to go to the crows once," Sostratos answered.
"That's all I know."

"Sounds like Stratonikos told everybody to go to the crows,"
Menedemos said. "That doesn't make this Areios out to be
anybody special. I wonder if we should bother seeing him."

"What else is there to do in Salamis of nights?" Sostratos
asked.

"Get drunk. Get laid." Menedemos named the two obvious
choices in any harbor town. They were, when he thought
about it, the two obvious choices in towns that didn't lie by the
coast, too.

"We can drink and listen to Areios at the same time," his
cousin said. "And if you decide you want a woman or a boy,
you can probably find one not far away."

"He's right, skipper," Diokles said.

"Well, so he is," Menedemos agreed. "He's right a lot of the time." He nudged Sostratos in the ribs. "If you're so smart, why aren't you rich?"

"Because I sail with you?" Sostratos asked innocently. Before Menedemos could get angry, his cousin went on, "A couple of hundred years ago, people asked Thales of Miletos that same question till he got sick of hearing it. He cornered the olive-oil market in those parts one year, and after that he *was* rich."

"Good for him. I don't suppose there's any law that says philosophers can't enjoy silver just like anybody else," Menedemos said. "And I don't suppose he got rich by trying to sell his oil to all the neighboring poleis that already had plenty of their own."

Sostratos grimaced. "No, I don't suppose so, either. We just have to do the best we can with it, that's all."

The answer was soft enough to keep Menedemos from going any further with his complaints. And he knew Sostratos didn't want to have the oil aboard the *Aphrodite,* either, even if it had come from his brother-in-law's groves. With a sigh, he turned to Diokles. "Whereabouts is this Areios playing?"

"It's not far," the oarmaster answered. "I was going to go over there myself, listen for a while, and see how overpriced the wine is. You gents coming?"

"Why not?" Menedemos said, and Sostratos dipped his head, too.

Diokles led them to the tavern where the kitharist was performing. When Menedemos saw where it was, he started to laugh. So did Sostratos, who said, "Call it Stratonikos' revenge." Nikokreon's cenotaph stood only fifteen or twenty cubits away, with the statue of the late king of Salamis looking back toward the tavern.

"Play loud, Areios," Menedemos said. "Let's hope Nikokreon's shade is listening."

The place was crowded when Menedemos, his cousin, and the keleustes went inside. He heard the archaic Cypriot dialect,

Macedonian, several less unusual varieties of Greek, and assorted retching gutturals from a table full of Phoenicians.

"By the dog of Egypt!" Menedemos exclaimed. "Isn't that Ptolemaios?" He pointed to a blunt-featured, middle-aged man sitting at the best table in the place.

"It can't be," Sostratos answered. "He went back to Alexandria from Kos this past fall with his new baby." He snapped his fingers. "This must be Menelaos, his brother. He commands here on Cyprus."

"Mm, I suppose you're right," Menedemos said after a second glance. "Sure does look like him, though, doesn't it?"

Perhaps sensing their eyes on him, Menelaos looked their way. He smiled and waved. Menedemos found himself waving back. Ptolemaios' brother seemed friendlier than the lord of Egypt. "He has less on his shoulders than Ptolemaios does," Sostratos said when Menedemos remarked on that.

Menedemos thought it over, then dipped his head. "I wouldn't be surprised if you were right."

Where Menelaos and his officers got the best seats in the house, a Rhodian merchant skipper and a couple of his officers had to take whatever they could get. Sostratos, of all people, was the one who spotted a table in the back of the tavern. All three Rhodians rushed to claim it. They got there just ahead of somebody who, by the gold rings on his fingers and his crimson-bordered himation, might have bought and sold them. The fellow gave them a sour stare before looking for somewhere else to sit.

Once his own fundament was on a stool, Menedemos discovered he could barely see the raised platform where Areios would perform. "He's not a flute-girl at a symposion," Sostratos said when he complained. "We came to listen to him, not to watch him dance or take his clothes off."

"I know, but I would like to have some idea what he looks like," Menedemos answered.

Before he could do any more grumbling, a serving woman came up and asked, "What are ye fain to drink, gentles?"

Menedemos hid a smile. He enjoyed listening to Cypriots

talk; it was almost like hearing Homer and his contemporaries come to life. "What have you got?" he asked.

"We've wine from Khios and Kos and Lesbos and Thasos and Naxos and . . ." The woman went on to name almost every island in the Aegean and every part of the mainland adjacent to it. She finished, "And, of course, we've the local, and also wine of dates, in the which the Phoenicians take much pleasure."

"A cup of the local will suit me fine," Menedemos said.

"Same for me," Diokles said.

The serving woman's eyes called them both cheapskates. Menedemos didn't care. A place like this was liable to pad its profits by claiming a cheap wine was really something more and charging three times as much for it as would have been right. With the local, at least he knew what he was getting.

"And what of you, most noble?" the woman asked when Sostratos didn't answer right away.

"Let me have a cup of date wine, if you please," Sostratos said. With a shrug, the serving woman went away.

"Why do you want to drink that horrid nasty stuff, young sir?" Diokles said.

"We're going to Phoenicia. I might as well find out what the Phoenicians like, don't you think?" Sostratos said. "If it is nasty, I won't drink it again."

After longer than she should have taken, the serving woman brought them their drinks. Menedemos tasted the local and made a face. He hadn't expected much, and he hadn't got it, either. Diokles drank without a word of complaint. Menedemos took another sip. He shrugged. It wasn't *that* much worse than the wine the *Aphrodite* carried for the crew.

"What about yours, Sostratos?" he asked.

His cousin held out the cheap earthenware cup. "Have a taste yourself, if you care to."

"Why not?" Menedemos said, though that was a question with an obvious answer. He sipped cautiously, then handed the cup back to Sostratos. "Too sweet for my taste, and thick as glue. The Phoenicians are welcome to it, as far as I'm concerned."

"I wouldn't drink it every day, either," Sostratos said, "but I don't think it's as nasty as Diokles made it out to be. Better than drinking water, that's certain."

"I should hope so," Menedemos said. "After all, what isn't?"

"There's that sour stuff the Egyptians and Thracians and Kelts brew from barley," Sostratos said. "By all accounts, beer's pretty bad. This tastes as though it wants to be wine, anyhow." He drank some more, then thoughtfully smacked his lips. "Yes, it could be worse."

"Thracians use butter instead of olive oil, so it's plain they have no taste," Menedemos said. Sostratos and Diokles both dipped their heads; for good measure, the oarmaster also made a disgusted face.

A fat, bejeweled man—Menedemos guessed he was the fellow who owned the tavern—came up onto the platform and spoke in throaty, Phoenician-accented Greek: "Hail, best ones! Hail also to the lovely ladies we have with us this evening."

That made Menedemos look around. It also made Sostratos cough sharply. "You stop that," Menedemos told him. "Hetairai aren't wives." Sostratos spread his hands, admitting as much. Menedemos did spot a couple of women; they wore veils, as if they were respectable, but they wouldn't have come to a tavern if they had been. One sat with a big Macedonian a couple of tables away from Menelaos and his comrades. The other accompanied a man with the sleek look of a rich landowner.

Menedemos had missed some of what the tavernkeeper had to say. "—Here direct from appearances in Athens and Corinth and Alexandria," the man went on. "My friends, I give you the famous . . . Areios!"

He clapped his hands, holding them above his head to signal everyone else to applaud, too. Menedemos clapped a few times. So did Diokles. Sostratos, Menedemos noted, sat quietly, waiting to find out whether the kitharist would be worth hearing. Sometimes Sostratos was too sensible for his own good.

"Thank you very much!" Areios waved to the crowd as he came out onto the platform. Lean and spare, he spoke a polished Attic Greek. He'd probably been a striking youth. Even now, though the gray in his hair argued that he had to be close to fifty, he shaved his face to make himself look younger. By lamp- and torchlight, the illusion worked remarkably well. "I'm very pleased to be here," he went on with a grin. "By the gods, I'm very pleased to be anywhere that isn't apt to get sacked in the next hour."

He got his laugh. Menelaos called, "That won't happen in Cyprus. Cyprus belongs to my brother, and he'll keep it!"

"As long as he keeps it till after I've sailed away, that's fine with me," Areios replied, and won a louder laugh.

"Another kitharist who thinks he can make fun of powerful men," Menedemos said. "Doesn't he remember what happened to Stratonikos here?" He paused. "Menelaos does seem a more cheerful sort than Nikokreon was—I will say that."

"I wonder how he feels about being the second most important man in Ptolemaios' realm," Sostratos said. "Does he ever wonder what things would have been like if he'd been born before his brother?"

"Why ask me?" Menedemos said. "Why not go over there and ask him?"

For a bad moment, he thought Sostratos would get up and do justthat. But his cousin was only shifting on the stool. Sostratos pointed to the kithara Areios cradled in his arms. "Have you ever seen a finer instrument?"

Menedemos had to crane his neck to see it at all, but answered, "I don't believe I have."

Large and heavy, the kithara was the instrument of choice of professional musicians. It had seven strings, and an enormous sound box that amplified the tones the kitharist struck from them. Areios' kithara was of pale oak, and gleamed as if rubbed with beeswax. It had inlays of ivory and of some dark wood, perhaps walnut, perhaps something more exotic—and more expensive. From supporting the instrument he played, Areios' arms were as muscular as a pankratiast's.

But then Areios ran his fingers over the strings, and Menedemos stopped noticing anything but the music. Not only was his one of the most beautiful kitharas Menedemos had ever seen, it was also one of the most perfectly tuned he'd ever heard. Tuning the kithara—or its relatives, the lyre, the barbitos, and the phorminx—was anything but easy. Like anyone who'd been to school, Menedemos had learned to play the lyre . . . after a fashion.

The strings—four in a lyre, more in the other instruments— were attached to the sound box at the bottom by a string bar and bridge. Things were more complicated at the other end. The strings were wound around the crosspiece and held in place by a piece of hide cut from the neck of a cow or goat and rubbed with sticky grease to make them adhere to it. Menedemos remembered endless plucking, endless adjustments—and the schoolmaster's stick coming down on his back when he couldn't get the tone right no matter what. And even when he managed to persuade the strings to yield notes somewhere close to what they should have been, a little playing would put them out again. It was enough—more than enough—to drive anybody mad.

Here, though, the tones weren't close to what they should have been. They were exactly right and seemed to pierce Menedemos' very soul. "Pure as water from a mountain spring," Sostratos whispered. Menedemos dipped his head, and then waved his cousin to silence. He didn't want to hear anything but the music.

Areios played a little bit of everything, from the lyric poetry of the generations following Homer to the latest love songs out of Alexandria. Everything he did play had a slight sardonic edge to it. He chose Arkhilokhos' old poem about throwing away his shield and leaving it for some Thracian to find. And the Alexandrian song was about a woman trying to bewitch her lover away from her rival—a boy.

At last, the kitharist struck one more perfect chord, bowed very low, said, "I thank you, most noble ones," and left the stage.

Menedemos clapped till his palms were sore. He wasn't the only one, either; a tremendous din of applause filled the tavern, enough to make his head ring. Cries of *"Euge!"* rang out from all sides.

"How is he next to Stratonikos?" Menedemos asked as they left the building.

"It's been a while since I heard Stratonikos," Sostratos replied, judicious as usual. "I think Areios is at least as good with the kithara itself—and I've never heard one better tuned—"

"Yes, I thought the same thing myself," Menedemos said. Diokles dipped his head. "Me, too."

"But Stratonikos, if I remember rightly, had a better voice," Sostratos finished.

"I'm glad we went," Menedemos said. He clapped the keleustes on the back. "Good thing you heard he was playing, Diokles—and I hope Nikokreon's shade got himself an earful tonight."

SOSTRATOS WASN'T SORRY to see Cyprus recede behind the *Aphrodite*'s goose-headed sternpost and the boat the akatos towed in her wake. He also was not eager to face Phoenicia or the land of the Ioudaioi. What he was was coldly furious at his brother-in-law. "When we get back to Rhodes," he said, "I'm going to pour melted cheese and garlic over Damonax and fry him in his own olive oil. We'll have plenty left to do the job, with some left over for the barley rolls we'll serve with his polluted carcass."

"You must be angry, if you've got the whole menu planned," Menedemos said.

"Herodotos puts the Androphagoi far to the north of the Skythian plains, beyond a great desert," Sostratos replied. "I wonder what he would have thought if he'd heard a Rhodian wanted to become a man-eater."

"He'd probably wonder what wine went best with brother-in-law," Menedemos said. "Something sweet and thick, I'd say."

"Gods bless you, my dear," Sostratos said, "for you're the best man I've ever known when it comes to helping someone along with his mood, whatever it happens to be. I'm not surprised men often choose you symposiarch when they throw a drinking party—you're the one to take them where they want to go."

"Well, thank you, O best one," Menedemos answered, raising his right hand from the steering-oar tiller to give Sostratos a salute. "I don't know that anyone's ever said anything kinder of me."

"Now that I think about it," Sostratos went on in musing tones, "that's probably the same sort of knack that gets you so many girls, isn't it?"

"I hadn't really thought about it," Menedemos said.

"Papai!" Sostratos exclaimed, now dismayed. He stared at his cousin, hardly believing what he'd heard. "Why not? Don't you know what Sokrates said?—'The unexamined life is not worth living.' He's right."

"I don't know about that," Menedemos said. "I'm usually too busy *living* my life to step back and take a look at it."

"Then how do you know if you're living well or not?"

Menedemos frowned. "If we go down this road, I'm going to get all tangled up. I can see that coming already." He wagged a finger at Sostratos. "I can see you looking forward to it, too."

"Who, me?" Sostratos said, not quite innocently enough. "Answer my question, if you please."

"How do I know if I'm living well?" Menedemos echoed. Sostratos dipped his head. His cousin frowned in thought. "By whether I'm happy or not, I suppose."

"Amazing, O marvelous one!" Sostratos said. Menedemos shot him a dirty look. Sostratos went on, "Could a dog or a goat speak, it would give the same answer. For a dog or a goat, it would be good enough, too. But for a man? No. Artaxerxes Okhos, the Great King of Persia, was happiest when he was killing people, and he killed a lot of them. Does that mean he lived well?"

"No, but killing people doesn't make me happy." Menedemos fixed Sostratos with a mild and speculative stare. "For certain people, I might make an exception."

"You're still talking around the question," Sostratos said. "Just think, too: if you knew why you were so charming, you might get more women yet."

That made Menedemos look sharply at him. Sostratos had thought it might. "Do you think so?" his cousin asked.

"I don't see why it wouldn't," Sostratos replied. "An archer who knows what he's doing is more likely to hit the target than one who just picks up the bow and lets fly, isn't he?"

"Well, yes, I suppose so." But Menedemos sounded suspicious. A moment later, he explained why: "I still think you're trying to turn me into a philosopher behind my back."

"Would I do such a thing?" Again, Sostratos sounded as innocent as he could.

He sounded so very innocent, in fact, that both Menedemos and Diokles burst out laughing. "Oh, no, my dear, not you," Menedemos said. "No, indeed. Never you. The thought wouldn't cross your mind." He laughed some more, louder than ever.

"What I'd like to know," Sostratos said with more than a little heat, "is what's so dreadful about the notion that one man should want to persuade another to love wisdom and look for it, instead of just stumbling over it when he chances upon it or turning his back on it altogether. Can you tell me that?"

"Philosophy's too much like work," Menedemos said. "I've got real work to do, and I haven't got the time to worry about becomingness or essences or any of that other philosophical nonsense that makes my head ache."

"Do you have time to think about whether you're doing the right thing, and why?" Sostratos asked. "Is anything more important than that?"

"Getting the *Aphrodite* to Phoenicia and not sinking on the way," his cousin suggested.

"You're being troublesome on purpose," Sostratos said. Menedemos grinned at him. Sostratos went on, "Yes, you want to survive. Any living thing wants to survive. But when you get to Phoenicia, will you do good or evil?"

"Good to my friends, evil to my enemies," Menedemos replied at once.

Any Hellene who answered without thinking was likely to say something much like that. Sostratos tossed his head. "I'm sorry, my dear, but what was good enough for Homer's heroes isn't any more."

"And why not?" Menedemos demanded. "If anybody does me a bad turn, I'll give him a knee in the balls first chance I get."

"What happens then? He'll give you one back, or his friends will."

"And then I'll get my own back, or I'll have a friend help me against his friend," Menedemos said.

"And your faction fight will go on for years, maybe for generations," Sostratos said. "How many poleis have been ruined by feuds like that? How many wars between poleis have started through feuds like that? By the gods, if the poleis of Hellas hadn't spent their time fighting amongst themselves, could the Macedonians have beaten them?"

He thought that was an invincible argument. But Menedemos said, "Ha! Now I've got you!"

"You do not!"

"I do so." His cousin leered at him. "For one thing, the Macedonians fight amongst themselves, too, even worse than regular Hellenes. Go ahead—tell me I'm wrong. I dare you." He waited. Sostratos stood silent. He couldn't disagree. "Ha!" Menedemos said again. "And, for another, if Philip of Macedon hadn't whipped the Hellenes into line, and if Alexander hadn't come along right afterwards, who'd be running Phoenicia now? The Great King of Persia, that's who. So I say hurrah for feuds, I do."

Sostratos stared at him, then started to laugh. *"Euge!"* he exclaimed. "That's the best bit of bad argument I think I've ever heard. Some people learn to argue from Platon and what he says of Sokrates. You took your model from Aristophanes' *Clouds*."

"Bad Logic there, you mean?" Menedemos asked, and Sostratos dipped his head. Not a bit abashed, Menedemos made as if to bow. "Bad Logic won, remember. Good Logic gave up and went over to the other side. And it looks like I've outargued you."

He waited to see whether Sostratos would challenge that. Sostratos didn't, but gave back the same sort of bow he'd got. "Every once in a while, I surprise you when we wrestle in the gymnasion." He towered over his cousin, but Menedemos was quicker and stronger and more agile. "Every once in a while, I suppose you can surprise me when we aim winged words at each other."

"Winged words?" Menedemos echoed. "You knew the Aristophanes, and now you're quoting Homer. By the dog, which of us is which?"

"Oh, no, you don't. You won't get away with that, you rascal. If you say you're me and I'm you, you get out of the oath you gave me in Salamis."

They both laughed. Menedemos said, "Well, it wouldn't be hard for you to keep. You don't go looking to sleep with other men's wives anyhow."

"I should hope not," Sostratos answered. "But you can't be me, because you didn't spend all that time over the winter learning Aramaic."

"I'm glad I didn't, too. You sound like you're choking to death every time you speak it." Menedemos put on a horrible Phoenician accent: "Dis iz vat joo zound lige."

"I hope not," Sostratos said.

"Go ahead and hope. You still do."

They kept on chaffing each other as Menedemos sailed the *Aphrodite* southeast. Going due east from Salamis would have shortened their journey across the Inner Sea, but then they would have had to crawl south along the Phoenician coast to get to Sidon, the city from which Sostratos wanted to set out and explore the interior. At this season of the year, with the sun hot and bright and the sea calm, the risk seemed worth taking.

Sostratos looked back toward Salamis. Already, the coast of Cyprus was no more than a low line on the horizon. The akatos would be out of sight of land for three days, maybe four, on the way to Phoenicia. Except for the journey south from Hellas and the islands of the Aegean to Alexandria, it was the longest journey over the open sea a ship was likely to have to make.

"I wouldn't want to do this in a round ship," Sostratos said. "Suppose you got halfway across and the wind died? Sitting out there, bobbing in the middle of nothing, hoping you wouldn't run out of water and wine . . ." He tossed his head. "No, thanks."

"That wouldn't be much fun," Menedemos agreed. "I don't like the idea of riding out a storm out of sight of land, either. When that happened on the way west from Hellas to Italy a couple of years ago, we were lucky to make as good a landfall as we did."

"There ought to be a better way to navigate out on the open sea," Sostratos said. "Sun and stars, wind and waves, just aren't enough. Ships that set out for Alexandria can end up almost anywhere along the Egyptian coast, in the Delta or in the desert to the west, and then have to beat their way back."

"I won't say you're wrong, because you're right," Menedemos replied. "But how would you do such a thing? What else is there but sun and stars, wind and waves?"

"I don't know," Sostratos said fretfully. He'd feared Menedemos would ask him that, for he had no answer to give. "Maybe there's *something,* though. After all, I don't suppose the very first sailors knew enough to cast a line down to the seabed so the lead's hollow bottom, full of tallow, would bring up sand or marl that helped tell them where they were."

"That's . . . probably true," Menedemos said. "I don't remember Homer talking about sounding leads in the *Iliad* or the *Odyssey*, and resourceful Odysseus would surely have used one if he'd known about it."

"Herodotos *does* mention them, so they've been known for more than a hundred years," Sostratos said. "Some time between the Trojan War and the Persian Wars, some clever fellow figured that out. I wonder who. I wonder when. I wish I knew. That's a man whose name deserves to live. I wonder if he was a Hellene or a Phoenician or a gods-detested Lykian pirate. I don't suppose anyone will ever know for certain."

His cousin gave him an odd look. "It hadn't even occurred to me that the fellow who came up with the lead could have been anything but a Hellene."

"We've borrowed all sorts of things," Sostratos said. "The Phoenicians gave us the alpha-beta. Theirs is older than ours, and you should have heard Himilkon go on and on about how they're happy with it just the way it is. The Lydians were the first ones to mint real coins, or so Herodotos says— before that, everybody had to weigh out scrap gold and silver. And even Dionysos is supposed to come from out of the distant east, so maybe we learned to make wine from barbarians, too."

"Wherever we learned it, it's a good thing we did," Menedemos said. "I wouldn't want to spend my whole life drinking water. Or it could be even worse than that. We could drink milk the way the Thracians and the Skythians do." He made a revolted face, sticking out his tongue like a Gorgon painted on the facing of a hoplite's shield.

"That would be dreadful." Sostratos made a nasty face of his own. "Cheese is all very well—cheese is better than all very well, as a matter of fact—but milk?" He tossed his head. "No, thanks."

"We found out the Syrians don't fancy seafood, remember," Menedemos said. "Now *that's* ignorance, nothing else but."

"Of course it is," Sostratos said. "And that strange god the

Ioudaioi worship won't let them eat pork." He sent his cousin a warning look. "You're going to start talking about Pythagoreans and beans and farting again, aren't you? Don't."

"I wasn't going to do any such thing," Menedemos insisted. Sostratos didn't believe him for a moment. But then his cousin went on, "What I *was* going to do was tell you there's a little tiny island between Lesbos and the Anatolian mainland that's called Pordoselene."

"What? Fartmoon?" Sostratos exclaimed. "I don't believe it."

"Apollo smite me if I lie," Menedemos said solemnly. "It even has a polis of the same name. And there's another island, even smaller, also called Pordoselene, in front of the polis, and that island has a temple to Apollo on it."

"Fartmoon," Sostratos said again, and shrugged in bemusement. "We're not even out of sight of land yet, but we're already getting . . . peculiar. By the time we spy the Phoenician coast, I expect we'll all be raving mad." He sounded as if he was looking forward to it.

"SHIP HO!" ARISTEIDAS CALLED FROM THE Aphrodite's *small* foredeck. He pointed. "Ship off the starboard bow!"

Menedemos peered in that direction. "I don't see a sail," he said, but swung the merchant galley a little to the south anyway. Over the past couple of years, he'd come to rely on Aristeidas' eyesight.

"No sail, skipper," the lookout said. "There's the hull—do you see it? Fishing boat, I'd guess."

"Ah." Menedemos had been looking for the wrong thing. As soon as Aristeidas told him what he ought to see, he spotted it. "We'll come up to him, and he can tell us just where we are."

The coastline of Phoenicia had come into view a little while before: a low, dark smudge of land rising up out of the endless blue flatness of the waters of the Inner Sea. Had Menedemos sighted land in Hellas, he wouldn't have needed to figure out where he was. But neither he nor anyone else aboard the akatos had ever come so far east before; the silhouettes of the hills against the sky didn't tell him where the ship was, as they would have in lands he'd already visited.

"He's making sail, skipper," Aristeidas called, and Menedemos dipped his head—he saw the pale square of linen coming down from the yard, too. The lookout added, "He must think we've got a pirate ship. A lot of these little boats do."

"Well, we'll keep after him anyhow," Menedemos said. "We'd make a pretty sorry excuse for a pirate if we couldn't catch up with a tubby scow like that, now wouldn't we?" He raised his voice: "Sostratos!"

His cousin, as far as he could tell, might not have noticed the boat at all—he was watching dolphins leaping and cavorting off to port. He started at the sound of his name and looked around wildly, as if wondering what had been going on while his mind was elsewhere. "What is it?" he asked apprehensively.

"See that fishing boat?" Menedemos said. By Sostratos' expression, he might never have heard of fishing boats, let alone seen one before; when he thought about other things, he thought hard. Patiently, Menedemos pointed it out. He was relieved to see the light of intelligence appear on his cousin's face, and went on, "How would you like to practice your Aramaic with whoever's aboard her?"

"I can do that, I suppose," Sostratos said. "What do you want me to say?"

Maybe that hadn't been the light of intelligence after all. Menedemos drummed his fingers on the steering-oar tiller.

"Do *you* know where we are, my dear?" he asked sweetly. "Do *you* have any idea which Phoenician city we're closest to?"

"Of course not." Sostratos sounded affronted. "How could I know that?"

"Well, one good way might be to ask the people on the boat there, don't you think?"

"Oh," Sostratos said. This time, it really was the light of intelligence, or something like it, anyhow. Still sounding slightly peevish, Sostratos asked, "Why didn't you tell me to do that before?"

Menedemos drummed his fingers on the tiller again. "Never mind," he said; he didn't feel like arguing with his cousin. "Just take care of it when we catch up with them, all right?"

"Certainly, O best one," Sostratos replied with such dignity as he could muster. "And it goes to show some people in these parts *do* catch fish, doesn't it?" Menedemos supposed it did. He hadn't thought of that.

The fishermen in that boat were good sailors. They got the sail down with commendable haste and wrung every digit of speed they could from their little craft. That made the *Aphrodite* take longer to catch up to them but never gave them the slightest chance of escaping her. They were much too far out to sea to get to shore before she came up alongside them. Even then, they were ready to fight. A couple of them brandished what were either gutting knives or shortswords. A third shot an arrow that splashed into the sea fifteen or twenty cubits short of the merchant galley.

"Tell them we're friendly. Tell them we don't want to murder them or sell them into slavery," Menedemos said. The fisherman with the bow let fly again. This arrow came closer. Menedemos scowled. "I get more tempted every minute, though."

His cousin shouted something in Aramaic. The fishermen shouted back. Menedemos raised a questioning eyebrow. Sostratos coughed. Then he said, "They're telling me to do things to my mother Sophokles never thought of in *Oidipous Tyrannos.*"

"Barbarians curse that way, don't they?" Menedemos said.

"They're not paying me compliments, my dear," Sostratos answered.

"Heh," Menedemos said. "All right. Find out what we need to know. And tell them that if they don't learn manners we cursed well *will* ram them and sink them, just to teach them to respect their betters."

"I don't think I can say all that in Aramaic," Sostratos warned.

"Try."

Sostratos dipped his head. He made what to Menedemos sounded like horrible choking noises. The Phoenicians in the fishing boat shouted back. This time, they seemed less impassioned. So did Sostratos when he replied to them. After a bit, he turned to Menedemos and said, "*Euge,* my dear. Sidon is a couple of hours' sail to the south. A very nice bit of navigating."

"*Euge* is right, skipper," Diokles agreed. "All that water to cross, and then to make it to the coast almost right where we wanted to be . . ." He raised his voice, calling out to the sailors, "Give the captain a cheer, boys! He put us right where he wanted to."

"*Euge!*" the men called. Menedemos grinned and waved. Somebody added, "The skipper always puts it right where he wants to." Menedemos laughed at that. After a moment, though, he felt like scowling again. Thanks to his bargain with his cousin, he might not have the chance to put it where he wanted to.

"Shall I send them on their way?" Sostratos asked.

"Yes, go ahead," Menedemos answered. "We've found out what we needed to know. If they're telling the truth, that is."

"Not much point to lying about something like that," Sostratos said. "We'd find the truth soon enough, and their lie wouldn't do us any harm, no matter how much they might wish it would." He shouted once more, in incomprehensible

Aramaic. The fishermen understood it well enough, though, whether Menedemos did or not. They steered away from the *Aphrodite,* and were no doubt delighted when the akatos, which dwarfed their little boat, did not match their course.

Sidon, once the merchant galley reached it, proved to lie on a small promontory behind a line of islets running parallel to the coast. "It's not a very big place, is it?" Menedemos said, none too happily—he wanted a good market for the *Aphrodite*'s wares.

"But look at the buildings," Sostratos said. "I've heard the Phoenicians build tall, and now I see it's true. They go up and up and up."

He was right. Few buildings in a polis full of Hellenes rose more than two stories above the street, so that the temples and other public structures stood out. Sidon was different. Every other building seemed to tower four or five stories high. Menedemos said, "The Sidonians must have strong legs, from going up and down all those stairs so often."

"I wouldn't be surprised if you're right," his cousin answered. "They have to get their exercise somewhere, I suppose. There certainly doesn't look to be room in the town for a gymnasion." He paused, then laughed. "In fact, the very idea of a gymnasion in a place like Sidon is absurd."

"Why?" Menedemos asked. "They could squeeze one in if they wanted to badly enough."

Sostratos gave him the sort of look he hated, the look that said he'd been so blatantly stupid, he should have been ashamed of himself. Menedemos scratched his head. He couldn't see why, which only made things worse. Holding on to patience with both hands—and making a point of doing so—Sostratos said, "What *is* a gymnasion? Literally, that is—what does the word mean?"

"A place to go nak—" Menedemos stopped. "Oh. Phoenicians don't go naked, do they?"

He could see they didn't for himself. The day was warm, warmer than it was likely to have been in Rhodes at this season of the year. It was more than warm enough for a lot of male Hellenes to have stripped off their chitons and gone through the streets bare without a second thought. They took nudity in stride and took it for granted.

But almost all the people he could see in Sidon covered themselves in cloth all the way down to their feet. The only exceptions were men—probably slaves—bearing heavy burdens, and even they wore loincloths. Those were the only exceptions Menedemos spotted, at any rate. Sostratos pointed to a knot of men on a quay and said, "Look. They're Hellenes, or maybe Macedonians."

He was right. He usually was. Some of the men he'd spotted wore short tunics like the ones he and Menedemos had on. A couple of others were in linen corselets and bronze helms with tall horsehair crests. Menedemos couldn't imagine why they wanted to show they were soldiers in a town unlikely to be attacked. All it would do was make them sweat more than they had to. But that was their worry, not his.

Sostratos did some more pointing, this time at some of the ships and, more important, at the large ship sheds by the water's edge. "Look at all the war galleys Antigonos has here," he said. "Do you suppose Menelaos knows about that, over in Salamis?"

Menedemos laughed. No matter how much Sostratos knew, he could be naive as a child. "My dear, think about how many ships go back and forth between here and Salamis," Menedemos said. "If I were Menelaos, I wouldn't just know how many ships old One-Eye has here. I'd know the name of every rower on every one of them, and I'd know the name of every rower's father, too. And you can bet your last obolos that Menelaos does."

Now it was his cousin's turn to say, "Oh," in a gratifyingly small voice. "Yes, that is reasonable, isn't it?"

Menedemos guided the *Aphrodite* to a mooring place at the end of a quay. The longshoremen who caught the lines to make the ship fast stared at the scantily clad Hellenes aboard her. They shouted questions in their harsh language. Sostratos gave halting answers. Menedemos caught the merchant galley's name, those of his father and uncle, and that of Rhodes. But for the handful of names, he understood not a word his cousin was saying.

A big round ship was tied up next to the akatos. More longshoremen carried sacks of grain off her, down the quay, and into the city. As they worked, they chanted: "*Hilni hiya holla—ouahillok holya.*"

"What does that mean?" Menedemos asked Sostratos.

"What does what mean?" his cousin answered. Menedemos pointed to the men unloading the round ship. Sostratos cocked his head to one side. Menedemos got the idea he hadn't even noticed the chant till it was pointed out to him. After a bit, Sostratos shrugged. "I don't know. I don't think it means anything at all, though I wouldn't swear to that. If I had to guess, I'd say it was something rhythmic they sing to help the time pass while they work."

"Could be," Menedemos said. "We have chants like that. I just wondered if this one made any sense."

"Not to me." Sostratos pointed toward the far end of the wharf. "And here comes an officer to ask us questions."

"Oh, hurrah," Menedemos said, meaning anything but, "Gods-detested arrogant snoops, the lot of them. I don't care if they work for Antigonos or Ptolemaios or one of the other Macedonian marshals. To the crows with 'em all."

Antigonos' man was quite tall—several digits taller than Sostratos and close to twice as wide through the shoulders. He had blue eyes, blondish hair, and a once-fiery beard now streaked with gray. Menedemos wondered for a moment if he was a Keltic mercenary, but he proved to be a Macedonian. "Who are you, and where are you from?" he asked, not bothering to sharpen his slurred accent. "Don't see many strange Hellenes here, and that's a fact."

"This is the *Aphrodite,* out of Rhodes," Menedemos told him.

"Rhodes, eh?" The Macedonian didn't seem to know what

to make of that. "Your little island built some ships for Antigonos, but you do a lot of business with Ptolemaios, too."

"Yes, we're neutral," Menedemos said, wondering if there were any such thing with the world as it was these days. "We have no quarrel with anybody."

"Ah, but what happens when somebody has a quarrel with *you*?" the Macedonian asked. Then he shrugged. "What are you carrying?"

"We've got papyrus and ink, Koan silk, fine Rhodian perfume, some of the best olive oil you'll ever see, Lykian ham, smoked eels from Phaselis, and a nice stock of books to help pass the time."

Antigonos' officer didn't laugh at the olive oil. The way things had gone, Menedemos took that as good news. The Macedonian said, "Books, eh? Why would you bring books?"

"Didn't Alexander himself travel with them?" Menedemos replied. "If they were good enough for him, why not for you?"

"On account of he had his letters, and I don't." The Macedonian's expression sharpened. "Coming from the west, you'd've stopped in Salamis, wouldn't you?"

"That's right," Menedemos said.

"Well, what did you see there?" the officer demanded. "How many war galleys in the harbor? Are they building more? Is Menelaos in town, or is he somewhere else on Cyprus? What's he up to?"

Before answering, Menedemos sent Sostratos a significant look. If Antigonos' men were so interested in learning what was happening on Cyprus, how could his cousin doubt that Ptolemaios' forces on the island also closely questioned sailors coming from Phoenicia? "Didn't pay much attention to the harbor," Menedemos said.

"Oh, yes—likely tell." Antigonos' officer curled his lip in what he no doubt thought to be an aristocratic sneer.

"By the gods, it's true," Menedemos said. "I don't care about war galleys; they've got nothing to do with me. If there'd been a couple of other akatoi in the harbor, you can bet

I'd've noticed them. We did see Menelaos, though. He's there."

"Ah, that's something." The Macedonian eagerly snatched the bone Menedemos tossed him. "Where'd you see him? What was he doing?"

"He was at a tavern, not far from the harbor," Menedemos answered.

"What was he doing? Was he getting drunk?" Yes, the officer was eager, all right. "Do you know if he gets drunk a lot?" Given the Macedonian reputation for pouring down cup after cup of neat wine, the questions weren't so surprising. If Cyprus' commander were drunk all the time, the place would be easier for Antigonos' men to attack.

But Menedemos and Sostratos both tossed their heads. Sostratos said, "He didn't seem drunk at all. He came to the place for the same reason we did: to hear Areios the kitharist play and sing."

That drew the Macedonian's interest, too, but not in the way Menedemos would have expected. "Really?" he said. "How was he? I've heard of him, but I've never seen him perform. I saw Stratonikos a few times when I was back in Hellas. He's the best I know—but the tongue on that man! If a viper had it, he wouldn't need to bite you—he'd just stick out that tongue and you'd fall over dead."

"That's the truth!" Sostratos said, and he and the Macedonian spent the next quarter hour chatting—sometimes arguing—about the virtues of various kitharists and swapping stories about Stratonikos. For all his uncouth accent, the officer plainly knew what he was talking about. Menedemos listened in growing bemusement. He would no more have expected the fellow to care about the kithara than he would have thought a Phoenician might set up as a philosopher. *You never can tell,* he thought.

At last, with obvious reluctance, Antigonos' officer tore himself away. Sostratos had succeeded in charming him; he said, "I enjoyed the talk, O best one. Gods give you profit here in Sidon." He went back into the city whistling the tune to one of Areios' Alexandrian love songs, which Sostratos had taught him.

"He wasn't a donkey after all," Menedemos said.

"No, but he brayed like one. Macedonians!" Sostratos answered. "When he got excited there, I was missing about one word in four."

"That doesn't matter," Menedemos said. "What matters is, he liked you, and so he'll give us a good character. Well done, my dear."

"Thanks," Sostratos said. "And tomorrow we'll see what we can find here in Sidon."

"Yes." Normally, one of the things Menedemos would have looked for in a new city was the bored wife of a merchant or an officer. Because of his oath, he wasn't supposed to do that. *Harlots all summer,* he thought, and sighed. Then he shrugged. It wasn't as if Sostratos had asked him to stay away from women altogether. His cousin knew him better than *that.*

WALKING THROUGH THE narrow streets of Sidon, Sostratos kept craning his neck up and up. He didn't particularly want to do it, but he couldn't help himself. When he glanced over at Menedemos, he was relieved to find his cousin doing the same thing. Menedemos gave him a sheepish look. "I know the buildings won't fall down on us, but I can't stop thinking they might," he said.

"Yes, I know. I feel like that, too," Sostratos said. "I wonder why they build so tall. And what happens when there's an earthquake?"

"Things fall down, I suppose." Menedemos spat into the bosom of his tunic to turn aside the evil omen. After another couple of paces, Sostratos imitated him. Logically, he saw no connection between the act of spitting and an earthquake that might come in the next instant or might not come for the next hundred years or more. How the one could keep the other from happening was beyond him.

He spat anyhow. The training in logic and analysis he'd had at the Lykeion in Athens warred with the superstitions he'd picked up at sea. At least as often as not, superstition won. For one thing, he spent his time these days around sailors, not around philosophers. For another, he didn't see how spitting could hurt, and so. . . .

"Why not?" he muttered.

"What's that?" Menedemos asked.

"Nothing," Sostratos said, embarrassed Menedemos had heard him.

The Sidonians took their towering buildings as much for granted as Sostratos took the shorter ones of Rhodes and other Hellenic poleis. They swarmed around the two Rhodians, sometimes grumbling at the slow-moving, gawking foreigners. All the men wore beards; though shaving was popular among Hellenes, especially of the younger generation, it hadn't caught on here. Some of their robes—often boldly striped in deep blue or rusty red—had fancy fringes on the hem; they used one hand to keep those fringes from trailing in the dust. They wore tall cylindrical caps or lengths of cloth—again, often brightly colored—wrapped around their hair.

More women went out in public than would have in a polis full of Hellenes. Some of them were veiled against the gaze of strange men, but many weren't. Quite a few stared in frank curiosity at the Rhodians. Sostratos needed a little while to figure out why. "We're a novelty here," he said. "Hellenes, I mean."

"Well, of course," Menedemos answered. "I haven't seen many Phoenician women till now. They're not bad, are they?"

"No," Sostratos admitted; he'd noticed bright eyes and red lips and white teeth himself. "They put on more paint than our women do—except for hetairai, of course."

"They're more used to being *seen* than our women are," Menedemos said. "They aim to take advantage of it."

"I think you're right." Sostratos dipped his head. Then he paused and sniffed. "Sidon doesn't smell the way I thought it would."

"It smells like a city—smoke and people and animals and shit," Menedemos said. "Maybe it smells a little worse than a lot of places—all those rotting shellfish they use to get their crimson dye. But what did you expect?"

"I don't know." But Sostratos *did* know, and at last, sheepishly, he owned up to it: "I thought it might smell like spices and incenses, because so many of them come through here on their way to Hellas: pepper and cinnamon and myrrh and frankincense and I don't know what all else. But"—he sniffed—"you'd never know it by your nose."

"No, you wouldn't," Menedemos agreed. "Sidon smells like the garbage on a hot day after Sikon did up seafood the night before."

"You're right—it does," Sostratos said. "That's *just* what it smells like, as a matter of fact. Your family has a good cook there. Father would buy him in a heartbeat if Uncle Philodemos ever decided to sell him."

"Not likely!"

"I didn't think it was," Sostratos replied. "I wouldn't even have mentioned it if he weren't going around Rhodes with his face like a thundercloud. Father and I have both noticed it. If Sikon's having trouble with your father—"

"No, no, no." Menedemos tossed his head. "It's not Father. Father wants to keep him and wants to keep him happy, too. Like I told you before, Baukis is the one who thinks Sikon spends too much silver on our opson, and so they fight."

"Yes, I understand that," Sostratos said. "I can see how it would be a problem, but I still think your father ought to come between his wife and his cook so they don't fight any more. Why doesn't he?"

"Why?" Menedemos laughed. "I told you that before, too, my dear. For the same reason nobody comes between Antigonos and Ptolemaios, that's why. They'd squash him between them, and then they'd go right on fighting. He's smart enough to know it, too. He sometimes thinks he can just lay down the law"—by the way Menedemos' mouth twisted, Uncle Philodemos often thought that around him—"but he hasn't tried it there."

"He could use you as his go-between," Sostratos remarked.

He wasn't ready for what happened next. His cousin's face slammed shut, as if it were a door slammed in the face of an unwelcome guest. "No," Menedemos said in a voice like a Thracian winter. "He couldn't do that. He couldn't do that at all."

"Why not?" Sostratos asked. "It would seem to make good logical sense, and—"

Still in that gelid voice, Menedemos broke in: "A lot of things that seem to make good logical sense are amazingly stupid when you try them out in the real world. You never have figured that out, have you? But believe me, this is one of them."

"Well, excuse me for existing," Sostratos said, not only affronted but also confused, for he didn't know how he'd managed to irk his cousin this time.

"I'll think about it, my dear," Menedemos replied. Had he stayed coldly angry, they would have had a real row. This time, though, something of the old sardonic glint returned to his voice and to his eye. Sostratos didn't ask him for any more family details, but he didn't feel like hauling off and kicking him any more, either.

They walked past a temple. With its colonnaded front, at first glance it put Sostratos in mind of a shrine in a Hellenic polis of no particular account. But the terra-cotta figurines decorating the pediment were done in a style different from any he would have seen where Hellenes lived. And the reliefs on the frieze were not only stiff and square and blocky— plainly the product of a sculptural tradition different from his own—but also acting out a mythological scene about which he knew nothing.

Menedemos noticed something else about the temple. Pointing, he asked, "What does all the funny writing say?"

Sostratos tried to decipher it, but then tossed his head. "Give me time and I can probably puzzle it out," he said. "But

I can't just sound it out and read it, the way I could if it were Greek. Sorry." When someone asked him something, he hated not being able to give a precise, detailed answer. That, after all, was one of the things he was best at.

But Menedemos said, "Well, don't worry about it, my dear. I wondered, that's all." As he had in Patara, he added, "If it's not in Greek, it can't be very important, can it?"

What would Himilkon have said had he heard that? Something memorable, Sostratos suspected. The Phoenician trader mocked Hellenes for their ignorance of languages other than their own. Back on Rhodes, Sostratos hadn't taken him seriously. Why should he have, in a polis where Greek, naturally, ruled? But here in Sidon, the purring, coughing, choking rhythms of Aramaic surrounded him. Who spoke Greek here? Antigonos' soldiers and clerks, along with a handful of Phoenicians who dealt with Hellenes. Drifting on this sea of strange words was intimidating, almost frightening.

It will be even worse in the country of the Ioudaioi, Sostratos thought glumly. *Nobody there deals with Hellenes, and, from everything I've heard, Antigonos doesn't bother sending many soldiers into the interior. Do I really want to try this without an interpreter?*

I do, he answered himself, more than a little surprised. *Why did I spend all that time and money with Himilkon, if not to do it myself?* He smiled. The truth was, he remained young enough to crave adventure. He'd been too young to go off to the ends of the earth with Alexander the Great. The men of the older generation, the ones who *had* gone conquering, had to look down their noses at him and his contemporaries, had to reckon them stay-at-homes who'd never measured themselves against the worst the world could do.

I can't conquer Persia or go fight along the Indus River, Sostratos thought. *That's been done. But I can do a little exploring of my own. I can, and I will.*

"When you go to Ioudaia, will you ride a horse or a donkey?" Menedemos asked as a donkey with several amphorai lashed to its back squeezed past the Rhodians.

"A donkey, I think," Sostratos said. "I'm no cavalryman, and never will be. Besides, bandits are less likely to want to steal a donkey than a horse."

"Bandits steal, and that's all you need to say about that," Menedemos answered. "You'd have a better chance to get away on horseback."

"Not unless all the sailors who come with me are on horseback, too," Sostratos said. "Or do you think I'd save my gore and let them perish?"

Menedemos shrugged. "Such things have been known to happen—but let it go, if the idea bothers you. Next question—will you hire your beast, or buy it outright?"

"Both, probably," Sostratos said. "I'll want one to carry things and one to ride. I'm thinking now of buying them, and then selling them again before we sail. With luck, that'll be cheaper than hiring them. If the dealers try to gouge me, that's when I'll think about doing it the other way."

"Of course they'll try to gouge you," Menedemos said. "That's why they're in business."

"Oh, I know. But there's a difference between gouging and *gouging,* if you know what I mean," Sostratos said. "Making a profit is one thing; cheating a foreigner is something else again, and I don't intend to put up with it."

His cousin dipped his head. "You make good sense. The only thing you have to be sure to do is get back several days before we sail, so you don't have to sell in a hurry and take the first offer you get, whatever it happens to be."

"If I can, certainly," Sostratos said. "I don't want to lose money on the deal—or as little as I can, anyhow—but I can't promise what I'll be doing in the country of the Ioudaioi, either."

"Whatever you're doing there, don't get so interested that you forget the season till it's wintertime," Menedemos said. "If you think we'll wait around for you and then risk sailing in bad weather, you're daft."

"You're the daft one, if you think I'd do anything like that,"

Sostratos retorted. Menedemos only laughed, and Sostratos realized his cousin had been teasing him.

Before he could say anything or even begin to plot a revenge, a skinny Phoenician of about his own age spoke to him and Menedemos in bad Greek: "You two, you Hellenes, yes?"

"No, of course not," Menedemos said, straight-faced. "We're Sakai from the plains beyond Persia."

The Phoenician looked confused. Sostratos gave Menedemos a dirty look. "Pay no attention to my cousin," he told the fellow. "Yes, we're Hellenes. What can we do for you?"

"You trader men?" the Phoenician asked. "You want to trade?"

"Yes, we're traders," Sostratos said cautiously. "I don't know if we want to trade with you or not. What have you got, and what do you want?"

"I got cinnamon, masters. You know cinnamon? You want cinnamon?"

Sostratos and Menedemos looked at each other. How likely was this scrawny, obviously poor man to have anything worth buying? A silent answer passed between them: *not very*. Still, Sostratos said, "Show us what you've got."

"I do." The fellow reached inside his robe and took out a folded cloth. "Hold out hands. I show." Sostratos did. The Phoenician poured some dried plants into his palm, saying, "Smell. Quality number one, yes?"

Sure enough, the sharp, tangy odor of cinnamon tickled Sostratos' nose. But he shifted from Greek to Aramaic to say, "You dog! You son of a dog! You thief! You sell trash, and say 'quality number one'? You liar!" Himilkon had taught him plenty of scornful expressions. "These are weeds with powdered cinnamon for smell. This is what they are worth." He threw them down and ground them under his foot.

He hadn't really expected to embarrass the Phoenician, and he didn't. The young man only grinned, not a bit abashed. "Ah, my master, you do know something of this business," he said in his own language. "We could work together, make much money off stupid Ionians."

"Go away," Sostratos said in Aramaic. That didn't convey much of what he wanted to get across, so he switched to Greek: "Go howl. To the crows with you."

"What was that all about?" Menedemos asked once the Phoenician, still unabashed, had gone his way. "I gather he was trying to trick us, but you were speaking his language, so I don't know how."

"Didn't you see what he gave me? He tried to pass off some worthless leaves and stems as cinnamon. He might have done it, too, if I didn't know what a quill of cinnamon was supposed to look like. And then, when I showed I did, he tried to get us to go into business with him and gull other Hellenes."

Menedemos laughed. "You almost have to admire such a thorough thief."

"Maybe you do," Sostratos said. "I don't. I just wish he'd jump off a cliff. He'll end up cheating some poor, trusting soul out of a lot of silver."

"As long as it's not me," Menedemos said.

Sostratos started to dip his head, then checked himself. "No," he said. "That's not right. You shouldn't want him to cheat anybody."

"Why not?" his cousin asked. "If someone else is dumb enough to let that Phoenician take advantage of him, why should I worry? It's the fool's lookout, not mine."

"Cheats shouldn't be allowed to do business," Sostratos said. "As a matter of fact, they *aren't* allowed to do business. Every polis has laws against people who sell one thing and say it's another, the same as every polis has laws against people who use false weights and measures."

"That still doesn't mean you aren't supposed to keep your eyes open," Menedemos replied. "If somebody you run into on the street tells you he's got all the treasure Alexander took and he'll sell it to you for two minai, don't you deserve to lose your money if you're stupid and greedy enough to believe him?"

"Of course you do," Sostratos answered. "You deserve to be a laughingstock, too. But that doesn't mean the other fellow shouldn't be punished for cheating you."

"Spoilsport. I admire a clever thief."

"How much would you admire one who was clever enough to cheat *you*?"

Menedemos didn't answer, not in words. But, by the way he strutted a little more than he had been doing, he clearly suggested such a thief was yet to be born. Sostratos also kept his mouth shut. Doubting his cousin too loudly would only start a fight, and he didn't want that.

When he and Menedemos came to the main market square in Sidon, they both stopped at the edge and stared before plunging in. Everything seemed much more tightly crowded than in an agora in a Hellenic polis. Stalls and tents and stands were everywhere, with only narrow lanes through them for customers—and for hawkers who walked about selling things like dates and cheap jewelry from trays they either carried or secured to their waists with harnesses of leather or rope.

When Sostratos did step into the maelstrom, he felt overwhelmed. Everywhere, people haggled and argued in guttural Aramaic. They gesticulated frantically, to bolster whatever points they were making.

He snapped his fingers. "*Heureka!*" he exclaimed.

"That's nice," Menedemos said. "What have you found?"

"Why this place isn't like one of our agorai."

"And the answer is?" his cousin asked.

"They're just talking business here," Sostratos said. "Business and nothing else. How much this costs, or how much of that they can buy for so many sigloi—'shekels,' they say in Aramaic. And that's all."

Menedemos yawned. "That's boring, is what it is. Business is all very well—don't get me wrong—but there are other things in life, too."

"I should hope so," Sostratos said. In a polis full of Hellenes, the agora wasn't only the place where people bought and sold goods. It was also the beating heart of a city's life. Men gathered there to talk politics, to gossip, to show off new clothes, to meet friends, and to do all the other things that made life worthwhile. Where did the Phoenicians do those things? *Did* the Phoenicians do those things? If they did, the market square gave no sign of it.

Looking around, Menedemos said, "It may not be a polis, but there's sure a lot for sale, isn't there?"

"Oh, yes, without a doubt. Nobody ever said the Phoenicians weren't formidable merchants. That's why we're here, after all," Sostratos said. "But the place feels . . . empty, if you're a Hellene."

"I think part of it's that everybody's speaking a foreign language," Menedemos said. "I noticed that in a couple of the Italian towns we visited, and Aramaic sounds a lot less like Greek than Oscan does."

"That's part of it," Sostratos admitted, "but only part. The Italians knew what an agora was for."

"Well, yes," his cousin said. "Even so, though, with us likely being here all summer long, I think I'm going to have to rent a room in the town. I don't see how I can do my business off the *Aphrodite*."

"I won't argue with you, my dear," Sostratos said. "Do what you have to do. Me, I'm going to look for a donkey tomorrow." He eyed Menedemos in a thoughtful way. "One I can ride, that is."

"Ha," Menedemos said. "Ha, ha. Ha, ha, ha. If you were half as funny as you think you are, you'd be twice as funny as you really are." Sostratos had to think that over before deciding his cousin had scored a point.

AS MENEDEMOS HAGGLED with an innkeeper, he wished he'd gone with Sostratos to learn a little Aramaic from Himilkon. The innkeeper spoke a rudimentary sort of Greek: he knew numbers and yes and no and a startling collection of obscenities. Even so, Menedemos was sure the fellow missed all the fine points of his argument.

"No," the Phoenician said now. "Too low. Pay more or—" He pointed toward the doorway.

The wretch had no style, no subtlety. Menedemos lost patience. "Hail," he said, and walked away.

He was almost to the doorway when the Phoenician said, "Wait."

"Why?" Menedemos asked. The innkeeper looked blank. Maybe nobody'd ever asked him such a philosophical question before. Menedemos tried again: "Why should I wait? For what? How much less do you say I'd have to pay?"

That finally got through to the fellow. He named a price halfway between what Menedemos had offered and what he himself had insisted on up till now. Menedemos tossed his head. The gesture meant nothing to the Phoenician. Remembering he was in a country full of barbarians, Menedemos shook his head, no matter how unnatural the motion seemed to him. For good measure, he started toward the door again.

"Thief," the innkeeper said. Menedemos found it interesting that he should know the word when his Greek was so limited. The Rhodian bowed, as if at a compliment. The Phoenician said something in his own language. By his tone, Menedemos doubted it was a compliment. He bowed again. The Phoenician added another string of harsh gutturals, but then cut the difference between his price and Menedemos' in half again.

"There, you see? You can be reasonable," Menedemos said. Odds were, the words went straight past the innkeeper. Menedemos raised his own price very slightly. The Phoenician made a wounded noise and clutched at his chest with both hands, as if Menedemos had shot him with an arrow. When that bit of theater failed to impress Menedemos, the barbarian nodded brusquely and stuck out his hand. "Deal," he said.

Clasping it, Menedemos wondered if he'd made a good bargain or a bad one. In Rhodes, he would have been pleased to rent a room for this price. But were prices here generally higher or lower than those back home? He didn't know. Figuring it out wasn't easy, either. Working back and forth between drakhmai and sigloi made his head ache; the local silver coins were worth just over two Rhodian drakhmai each. Sostratos seemed to have little trouble shifting from one to the other, but Sostratos had been born with a counting board between the ears. Menedemos' mathematical accomplishments were much more modest.

The room itself was about what he'd expected. It was small and close, furnished with a bed, a couple of rickety stools, and a chamber pot. Who'd been in the bed before? What bugs waited there for the next arrival? Just thinking of the question was enough to make Menedemos start scratching.

He knew he dared not leave anything in the room unguarded. He sighed. That would mean paying a sailor something extra to keep an eye on things while he went out to sell. The expense would make Sostratos grumble. Any expense made Sostratos grumble. But the expense of missing trade goods would be worse.

When Menedemos walked back from the room to the front of the inn, he found the Phoenician arguing with his wife. Menedemos had to fight to hold back a laugh. Here was one woman who wouldn't tempt him into adultery. She was fat and gray-haired, with a sickle of a nose dominating her face. She had a harsh voice that did nothing to soften the rough Aramaic language.

But when she saw Menedemos, she broke off berating her husband and, absurdly, batted her eyelashes at the Rhodian. "Good days," she said in Greek even worse than the innkeeper's. "How you is?"

"Well, thank you," Menedemos answered. Politely, he added, "And you?"

"Good." She smiled at him and, turning her face away from her husband, ran her tongue over her lips. Then she batted her eyelashes again.

Oh, by the gods! Menedemos thought in alarm. *Sostratos doesn't want me seducing anybody, and I don't want this harridan seducing me.* He wondered if he ought to find another inn. But he didn't feel like wasting his time in another dicker over another unappealing little chamber. *The less I'm here, the less I'll have to deal with her,* he told himself.

She said something in Aramaic to her husband. Whatever it

was, it started the argument once more. Menedemos didn't want to get stuck in the middle. He was about to retreat to his room when a man came in carrying a chunk of pork. Menedemos remembered Sostratos saying Ioudaioi didn't eat swine's flesh. That plainly didn't hold for Phoenicians. The newcomer gave the innkeeper a bronze coin. The innkeeper took the meat and threw it into hot oil. The oil bubbled and sizzled. A savory aroma filled the chamber.

But it wasn't so savory as it might have been. The meat couldn't have smelled better. The oil could have. It wasn't very fresh, and hadn't been very good to start with. Menedemos wrinkled his nose. So did the fellow who'd brought in the pork. He said something in Aramaic. Menedemos didn't know how the innkeeper replied, but he sounded defensive. The way he spread his hands also made that likely.

Menedemos had an inspiration. As the innkeeper turned the meat with a pair of wooden tongs, the Rhodian asked him, "Do you want to buy some better olive oil?"

"What you say?" The fellow's Greek was horrible.

"Olive oil. *Good* olive oil. You buy?" Menedemos spoke as if to an idiot child—not that an idiot child would have been interested in buying olive oil, of course.

He wasn't sure the innkeeper understood the Greek for *olive oil,* and wished Sostratos were here to translate for him. But he had to do the best he could. He pointed into the pan and held his nose. The man whose pork was frying did the same thing.

"Olive oil? You? How much?" the innkeeper asked.

"Yes. Olive oil. Me." Menedemos started to dip his head, then remembered to nod instead. He named his price.

The Sidonian stared at him. He said something in Aramaic—Menedemos guessed it was the price, translated into his own language. The innkeeper's wife and the customer both exclaimed in what certainly sounded like horror. The innkeeper then doled out one word of Greek: "No."

That wasn't an invitation to haggle. It was rejection, plain and simple. As the innkeeper took the fried pork out of the pan, wiped oil off it with a bit of rag, and handed it to the man who'd brought it in, Menedemos asked him, "Well, what do you usually pay for olive oil?"

He had to simplify that before the innkeeper understood him. When the fellow told him, he let out a wistful sigh. The innkeeper bought oil as cheap as he could get. He wouldn't have been interested in Damonax's fine oil at any price that let Menedemos break even, let alone turn a profit. *So much for inspiration,* he thought.

The man with the fried pork walked out gnawing on it. The innkeeper and his wife didn't start quarreling again, but the woman did send Menedemos a wink and a leer. He retreated faster than the Persian king had after each battle against Alexander. The Phoenician woman let out a sigh doubtless intended to be alluring. It only made Menedemos retreat faster still.

When he told Sostratos about it on the *Aphrodite,* his cousin said, "Yes, now give me another story. You're trying to back out of your oath, is what you're doing."

"By the gods, I am not!" Menedemos said with a shudder. "Come to the inn with me and you'll see for yourself. I tell you, I wouldn't have this woman on a bet, and to the crows with me if I can understand why the barbarian married her."

"Maybe she brought a large dowry," Sostratos suggested.

"Maybe," Menedemos said. "That makes more sense than anything else I can think of, but even so. . . ." He shuddered again, then went halfway toward changing the subject: "I tried to sell the innkeeper some of your brother-in-law's olive oil."

"Did you? Well, thanks," Sostratos said. "Let me guess—no luck?"

"I'm afraid not, my dear. He was using some dreadful, nasty stuff to fry meat, and I hoped he might want something better, but no. He used the nasty oil because it was cheap, and he turned green when I told him what I wanted for ours—as green as if he were seasick, or as if he'd been tasting his own oil. I did try, though."

Sostratos sighed. "I already said thank you. I'll say it again. Gods only know how we're going to unload that stuff. It *is* good oil, but even so. . . ." He clicked his tongue between his teeth. "I wouldn't mind breaking an amphora of it over Damonax's head."

"Have you got your donkey yet?" Menedemos asked. "Besides your brother-in-law, I mean?"

"Heh," Sostratos said, and then tossed his head. "No, not yet. Prices for beasts of burden are higher than I want to pay, because Antigonos' soldiers have bought up—or maybe stolen, for all I know—so many of them. But there's one—a mule, actually, not a donkey—I have my eye on, if I can get the man who owns it down to something like a reasonable price."

"I wished I had you along today, so you could have told the innkeeper just how vile his olive oil was," Menedemos said. "Maybe I should have learned some Aramaic after all."

"I could say, 'I told you so,'" Sostratos remarked. But then he surprised Menedemos by continuing, "But I won't. I've been speaking it all day, and my head feels pounded flat."

"I believe you." Menedemos didn't really want to speak Aramaic. He wanted all the barbarians he dealt with to speak Greek. Doing things the other way round was, in his mind, a poor second best.

A big round ship made her slow, stately way into Sidon's harbor. Her entrance had to be slow and stately. The wind had brought her south past the promontory on which the Phoenician town sat, but that same wind blew dead against her when she tried to come about and sail in. That failing, the crew worked their sweeps and rowed the round ship into port. Her performance under oars was to the *Aphrodite*'s as a spavined ass' was to that of a Persian stallion.

When at last she tied up at a quay perhaps a plethron from the *Aphrodite,* she started disgorging soldiers. Some of them wore their corselets and crested bronze helms; more carried them. In this warm weather, Menedemos reckoned that sensible. He wouldn't have wanted to wear any more than he had to, either.

Sostratos' lips were moving. After the last trooper came off the merchantman, he said, "I counted two hundred and eight men there. The next interesting question is whether they'll stay here or go on to someplace else—someplace farther south, say."

"If they stay here, Antigonos or his general probably intends to use them against Cyprus," Menedemos said, and his cousin dipped his head in agreement. Menedemos went on, "If they move south, where will they be going? Against Egypt, do you think?"

"That seems likely," Sostratos said. "The next question is, how long will Ptolemaios or his brother Menelaos need to hear those men are here and they've done whatever they end up doing?"

"Only a few days' sail from here to Cyprus," Menedemos observed. "Not much more to Alexandria—maybe no more, because you're likely to have the wind with you all the way down to the Nile. If someone doesn't leave with the news before the sun sets tomorrow, I'd be astonished."

"So would I." Sostratos dipped his head once more. He went on, "I can hardly wait to start down toward the land of the Ioudaioi. I wonder how many Hellenes have ever gone there. Not many, unless I miss my guess."

"You could write a book," Menedemos said.

He didn't like the glow that lit his cousin's eyes. "You're right," Sostratos murmured. "I could, couldn't I? Every Hellene who ever set foot in India seems to have written down what he saw and heard there. Maybe I could do the same for this place."

"That's fine," Menedemos told him. "Or it's fine as long as you remember you're there first to buy balsam and whatever else you find. If you take care of that, whatever else you do is your own affair. If you don't, though, you'll have to explain to me and to your father—and to mine—why you didn't."

"Yes, my dear. I do understand that, I really do," Sostratos said patiently.

Menedemos wondered whether to believe him.

HAVING BOUGHT HIS mule, Sostratos wished he could leave Sidon without an escort. The more he thought about having several sailors with him, the less he liked it. But he'd made the bargain with Menedemos, and he had a merchant's horror of broken bargains. Then, after the first two men he asked to come with him to the land of the Ioudaioi turned him down flat, he began to wonder if he could keep this one.

What will I do if they all say no? he wondered nervously. *I'll have to hire guards here in Sidon, I suppose.* His mouth twisted. He didn't like that. Trusting himself to the company of strangers seemed more dangerous than going alone. He wondered whether his cousin would agree. He doubted it.

He walked up to Aristeidas. The sharp-eyed young sailor smiled and said, "Hail."

"Hail," Sostratos answered. "How would you like to come to Engedi with me, to serve as a bodyguard along the way?"

"That depends," Aristeidas answered. "How much extra will you pay me if I do?"

"A drakhma a day, on top of the drakhma and a half you already make," Sostratos said. The other two sailors had asked the same question. The extra money hadn't been enough to interest them. They were happier staying in Sidon and spending their silver on wine and women.

But Aristeidas, after a momentary hesitation, dipped his head. "I'll come," he said, and smiled again. Like most though not all men of his generation, he shaved his face, which made him look even younger than he was. He'd probably made a striking youth, though that might have gone unnoticed in someone growing up without wealth.

In any case, a youth's beauty did less for Sostratos than did a woman's. "Oh, very good!" he said. "I'll be glad to have you along." He meant it, and explained why: "It's not just that you've got good eyes. You've got good sense, too."

"Thank you very much," Aristeidas said. "I don't exactly know that that's true, but I like to hear you say it."

The next sailor Sostratos asked was Moskhion. He wasn't particularly young or particularly smart, but he had been smart enough to see that while pulling an oar wasn't an easy life, it beat the whey out of his former career of sponge diving. And he was big enough and strong enough to be worth more than a little in case of a brawl.

"Sure, I'll come," he said when Sostratos put the question to him. "Why not? With a little luck, all we'll have to do is go there and come back, right?"

"Yes, with a little luck," Sostratos answered. "But what will you do if our luck isn't so good? What will you do if we have to fight?"

"I expect I'll fight. What else?" Moskhion didn't sound worried.

Sostratos supposed that if you'd got used to jumping out of a boat with a trident in one hand and with a rock held against your chest in the other to make you sink faster, nothing that might happen on dry land was likely to faze you. He said, "I'm glad to have you along. You're a host all by yourself."

"Maybe. Maybe not, too," Moskhion said. "But people think so when they look at me. Every once in a while, that gets me into fights. More often, though, it keeps me out of them."

"That's what I want it to do here," Sostratos said. "I'm not looking to get into fights with the barbarians."

"Good," Moskhion said. "Some people fight for sport, but I'm not one of them."

"I wouldn't want you along if you were," Sostratos said. The next three men he asked all told him no. Annoyed at them, annoyed at the need to bring guards along, he went to Menedemos and asked if two would do.

His cousin annoyed him all over again by tossing his head.

"Get somebody else," Menedemos said. "The idea is to have enough men along to keep from giving bandits nasty ideas."

"I might take the whole crew and not manage that," Sostratos protested.

"I'm not asking you to take the whole crew," Menedemos said. "I am asking you to take one more man."

Since he was the captain, Sostratos had to pay attention to him. Sostratos liked getting orders no more than any other free Hellene. Indeed, he liked it less than a lot of other Hellenes might have. Here, though, he had to obey.

As he came down from the *Aphrodite*'s poop deck with a storm cloud on his face, one of the sailors said, "Excuse me, but if you're looking for somebody to go with you when you head inland, I'll do it."

"You, Teleutas?" Sostratos said in surprise—and not necessarily pleased surprise, either. "Why do you want to come?"

"Well, I'd be lying if I said I couldn't use the extra silver. A drakhma a day over and above the usual? That's not bad. Not half bad, matter of fact. And it ought to be pretty easy money, so long as everything goes well."

"Yes, but what if it doesn't?" Sostratos asked.

Teleutas took his time thinking about that. He was perhaps ten years older than Sostratos—in his mid- to late thirties. Rowing under the fierce summer sun had made his lean face dark and leathery, with lines like gullies, so that at first glance he seemed older than he was. His eyes, though, retained what was either a childlike innocence or a chameleonlike gift for hiding his true nature. He always did enough to get by, but only just, and had a habit of grumbling even about that. More than two years after first bringing him aboard the *Aphrodite,* Sostratos kept wondering if he'd made a mistake.

At last the sailor said, "Whatever happens, I expect I can handle it."

"Can you?" Sostratos meant the question. Once, in Italy, Teleutas might have left him and Menedemos in the lurch. He'd quickly returned to the agora in that town in Great Hellas with other sailors from the merchant galley. Maybe he'd only gone to get help. Maybe.

"I expect I can," he said now. Was his grin as open and friendly as it seemed, or an actor's mask to hide cowardice? Try as Sostratos would, he couldn't tell. Teleutas went on in reasonable, rational tones, as if arguing a point at the Lykeion: "I'm not likely to light out, am I, not in a countryside full of barbarians? You may like making those funny noises in the back of your throat, but I don't."

Isn't that interesting? Sostratos thought. *He knows I don't trust him, and he's giving me a reason why I should this time.* It was a good reason, too. Sure enough, why would Teleutas want to do anything but what he was paid to do when he spoke no Aramaic? He couldn't easily disappear among strangers here, as he could in a polis full of Hellenes. Sostratos plucked at his beard, considering.

Teleutas added, "I know a thing or two that might come in handy, too, the sort of thing you probably wouldn't."

"Oh? Such as?" Sostratos asked.

"This and that," the sailor answered. "You never can tell when it'd be useful, but it just might." Plainly, he didn't want to give details. Sostratos wondered what that meant. Had he been a bandit at one time or another? He spoke like a Rhodian, and few Rhodians needed to turn to brigandage to survive. But if, say, he'd been a mercenary and seen things go sour, who could guess what he'd had to do to keep eating? He didn't have a soldier's scars, but maybe he'd been lucky.

With sudden decision, Sostratos dipped his head. "All right, Teleutas. I'll take you on. We'll see what comes of it."

Teleutas gave him that charming grin again. "I thank you kindly. You won't be sorry."

"I'd better not be," Sostratos said. "If you make me sorry, I'll make you sorry, too. I promise you that. Do you believe me?"

"Yes," Teleutas said. But what would he say? More than a few people took Sostratos lightly because he used his wits more readily than his fists. He'd made some of them regret it.

He hoped he wouldn't have to worry about that with Teleutas.

When he told Menedemos he'd chosen his third escort, his cousin looked pained. "By the dog of Egypt, I wish you'd picked almost anybody else," Menedemos said. "Can you trust Teleutas when your back is turned? I wouldn't want to— I'll tell you that."

"I wouldn't want to in Hellas. I'd be lying if I said anything else," Sostratos replied. "But here? Yes, I think I can. He's not going to make friends with bandits when he can't speak their language, and he doesn't know any Aramaic. He should be safe enough."

"I hope so." Menedemos didn't sound convinced.

Since Sostratos wasn't altogether convinced, either, he couldn't get angry at his cousin. He said, "I think everything will be all right."

"I hope so," Menedemos said again, even more dubiously than before.

"What harm can he do me?" Sostratos asked. "I asked myself again and again, and I couldn't see any."

"I can't see any, either," Menedemos admitted. "But that doesn't mean there isn't any."

"We're on dry land now, my dear," Sostratos said with a smile. "We don't have to pay any attention to all our seagoing superstitions."

Menedemos had the grace to laugh. He, at least, knew he was superstitious. Many sailors would have indignantly denied it, at the same time spitting into the bosom of their chitons to take away the bad luck in the accusation. "All right. All right," Menedemos said. "I've got no real reason not to trust Teleutas. But I don't. Remember, he was about the last one we took on a couple of years ago, and he's still the first one I'd leave behind if I ever had to."

"Maybe you'll have a different idea when we come back from the land of the Ioudaioi," Sostratos said.

"Maybe. I hope I will," Menedemos answered. "But maybe I *won't,* too. That's what worries me."

Sostratos judged it a good time to change the subject, at

least a little: "When I leave Sidon, may I borrow your bow and arrows?"

"Oh, yes, of course." Menedemos dipped his head. "You'll get better use out of them there than I will here. I'm sure of that. Just try to bring the bow back in one piece, if you'd be so kind."

"What do you think I'd do to it?" Sostratos asked with as much indignation as he could muster.

"I don't know. I don't want to find out. All I know is, things sometimes go wrong when you handle weapons."

"That's not fair!" Sostratos said. "Haven't I shot pirates? Haven't you compared me to Alexandros in the *Iliad* when I did?"

His cousin dipped his head once more. "You have. I have. All true, every word of it. But I've seen you at the gymnasion in Rhodes, too, and there are times when you've looked like you hadn't the faintest idea what to do with a bow."

That hurt. It hurt all the more because Sostratos knew it was true. He would never make a really fine archer. He would never be anything that required large amounts of grace and strength. Try as he would, he didn't have them in him, not in large supply. *I've got my wits,* he told himself. Sometimes that brought him considerable consolation, for it let him look down his nose at people who were merely strong and athletic. Other times, such as today . . . He tried not to think about it.

Menedemos set a hand on his shoulder, as if to say he shouldn't make too much of it. "If the gods are kind, you won't have to worry about any of this. The only time you'll shoot the bow is for the pot."

"Yes, if the gods are kind," Sostratos agreed. But Teleutas wouldn't have any worries or any work to do if the gods were kind, either. Sostratos' gaze slid to Menedemos. In a way, his cousin reminded him of Teleutas (though Menedemos would have been anything but pleased to hear him say so). They both wanted things to be easy and convenient. There the resemblance ended. If things weren't easy or convenient, Teleutas, a man of no particular drive, would either withdraw or get through the difficulty or the inconvenience as best he could.

Menedemos was much more likely to try to reshape whatever was going on around him so that it suited him better—and had both the energy and the charm to get what he wanted most of the time.

With a laugh, Menedemos went on, "Of course, if we could be sure the gods would be kind, you wouldn't need to take guards along—or the bow, either, for that matter."

"You'd like that, wouldn't you?" Sostratos said. "Then you could forget about your half of our bargain."

His cousin wagged a finger at him. "That knife has two edges, and you know it. You don't want to travel with the sailors because they'll keep you from poking your nose into everything under the sun."

"It's not your nose you want to poke into everything under the sun," Sostratos retorted.

Menedemos laughed again, this time with a booming guffaw that made several sailors turn their heads to try to find out what was so funny. He waved them back to whatever they were doing, then said, "Ah, my dear, anyone would think you knew me."

"I'd better, after all these years of living side by side in Rhodes and even closer than that when we go to sea," Sostratos answered. "But how much does it matter? Not so much, I'd say, as whether you know yourself."

"That's one of your philosophers," Menedemos said accusingly. "I know you, too—you always try to sneak them in. You think you have to improve me, whether I feel like being improved or not."

Since that held no small amount of truth, Sostratos didn't waste time denying it. He said, "It's from one of the Seven Sages, sure enough. But it's also the inscription at Delphi. If it's good enough for the oracle there, shouldn't it be good enough for you, too?"

"Hmm. Maybe," Menedemos said. "I thought it would be Platon or Sokrates—they're the ones you usually trot out."

"Why shouldn't I?" Sostratos knew his cousin wanted to get his goat, and also knew Menedemos was succeeding. He couldn't keep the irritation from his voice as he continued, "Or do you think Sokrates was wrong when he said the unexamined life wasn't worth living?"

"Here we go again. I don't know about that," Menedemos said. Sostratos showed his teeth in a triumphant grin; even his cousin wouldn't have the nerve to quarrel there. But Menedemos did: "I do know that if you spend too much time examining your life, you won't have time to live it."

·Sostratos opened his mouth, then closed it again. He hoped he would never hear a better argument against philosophy. He made the best comeback he could, answering, "One of the Seven Sages also said, 'Nothing too much.'"

"I think we've had too much of this argument for now," Menedemos said. Sostratos dipped his head, glad to escape so easily. But then Menedemos added, "I also think we've got too much of your brother-in-law's olive oil."

"So do I," Sostratos said, "but sometimes you have to make allowances for family." He looked Menedemos in the eye. "Think of all the allowances I've made for you."

"I haven't the faintest idea what you're talking about," Menedemos said. "Here I thought I was the one making allowances for you. Didn't I let you wander over the Italian countryside when we were docked at Pompaia a couple of years ago, even though I was afraid somebody would knock you over the head? Didn't I let you lug that gryphon's skull all around the Aegean last summer, even though I was sure we wouldn't make back what we paid for it?"

"I don't know why you were so sure of that, when Damonax offered me enough silver to let me turn a big profit," Sostratos said tartly.

"You turned him down, which proves you're a fool," Menedemos said. "And he offered it, which proves *he's* a fool. If he's not a fool, why have we got so cursed much olive oil aboard the *Aphrodite*? See what I mean about making allowances for family?"

"What I see is—" Sostratos stopped and spluttered laughter. He wagged a finger at Menedemos. "Here, you're not going to like this, but I'll tell you what I see. I see a man who knows how to use logic but says he's got no use for philosophy. I see a man who'd like to love wisdom but—"

"Would sooner love pretty girls and good wine instead," Menedemos broke in.

Sostratos tossed his head. "Oh, no, my dear. You're not going to get away with a joke this time. You're going to let me finish. What I see is a man who'd like to love wisdom but can't bring himself to take anything seriously. And that, if you ask me, is a shame and a waste of a good mind."

Out in the harbor, a tern dove into the water. A moment later, it came out with a writhing fish in its beak. It swallowed the fish as it flew away. Menedemos pointed to it. "That bird has no philosophy, but it still gets its opson."

"It does not," Sostratos said.

"What? Are you blind? Did it catch a fish or didn't it?"

"Certainly it did. But what does a tern live on? Fish, of course—fish is its sitos, its staple. If you gave it a barley roll, that would be its opson, its relish, because it has to have fish but it could do without the roll."

Menedemos scratched his head in thought. Then he scratched again, this time in earnest. "I hope that miserable inn hasn't left me lousy. All right, you're right—fish, for a tern, is sitos, not opson. I suppose you'll tell me that's philosophy, too."

"I won't tell you anything of the sort. I'll just ask a question." If there was anything Sostratos enjoyed, it was the chance to play Sokrates. "If caring enough to use the right word isn't part of loving wisdom, what is it?"

"I don't suppose you'd put up with anything so ordinary as just trying to say the right thing, would you?"

"Is that all Homer was doing—just trying to say the right thing, I mean?"

"Homer always said the right thing." Menedemos sounded very sure. "And he never heard of philosophy."

Sostratos wanted to argue that, but soon decided he couldn't. "He doesn't use the word for wisdom at all, does he?"

"*Sophie?* Let me think." After a moment, Menedemos said, "No, that's not true. He uses it once, in the fifteenth—I think—book of the *Iliad*: 'And he who, thanks to the inspiration of Athene, knows well every skill.' But he's not talking about a philosopher—he's talking about a carpenter. And *sophie* in the *Iliad* doesn't mean abstract knowledge, the way it does with us. It means knowing how to do the things a carpenter does."

"You can still use it that way," Sostratos said, "but not, I admit, if you're going to talk about philosophy."

"No," Menedemos said. "Homer's a very down-to-earth poet. Even his gods on Olympos are down-to-earth, if you know what I mean."

"They certainly are—they behave like a bunch of bad-tempered Macedonians," Sostratos said, which made Menedemos laugh. More seriously, Sostratos went on, "They're so down-to-earth, in fact, that some people who love wisdom have trouble believing in them."

His cousin's expression curdled like sour milk. Sostratos hadn't included himself in that group, but he hadn't excluded himself from it. He suspected he knew why Homer said nothing about philosophy. The poet had lived a long time ago, before any Hellenes began seriously asking questions of the world around them and following logic wherever it took them. *We were as ignorant as any barbarians,* he thought, bemused. *And some of us still are, and don't want to be any different.*

Menedemos said, "Some people say they love wisdom when all they really love is making their neighbors uncomfortable." He gave Sostratos a pointed stare.

Sostratos returned it. "Some people think that just because their great-grandfathers believed something was so, it has to be so. If we all had that attitude, we wouldn't use iron—or even bronze, come to that—and we would have thrown back the alpha-beta like a worthless fish that nobody eats."

They glared at each other. Then Menedemos asked, "What do you suppose would happen if you made that argument to the Phoenicians or the Ioudaioi?"

"Nothing pretty. Nothing pleasant. But they're barbarians, and they don't know any better. We're Hellenes. What's the point of being a Hellene, if not to use the wits the gods—whatever they may be—gave us?"

"You think you have an answer for everything, don't you?"

"No. Not at all." Sostratos tossed his head. "I think we should use our wits, though, to try to find answers, and not rely on whatever our forefathers said. They might have been wrong. A lot of the time, they *were* wrong. If I'd managed to get that gryphon's skull to Athens, for instance, it would have shown people how wrong they were about the beasts."

"Yes, but how important are gryphons?" Menedemos asked.

"Gryphons *aren't* important, not by themselves," Sostratos said. "But the men of the Lykeion and the Academy would have looked at the evidence and changed their views to fit. They wouldn't have said, 'No, we won't believe what the skull tells us, because our great-grandfathers told us something else.' And that's important, don't you see?" He sounded as if he was pleading, and he sadly wondered whether Menedemos understood at all.

MENEDEMOS CLAPPED SOSTRATOS ON THE BACK, then cupped his hands and interlaced his fingers to give his cousin a leg-up. With his help, Sostratos swung up onto the back of the mule he'd bought. Sostratos looked around with a grin, saying, "I'm not used to being so far off the ground."

"Well, O best one, you'd better get used to it," Menedemos answered. "You're going to be on that mule for a while."

"That's right," Aristeidas agreed with a grin. "You'll come

back to Sidon all bowlegged." He stumped around with his legs splayed wide apart.

"Go howl!" Sostratos said, laughing.

"No, Aristeidas is right, or he should be. I like that," Menedemos said, laughing, too. "Your legs'll look like an omega, thus." He wrote the letter—W—in the dust of the street with his right big toe, then he also imitated a bowlegged man. "And when you get back, you won't be any taller than I am."

"In your dreams," Sostratos retorted. That held more truth than he might have guessed, for Menedemos, especially when they were both growing up, *had* dreamt of matching his gangling cousin's height. Sostratos went on, "You'd burst like a squashed melon if Prokroustes tried stretching you on his rack till you were my size."

"Ha!" Menedemos said. "Prokroustes'd be cutting you down to size if he ever got you to sleep in his bed, and he'd start with your tongue."

Sostratos stuck out the organ in question. Menedemos made as if to grab for his belt knife. Sostratos looked from him to Aristeidas, Teleutas, and Moskhion. The former sponge diver carried a pike as tall as he was, while the other two men wore swords on their hips. "Some bodyguards," Sostratos said. He had a sword himself; a leather bowcase held Menedemos' bow, several spare bowstrings, and twenty arrows. All four men wore cheap bell-shaped bronze helmets that would keep a club from knocking their brains out. The helms offered no protection for the face, but were far lighter and cooler than the all-enclosing ones hoplites used.

"I think we're ready," Sostratos said. As if to agree with him, Aristeidas picked up the lead rope of the donkey that carried their trade goods and money. The donkey brayed in protest. A moment later, the mule joined in, its voice louder and deeper.

"Wing-foot Hermes keep you safe," Menedemos said. He set his hand on Sostratos' leg for a moment. His cousin covered it with his own hand. Then Sostratos flicked the reins and squeezed the mule's barrel with his knees and calves. The beast brayed again. For a moment, Menedemos thought it would do no more. But, ears twitching resentfully, it began to walk. Aristeidas had to yank on the ass' lead line to get it to follow. The four Hellenes and two animals left the harbor and disappeared into Sidon. Before long, they'd be off in the wilds of the land of the Ioudaioi.

"Keep an eye on him, all of you," Menedemos muttered. He wondered if he was talking to the sailors from the *Aphrodite* who accompanied Sostratos or to the gods high above. By then, the sailors were too far away to hear him. He hoped the gods weren't.

Sighing, he walked back up the pier to the *Aphrodite*. Diokles said, "Hope everything goes good for him, skipper."

"Yes. So do I," Menedemos replied.

"He's a clever fellow, your cousin," the oarmaster said, doing his best to sound reassuring. "He'll be fine."

Menedemos remained unreassured. "Oh, yes, Sostratos is very clever," he said. "But has he got any common sense? There are times when I don't think he's got as much as the gods gave a gecko."

"He's got more than you think," Diokles said. "The two of you, you're kin, so of course you can't see each other straight."

"Maybe you're right. I hope you're right," Menedemos said. "Still and all, though, I wish he weren't wandering around among the barbarians. When he goes and does something strange, Hellenes know how to make allowances: almost everybody's seen someone who's more cut out to be a philosopher than to live in the real world. But what do these silly Ioudaioi know about philosophy? Not a thing. Not a single, solitary thing. How could they? They're just barbarians. They'll think he's crazy, is what they'll think."

"Your cousin doesn't do that stuff all the time, or even very often," Diokles said.

"I hope you're right," Menedemos repeated. If the keleustes was right, Sostratos would, or at least might, come back with balsam and with profit. If, on the other hand, he was wrong . . . Menedemos didn't want to dwell on that but couldn't help it. He said, "If Sostratos has all this common sense, why did he take Teleutas for one of his guards? Why not anybody else? I wish I hadn't let him."

Diokles put the best face on it he could: "Nobody's ever been able to prove anything bad about Teleutas. Everything he does, there's always a good reason for it, or there always could be one, anyway. Otherwise, you wouldn't have let him ship with us last year, let alone this year."

"It could be," Menedemos admitted. "Yes, it could be. But when he's one of forty-odd men aboard the *Aphrodite,* that's one thing. When he's one of four Hellenes in the middle of nowhere, that's something else—or it's liable to be something else, anyhow."

Diokles didn't argue with him. He wished the keleustes would have. He wanted to think he was wrong, not that he was right. What Diokles did say was, "While your cousin's traveling, what will you do?"

"The best I can," Menedemos answered. "Gods only know how I'm going to unload the olive oil we're carrying, but we'll see about that. I do have hopes for the rest of the food and the perfume and the silk and especially the books. Sostratos was clever there. I wouldn't have thought of them by myself, and we'll make a fine profit from them—or I hope we will."

"That'd be nice," the oarmaster said agreeably. "How do you propose to go about selling 'em, though? You can't just take 'em to the market square. Well, I suppose you *could,* but how much good would it do you? Mostly Phoenicians there, and they won't care anything about our books."

"I know. I've been thinking about that," Menedemos said. "What I have in mind doing is . . ." He explained. "What do you think of that?"

"Not bad, skipper." Diokles grinned and dipped his head. "Matter of fact, not half bad. I'd love to see you when you bring it off, I would."

"Well, why don't you come along?" Menedemos said.

"And who'd keep an eye on the ship if I did?" Diokles asked. "If your cousin were here, if Aristeidas were here, even, that'd be different. But the way things are, I think I'd better stick around when you're away."

Menedemos clapped him on the back. "You're the best keleustes I've ever known. You ought to have a ship of your own. I'm sorry things haven't broken the way they might have for you."

With a shrug, Diokles said, "One of these days, maybe. I've had the same thought. I'd like to be a captain. I won't say any different. But things could be a lot worse, too. If I hadn't been lucky, I'd still be pulling an oar somewhere." He held out his hands, palms up, to show the thick rower's calluses they still bore.

In a way, Menedemos admired the oarmaster's patience and willingness to make the best of things. In another way . . . He tossed his head. When he was unhappy about how life treated him, everybody around him knew he was unhappy. Sometimes that only succeeded in annoying everybody. More often, though (he thought it was more often, anyhow), letting people know what he wanted and that he wouldn't be satisfied till he got it helped him get it. He wondered whether he ought to tell Diokles as much. After a moment, he tossed his head. He doubted Diokles was one who could profit from the advice.

Later that day, he put several books in a wicker basket with a lid, which he took care to fasten down securely. Then he made his way through Sidon's narrow, brawling streets—canyons, they seemed to him, on account of the tall buildings to either side—looking for the barracks housing the Macedonians and Hellenes of the garrison.

He got lost. He'd known he would. He'd got lost before, in plenty of towns. It didn't usually worry him. Here, it did. Most places, if he got lost, he could ask for directions. Here, people stared at him as if he was speaking a foreign language when he asked, "Do you speak Greek?"—and so, to them, he was. He couldn't even steer by the sun. In Sidon, the tall buildings mostly kept him from seeing it.

He was beginning to wonder if he'd ever manage to find his way to the barracks or back to the harbor when he ran into a Macedonian. That was literally what he did—the fellow was coming out of an armorer's shop, a stout mace in hand, when Menedemos bumped him. "I'm sorry. Please excuse me," Menedemos said automatically, in Greek.

"It's all right. No harm done," the fellow answered. He certainly stood out from the locals. His skin was ruddy rather than olive, his face freckled, his eyes green, and his hair halfway between brown and blond. His nose was short and blunt—and leaned to the right, the result of a long-ago encounter with something hard and blunt.

"Oh, gods be praised! Someone I can understand!" Menedemos said.

Now the Macedonian laughed. "Hellenes don't always say that about the likes of me. When I start talking the way I did back home on the farm, I . . ." He drifted into Macedonian dialect, which, sure enough, Menedemos couldn't follow.

He waved that aside. "Doesn't matter, O best one. You *can* speak Greek if you want to, but these Phoenicians don't come close. Can you tell me where your barracks are?"

"I'll do better than that. I'm on my way back, and I'll take you there," the Macedonian said. "I'm Philippos son of Iolaos." He waited for Menedemos to give his own name, his father's name, and his birthplace, then asked, "Why do you want to find the barracks, Rhodian?"

Menedemos held up the basket. "I'm a merchant, and I've got things to sell in here."

"Things? What kind of things?"

"Books," Menedemos answered.

"Books?" Philippos echoed in surprise. Menedemos dipped his head. "Who'd want to buy a book?" the Macedonian asked him.

"Can you read and write?" Menedemos asked in return.

"Not me." Philippos spoke with a certain stubborn pride Menedemos had heard before. "Letters are just a bunch of scratches and squiggles, far as I'm concerned."

Even in Rhodes, far more men would have answered that way than not. Menedemos said, "Well, in that case, you wouldn't know what I was talking about even if I explained, so I'm not going to waste my time. I might as well try explaining music to a deaf man. But a lot of men who have got their letters do enjoy reading."

"I've heard that, but to the crows with me if I know whether to believe it or not," Philippos said. "Tell you what, pal— we're almost to the barracks. Bet you a drakhma you don't sell any of your silly scribbles."

"Done!" Menedemos said, and he clasped hands with the Macedonian to seal the wager.

They rounded a corner. Like so many buildings in cramped Sidon, the barracks towered five stories into the air. Sentries in Hellenic armor stood guard outside the entrance. Soldiers and hucksters went in and out. Menedemos heard the sweet, rising and falling cadences of Greek and those of Macedonian, which sounded the same at a distance but, to his ear, didn't resolve into meaning when he drew closer.

Philippos said, "I'm going to stand right here beside you, friend. By the gods, I won't jog your elbow. But if you can sell books, you're going to do it where I can see you."

"That's fair," Menedemos agreed. He planted himself a couple of cubits in front of the sentries and launched into the *Iliad:* "'Rage!—Sing, goddess, of Akhilleus'. . . .'" He wasn't a rhapsode, one of the traveling men who'd memorized the whole poem (or, sometimes, the *Odyssey*) and made their living by going from polis to polis and reciting in the agora for a few khalkoi here, an obolos there. But he knew the first book well, and he was livelier than most rhapsodes; they'd repeated the epics endless times and squeezed all the juice from thèm. Menedemos was really fond of the poet, and that showed as hexameter after hexameter flowed from him.

A soldier going into the barracks stopped to listen. A moment later, so did another one. Somebody stuck his head out a third-story window to hear Menedemos. After a bit, the fellow pulled it back in again. He came downstairs to hear better. By the time a quarter of an hour passed, Menedemos had drawn a fair crowd. Two or three soldiers had even tossed coins at his feet. He didn't bother to pick them up, but kept on reciting.

"You're not selling books," Philippos said. "You're doing the poem yourself."

"Shut up," Menedemos hissed. "You told me you wouldn't queer my pitch." The Macedonian subsided.

Menedemos went on with the *Iliad*:

"'Thus he spoke. Peleus' son grew troubled, his spirit
Pondering, divided in his shaggy breast,
Whether to draw his keen sword from beside his thigh,
Break up the assembled men, and slay the son of Atreus,
Or to contain his anger and curb his spirit.'"

He stopped. "Here, go on!" one of the soldiers exclaimed. "You're just getting into the good stuff." A couple of other men dipped their heads.

But Menedemos tossed his. "I'm no rhapsode, not really. I'm just a man who loves his Homer, the same as you're men who love your Homer. And why not? How many of you learned to read and write from the *Iliad* and the *Odyssey*?"

Several soldiers raised their hands. Philippos the Macedonian let out a low, admiring whistle. "Crows take you, Rhodian—I think you're going to cost me money."

"Hush," Menedemos told him, and went on with his sales pitch: "Don't you want the poet always with you, so you can enjoy his words whenever you please? The divine Alexander did: he took a complete *Iliad*, all twenty-four books, with him when he went on campaign in the east. That's what people say, anyhow."

"It's the truth," one of the soldiers, an older man, said. "I saw his *Iliad* with my own eyes, I did. He wanted to be as great a hero as Akhilleus. Me, I'd say he did the job, too."

"I wouldn't want to argue with you, my friend," Menedemos said. "Of course, a complete *Iliad*'s an expensive proposition. What I've got here, though"—he hefted the basket—"are copies of some of the best books in the *Iliad* and in the *Odyssey,* too, so you can read about the anger of Akhilleus or his fight with Hektor or about Odysseus and the way he tricked Polyphemos the Cyclops, as often as you like. The finest scribes in Rhodes wrote 'em out; you can be sure you've got the words just as Homer sang them all those years ago."

He knew he was stretching things. He wasn't sure himself any more just what Homer had sung. And Rhodes had so few scribes that speaking of them in the plural necessarily lumped in just about all of them. But he didn't intend to mention to the soldiers the hopeless, hapless drunk Sostratos had dealt with. They didn't need to know such things—and, after all, poor Polykles hadn't copied any of these books. Besides, though Rhodes had only a handful of scribes, it surely boasted more than any other cities except Athens and Ptolemaios' bumptious upstart of a capital, Alexandria.

"How much do you want for one of your books?" asked the soldier who'd seen Alexander's *Iliad.*

Menedemos smiled his smoothest smile. "Twenty drakhmai," he replied.

"That's bloody robbery, buddy, that's what that is," another man squawked. By his accent, he sprang from Athens. "Where I come from, five drakhmai's a fair price for a book."

"But you're not where you come from, are you?" Menedemos said, still smoothly. "I had to get these books copied in Rhodes, then dodge pirates all the way from there to here to bring them to Sidon. If you want a book here, I don't think you'll go to a Phoenician scribe to get one written out. The Phoenicians' letters don't even run the same way ours do; they read from right to left." If his cousin hadn't complained about that, he never would have known it, but he happily used it as part of his argument. "Besides," he added, "what else would you rather spend your silver on?"

"Wine," said the mercenary from Athens. "Pussy."

"You drink wine, and an hour later you piss it out. You lay a woman, and a day later your spear stands stiff again," Menedemos said. "But a book's different. A book is a possession for all time." He'd heard that phrase from Sostratos, too; he supposed Sostratos had got it from one of the historians he liked so much.

A couple of the men who'd listened to him looked thoughtful. The Athenian said, "That's still an awful lot of money."

Dickering started there. Not even the Athenian had the gall to offer only five drakhmai. The soldiers started at ten. Menedemos tossed his head—not derisively, but with the air of a man who didn't intend to sell for that price. One of them went up to twelve with no more prodding than that. Menedemos had to fight to keep a smile off his face. It wasn't supposed to be so easy. He didn't have to come down very far at all: only to seventeen drakhmai, three oboloi for each book.

"You'll sell for that?" the Athenian asked, to nail it down. With the air of a man making a great concession, Menedemos dipped his head. Eight or nine soldiers hurried into the barracks. Even before they came back, Philippos son of Iolaos handed Menedemos a drakhma. "Well, Rhodian, you taught me a lesson," he said.

"Oh? What lesson is that?" Menedemos asked. "My cousin collects them."

"Don't bet against a man who knows his own business. Especially don't push the bet yourself, like a gods-detested fool."

"Ah." Menedemos considered. "I think Sostratos already knows that one. I hope he does, anyhow."

SOSTRATOS HAD NEVER wanted to be a leader of men. In the generation following Alexander the Great, when every fisherman dreamt of becoming an admiral and every dekarkhos imagined he would use the ten men he commanded to conquer a kingdom full of barbarians and set a crown on his head, that made the Rhodian something of a prodigy. Of course, hardly any of the men with big dreams would fulfill them. Sostratos, with no ambitions along those lines, found himself in a role he didn't want to play.

"Trust me to get too much of what I don't want," he muttered from atop his mule. He didn't like the animal, either.

"What's that?" Aristeidas asked.

"Nothing," Sostratos said, embarrassed at being overheard. He liked Aristeidas and got on fine with him aboard the *Aphrodite,* not least because he hardly ever had to give him orders there. Here on dry land, though, almost everything he said took on the nature of a command.

The mule's and donkey's hooves and the feet of the sailors accompanying him raised dust from the road. The sun blazed down, the weather warmer than it would have been in Hellas at the same season of the year. Sostratos was glad for the broad-brimmed traveler's hat he wore in place of his helmet. Without it, he thought his brains might have cooked.

Apart from the heat, though, the countryside could easily have been inhabited by Hellenes. The grain fields lay quiet. They would be planted in the fall, when the rains came, for harvesting at the beginning of spring. Olive groves, with their silver-green leaves and gnarled, twisted tree trunks, looked much the same as they would have on Rhodes or in Attica. So did the vineyards. Even the sharp silhouettes of mountains on the horizon could have come straight from a land where Hellenes dwelt.

But the farmers tending the olive trees and grapevines stared at the men from the *Aphrodite.* Like the Sidonians, the men in the interior wore robes that reached down to their ankles. Most of them just draped a cloth over their heads to hold the sun at bay. The Hellenes' tunics, which left their arms bare and didn't reach their knees, marked them as strangers. Even Sostratos' hat seemed out of place.

Teleutas didn't want to bother with his chiton. "Why can't I shed it and go naked?" he said. "This weather's too stinking hot for clothes."

"These people pitch fits if you run around bare, and it's their country," Sostratos said. "So no."

"It's not their country—it's Antigonos' country now," Teleutas said. "Do you think old One-Eye cares a fart whether I wear my chiton or not?"

Sostratos wondered why he'd let Teleutas talk his way into coming along on this journey. Here they were, only a day out of Sidon, and the sailor was already starting to whine and fuss. Sostratos said, "What I think is, Antigonos is back in Anatolia, keeping an eye on Ptolemaios. The Phoenicians, though, the Phoenicians are *here.* They don't like people going naked. I don't want them throwing rocks at us or whatever else they decide to do."

"How do you know they'd do that?" Teleutas demanded. "How do you—"

"I don't *know* they'd do that," Sostratos said. "What I do know, O marvelous one, is that you're about a digit's breadth away from going back to Sidon and explaining to my cousin that I couldn't use you here after all. If you're going to come along, you'll do what I tell you, the same as you do what Menedemos tells you when we're at sea. Have you got that?" He was breathing hard by the time he finished. He didn't like launching into a tirade like that. He'd hoped he wouldn't have to. *And maybe I wouldn't,* he thought resentfully, *if I'd picked somebody besides Teleutas.*

But he had picked Teleutas, and so he was stuck with him. The sailor looked resentful, too. He plainly had not the faintest notion why Sostratos had come down on him so hard. Had he understood such things, he wouldn't have annoyed Sostratos in the first place. Now, glaring, he said what he had to say: "All right. All right. I'll keep my chiton on. Are you happy?"

"Delighted," Sostratos answered. Aristeidas snickered. Even Moskhion smiled, and he was hardly a man to notice subtleties. But Teleutas just went on glaring. Either he couldn't recognize sarcasm when he heard it or he was more comprehensively armored against it than anyone Sostratos had ever met.

Aristeidas pointed and asked, "What's that up ahead?"

As usual, he'd seen something before anyone else did. After riding on for a little way, Sostratos said, "I think it's a little roadside shrine, like a Herm at a crossroads back in Hellas."

The sandstone stele stood about half as tall as a man. It had the image of a god, now much weathered, carved in low relief on each of its four sides. There had been letters beneath the god's images, but they were too worn to make out, at least for someone as little familiar with Phoenician writing as Sostratos.

A couple of bundles of dried flowers and a loaf of bread, now half eaten by animals, lay by the base of the stele. "Let's leave some bread of our own," Moskhion said. "We ought to get the gods here on our side, if we can."

Sostratos doubted an offering would do anything of the sort, but he didn't suppose it could hurt. If it made Moskhion and the other sailors feel better, it might even do some good. "Go ahead," he told the former sponge diver.

Moskhion took a barley roll from a leather sack on the pack donkey's back. He set it by the old loaf. "I don't know what prayers you're used to," he told the god whose image adorned the stele, "but I hope you'll look kindly on the Hellenes passing through your land." He bobbed his head up and down. "Uh, thank you."

It wasn't the worst prayer Sostratos had heard. "May it be so," he added. "Shall we press on now?"

No one said no. Before long, a Phoenician leading a donkey came up the road toward the Hellenes. He stared at them. Plainly, he'd seldom seen men who looked like them or dressed like them. But they were four to his one, so he kept to himself whatever opinions he might have had.

"Peace be unto you," Sostratos said in Aramaic—the phrase most often used as a greeting or farewell in that language.

The Phoenician blinked. He must not have expected a for-

eigner to use his tongue. "And to you also peace," he replied.
"What manner of men are you?"

"We are Hellenes," Sostratos said. That was what it meant,
anyway; as always in Aramaic, the literal meaning was, *We
are Ionians.* "Who are you, my master? What does your beast
carry? Maybe we can trade."

"Hellenes!" The Phoenician's dark eyebrows rose. "I have
seen soldiers who called themselves by that name, but never
traders till now. I thought all Hellenes were soldiers and robbers. It does my heart good to learn I am wrong." That told
Sostratos more than he might have wanted to hear about the
way his countrymen behaved hereabouts. The Phoenician
bowed and went on, "Your servant is Bodashtart son of Tab-
nit. And you, sir?"

"I am called Sostratos son of Lysistratos," Sostratos answered. "I come from the island of Rhodes." He pointed
westward.

"And you come here from this island to trade?" Bodashtart
asked. Sostratos started to dip his head, then remembered to
nod as a barbarian would have done. Bodashtart pointed to
the pack donkey. "What do you carry there?"

"Among other things, fine perfume. Rhodes is famous for
it," Sostratos told him. "The name of the island—and the
name of the city on the island—means 'rose.'"

"Ah. Perfume." The Phoenician nodded again. "If it is not
too expensive, I might want some for my concubine, and
maybe for my wife, too."

A man who could afford to keep both a concubine and a
wife could probably afford perfume. Sostratos gave him another bow, asking, "Would you buy for silver, my master? Or
would you trade?" Bodashtart hadn't told him what his donkey was carrying.

"My lord, I have with me beeswax and fine embroidered
linen from the east," the man said now. He had to pause and
explain what beeswax was; Sostratos hadn't heard the word
before. That done, he went on, "I was taking them to Sidon to

sell them for what they might bring. Truly Shamash shines on the hour of our meeting."

Shamash, Sostratos remembered, was the Phoenician name for Apollo, the god of the sun. "Truly," he echoed. "I can use beeswax, I think. You buy perfume for yourself only? Or you want some to sell later?"

"I may want some to sell. Indeed, my master, I may," Bodashtart replied. "But it depends on price and quality, eh?"

"And what does not?" That earned Sostratos the first smile he'd got from the Phoenician. He slid down off his mule. The muscles in his inner thighs weren't sorry to escape the beast. Trying not to show how sore he was, he walked over to the pack donkey.

"What's going on?" Aristeidas asked. "We can't understand a word you're saying, remember."

"He has beeswax and embroidered linen," Sostratos answered. "He's interested in perfume. We'll see what we can work out."

"Ah, that's fine, sir. That's very fine," the sharp-eyed young sailor said. "But remember that you'll want to have some perfume left when we get to that Engedi place, so you can trade it for balsam."

"I'll remember," Sostratos promised. He hesitated; Aristeidas deserved better than getting brushed off like that. "It's good you remembered, too," Sostratos said. "If you can keep such things in mind, maybe you'll make a trader yourself one day."

"Me?" Aristeidas looked surprised. Then he shrugged. "Don't know that I'd want to. I like going to sea the way I do."

"All right. I didn't say you had to make a trader. I said you might." Sostratos fumbled with the lengths of rope lashing the pack donkey's burden to its back. Bodashtart watched with growing amusement, which only made Sostratos fumble worse. He was about to pull out his knife and solve the problem the way Alexander had solved the Gordian knot when Moskhion stepped up and helped undo the knots. "Thanks," Sostratos muttered, half grateful, half mortified.

One large leather sack held the jars of perfume, which lay nestled in wool and straw to keep them from smashing together and breaking. Sostratos pulled out a jar and held it up. Bodashtart frowned. "It isn't very big, is it?"

"My lord, the perfume is . . . strong." Sostratos wanted to say *concentrated,* but had no idea how to do so in Aramaic, or even if the word existed in that language. It wasn't the first time he'd had to try to talk his way around holes in his vocabulary. He pulled the stopper out of the jar. "Here—smell for yourself."

"Thank you." Bodashtart held the jar under his nose, which was long and thin and hooked. In spite of himself, he smiled at the fragrance. "That is very sweet, yes."

"And the odor stays," Sostratos said. "Perfume is in olive oil, not water. Not wash off easily."

"That is good. That is clever," Bodashtart said. "I have heard you Hellenes are full of clever notions. Now I see it is so. Here, let me show you the beeswax I have."

"Please," Sostratos said. The Phoenician had no trouble with the ropes securing *his* ass' load. Sostratos sighed. He'd thought he was used to the idea that most people were more graceful and dexterous than he. Every once in a while, though, it upped and bit him. This was one of those times.

"Here you are, my master." Bodashtart held up a lump of wax bigger than Sostratos' head. "Have you ever seen any so fine and white? White as the breasts of a virgin maid, is it not so?" He had to eke out his words with gestures; that wasn't vocabulary Himilkon had taught Sostratos.

When the Rhodian understood, he chuckled. He didn't think a Hellene would have tried to sell him wax with that particular sales pitch. From his point of view, Phoenicians were even worse than bad tragedians for overblown comparisons and figures of speech. Of course, they probably found most Hellenes bland and boring. *Custom is king of all,* Sostratos reminded himself once more. To Bodashtart, he said, "Let me see that wax, if you please."

"I am your slave," the Phoenician replied, and handed him the lump.

He sniffed it. It had the distinctive, slightly sweetish odor of good wax. Bodashtart hadn't cheapened it with tallow, as some unscrupulous Hellenes were known to do. Sostratos took his belt knife from its sheath and plunged it deep into the mass of wax, again and again.

"I am no cheat," Bodashtart said. "I have not hidden rocks or anything else in the middle of the beeswax."

"So I see," Sostratos agreed. "You have not. But I do not know you. I meet you on the road. I have to be sure."

"Shall I open every jar of perfume I get from you, to make sure you have not given me one that is half empty?" Bodashtart asked.

"Yes, my master, if you like," Sostratos answered. "Fair is fair. How can I say, do not make yourself safe? I cannot."

"Fair is fair," Bodashtart echoed. He bowed to Sostratos. "I had heard that all Hellenes were liars and cheats. I see this is not so. I am glad."

Sostratos politely returned the bow. "You too seem honest. I want this beeswax. How many jars of perfume for it?" He had a good notion of the price he might get for about ten minai of beeswax back in Rhodes. Sculptors and jewelers and others who cast metal used as much of the stuff as they could lay their hands on, and paid well for it.

Bodashtart said, "Ten jars seems right."

"Ten?" Sostratos tossed his head, then shook it back and forth in barbarian style. "You are no cheat, my master. You are a thief."

"You think so, do you?" the Phoenician said. "Well, how many jars would you give me for my wax?"

"Three," Sostratos answered.

"Three?" Bodashtart laughed scornfully. "And you call me a thief? You are trying to steal from me, and I will not have it." He drew himself up to his full height, but was still more than a palm shorter than Sostratos.

"Maybe we have no deal," Sostratos said. "If no deal, I am pleased to meet you even so."

He waited to see what would happen next. If Bodashtart didn't want to trade, he would take back the beeswax and go on his way toward Sidon. If he did, he would make another offer. The Phoenician bared his teeth in what was anything but a friendly grin. "You are a bandit, a robber, a brigand," he said. "But to show that I am just, that I uphold fair dealing, I will take only nine jars of perfume for this splendid, precious wax."

Now Bodashtart waited to see if the Rhodian would move. "I maybe give four jars," Sostratos said reluctantly.

They shouted at each other again and accused each other of larcenous habits. Bodashtart sat down on a boulder by the side of the road. Sostratos sat down on another one a couple of cubits away. The sailors escorting him started throwing knuckle-bones for oboloi while he haggled. His mule and ass and Bodashtart's donkey began to graze.

After a fair number of insults, Sostratos got up to six jars of perfume and Bodashtart got down to seven. There they stuck. Sostratos suspected six and a half would have made a decent bargain, but perfume, except to cheaters, didn't come in half-jars. Bodashtart showed no inclination to accept only six, and Sostratos didn't want to part with seven. The market for beeswax wasn't enormous, and did fluctuate. If someone close to home came up with a lot of it, he'd lose money even paying only six jars of perfume for this lump.

He and Bodashtart glared at each other, both of them frustrated. Then the Phoenician said, "Look at the cloth I have to sell. If I give you a bolt of that—it's about three cubits long—with the wax, will you give me seven jars of your perfume?"

"I know not," Sostratos answered. "Let me see it."

Bodashtart got up and opened a leather sack on the ass' back. Sostratos would have carried fine cloth inside an oiled-leather sack, too, to make sure water didn't damage it. Rain at this season of the year would have been unlikely in Hellas and, he judged, was even more so here, but Bodashtart's donkey might have to ford several streams between here and Sidon.

When the Phoenician held out the length of cloth, all three of Sostratos' escorts inhaled sharply. In Greek, Sostratos snapped, "Keep quiet, you gods-detested fools! Do you want to mess this up for me? Turn your backs. Pretend you're looking out to the hills for bandits if you can't keep your faces straight."

To his relief, they obeyed. Bodashtart asked, "What did you say to them? And will the cloth do?"

"I said they should watch for bandits in the hills." Sostratos feared he'd made a hash of indirect discourse; the Aramaic construction was quite different from the accusative and infinitive Greek used to show it. But Bodashtart nodded, so he must have made himself understood. He went on, "Let me have a better look, please."

"As you say, my master, so shall it be," Bodashtart replied, and brought it up to him.

The closer the Phoenician came, the more splendid the cloth appeared. Sostratos didn't think he'd ever seen finer embroidery. The hunting scene might have come straight from real life: the frightened hares, the thorn bushes beneath which they crouched, the spotted hounds with red tongues lolling out, the men in the distance with their bows and javelins. The detail was astonishing. So were the colors, which were brighter and more vivid than those in use back in Hellas.

He'd managed to keep his men from exclaiming over the piece. Now he had to fight to keep from exclaiming over it himself. To him, it had to be worth more than the beeswax. Doing his best to keep his voice casual, he asked, "Where did it come from?"

"From the east, from the land between the rivers," Bodashtart told him.

"Between which rivers?" Sostratos asked. But then the Greek equivalent of what the Phoenician had said formed in his mind. "Oh," he said. "From Mesopotamia." That, of course, meant nothing to Bodashtart. Sostratos knew Mesopotamia lay too far east for him to go there himself. He would have to get this work from middlemen like the fellow with whom he was haggling.

"Will it do?" Bodashtart asked anxiously. To him, the embroidery seemed nothing out of the ordinary: just a small extra he could throw in to sweeten the price for perfume he really wanted.

"I . . . suppose so." Sostratos had trouble sounding as reluctant as he knew he should. He wanted the embroidered cloth at least as much as the wax. Only later did he realize he might have asked for two cloths. Menedemos would have thought of that right away and would have done it, too. Menedemos automatically thought like a trader, where Sostratos had to force himself to do so.

Bodashtart, fortunately, noticed nothing amiss in Sostratos' answer. He smiled. "We have a bargain, then—the cloth and the wax for seven jars of perfume." He thrust out his hand.

Sostratos took it. "Yes, a bargain," he agreed. "Seven jars of perfume for the wax and the cloth." They exchanged the goods. The Phoenician put the perfume into a leather sack and led his ass on toward Sidon.

"You cheated him good and proper," Teleutas said as Sostratos loaded the beeswax and the embroidered cloth onto his pack donkey.

"I think I got the better of him, yes," Sostratos answered. "But if he makes a profit with the perfume, then no one cheated anybody. That's the way I hope this trade works out."

"Why?" the sailor asked. "Why not hope you diddled him good and proper?" He had a simple, selfish rapacity that wouldn't have been out of place on a pirate.

Patiently, Sostratos answered, "If both sides profit, they'll both want to deal again, and trade will go on. If one cheats the other, the side that gets cheated won't want to deal with the other the second time around."

Teleutas only shrugged. He didn't care. He had no eye for the long term, only for quick gain. Some merchants were like that, too. They didn't usually stay in business long, and they fouled the nest for everyone else. Sostratos was glad he had more sense than that. Even Menedemos had more sense than that. Sostratos hoped his cousin had more sense than that, anyhow.

He walked over to the mule. "Someone give me a leg-up," he said. "We can get some more travel in before the sun goes down."

MENEDEMOS WAS BEGINNING to feel at home in and around the barracks that housed Antigonos' garrison in Sidon. He preferred working the barracks to going into the market square. Not enough people in Sidon spoke Greek to make selling in the agora worthwhile for him. Around the barracks, he was dealing with his own kind. He was even starting to understand bits of Macedonian. It wasn't so big an accomplishment as Sostratos' learning Aramaic, but it made Menedemos proud.

When he came up to the barracks one morning, a guard who'd seen him before said, "Haven't you sold all your books yet?"

"I've still got a couple left," Menedemos answered. "Want to buy one?"

The soldier tossed his head. "Not me. Only use I'd have for papyrus is wiping my arse, on account of I can't read."

"You wouldn't want it for that. It's scratchy," Menedemos said, and the sentry laughed. Carefully keeping his voice casual, Menedemos asked, "What's the name of your quartermaster here, eh?"

"What do you want to talk with Andronikos for?" the soldier replied. "With his shriveled-up little turd of a soul, *he* won't want to buy your books."

"Well, maybe you're right and maybe you're not," Menedemos said easily. "I'd still like to find out for myself."

"All right, Rhodian." The sentry stood aside to let him into the building. "He's got an office on the second floor. But don't say I didn't warn you."

Menedemos had to be content with that less than ringing endorsement. He paused inside the barracks to let his eyes adjust to the gloom. Someone on the first floor was reading aloud the story of Akhilleus' fight with Hektor. Menedemos dared hope it was from a copy of the relevant book of the *Iliad* he'd sold. He didn't stop to find out, though. He made his way to the stairs and went up them.

"I'm looking for Andronikos' office," he told the first Hellene he saw when he came out onto the second floor. The man jerked his thumb to the right. "Thanks," Menedemos said, and went down the hallway leading in that direction.

Four or five people were in front of him. He waited for perhaps half an hour as the quartermaster dealt with them one by one. They didn't emerge from Andronikos' office looking happy, though Andronikos seldom if ever bothered raising his voice.

In due course, it was Menedemos' turn. By then, a couple of more Hellenes had joined the line behind him. When Andronikos called, "Next," he hurried into the office, a broad, friendly smile on his face.

That smile survived his first glimpse of the quartermaster, but barely. Andronikos was in his late forties, with a permanent fussy frown on his pinched features. "Who are you?" he asked. "Haven't seen you before. What do you want? Whatever it is, make it snappy. I haven't got time to waste."

"Hail, O best one. I'm Menedemos son of Philodemos, of Rhodes," Menedemos said. "My bet is, you're having more trouble keeping this garrison fed than you wish you did. Am I right or am I wrong?"

"You're the Rhodian, eh? Hail." Andronikos rewarded him with a dry grimace doubtless intended for a smile. "What do you care what the soldiers eat? You can't sell them papyrus."

"No, indeed, most noble, though I can sell you papyrus and first-quality Rhodian ink for record-keeping, if you're so inclined." Menedemos kept trying his best to be charming. Andronikos' unwaveringly sour expression told him he was wasting his time. He continued, "The reason I'm asking is that I also have some top-notch olive oil aboard my akatos, oil fit for the highest-ranking officers in the garrison here. And I've got fine Pataran hams and a few smoked eels from Phaselis, too."

"If the officers want fancy grub, they buy most of it themselves. As for you—you sailed an akatos here from Rhodes, and you're carrying oil?" Surprise made the quartermaster sound amazingly lifelike. "You believe in taking chances, don't you?"

Menedemos winced. It wasn't as if he hadn't been telling himself the same thing—he had. But having someone he'd just met throw it in his face rankled. *I'm going to hit Damonax over the head with a brick when we get home,* he thought. Aloud, all he could say was, "It's prime-quality oil, believe you me it is."

"I can get plenty of ordinary oil for not very much," Andronikos pointed out. "Why should I spend silver when I don't have to? Tell me that, and quick, or else go away."

"Because this isn't ordinary oil," Menedemos answered. "It's the best oil from Rhodes, some of the best oil anywhere. You can give common soldiers ordinary oil to eat with their bread, and they'll thank you for it. But what about your officers? Don't they deserve better? Don't they ask you for better?"

He hoped Antigonos' officers asked the quartermaster for better. If they didn't, he hadn't the faintest idea what he'd do with all that oil. Andronikos muttered something under his breath. Menedemos couldn't make out all of it; what he could hear was distinctly uncomplimentary to the officers in Antigonos' service, mostly because they made him spend too much money.

At last, with the air of a man whose stomach pained him, Andronikos said, "Bring me an amphora of this wonderful oil. We'll let a dozen soldiers dip bread in what they're using now and in what you bring. If they can tell the difference, we'll talk some more. If they can't"—he jerked a thumb toward the doorway through which Menedemos had come—"many goodbyes to you."

"What about the hams and the eels?"

"I already told you, I'm not interested. Maybe some of the officers will be—with their own silver, of course."

"All right, most noble one. Fair enough. A chance to show how good my oil is is all I ask." As usual, Menedemos spoke boldly. He did his best to hide the alarm he felt inside. Just how good *was* the oil Sostratos' new brother-in-law had foisted on the *Aphrodite*? Good enough to let men tell the difference at a single taste? He didn't know. He was about to find out. He did say, "Since you'll be buying the oil mostly for officers, some of the men who try it should be officers, too."

Andronikos considered, then dipped his head. "Agreed," he said. "Go fetch your oil. I'll get the men together, and some bread, and some of our local oil. And then, Rhodian, we shall see what we shall see."

"So we shall," Menedemos said, in what he hoped wasn't too hollow a voice. He hurried back to the harbor and freed a jar of olive oil from the rope harness and dunnage of twigs and branches that kept it from fetching up against other amphorai and smashing.

"What's going on, skipper?" Diokles asked. Menedemos explained. The keleustes whistled and said, "That's a roll of the dice, isn't it? Any which way, though, you can't lug that jar back to the barracks yourself. How would it look, a captain doing stevedore's work? Lapheides!"

"What is it?" said the sailor, who'd been paying no attention to the conversation between oarmaster and captain.

"Come get this amphora and carry it for the skipper," Diokles answered.

Lapheides looked no more delighted at that prospect than anyone else would have, but he came up and grabbed the jar by its handles. "Where to?" he asked Menedemos.

"Barracks," Menedemos told him. "Just follow me. You'll do fine." He hoped Lapheides would do fine. The sailor was a scrawny little man, and the full amphora probably weighed half as much as he did.

By the time they got back to the barracks, Lapheides was

bathed in sweat, but he'd done a good game job of carrying the amphora. Menedemos gave him three oboloi as a reward for his hard work. "Thanks, skipper," he said, and stuck the coins in his mouth.

One of the sentries, plainly forewarned, escorted Menedemos and Lapheides up to Andronikos' office. In the next room, the quartermaster had set up a table that held a loaf of bread and half a dozen shallow bowls. He—or, more likely, a slave—had poured yellow oil into three of the bowls. The other three waited, empty.

Menedemos used his belt knife to chip away at the pitch around the clay stopped to the amphora he'd had Lapheides bring. Once the stopper was out, he poured Damonax's oil into the empty bowls. It was greener than the oil Andronikos had got locally; Menedemos' nostrils quivered at its odor—fresh, fruity, almost spicy. The Rhodian breathed a silent sigh of relief. By all the signs, this *was* good oil.

He nodded to Andronikos. "Bring in your men, O best one."

"I intend to." The quartermaster walked down the hall, returning a moment later with what looked like a mix of ordinary soldiers and officers. To them, he said, "Here, my friends, we have one oil in these bowls and another in these. Taste them both, and tell me which is better."

"Please wait till you've all tasted both before speaking," Menedemos added. "We don't want one man's words coloring another man's thoughts."

A couple of soldiers scratched their heads. But the men wasted no time in tearing the bread into chunks and dipping those chunks first into one olive oil, then into the other. They chewed solemnly and thoughtfully, looking from one to another to see when they'd all sampled both oils. By then, only a few crumbs of the loaf were left.

A scarred veteran who wore a fat gold hoop in his right ear pointed to one of the bowls Menedemos had filled. "That oil there is better," he said. "Tastes like it's squeezed from the very first olives of the season. When I was a lad, I spent plenty of autumns whacking the olive trees with sticks to bring down the fruit, I did. Reckon I know a first-rate early oil when I taste one."

Another man dipped his head. "Hippokles is right, by Zeus. I haven't tasted oil like that since I left my old man's farm to go soldier. Tastes like it came out of the press yesterday, to the crows with me if it doesn't." He smacked his lips.

Then all the soldiers were talking at once, and all of them praising Menedemos' oil. No, all of them but one. The stubborn holdout said, "I'm used to this stuff here"—he pointed to a bowl of the local oil. "This other oil tastes different."

"That's the idea, Diodoros," Hippokles said. "The stuff we've been eating is tolerable, I guess, but if we can get this other oil, what we've been using ought to go into lamps instead, far as I'm concerned." His comrades agreed, some of them more heatedly.

Diodoros tossed his head. "I don't think so. I like *this* oil fine."

Menedemos glanced toward Andronikos. The quartermaster didn't seem to want to meet his eye. With his confidence restored, Menedemos didn't let that stop him. He shooed the soldiers out of the testing room, saying, "Thank you, most wise ones. Thank you very much. I'm sure we can arrange for you to have some of this oil you like—and I've got smoked eels and hams to sell, too, back at my ship." Once they were gone, he rounded on Andronikos. "Can't we arrange that?"

"Depends on what you want for it," the quartermaster said coolly. "If you think I'm going to throw silver at you like a young fool in love with his first hetaira, you'd better think again."

"Do you suppose your men there will keep quiet about what they just did?" Menedemos asked. "Can you afford not to buy? Will you wake up with a scorpion in your bed if you don't?"

Andronikos said, "I've squashed scorpions before. And I'll squash you, too, if you try to cheat me. What do you want for your fancy Rhodian oil? Just so you know, I'm paying seven sigloi the amphora for what I buy hereabouts."

Menedemos reminded himself that one Sidonian siglos held about twice as much silver as two Rhodian drakhmai. Sostratos was bound to know the exact conversion factor. When Menedemos tried to do anything but two for one, he felt as if his brains would start leaking out of his ears.

"You've seen for yourself that what I sell is better than what you're getting here," he said. "And it comes from Rhodes."

"So what?" Andronikos retorted. "You can bring it all that way by sea as cheaply as I can get oil from a day's journey away by land."

"That might be true on a round ship, best one, but I'm afraid it's not on an akatos," Menedemos said. "I have to pay my rowers, you know."

"Which gives you an excuse to gouge me," the quartermaster growled.

"No," Menedemos said, thinking, *Yes*. He went on, "All in all, I think thirty-five drakhmai the amphora is reasonable."

"I wish this chamber were on a higher floor, so I could throw you out the window and be sure I was rid of you once for all," Andronikos said. "You whipworthy rogue, do you think I'd give you more than twenty?" He had no trouble shifting from sigloi back to drakhmai.

"I certainly do think so, because I'm not going to lose money by selling you my oil," Menedemos answered. "What will your men—and especially your officers—say when they hear you're too cheap to buy them anything good?"

"My superiors will say I'm not wasting Antigonos' money," Andronikos told him. "That's my job—not wasting his money." He scowled at Menedemos. "What will your principal say when you go back to Rhodes with that olive oil still in the belly of your ship? How will you pay your rowers on no money at all?"

Menedemos hoped his flinch didn't show. Andronikos was a quartermaster, all right, and a ruthless specimen of the

breed. Despite all of Menedemos' persuasive powers, he refused to go higher than twenty-four drakhmai.

"I can't make any money on that," Menedemos said.

"Too bad. Here." Andronikos gave him three sigloi. They
showed the battlemented walls and towers of a city—presum-
ably Sidon—on one side and a king slaying a lion on the
other. "I'm not a thief. This more than pays for the oil you
used. Now close up your jar there and go."

"But—" Menedemos said.

The quartermaster tossed his head. "Go, I told you, and I
meant it. You don't want my best price, and I won't go higher.
Good day."

Rage threatened to choke Menedemos. He wanted to choke
Andronikos. He didn't. Nor would he give the older man the
satisfaction of seeing how badly he was wounded. He'd expected to sell the olive oil after his successful demonstration.
The quartermaster's shot had been all too shrewd. Taking it
back to Rhodes was the last thing he wanted to do. But all he
said was, "Seal up the jar, Lapheides. We're leaving."

He kept hoping Andronikos would ask him to stop or call
him back as he started out of the chamber. Andronikos didn't.
He stood silent as a stone. Menedemos slammed the door on
the way out, hard enough to rattle it on the pivoting pegs set
into the floor and the lintel. That made him feel better for a moment, but it did nothing to bring back the business he'd hoped
to have.

Lapheides was not a man he would have called particularly
clever. The sailor did have the sense to wait till they'd left the
barracks before asking, "What do we do now, skipper?"

It was a good question. It was, in fact, an excellent question.
Menedemos wished he had an excellent answer for it, or even
a good one. Being without either, he shrugged and said, "We
go back to the *Aphrodite* and see what happens next. Whatever it is, I don't see how it can be much worse than this."

After a couple of heartbeats of thought, Lapheides dipped
his head. "Neither do I," he said. Menedemos would sooner
have had consolation. Since he could find none himself,

though, he didn't see how he could blame Lapheides for also being unable to come up with any.

SHEEP GRAZED AND bleated around the little village nestled between hills and flatlands. Dogs barked at Sostratos and his sailors as they walked into the place. As often happened, some of the bigger, fiercer dogs made rushes at them. Teleutas scooped up an egg-sized stone and flung it. It caught the biggest, meanest dog right in the nose. The beast's snarls turned to yips of pain. It turned tail and ran. The rest of the dogs suddenly seemed to have second thoughts.

"*Euge!*" Sostratos said. "Now we won't have to beat them back with our spearshaft and swords. I hope we won't, anyhow. People don't like it when they see us laying into their animals."

"They don't care when they see the gods-detested dogs trying to bite us, though," Teleutas said. "They think *that's* funny. Pestilence take 'em, far as I'm concerned."

Aside from the dogs—some of which still barked and growled from a safe distance, which argued they'd had more than a few rocks thrown at them before—the hamlet was quiet. No sooner had that crossed Sostratos' mind than he tossed his head. It didn't just seem quiet. It seemed more nearly dead.

But a dead village wouldn't have had flocks grazing around it. Its buildings wouldn't have been in such good repair. Smoke wouldn't have risen from the vent holes in several roofs.

On the other hand, when strangers came to most villages, the locals came tumbling out of their houses to stare and point and exclaim. Up till now, that had seemed as much a truth in these parts as it would have back in Hellas. Not here. Everything stayed quiet except for the dogs.

Just before Sostratos and the sailors got to the center of the hamlet, an old man who wore a head scarf in place of a hat came out of one of the bigger houses and looked them over. "May the gods bless you and keep you, my master," Sostratos said in his best Aramaic. "Please tell us the name of this place."

The old man stared back without a word for an unnervingly long time. Then he said, "Stranger, we do not speak of the gods here. We speak of the one god, the true god, the god of Abraham and Isaac and Jacob. This village is called Hadid."

Excitement tingled through Sostratos. "The one god, you say?" he asked, and the old man nodded. Sostratos went on, "Then I have come to the land of Ioudaia?"

"Yes, this is the land of Ioudaia," the old man said. "Who are you, stranger, that you need to ask such a thing?"

Bowing, Sostratos answered, "Peace be unto you, my master. I am Sostratos son of Lysistratos, of Rhodes. I have come to trade in this land."

"And to you also peace. Sostratos son of Lysistratos." The local tasted the unfamiliar syllables. After another long pause, he said, "You would be one of those Ionians, wouldn't you?"

"Yes," Sostratos said, resigned to being an Ionian in these parts despite his Doric roots. "What is your name, my master, if your slave may ask?"

"I am Ezer son of Shobal," the old man replied.

"Is all well here?" Sostratos asked. "No pestilence, nothing like that?"

Ezer had formidable gray eyebrows and a beaky nose. When he frowned, he looked like a bird of prey. "No, there is no pestilence. May the one god forbid it. Why do you ask?"

"Everything is very quiet here." Sostratos waved his arms to help show what he meant. "No one works."

"Works?" Ezer son of Shobal frowned again, even more fiercely than before. He shook his head. "Of course no one works today. Today is the sabbath."

"Your slave prays pardon, but he does not know that word," Sostratos said.

"You did not learn this tongue from a man of Ioudaia, then," Ezer said.

Once more, Sostratos had to remember to nod instead of dipping his head. "No, I did not. I learned from a Phoenician. Truly you are very wise." Yes, flattery seemed built into Aramaic.

"A Phoenician? I might have known." By the way Ezer said it, he had as much scorn for Phoenicians as Himilkon had for Ioudaioi. "The one god commands us to rest one day in seven. That is the sabbath. Today is the seventh day, and so . . . we rest."

"I see." What Sostratos saw was why these Ioudaioi had never amounted to anything in the wider world, and why they never would. If they wasted one day in seven, how could they keep up with their neighbors? He marveled that they hadn't already been altogether swept away. "Where can my men and I buy food?" he asked. "We have come a long way today. We too are tired."

Ezer son of Shobal shook his head again. "You do not see, Ionian. Sostratos." He carefully sounded out the name. "I told you, this is the sabbath. The one god decrees we may not work on this day. Selling food is work. Until the sun sets, we may not do it. I am sorry." He sounded not the least bit sorry. He sounded proud.

Himilkon had warned that the Ioudaioi had set ideas about their religion. Sostratos saw he'd known what he was talking about. "Will someone draw water from the well for us?" he asked. "You have a well, I hope?"

"We have a well. No one will draw water for you, though, not till after sunset. That is also work."

"May we draw water ourselves?"

Now Ezer nodded. "Yes, you may do that. You are no part of us."

No, and I wouldn't want to be any part of you, either, Sostratos thought. He wondered how he would live in a land where religious law so closely hemmed in everything these people did. His first thought was that he would simply go mad.

But then he wondered about that. If he'd been raised from childhood to find that law right and proper and necessary, wouldn't he come to believe it was? Even in Hellas, thoughtless people blindly believed in the gods. Here in Ioudaia, it seemed, everyone believed in their strange, invisible deity. *If I'd been born a Ioudaian, I suppose I would, too.*

The more Sostratos thought about that, the more it frightened him. He bowed to Ezer. "Thank you for your kindness, my master."

"You are welcome," the old man replied. "You cannot help it that you are not one of us, and so cannot know and obey the sacred laws of the one god."

He means that, Sostratos realized in astonishment. Ezer son of Shobal was as proud to belong to his narrow little backwoods tribe as Sostratos was to be a Hellene. It would have been funny if it hadn't been so sad. *I wish I could show him how ignorant he is.* Sostratos had had that same urge with Hellenes, too. With his own folk, he could act on it. Sometimes he managed to convince them of the error of their ways. More often, though, even Hellenes chose to cling to their own ignorance rather than accepting someone else's wisdom.

"What are you and this big-nosed old geezer going on about?" Teleutas asked.

Ezer didn't change expression. *No, of course he doesn't speak Greek,* Sostratos told himself. All the same . . . "You want to be careful how you talk about people here. You never can tell when one of them may understand some of our tongue."

"All right. All right." Teleutas dipped his head with obvious impatience. "But what *is* going on?"

"We can't buy any food till after sundown," Sostratos answered. "They have a day of rest every seventh day, and they take it seriously. We can get water from the well, though, as long as we do it ourselves."

"A day of rest? That's pretty stupid," Teleutas said, which was exactly Sostratos' opinion. The sailor went on, "What happens if they're in a war and they have to fight a battle on this special day of theirs? Do they let the enemy kill them because they're not supposed to fight back?"

"I don't know." That intrigued Sostratos, so he turned it into Aramaic, as best he could, for Ezer.

"Yes, we would die," the Ioudaian answered. "Better to die than to break the law of the one god."

Sostratos didn't try to argue with him. Ezer sounded as passionate as a man who was busy wasting his inheritance on a hetaira and didn't care if he ruined himself on her behalf. A man who wasted his inheritance on a hetaira at least had the pleasure of her embraces to recall. What did a man who wasted his life on devotion to a foolish god have left? Nothing Sostratos could see. Such mad devotion might even cost a worshiper life itself.

He didn't care to point that out to Ezer son of Shobal. The Ioudaian had made it plain he could see it for himself. He'd also made it plain he was willing to take the consequences. How could a man's devotion to a god be greater than his devotion to life itself? Sostratos shrugged. No, it made no rational sense.

The Rhodian did find a rational question to ask: "My master, where is the well? We are hot and thirsty."

"Go past this house here"—Ezer pointed—"and you will see it."

"Thank you." Sostratos bowed. Ezer returned the gesture. However mad he might be in matters pertaining to his god, he was polite enough when dealing man to man. Sostratos went back to Greek to tell the sailors with him where the well was.

"I'd sooner have wine," Teleutas said.

That wasn't quite pure complaint, or it might not have been pure complaint, anyhow. Aristeidas dipped his head, saying, "So would I. Drinking water in foreign parts can give you a flux of the bowels."

He was right, of course, but Sostratos said, "Sometimes it can't be helped. We *are* in foreign parts, and we have to drink water by itself now and again. The country isn't swampy or marshy. That makes the water likelier to be good."

"I don't care how good it is. I don't care if it's water from the Khoaspes, the river the Persian kings used to drink from," Teleutas said. "I'd still sooner have wine." He hadn't cared about his health, then—only about his palate and the way wine would make him feel. *Why am I not surprised?* Sostratos thought.

As Hellenes often did, the Ioudaioi had circled the well with rocks to the height of a cubit or so, to keep animals and children from falling in. They'd also put a wooden cover over the top of the well. When the sailors took it off, they found a stout branch lying across the opening, with a rope attached to it.

"Let's haul up the pail," Sostratos said.

The men got to work, taking turns at it. Teleutas groaned and grumbled as he hauled on the line; he might almost have been sentenced to torture. From everything Sostratos had seen, Teleutas reckoned work the equivalent of torture. Then again, hauling up a large, full bucket wasn't easy. Sostratos wondered if there were some easier way to raise a bucket of water than yanking it up one pull at a time. If so, it didn't occur to him.

"Here we are," Aristeidas said at last. Moskhion reached out and grabbed the dripping wooden pail. He raised it to his lips; took a long, blissful pull; and then poured some over his head. Sostratos said not a word when Teleutas and Aristeidas took their turns before passing him the pail. By bringing it up from the bottom of the deep well, they'd earned the right.

"Water seems good enough," Aristeidas said. "It's nice and cool, and it tastes sweet. I hope it's all right."

"It should be." Sostratos drank. "Ahh!" As his men had, he poured water over his head, too. "Ahh!" he said again. It felt wonderful running down his face and dripping from his nose and the end of his beard.

Every now and then, he spied a face staring from the windows of the stone and mud-brick houses. No one but Ezer son of Shobal came out, though. In fact, Sostratos waved the first time he saw one of those curious faces. All that did was make it disappear in a hurry.

Aristeidas noticed the same thing. "These people are funny," he said. "If we came into a village full of Hellenes, they'd be all over us. They'd want to know who we were and where we were from and where we were going next and what

news we'd heard lately. The rich ones would want to trade
with us, and the poor ones would want to beg from us. They
wouldn't just leave us alone."

"I should say not," Teleutas agreed. "They'd try to steal
anything we hadn't nailed down, too, and they'd try to pry up
the nails."

Sostratos raised an eyebrow. It wasn't that Teleutas was
wrong. The sailor was, without a doubt, right—Hellenes
would act like that. But the notion of thievery seemed to occur
to him very quickly. Not for the first time, Sostratos wondered
what that meant.

He could have pushed on from Hadid, but he did want to
buy food, and Ezer had made it very plain he couldn't do that
till after sunset. He and the sailors rested by the well. After a
while, they refilled the bucket and hauled it up again. They
drank deep and poured the rest over themselves.

As he might have done in Hellas, Teleutas started to pull
off his tunic and go naked. Sostratos held up a hand. "I already told you once, don't do that."

"It'd be cooler," Teleutas said.

"People here don't like showing off their bodies."

"So what?"

"So what? I'll tell you so what, O marvelous one." Sostratos waved a hand. "There probably aren't any other Hellenes closer to this place than a day's journey. If we get people
here up in arms against us, what can we do? If they start
throwing rocks, say, what can we do? I don't think we can do
anything. Do you?"

"No, I guess not," Teleutas said sulkily. He left the chiton on.

After the sun went down, the locals emerged from their
houses. Sostratos bought wine and cheese and olives and
bread and oil (he tried not to think about all the oil Damonax
had made him carry on the *Aphrodite,* and he hoped
Menedemos was having some luck getting rid of it). Some
people did ask questions about who he was, where he was
from, and what he was doing in Ioudaia. He answered as best
he could in his halting Aramaic. As twilight deepened, mos-

quitoes began to whine through the air. He slapped a couple of times, but still got bitten.

A few of his questioners were women. Though they robed themselves from head to foot like the local men, they didn't wear veils, as respectable Hellenes would have. Sostratos had noticed that back in Sidon, too. To him, seeing a woman's naked face in public came close to being as indecent as seeing his—or Teleutas'—naked body would have been for the Ioudaioi.

He wished he could ask them more about their customs and beliefs. It wasn't so much that his Aramaic wasn't up to the job. But, as he hadn't wanted Teleutas to offend them, he didn't want to do so himself. He sighed and wondered how long it would be till his curiosity got the better of his common sense.

"HOW YOU IS?" THE INNKEEPER ASKED WHEN Menedemos came out of his room one morning. His name, the Rhodian had learned, was Sedek-yathon.

"Good," Menedemos answered in Greek. Then he said the same thing in Aramaic, of which he'd picked up a few words.

Sedek-yathon grunted. His wife, who was called Emashtart, smiled at Menedemos. "How clevers you am," she said in her dreadful Greek. She rattled off a couple of sentences of Aramaic much too fast for him to follow.

"What?" Menedemos said.

Emashtart tried to explain it in Greek, but she lacked the vocabulary. She turned to her husband. Sedek-yathon was busy putting a new leg on a stool. He showed no interest in translating. His Greek was bad, too; odds were he couldn't have done it if he'd wanted to. When he refused even to try, Emashtart started screeching at him.

"Hail," Menedemos said, and left the inn in a hurry. He spent as little time there as he could. The innkeeper's wife kept making unsubtle advances at him. His oath to Sostratos had nothing to do with anything. He didn't want the woman, whom he found repulsive, and he didn't want Sedek-yathon thinking he did want her and trying to kill him as a result.

Though the sun hadn't been up long, the day promised brutal heat. The breeze came, not from the Inner Sea, but from the hills east of Sidon. When it swept down off them, Menedemos had learned, the heat got worse than anything he'd ever known in Hellas.

He stopped at a baker's and bought a small loaf of bread. With a cup of wine from the first fellow he saw carrying a jug, it made a good enough breakfast. The cup, fortunately, was small; unlike Hellenes, Phoenicians didn't believe in watering their wine and always drank it neat. A big mug of unmixed wine first thing in the morning would have set Menedemos' head spinning.

Sidon was already bustling as he made his way through its narrow, winding streets toward the harbor and the *Aphrodite*. On days like this, the locals often tried to pack as much business as they could into the early morning and the late afternoon. When the heat was at its worst, they would close their shops and sleep, or at least rest, for a couple of hours. Menedemos wasn't used to doing that, but he couldn't deny it made a certain amount of sense.

Diokles waved to him when he came up the wharf. "Hail," the oarmaster called. "How are you?"

"Glad to be here," Menedemos answered. "Yourself?"

"I'm fine," Diokles said. "Polykharmos came back to the ship last night shy a front tooth, though. Tavern brawl." He shrugged. "Nobody pulled a knife, so it wasn't a bad one. He was pretty drunk, but he kept going on about what he did to the other fellow."

"Oh?" Menedemos raised an eyebrow. "Didn't anybody ever tell him he shouldn't lead with his face?"

The keleustes chuckled. "I guess not. Hasn't been *too* bad here—I have to say that. Nobody's been stabbed; nobody's been badly hurt any other way. As often as not, you lose a man or two on a trading run."

"I know." Menedemos spat into the bosom of his tunic to turn aside the evil omen. Diokles did the same. "Gods prevent it," Menedemos added.

"Here's hoping," Diokles agreed. "What are you going to do about Damonax's olive oil and the rest of the food now, skipper?"

"To the crows with me if I know." Menedemos melodramatically threw his hands in the air. "I thought I had a bargain with that whipworthy rogue of an Andronikos, but the abandoned catamite wouldn't give me a decent price."

"Quartermasters are cheese-parers," Diokles said. "They always have been, and I expect they always will be. They don't care if they serve their soldiers slop. If giving the men something better means costing them an extra obolos, they won't do it. They figure you can fight as well on stale, moldy bread as on fresh—maybe better, because bad food makes you mean."

"Every word you say is true, but there's more to it than that," Menedemos answered. "A lot of the time, every obolos a quartermaster doesn't spend on his soldiers is an obolos he gets to keep for himself."

"Oh, yes. Oh, yes, indeed." The oarmaster dipped his head. "Still, though, if I were in Antigonos' army, I'd be careful about playing games like that. If old One-Eye caught me at 'em, I'd end up on a cross like *that*." He snapped his fingers.

"May Antigonos catch Andronikos, then. May he—" Menedemos broke off. Someone was coming up the pier toward the *Aphrodite*: a Hellene, surely, for no Phoenician would have worn a tunic that bared his arms to the shoulders and his legs to above the knee. Menedemos raised his voice: "Hail, friend! Do something for you?"

"You're the fellow who brought that good olive oil to the

barracks the other day, aren't you?" the newcomer said. Before the Rhodian could answer, the man dipped his head and answered his own question: "Yes, of course you are."

"That's right." Menedemos didn't bother hiding his bitterness. "Your polluted quartermaster doesn't want anything to do with it, though."

"Andronikos can take it up the arse like a slave in a boy brothel for all of me," the Hellene replied. "I know what he gives us, and I was one of the people who tasted what you've got. He may not want to buy any, but I do. How much do you want for a jar?"

"Thirty-five drakhmai," Menedemos answered, as he had at the beginning of the failed dicker with Andronikos.

He waited to see what counteroffer the Hellene would make. *Hippo-kles, that's what his name is,* Menedemos remembered. He'd liked the oil a lot when he tried it. And now he didn't make any counteroffer. He just dipped his head and said, "I'll take two amphorai, then. That'd be thirty-five sigloi, near enough, right?"

"Right," Menedemos said, doing his best to hide his surprise.

"Good." Hippokles turned on his heel. "Don't go anywhere. I'll be back. I've got to get the money and a couple of slaves to haul the jars." Away he went.

"Well, well," Menedemos said. "That's better than nothing." He laughed. "Of course, I would've sold Andronikos a lot more than two jars."

Less than an hour later, Hippokles returned with two scrawny men in tow. He gave Menedemos a jingling handful of Sidonian coins. "Here you are, pal. Now I'll put these lazy wretches to work."

Menedemos counted the sigloi. Hippokles hadn't tried to cheat him. Some of the coins bore inscriptions in the angular Aramaic script. The letters meant nothing to Menedemos. That Hippokles had plenty of silver did. "Would you like to buy some smoked eels from Phaselis, too?" he asked. "Two sigloi each."

That was four times what Sostratos had paid for them in the

Lykian town. And Hippokles, after tasting a tiny sample, dipped his head and bought three. He took care of them himself. The slaves, grunting, picked up the jars of oil and carried them back down the quay after him into Sidon.

"Not bad," Diokles said.

"No. I got premium prices there, no doubt about it." Menedemos ducked under the poop deck and stowed his fat handful of silver in an oiled-leather sack. He'd just made about a day's wages for the crew of the merchant galley. Of course, not all of it was profit; the olive oil and eels hadn't come on board for nothing. Even so, it was the best he'd done since putting in at Sidon.

And Hippokles turned out not to be the only soldier who, after trying Damonax's olive oil, wanted some for himself. The mercenary hadn't been gone long before another officer came up the pier to the *Aphrodite*. This fellow didn't need to go back and fetch a slave to take away his purchase; he'd brought a man along. Like Hippokles, he had only Sidonian coins on him. "I've been here three years, ever since we took this place back from Ptolemaios," he told Menedemos. "Whatever drakhmai I had once upon a time are long since spent."

"Don't you worry, best one," Menedemos said smoothly. "I'll figure out how many sigloi make thirty-five drakhmai, never fear." Sostratos would have done it in his head. Menedemos had to flick beads on a counting board. With the board, he got the answer about as quickly as his cousin would have: "Seventeen and a half."

"Sounds about right." The other Hellene counted out sigloi one by one and gave them to Menedemos. ". . . sixteen . . . seventeen." He handed the Rhodian a smaller coin. "And here's the half-siglos to make it square."

"Thanks very much," Menedemos said. "I've got hams from Patara, too, if you'd be interested in one of those. . . ."

"Let me try a bit," the officer said. Menedemos did. The officer grinned. "Oh, by the gods, yes—that pig died happy." He made Menedemos happy, too, with the price he paid. Turning to his slave, the fellow added, "Come on, Syros. Sling that ham over your shoulder—may I scrounge a bit of rope from you, Rhodian?—grab that amphora, and get moving."

"Yes, boss," the slave replied in halting, Aramaic-accented Greek. Sweat poured from him as he followed his master off the ship. He was shorter and much skinnier than the Hellene, but it would have gone against his master's dignity to stoop to manual labor himself when he had a slave to do it for him.

Menedemos and Diokles watched the two men go. "How about that?" the oarmaster said. "If one soldier had come here, I'd've said it was a nice happenstance and forgotten about it the next day. But if two do it of a morning . . ."

"Yes." Menedemos dipped his head. He looked down at his new handful of silver. "I wonder how many more we'll get." Something else occurred to him. "And I wonder if the other oil Andronikos had in that room was some of the best he serves out, not the everyday stuff. Wouldn't surprise me. Even if it was, it wasn't good enough."

"He's the only one who knows for sure," Diokles answered. "One thing, though: at least now *we* know the olive oil we've got really is as good as we've been saying."

"Yes. The same thing occurred to me." Menedemos sighed. "All the trouble we've had getting rid of it, I was worrying about that myself. Harder to make sure you get top quality from in-laws, but you'd better. Otherwise, who's going to trust you when you come back to a place in a year or two?"

Diokles laughed. "It might not matter here, skipper. If we come back to this place in a couple of years, we're liable to find Ptolemaios' garrison here, not Antigonos'."

"Well, I can't tell you you're wrong, and I won't even try," Menedemos answered. "Or, of course, we might find that Ptolemaios' men had been here, and Antigonos' had run them out again."

"That, too," the oarmaster agreed. "It's like the pankration with those two—they'll keep pounding away till one of them can't pound any more."

"And with Lysimakhos, and with Kassandros," Menedemos added. "And if one of them does go down, somebody else will probably rise up to take his place—that Seleukos, maybe, out in the east. Somebody. I don't think anyone can fill Alexander's shoes, but nobody's willing to leave them empty, either."

"The marshals don't care what they step on while they're fighting," Diokles said. "They'll step on Rhodes if they get the chance."

"Don't I know it," Menedemos said. "We really are a free and autonomous polis, and even Ptolemaios, who's the best friend we've got among the Macedonians, even he thinks it's funny we want to stay that way. He'll humor us—we're the middlemen for his grain trade, after all—but he thinks it's funny. I saw that in Kos last year."

Instead of taking the political talk further, Diokles pointed down to the base of the quay. "Furies take me if those don't look like more soldiers looking around for the *Aphrodite*."

"You're right," Menedemos murmured. "Maybe that session at the barracks is going to pay off pretty well after all, even if that abandoned rascal of an Andronikos didn't do any buying himself."

Up the pier came the Hellenes. They remained tentative till Menedemos waved and called to them. Then they sped up. One of them said, "You're the trader with the good oil?"

"That's me, sure enough." Menedemos looked from one man to the next. "How do you know about it? I've got a good memory for faces, and I don't think any of you were at the quartermaster's taste test."

"No, but we heard about it, and we know what he feeds us," replied the soldier who'd spoken before. He made a face to show what he thought of it. "We figured we'd club together, buy an amphora of the good stuff, and share it amongst us. Isn't that right, boys?" The other mercenaries dipped their heads to show it was.

"Fine with me," Menedemos said. Then he told them what a jar cost.

"*Papai!*" their spokesman said as the others flinched in dismay. "Can't you give us a break on that? It's pretty steep for ordinary mortals."

"I've already sold three jars for that price this morning," Menedemos answered. "If I sell it to you for less, your pals will come by and say, 'Oh, you gave it to good old What's-his-name for twenty drakhmai, so let us have it for twenty, too.' There goes my profit—you see what I mean?" He spread his hands to show he was sorry, but he held firm.

The soldiers put their heads together. Menedemos ostentatiously didn't listen to their low-voiced argument. At last, they separated again. The fellow who did the talking for them said, "All right, thirty-five drakhmai it is. This is supposed to be good stuff, so we'll pay for it this once."

"And I do thank you very much, most noble ones," Menedemos said. "Come aboard, then, and choose the amphora you want." They were as near identical as one ear of barley to another, but he'd seen before that giving—or rather, seeming to give—customers such choices made them happier. As they picked their jar, he added, "Would you like to buy some ham or some smoked eels?"

Antigonos' men put their heads together again and then spent some more money on eels. Menedemos ended up happy when they paid him, too. Some of the coins they used were Sidonian sigloi, which he accepted as equaling two Rhodian drakhmai. But others were drakhmai and didrakhms and tetradrakhms from all over Hellas. Athenian owls and turtles from Aigina were considerably heavier than Rhodian coins. To the soldiers, one drakhma was as good as another. Menedemos knew better—and also knew better than to say anything about the extra profit he was making.

Before long, another party of soldiers came up the pier toward the *Aphrodite*. "You may end up thanking that quartermaster for turning you down, not cursing him," Diokles remarked.

Menedemos thought about how very many amphorai of olive oil remained aboard the akatos. But then he thought about how large Antigonos' garrison in Sidon was. If Damonax's oil became a fad . . . "By the dog of Egypt," he said slowly, "so I may."

As SOSTRATOS TRAVELED father into Ioudaia, he began to see why Hellenes knew so little about the land and its folk. The people stuck together, clinging to their own kind and having as little to do with outsiders as they could. And the land worked with them. It was broken and hilly and hot and poor. As far as he could see, the Ioudaioi were welcome to it. Who in his right mind would want to take it away from them?

He knew he couldn't have been so very many stadia from the Inner Sea. There it lay, off to the west, the broad highway that could swiftly waft him back to Rhodes. But the Ioudaioi turned their backs on it. They had their flocks of sheep and cattle, their olive trees and their vineyards, and they seemed content with those—and with their strange god, whose face no one ever saw.

In every village and town through which he passed, Sostratos had looked for a temple to this mysterious god. He never found one. At last, he'd asked a Ioudaian who'd proved friendly enough over a couple of cups of wine in a tavern. The fellow had shaken his head and looked amused at the question: amused and pitying, as if Sostratos couldn't be expected to know any better.

"Our god has only one temple, where the priests offer prayer and sacrifice," he'd said. "That is in Jerusalem, our great city."

Everywhere in Ioudaia, people spoke of Jerusalem as Hellenes spoke of Athens or Alexandria. Every other town, they said, was as nothing beside it. And they spoke of their temple as Athenians might have spoken of the Parthenon—as the most perfect and beautiful building in the world.

They were only barbarians, and provincial barbarians at
that, so Sostratos did discount a fair amount of what he heard.
Even so, he wasn't prepared for his first sight of Jerusalem,
which he got from a rocky ridge a couple of hours' travel
north and west of the city.

He pointed ahead. "That's it," he said. "That has to be it.
But is that all there is? *That's* what all the Ioudaioi we've met
were swooning over?"

"Doesn't look like so very much, does it?" Aristeidas said.

"Now that you mention it, no," Sostratos answered. The al-
legedly great city of the Ioudaioi straggled along a rise between a sizable valley to the east and a smaller, narrower
ravine to the west. It might have been half a dozen stadia long;
it was nowhere near half a dozen stadia wide. Some more
homes—suburbs, though they hardly deserved the name—
dotted the rise west of the narrow ravine. Smoke hung above
everything: the unfailing mark of human habitation. Giving
the place the benefit of the doubt, Sostratos said, "There are
poleis that are smaller."

"I can't think of any that're uglier," Teleutas said.

Sostratos didn't find that quite fair. The walls around
Jerusalem and the bigger buildings he could see were built
from the local stone, which had a golden color his eye found
pleasing. He couldn't make out any details, not at this range,
and doubted even lynx-eyed Aristeidas would be able to. "One
of those big buildings will probably be the temple the Ioudaioi
talk about."

"I don't see anything that looks like a proper temple, with
columns and all," Aristeidas said, leaning forward to peer at
the distant city on the hill.

"They're barbarians, and peculiar barbarians at that,"
Moskhion said. "Who knows if their temples look the way
temples are supposed to?"

"And they worship this silly god nobody can see," Teleutas
added slyly. "Maybe they've got a temple nobody can see, too."

"It could be," Sostratos said. "The Kelts worship their gods in groves of trees, I've heard." He looked around. "I admit there are bound to be more trees in the land of the Kelts than there are here." After a little more thought, he went on, "I take it back. I do think one of those buildings *is* the temple, for the Ioudaioi wouldn't have talked about the place the way they have if it were only a sacred grove—or, for that matter, if it weren't there at all."

He stopped, pleased by his logic. But when he looked from one of his escorts to another to find out if it had impressed them, too, he caught Teleutas muttering to Aristeidas: "By the dog, I can't even make a joke without getting a lecture back."

Sostratos' ears burned. *Well, you wanted to find out what they thought,* he told himself. *Now you know.* He hadn't intended to lecture. He'd just been making a point. Or so he'd thought, anyhow. He sighed. *I have to watch that. I really do need to be careful. If I'm not, I'll end up boring people. That's the last thing a merchant can afford to do, because—*

He broke off. He did some muttering of his own, some fairly pungent muttering. He'd started lecturing himself about not lecturing. "Let's go," he said aloud. That was brief enough and enough to the point that not even Teleutas could try to improve it.

The road to Jerusalem meandered through olive trees and fields that would have been richer had they not gone uphill at such a steep slope. The closer the Hellenes got to the city, the more impressive its fortifications looked. The walls cunningly took advantage of the ground. The northern part of the place had especially strong works. Even Teleutas said, "I wouldn't want to try storming this place."

"No, indeed." Aristeidas dipped his head. "You'd have to try to starve it out. Otherwise, you could throw away an army in nothing flat."

On approaching the western gate, Sostratos found some of the guards to be Hellenes and others—who carried spears and shields and wore helmets, but had no body armor— swarthy, hook-nosed Ioudaioi. One of the Hellenes stared at the short chitons Sostratos and the sailors from the *Aphrodite* had on. He nudged his comrades. They all pointed toward the newcomers. The man who'd first noticed them called out, *"Hellenizete?"*

"Malista." Sostratos dipped his head. "Of course we speak Greek."

"Poseidon's prick, man, what are you castaways doing in this gods-forsaken place?" the gate guard asked him. "We have to be here, to keep Moneybags in Egypt from taking this town away from Antigonos again, but why would anybody in his right mind come here if he didn't need to?"

"We're here to trade," Sostratos said. "We're bound for En-gedi, to buy balsam there, but we'll do business along the way, too."

"Not much business *to* do in these parts," another guard said, which did nothing to gladden Sostratos' heart. But then he went on, "What there is of it, though, you'll do in Jerusalem."

"Well, that's good to hear," Sostratos said. He gave the Ioudaioi at the gate a polite nod, aping barbarous manners as best he could, and switched to Aramaic: "Peace be unto you, my masters."

The Ioudaioi exclaimed in surprise. So did the Hellenes. "Listen to him make bar-bar noises!" one of them said. "He can talk with these polluted Ioudaian maniacs. He doesn't have to point and do dumb show and hope you can find one of them who's picked up a few words of Greek."

"Where'd you learn this language, pal?" another Hellene asked.

"From a Phoenician merchant on Rhodes," Sostratos answered. "I don't speak all that much of it."

"Better than I can do, and I've been out here a couple of years," the guard told him. "I can ask for a woman—they don't like you to ask for a boy, on account of they say their god doesn't go in for that—and for wine and bread, and I can say, 'Hold still! Hands up!' And that's about it."

In Aramaic, Sostratos asked the Ioudaioi if they spoke Greek. They all shook their heads. By the way a couple of them had looked back and forth when he and the guard were talking, he suspected they understood more than they let on. "Why do they share this duty with you?" he asked the Hellenes.

"Because they shared it with the Persians," one of them answered. "That's the deal we've got here—whatever the Ioudaioi had under the Persians, they've still got under us. *They* say Alexander went through here and set that up himself."

"Bunch of drivel," another Hellene said. "Like Alexander would come to the middle of nowhere while he was on his way to Egypt. Fat chance! But we smile and play along. It saves trouble, you know what I mean? As long as we don't mess with their god, everything's fine. You know about that? You can get into a lot of trouble awful quick if you're not careful to be nice to their god."

"Oh, yes," Sostratos said. "I do know about that. My men and I did well enough coming down here from Sidon, anyhow."

"All right, then," the guard said. He and his friends stood aside. "Welcome to Jerusalem."

Such as it is, Sostratos thought. But he kept that thought to himself, not knowing whether the Ioudaioi with the Hellenes had picked up any Greek. He was perfectly wiling to insult Ioudaia in general and Jerusalem in particular, but he didn't care to do it where the locals might understand. That was bad business.

What he did say was, "Thank you." After a moment, he added, "Where is the market square in the city, and can you recommend an inn not too far from it?"

"It's not far from the temple, in the north end of town," the guard answered. "You know about the temple?"

"Some." Sostratos dipped his head. "We were trying to spot it as we came up to the town. I'd like to, and to have a look around the place when I get the chance."

"You can do that." The guard who'd spoken tossed his head. "I take it back—you can do some of that. But only the outer parts are open to people who aren't Ioudaioi. Whatever you do, *don't* try going where you're not supposed to. For one thing, the barbarians are liable to murder you. For another, if they don't, *we're* liable to. Poking your nose in where it doesn't belong is bound to start a riot, and the Ioudaioi get excited enough as things are."

"All right." Sostratos hid his disappointment; he'd looked forward to poking his nose in wherever he could. "What about the inn?" he asked again.

"Ask these fellows." The Hellene pointed to the Ioudaian guards. "You can make the funny noises they do, and they know this miserable place better than we do."

"Good idea." Sostratos switched to Aramaic: "My masters, can you tell me where to find an inn near the market square?"

That almost touched off a riot by itself. Every Ioudaian seemed to have a cousin or a brother-in-law who ran an inn. Each of them praised his relative's establishment and scorned all the others. Their snarling gutturals got louder every minute. They began to shake fists and brandish weapons.

Then one of them said, "*My* brother-in-law already has an Ionian staying at his inn."

"What is your brother-in-law's name? How can I find his inn?" Sostratos asked. The chance to speak his own language with someone else at the inn struck him as too good to pass up.

"He is Ithran son of Akhbor," the guard replied. "His inn is on the Street of Weavers, near the Street of Coppersmiths."

"I thank you," Sostratos said, and gave him an obolos.

One of the Hellenes said, "You paid him too much. Around here, the governors coin these little tiny silver bits, so small it takes ten or twelve of 'em to make a drakhma. They don't even bother counting 'em most of the time—they just weigh 'em. One of those would have been about right."

With a shrug, Sostratos said, "I'm not going to worry about an obolos." He had some of those tiny silver coins, but hadn't known whether giving the Ioudaian guard so small a gift would have been reckoned an insult. He waved to the sailors. "Come on," he told them, and booted his mule into motion. They passed into Jerusalem.

In one way, the place seemed more like a polis than Sidon had. Unlike the Phoenicians, the Ioudaioi didn't build so high as to seem to scrape the sky. Their homes and shops and other buildings had only one or two stories, like those of the Hellenes. In another way, though, Jerusalem was startlingly different from any Hellenic city. Sostratos didn't notice that himself; Aristeidas did. After the Rhodians had got about halfway to Ithran's inn—or so Sostratos thought, anyhow—the sharp-eyed sailor said, "Where are all the statues?"

"By the dog!" Sostratos exclaimed in surprise. "You're right, Aristeidas. I haven't seen a one—not a Herm, not a carved face anywhere."

Even the meanest, poorest polis would have had Herms—carved pillars with Hermes' face and genitals—in front of houses for luck. It would have had images of the gods, too, and of figures from myth and legend, and, these days, perhaps of prominent citizens as well. Sidon had been similar. The statues had been of a different style and had commemorated different gods and different legends, but they'd been there. In Ioudaia, though . . .

Slowly, Sostratos said, "I don't think we've seen a single statue since we came into this country. Do any of you boys remember one?"

After some thought, the three sailors tossed their heads. Moskhion said, "I wonder why that is. Pretty strange, you ask me. Of course, everything in this polluted land is pretty strange, you ask me."

He used such comments to keep his curiosity from getting loose. Sostratos wanted his to run free. When a plump, prosperous-looking Ioudaian came up the street toward him, he spoke in Aramaic: "Excuse me, my master, but may your humble slave ask a question without causing offense?"

"You are a foreigner. Your being here causes offense. I do not wish to speak with you," the Ioudaian answered, and pushed on past him.

"Well, to the crows with *you*, friend," Sostratos muttered.

He and the sailors pressed on toward the inn. A couple of blocks later, he asked another man if he could ask.

This fellow also looked at him as if he was less than welcome in Jerusalem, but said, "Ask. If I do not like the question, I will not answer it."

"Well enough, my master," Sostratos said. When he tried to ask what he wanted to know, he discovered he had no idea how to say *statue* in Aramaic. He had to describe what he meant instead of simply naming it.

"Oh," the Ioudaian said after a little while. "You mean a graven image."

"Thank you," Sostratos told him. "Why no graven images here in Jerusalem? Why none in Ioudaia?"

"Because our god commands us not to make them—it's as simple as that," the Ioudaian answered.

I might have known, Sostratos thought. But that didn't tell him all he wanted to know. And so he asked another question: "Why does your god command you not to make graven images? Again, my master, I mean no offense."

"Our god made mankind in his own image," the Ioudaian said. Sostratos dipped his head, then remembered to nod instead. Hellenes believed the same thing. The Ioudaian went on, "We are forbidden to make graven images of our god, so how can we make them of ourselves, when we are made in his image?"

His logic was as pure as any a Hellenic philosopher might have used. His opening premise, on the other hand, struck Sostratos as absurd. Even so, the Rhodian said, "My thanks." The Ioudaian nodded and went on his way. Sostratos scratched his head. The fellow had shown him a flaw in logic he hadn't thought enough about: if the premise from which it began was flawed, everything springing from that premise would be worthless, too.

It's a good thing we Hellenes don't use such foolish premises. Otherwise, we might make mistakes when we reason and never even notice ourselves doing it, he thought. He rode on for another half a block, feeling pleased with himself for noticing the holes in the barbarian's logic. Then, abruptly, he was much less happy. *Suppose some of the premises from which we reason are flawed. How would we know? Our logic would be only as good as that Ioudaian's.*

He spent some little while chewing on that and found no answer that satisfied him. He might have kept right on chewing on it, too, had Teleutas not asked, "Are we getting close to this miserable inn? I've been walking for a long, long time—feels like forever—and I'd like to get off my feet for a while."

"I'll ask," Sostratos said with a sigh.

He didn't like asking such practical questions of strangers even in Greek. Historical or philosophical queries were a different matter—there his curiosity overcame everything else. But something as mundane as directions? He wished he could get away without them.

Here, though, he obviously couldn't. Taking a deep breath, he made himself beard another Ioudaian: "I crave pardon, my master, but could you direct your servant to the inn of Ithran son of Akhbor?"

The fellow pointed. The flood of words that followed flowed too swiftly for Sostratos to understand.

"Slow! Slow!" he exclaimed.

More pointing. More quick, guttural Aramaic. Sostratos threw his hands in the air. More than any of his own words, the despairing gesture got through to the Ioudaian. On his third go-round, the man really did slow down, enough so that Sostratos could actually figure out most of what he was saying.

"Four blocks up, two to the right, and then one more up? Is that right?" Sostratos asked.

"Yes, of course. What did you think I said?" the Ioudaian asked.

"I was not sure," Sostratos answered truthfully. He gave the man one of the tiny silver coins the local governors issued. The Ioudaian put it in his mouth, as a Hellene might have. It was so small, Sostratos wondered if he would swallow it without noticing.

Ithran's inn proved to be a large, noisy, ramshackle place. When Sostratos and the sailors from the *Aphrodite* got there, the innkeeper was patching a crack in a mud-brick wall with what looked and smelled like a mixture of clay and cow dung. He wiped his hands on his robe, but still had second thoughts about clasping hands with Sostratos. Instead, bowing, he said, "How may I serve you, my master?"

"A room for me. A room for my men," Sostratos replied. "And stalls for the animals."

Ithran bowed again. "It shall be just as you require, of course," he said. He was a few years older than Sostratos, tall and lean, handsome in a swarthy way, with a scar on one cheek that vanished into his bushy black beard.

Sostratos snapped his fingers, remembering something. "Is it not true, sir, that another Ionian is here?" When the innkeeper nodded, Sostratos switched to Greek and asked, "Do you speak the tongue of the Hellenes, then?"

"Speak little bit," Ithran answered in the same language. "Was soldier for Antigonos before wound." He touched his face to show what he meant. "Learn Greek from soldiers." Had he not told that to Sostratos, his accent would have. It was one of the strangest the Rhodian had ever met: half guttural Aramaic, half broad Macedonian. If he hadn't already heard foreigners mangle Greek a lot of different ways, he wouldn't have been able to make head or tail of it.

"How much for the lodgings?" he asked.

When Ithran told him, he thought he'd misheard. The Ioudaian had replied in Aramaic. Sostratos went over to Greek again, but the answer didn't change. He did his best not to show how astonished he was. He haggled a little for form's sake, but he would have been content to take the first price the innkeeper quoted. In Rhodes or Sidon, he would have paid three times as much.

Once he and the sailors from the *Aphrodite* got to their rooms, he remarked on that. He all but chortled with glee, as a matter of fact. But Teleutas put things in perspective. "Of course rooms are cheap here," he said. "You go to Sidon or

Rhodes, those are places people really want to visit. But who in his right mind would want to come to this miserable sheep turd of a town?"

Sostratos considered what he'd seen walking through Jerusalem's narrow, winding, smelly streets. He heaved a sigh. "I hadn't thought of it like that," he admitted, "but to the crows with me if I can tell you you're wrong."

A MACEDONIAN TROOPER TOO far down on the social scale to care about whether he did his own work lugged an amphora of olive oil and a Lykian ham off the *Aphrodite,* down the pier, and back into Sidon. As soon as he was off the ship, Menedemos stopped paying much attention to him. Instead, the Rhodian merchant looked down at the gleaming silver that filled his hands: a mixture of Sidonian silver and coins from all over Hellas.

"By the dog, I really am almost starting to think that pimp of an Andronikos did us a favor when he wouldn't buy our whole shipment of oil," he said. "Garrison troops just keep coming in and taking it away a jar at a time."

"And paying a lot more per jar than he would have," Diokles said.

"Sure enough," Menedemos agreed. "We won't have to unload all the oil to come back to Rhodes with a decent profit." He laughed. "I never would have said anything like that half a month ago—you'd best believe I wouldn't."

He wouldn't have laughed half a month before, either. He'd been sure he would end up stuck with every last amphora of Damonax's olive oil. He'd unloaded much more of it by now than he'd ever thought he would after Antigonos' quartermaster turned him down.

A Phoenician came up the quay toward the akatos. The man wore gold hoops in his ears and a massy gold ring on one thumb; he carried a gold-headed walking stick. "Hail! This ship is from the island?" he said in accented but fluent Greek.

"That's right, best one," Menedemos answered. "What can I do for you today?"

"You sell olive oil, fine olive oil?" the Phoenician asked.

Menedemos dipped his head. "Yes, I do. Ah, if you don't mind my asking, how did you know?"

The Phoenician smiled a thin smile. "You Hellenes can do many marvelous things. You have astonished the world. You have overthrown the Persians, who ruled their great kingdom for generation upon generation. You have cast down the mighty city of Tyre, a city any man would have thought could stand secure forever. But I say this, and I say true: there is one thing you Hellenes cannot do. Try as you will, you cannot keep your mouths shut."

He was probably right. As a matter of fact, from everything Menedemos had seen, he was almost certainly right. The Rhodian found no point to arguing with him. "Would you care to come aboard and sample the oil, ah . . . ?" He paused.

With a bow, the Phoenician said, "Your servant is called Zimrida son of Luli. And you are Menedemos son of Philodemos, is it not so?" He walked up the gangplank, his stick tapping against the timber at each step.

"Yes, I am Menedemos," Menedemos answered, wondering what else Zimrida knew about him and his business. By the way the Phoenician spoke, by the amused glint in his black, black eyes, he was liable to have a better notion of how much silver was aboard the *Aphrodite* than Menedemos did himself. Trying to hide his unease, Menedemos drew the stopper from an already-open jar of oil, poured out a little, dipped a chunk of barley roll in it, and offered the roll and oil to Zimrida.

"I thank you, my master." The Phoenician murmured something in his own language, then took a bite.

"What was that?" Menedemos asked.

"A . . . prayer we use over bread," Zimrida answered, chewing. "In your tongue, it would be, 'Blessed be you, gods who made the universe, who make bread come forth from the earth.' In my speech, you understand, it is a poem."

"I see. Thanks. What do you think of the oil?"

"I will not lie to you," Zimrida said, an opening that immediately made Menedemos suspicious. "It is good olive oil. It is very good, in fact." As if to underscore that, he dipped the barley roll again and took another bite. "But it is not worth the price you are getting for it."

"No?" Menedemos said coolly. "As long as I am getting that price—and I am—I would have to tell you you are wrong."

Zimrida waved that aside. "You are getting that price for an amphora here, for two amphorai there. How much oil will you have left when you must leave Sidon? More than a little, is *that* not so?"

"Then I'll sell the rest somewhere else," Menedemos answered, again trying to sound unworried. Sure enough, Zimrida was liable to know the last obolos lurking half forgotten between a sailor's cheek and gum.

"Will you?" the Phoenician said. "Perhaps. But perhaps not, too. Such things are in the hands of the gods. You will surely know that."

"Why should I sell to you for less than what I'm getting?" Menedemos demanded once more.

"For the sake of getting rid of all your cargo," Zimrida answered. "You would have sold it to Andronikos for a good deal less than the seventeen and a half shekels you are getting. . . . Excuse me, I should say *sigloi* in Greek, eh? You would have sold it to Andronikos for less, I tell you again, and so, if I buy a lot of what you have, you should also sell to me for less. It only stands to reason."

"But I couldn't make a bargain with Andronikos," Menedemos reminded him.

"I know this Hellene," Zimrida said. "I know you Hellenes say we Phoenicians are grasping and money-grubbing and care for nothing in all the world except silver. I tell you, Rhodian, this quartermaster of Antigonos' is the meanest man I have met in all my days, Phoenician or Hellene—or Persian, come to that. If he could save his father's life with a drakhma's worth of medicine, he would try to haggle the price down to three oboloi—and woe betide the old man if he failed."

Menedemos let out a startled bark of laughter. That summed up Andronikos pretty well, all right. "How do I know you'll do any better for me, though?" he asked.

"You might try finding out," the Phoenician said tartly, "instead of saying, 'Oh, no, I'll never sell to you, because I'm making too much money the way things are'"

"All right." Menedemos dipped his head. "All right, by the gods. If you buy in bulk, how much the amphora will you give me?"

"Fourteen sigloi," Zimrida said.

"Twenty- . . . eight drakhmai the jar." Menedemos made the translation into money more familiar to him. Zimrida nodded. Menedemos also translated that into its Hellenic equivalent. He said, "Is that enough profit to satisfy you, buying at twenty-eight and selling at thirty-five, when you know you may not sell all of what you buy?"

The Phoenician's eyes were dark and distant and utterly opaque. "My master, if I did not think so, I would not make the offer, is it not so? I do not ask what you will do with my silver once you take it. Do not ask me what I will do with the oil."

"I won't sell it all to you at that price," Menedemos said. "I'll hold back fifty jars, because I think I may move that many at my price. The rest, though . . . twenty-eight drakhmai is a fair price, and I can't deny it."

I'll be rid of Damonax's miserable oil. By the gods, I really will, he thought, trying to hide his growing delight. *And I'll have plenty of silver to buy things that are cheap here but expensive back in Rhodes.*

"Have we a bargain, then?" Zimrida asked.

"Yes. We have one." Menedemos thrust out his right hand. Zimrida clasped it. His grip was hard and firm. "Twenty-eight drakhmai or fourteen sigloi the amphora," Menedemos said while they held each other, leaving no room for misunderstanding.

"Twenty-eight drakhmai or fourteen sigloi," the Phoenician agreed. "You say you will keep fifty jars. I do not object to

that. And you will already have sold close to a hundred jars."
Sure enough, he knew Menedemos' affairs very well indeed.
The Rhodian didn't even try to deny it—what point? Zimrida
went on, "Then you will sell me . . . two hundred fifty jars,
more or less?"

"About that, yes. Do you want the exact count now, O best
one, or will tomorrow do?" Menedemos asked. He suspected
Zimrida would have an exact count by tomorrow whether he
gave it to the Phoenician or not.

"Tomorrow will do well enough," Zimrida said. "I am glad
we have made this bargain, Rhodian. We will both profit from
it. You will be here at sunrise?"

"Not long after, anyhow," Menedemos answered. "I've
taken a room at an inn." He mimed scratching at bedbug bites.

Zimrida smiled. "Yes, I know the place where you are staying," he said—which, again, surprised Menedemos not at all.
"Tell me, is Emashtart trying to lure you into her bed?"

Hearing that, Menedemos began to wonder if there were
anything at all about Sidon that Zimrida didn't know. "Well,
yes, as a matter of fact," he answered. "Who on earth would
have told you that?"

"No one. I did not know, not for certain," Zimrida told him.
"But I am not surprised. You are not the first, and I do not suppose you will be the last." He started up the gangplank, tapping with his stick at each step.

"Why doesn't her husband keep her happy?" Menedemos
asked. "Then she wouldn't have to play the whore." *Am I saying that?* he wondered. *How many wives have I lured away
from their husbands' beds?* He didn't know, not exactly.
Maybe Sostratos could have given him a precise number; he
wouldn't have been surprised to learn his cousin had been
keeping a tally. But the difference here was simplicity itself:
he didn't want the innkeeper's wife. He couldn't remember
the last time he'd been pursued by a woman who interested
him less.

"Why?" Zimrida echoed. "You have seen her, is it not so?

Having seen her, you can answer the question for yourself. And I will tell you one thing more, my master. Two doors down from the inn lives a potter with a friendly, pretty young wife. She is even friendlier than he thinks."

"Is she?" Menedemos said. Zimrida son of Luli nodded. Menedemos' opinion was that she would have to be friendly to the point of madness to find Sedek-yathon attractive, but women had peculiar taste.

"Good day," Zimrida told him. "I will be here tomorrow with the silver, and with slaves and donkeys to take away the olive oil." Down the pier he went.

"Not bad, skipper," Diokles said when the Sidonian was out of earshot. "Not bad at all, tell you the truth."

"No," Menedemos agreed. "This is better than I hoped for. We really *are* rid of Damonax's oil. I feel so glad to be out from under it, too—as if Sisyphos didn't have to roll his stone up the hill any more."

"I believe that," the oarmaster said. "Now the only worry is, will he really pay us what he said he would?"

"Did you see all the gold he was wearing?" Menedemos said. "He can afford it; I'm sure of that. And he wasn't putting on the dog to try to impress us, the way a cheat would. His robe was fine wool, and it was well worn, too. He hadn't just borrowed it to make himself look richer than he was."

"Oh, no. That's not what I meant. You're right—I'm sure he can afford to pay. But will he try to stiff us some kind of way? You never can tell with barbarians . . . or with Hellenes, either, come to that."

"I only wish I could say you were wrong," Menedemos told him. "Well, we'll find out."

Diokles pointed toward the base of the pier. "Now who's this fellow coming our way, and what's he going to want? Besides our money, I mean?"

"He's selling something—something to eat, I bet. Look at that big, flat basket he's carrying. You see hucksters with that kind of basket all the time back in Hellas," Menedemos said.

"There, they'd have fried fish on it, or songbirds, or most likely fruit. What do you want to bet he's got raisins or plums or figs or something like that?"

They had to wait a little while to find out. The peddler stopped at every ship tied up along the quay. He called out the name of whatever he was selling in Aramaic, which did Menedemos no good at all. Seeing Hellenes aboard the akatos, though, the fellow switched to Greek: "Dates! Fresh dates!"

"Dates?" Menedemos echoed, and the Phoenician nodded. "*Fresh* dates?" The peddler nodded again, and invitingly held out the basket.

"Well, well," Diokles said. "Isn't that interesting?"

"It certainly is," Menedemos said. "Sostratos would be fascinated. I wonder if he's seen any." A few date palms grew in Rhodes; Menedemos had seen them on the islands of the Kyklades, too, and had heard they were also found on Crete. But no date palm anywhere in Hellas gave forth fruit; the climate wasn't warm enough to let the trees come to full maturity. All the dates that reached the land of the Hellenes from Phoenicia and Egypt were sun-dried like raisins or, often, figs.

"You want?" the peddler asked.

"Yes, I want," Menedemos answered. To Diokles, he went on, "We wouldn't be able to take 'em back to Rhodes; they won't keep for us any more than they do for anybody else. But they're still something to talk about."

"Sounds good to me, skipper," the keleustes answered. "I'm always game for something new."

An obolos bought a handful for each of them. Menedemos exclaimed in delight at the sweet taste of his. He'd had dried dates often enough. They cost more than figs, but that didn't always stop Sikon from keeping them in the house. Menedemos tossed his head. It *hadn't* always stopped Sikon from keeping them in the house. With Baukis quarreling over every obolos—no, every khalkos—who could say whether the cook still dared buy them?

Menedemos sighed. He'd mostly been too busy to think

about his father's second wife since sailing out of Rhodes. That was one of the reasons, and not the least, he was so glad when winter ended and good weather returned. Brooding about Baukis could only lead to misery, and to trouble.

To try to get her out of his mind, he asked the huckster, "Do you also sell dried dates?"

The Phoenician didn't speak a lot of Greek. Menedemos had to repeat himself and point to the sun before the fellow got the idea. When he did, he nodded again. "Sell sometimes," he answered. His expression was scornful, though. "Dried dates for servants, for slaves. Fresh dates proper food, good food."

"Did he say what I think he did?" Diokles asked after the huckster went on to the next pier. "Back in Hellas, we eat for a treat what's slave food here? I like our kind of dates. But for honey, you can't find anything much sweeter. Don't know that I'll want 'em any more, though."

"Can't be helped," Menedemos said. "Like I said, fresh dates won't keep on a voyage back to Hellas, any more than fresh grapes would."

"Well, maybe not," the oarmaster said. "But it still galls me that the Phoenicians send us their leavings and keep the best for themselves. There was that miserable fellow with his cheap basket, and he's selling something nobody in Hellas can have. It doesn't seem right."

"Maybe it doesn't, but I don't know what to do about it, either," Menedemos answered. "Fresh is fresh, in figs as in pretty boys, and it won't keep in either one. Boys sprout hair and figs sprout mold, and there's nothing anybody can do to it."

"There ought to be," Diokles insisted.

Menedemos laughed. This was almost the sort of argument he and Sostratos would have all the time. The difference was, Sostratos knew enough in the way of logic to keep the discussion moving in one direction. Diokles didn't, and neither did Menedemos himself. When hashing things out with his cousin, it hadn't mattered. Now it did, and he felt the lack.

He wondered how Sostratos was doing among barbarians who not only didn't have much in the way of logic, but who'd probably never even heard of it. "Poor wretch," Menedemos muttered; if anything could be calculated to drive Sostratos mad, it was people who couldn't think straight.

SOSTRATOS SAT IN Ithran's inn, snacking on fresh dates and on chickpeas fried in cumin-flavored oil and drinking wine. The wine wasn't particularly good, but it was strong; like the Phoenicians, the Ioudaioi drank it unmixed. This was only his second cup, but his head had already started to spin.

Aristeidas and Moskhion had taken some of their pay and gone to visit a brothel. Teleutas would take his turn when one of them got back. The sailors from the *Aphrodite* seemed to have decided Menedemos would kill them if they left Sostratos alone for even a minute. He'd tried to convince them that that was nonsense. They'd paid no attention to his elegant logic.

Ithran's wife was a handsome woman named Zilpah. She came up to Sostratos and Teleutas with a pitcher. "More wine, my masters?" she asked in Aramaic; she spoke no Greek.

"Yes, please," Sostratos replied in the same language. When she poured his cup full, Teleutas also held out his and got it filled again. The idea of drinking neat wine all the time didn't bother him—on the contrary.

His eyes followed Zilpah as she walked away. "What a slut she is, to come and talk with us without even trying to cover her face."

Sostratos tossed his head. "That's our custom, not theirs. She has no reason to follow it. She seems a good enough woman to me."

"Better than good enough," Teleutas said. "She'd be a piece and a half in bed, I bet. Ithran's a lucky dog. I'd sooner lay her than some bored whore who might as well be dead."

"Drag your mind out of the chamber pot, if you'd be so kind," Sostratos said. "Have you seen her paying attention to anyone but her husband? You'll get us thrown out—or worse—if you treat her like a loose woman when she plainly isn't."

"I haven't done anything with her. I haven't done anything to her. I don't intend to," Teleutas said. But he'd had enough wine to speak his mind: "I'm not the only one who keeps watching her all the time, though, and there's nobody can say I am." He sent Sostratos a significant glance.

"Me? Are you talking about me? Go howl, you whipworthy rogue!" Sostratos exclaimed, so sharply that Zilpah, who usually paid no attention to talk in Greek, looked back in surprise to see what the matter was.

Sostratos gave her a sickly smile. She frowned back. But, when neither he nor Teleutas pulled out a knife or started swinging a stool like a flail, she relaxed and went back to what she'd been doing.

"Ha!" Teleutas sounded disgustingly sly. "I knew I put that arrow right in the middle of the target. If you were your cousin, now, you'd already know what she's like under those robes. If she shows you her face, she'll show you the rest, too, easy as you please."

"*Will* you shut up?" Instead of shouting, as he wanted to do, Sostratos kept his voice to a furious whisper so as not to draw Zilpah's notice again. "And I keep telling you, going around unveiled doesn't mean the same thing here as it would back in Hellas. Besides, what would get me murdered faster than trying to seduce the innkeeper's wife?"

"Menedemos wouldn't worry about any of that," Teleutas said. "All he cares about is getting it in." He was, no doubt, right. He spoke with nothing but admiration. But what he saw as praiseworthy seemed blameworthy to Sostratos. Then the sailor added, "You only get in trouble if she doesn't like it. If she does, you're happy as a billy goat."

"That only shows how much—or how little—you know," Sostratos said. The women Menedemos seduced didn't complain and didn't betray him to their husbands. He commonly betrayed himself by taking insane chances to get what he wanted. He was lucky to have come out of Halikarnassos and Taras in one piece.

"I give up," Teleutas said. "But tell me you'd throw her out of bed if you found her in there. Go on—tell me. I dare you."

"It's not going to happen, so there's no point talking about it. Hypothetical questions have their uses, but that isn't one of them."

As he'd hoped, the formidable word gave Teleutas pause. Before the sailor could start up again, Aristeidas walked into the inn, a satisfied smirk on his face. Teleutas gulped down what was left of his wine, then hurried away. Aristeidas sat down on the stool he'd vacated. "Hail," he said to Sostratos.

"Hail," Sostratos answered. When Teleutas came back from the brothel, he would give a thrust-by-thrust description of what he'd done. Aristeidas didn't have that vice. He was content to sit there and keep an eye on Sostratos. To encourage him to do that and nothing more, Sostratos sipped at his wine and half turned away.

That meant his gaze swung toward Zilpah. *What would she be like in bed?* he wondered. It wasn't the first time the question had crossed his mind. He'd got angry at Teleutas not least for noticing. If the sailor had seen his curiosity (that seemed a safer word than *desire*), had Zilpah seen it, too? Worse, had Ithran?

He must know he has a good-looking, good-natured wife, the Rhodian thought. *Because they don't shut their women away from the world, as we do, he must know other men will get to know her, too. He shouldn't mind my admiring her, so long as I do it with my eyes and nothing more.*

Sostratos dipped his head. Yes, that made good logical sense. The only trouble was, logic was often the first thing out the window in dealings between men and women. If Ithran caught him staring at Zilpah, the Ioudaian might prove as jealous as any Hellene would have been on catching a man eyeing his wife.

And, then again, Sostratos found himself ever more

tempted to find out just how interested in straying Zilpah might be. Maybe that was just because he'd gone without a woman for a long time. Maybe a trip to a brothel would cure him of it. But maybe such a visit wouldn't, either. He was beginning to understand the attractions the game of adultery held for Menedemos. One willing woman might be worth several who lay down for a man because they had no choice.

His cousin had always insisted such things were true. Sostratos had always mocked him, scorned him. Now he discovered Menedemos had, at least to some degree, known what he was talking about. Few discoveries could have alarmed him more.

His eyes slid toward Zilpah again. Angrily, he made himself look away. *Did* she know what he was thinking? If she did, what did *she* think? Was it, *Oh, dear, here's another traveler who's liable to make a fool of himself?* Or was it, *He wants me. Do I want him, too?*

How do I find out? Sostratos wondered. He scowled and made a fist. Sure enough, he was liable to be walking down Menedemos' road. "No," he muttered.

"What do you mean, no?" Aristeidas asked.

"Nothing. Nothing at all," Sostratos said quickly, and sipped his wine. His ears heated. *How can I find out whether she wants me without putting my head on the block?* He liked that version of the question much better. *I won't take any chances to find out, not the way Menedemos does.*

That made him feel better, but only for a little while. If he hadn't been trained to root out self-delusion, it probably would have satisfied him longer. As things were, though, he had to wonder, *How do I know what I want? A man who wants a woman isn't likely to think straight.*

Aristeidas said, "Maybe you ought to go get laid, you don't mind my saying so. The girls at this place around the corner are pretty friendly—or they act like they are, anyhow."

If he hadn't added that last little bit, he might have persuaded Sostratos. As things were, he only reminded him of the difference between what was paid for and what was freely given. "Another time," Sostratos said.

"They're funny there, you know?" Aristeidas went on. "Our women always singe off the hair between their legs or else shave it off, the way you shave your face."

Sostratos plucked at his beard. "I don't shave my face," he pointed out.

"No, the way you would if you did," the sailor said confusingly. "The whores here don't shave their bushes, or singe them, or anything. They just let 'em grow. It looks funny, if you ask me."

"Yes, I guess it would," Sostratos agreed. Some men, he supposed, might find the difference exciting. Others might find it disgusting; Aristeidas seemed close to feeling that way. At first, Sostratos thought it wouldn't matter to him one way or the other. Then he imagined Zilpah with a hairy delta at the joining of her legs. The thought roused him more than he'd expected it to, but was that because he imagined hairy private parts or Zilpah's private parts? He wasn't sure.

Zilpah said, "Greetings, my master." She wasn't talking to Sostratos, but to another lodger who'd just walked into the inn.

"Hail," the newcomer replied in Greek. He paused for a moment inside the doorway, letting his eyes adjust to the gloom within. Seeing Sostratos and Aristeidas, he waved. "Hail, Rhodians," he said, and headed over to their table.

"Hail, Hekataios," Sostratos answered. "Always good to talk to a fellow Hellene."

Aristeidas didn't seem to share his opinion. The sailor got to his feet. "I'll see you later, young sir," he said. "I'm sure you'll still be around whenever I come back." He left before Hekataios perched on a stool.

Perched, Sostratos thought, was the operative word. Hekataios of Abdera—a polis on the southern coast of Thrace—was a birdlike man: small, thin, sharp-featured, quick-moving. "How are you?" he asked Sostratos, speaking Ionic Greek with a strong Attic overlay. Sostratos' Doric accent had that same overlay, so the two of them sounded more like each other than less educated, less traveled men from their home cities would have.

"Well, thanks," Sostratos answered.

Zilpah came up. "What would you like, my master?" she asked Hekataios.

"Wine. Bread. Oil," he replied in extremely rudimentary Aramaic.

"I would also like bread and oil, please," Sostratos told the innkeeper's wife.

As Zilpah went off, Hekataios returned to Greek: "I'm jealous of you. You really speak the language. I didn't think I'd need to when I started traveling through Ioudaia, but Hellenes are so thin on the ground here, I've had to start learning 'ow to go bar-bar-bar myself." Every once in a while, but only every once in a while, he would forget a rough breathing, as Ionians usually did.

"I'm not fluent," Sostratos said. "I wish I knew more."

"I'd have an easier time with my researches if I could make those funny grunting noises, but I do seem to manage even without them."

Zilpah came back with the food and drink. As Sostratos dipped a chunk of brown bread in olive oil, he said, "Jealous? Speaking of jealous, O best one, you have no idea how jealous I am of you. I have to buy and sell as I go. I can't travel about the countryside for the sake of love of wisdom." He was also jealous of the wealth that let Hekataios of Abdera do exactly that, but kept quiet about that bit of envy. To him, the other was more important.

Hekataios shrugged. "When I was in Alexandria, I got interested in the Ioudaioi. They're such a peculiar people." He rolled his eyes. "And so I decided to come here and find out about them for myself."

"You're lucky Antigonos' men didn't decide you were spying for Ptolemaios," Sostratos said.

"Not at all, my dear fellow." Hekataios tossed his head. "I

had written out for me a safe-conduct stating that I was a lover
of wisdom traveling for the sake of learning more about the
world in which I live, and so was not to be harassed by mere
soldiers."

"And it worked when you got to the frontier?" Sostratos
asked.

"Plainly not. Plainly I was seized and tortured and crucified," Hekataios answered. Sostratos coughed and flushed. He
could be sarcastic himself, but he'd met his match and then
some in Hekataios of Abdera. The older man relented: "As a
matter of fact, Antigonos' officers 'ave been more than a little
helpful. From everything I've heard and seen, Antigonos himself is a man of learning."

"I suppose so," Sostratos said. "I know Ptolemaios is. But I
wouldn't want to have either one of them angry at me, and
that's the truth."

"There I cannot argue with you in the least," Hekataios
agreed. "Then again, however, the weak are always wise not
to fall into the clutches of the strong. So it has been since the
gods—if gods there be—made the world, and so it shall re-
main as long as men stay men."

"It's a good thing you said that in Greek, and that Ithran
wasn't here to understand it," Sostratos observed. "Let a
Ioudaian hear 'if gods there be' and you've got more trouble
for yourself than you really want. They take their own invisible deity very, very seriously."

"I should say they do!" Hekataios dipped his head. "They
always have, as best I've been able to determine."

"Tell me more, if you'd be so kind," Sostratos said. "This
sort of thing is meat and drink to me. I wish I had the chance
to do what you're doing." *I wish I didn't have to worry about
making a living,* was what that boiled down to. Hekataios'
family had to own land out to the horizon up in Abdera, or to
have got wealthy some other way, to let him spend his life
traveling and learning.

He smiled what struck Sostratos as a superior smile. But

that half sneer didn't last. What could be more attractive than somebody who was interested in what one was doing? "As I was telling you the last time we talked," Hekataios said, "these Ioudaioi came here from out of Egypt."

"Yes, you did say that; I remember," Sostratos answered. "You were telling me some sort of pestilence there made them flee the country?"

"That's right." Hekataios smiled again, this time without a trace of superiority. "You *were* paying attention, weren't you?"

"Of course I was, best one. Did you doubt it?"

"As a matter of fact, yes. When you discover how few people have the least interest in the past and how it came to shape the present, you eventually begin to believe no one but yourself has any interest in such things at all. Being proved wrong is always a pleasant surprise."

"You've found me," Sostratos said. "Please do go on."

"I'd be glad to." Hekataios paused to sip his wine and gather his thoughts. Then he said, "When this plague arose in Egypt, the common people there believed some divinity had caused it."

"That's not surprising," Sostratos said. "They wouldn't have known of anyone like Hippokrates who might have offered a different explanation."

"No, indeed not." Hekataios of Abdera dipped his head. "Now Egypt at this time—it would have been about the time of the Trojan War, I believe—was full of all sorts of foreigners, and—"

"Excuse me, most wise one, but how do you know that?" Sostratos broke in.

"For one thing, the Egyptian priests say so," Hekataios answered. "For another, the Ioudaioi have a legend that they themselves came 'ere to this country from out of Egypt. Does that satisfy you?"

"Thank you. Yes, it does. But history is only as good as its sources and the questions you ask of them. I did want to know."

"Fair enough. You *do* understand the finer points, don't

you?" Hekataios said, and Sostratos wanted to burst with pride. The Abderan went on, "All these foreigners, naturally, worshiped their own gods and had their own rites. The native Egyptians' rituals were being ignored and forgotten. The Egyptians—I suspect that means their priests, but I can't prove it—feared their gods would never have mercy on them in respect to the plague unless they expelled the foreigners from their land."

"And so they did?" Sostratos asked.

"And so they did," Hekataios agreed. "The most outstanding foreigners banded together and went to places like Hellas: Danaos and Kadmos were some of their leaders."

"I've also heard Kadmos was a Phoenician," Sostratos said.

"Yes, so have I. Perhaps he stopped in Phoenicia on his way up to Hellas from Egypt. But most of the exiles ended up here in Ioudaia. This isn't far from Egypt, and in those days no one at all lived here, or so they say."

"I see," Sostratos said. "But how did the customs of the Ioudaioi become so strange?"

"I *am* coming to that, O best one," Hekataios answered. "Their leader at this time was a man outstanding for courage and wisdom, a certain Moüses. He refused to make any images of the gods, because he did not think his god was of human form."

"The Ioudaioi have kept that custom ever since," Sostratos said. "I've seen it."

"One could hardly help seeing it—or not seeing it—in this country," Hekataios said, a little superciliously. "That is the reason the sacrifices this Moüses established differ from those of other nations. So does their way of living. Because of their expulsion from Egypt, he introduced a way of life that was rather antisocial and hostile to foreigners."

"I don't know if they're truly hostile to foreigners, or if they simply want to be left alone," Sostratos said. "They haven't treated me at all badly. They just don't want me trying to tell them about the way we Hellenes live."

"Well, if that doesn't make them hostile to foreigners all by itself, I don't know what would," Hekataios said.

Sostratos frowned. He thought he saw a logical flaw in the other man's argument, but for once he let it go. Hekataios of Abdera had studied the Ioudaioi more thoroughly than he had—had studied them as he wished he might have, in fact. "Now that you've learned all these things, I hope you write them down so other Hellenes can have the benefit of your inquiries," Sostratos said.

"I intend to, when I get back to Alexandria," Hekataios answered. "I want my name to live forever."

"I understand," Sostratos said, and sighed. *You have to write one day, too,* he told himself, *or who will remember you once you're gone?* He sighed again, wondering if he would ever find the time.

"HAIL," EMASHTART SAID WHEN MENEDEMOS came out of his bedchamber to start another day. "How you?" the innkeeper's wife went on in her fragmentary Greek. "You to sleep good?"

"Yes, thank you, I slept well enough," Menedemos answered around a yawn. He scratched. Beyond any doubt, the room had bugs. He saw no point to complaining about it. What room at an inn didn't? Oh, a clean one happened now and again, but you had to be lucky.

Emashtart was kneading dough on a countertop. She looked up from the work with a sly smile. "You not alonely, to sleep all lone?"

"I'm fine, thanks," Menedemos said. She'd taken this tack

before. Her attempts at seduction would have been funny if they hadn't been so sad—and so annoying. *This is Sostratos' revenge on me,* Menedemos thought. *Here's a woman I don't want and never would, and what does she care about? Adultery, nothing else but.*

She wasn't subtle about it, either. "You to sleep better, you having woman with you. Woman make you all tired, no?"

"I'm plenty tired by the end of the day, believe me," Menedemos replied.

"Once upon a time, I famous beauty. Men to fight for me all over Sidon," the innkeeper's wife said.

Menedemos almost asked her whether that had been during Alexander's reign or that of his father, Philip of Macedon. Alexander had been dead for fifteen years now, Philip for almost thirty. Had Menedemos been only a few years younger, a few years crueler, himself, he would have done it. But Emashtart probably wouldn't have understood him. And, if she had, she would have been insulted. *She's enough trouble the way things are,* the Rhodian thought, and kept quiet.

When, as usual, he refused to rise to her bait, she sent him a venomous look. After pounding the dough harder than she really needed to, she asked, "Is true, what they to say of Hellenes?"

"I don't know," Menedemos answered innocently, though he had a pretty good idea what would come next. "What do they say about Hellenes?"

Emashtart glared at him again. Maybe she'd hoped he would help. But when he didn't, she wasn't shy about speaking her mind: "They say, Hellenes sooner to put up boy's arse than woman's pussy."

"Do they?" Menedemos exclaimed, as if he'd never heard of such a thing before. "Well, if we did that all the time, there wouldn't be any more Hellenes after a little while, now would there?" He waited to find out whether she understood. When he saw she did, he gave her his sweetest, most charming smile. "Good day," he said, and strolled out of the inn.

Behind him, the innkeeper's wife said several things in Aramaic. Menedemos understood not a word of them, but they sounded pungent. He wondered what Sostratos would have made of them. After a moment, he tossed his head. Not knowing might be better.

"Miserable old whore," he muttered. "Why doesn't her husband take charge of her?" A moment's thought gave him a couple of possible answers. Maybe Sedek-yathon feared his wife. Or maybe he didn't want her, either, and didn't care what she did. *Well, he can go howl,* Menedemos thought. He hurried off toward the *Aphrodite*. These days, he wished he'd stayed aboard the merchant galley instead of taking a room in Sidon. It would have been less comfortable but would have offered him more peace of mind.

"Hail," Diokles called as Menedemos came up the quay. The oarmaster was staying aboard the *Aphrodite*. Every so often, he'd make a sally into Sidon after wine or a friendly woman. Other than that, he seemed content to do without a roof over his head and a mattress under him. Indeed, he kept up his usual habit of sleeping sitting up on a rower's bench and leaning against the planking of the ship for support. Thinking about that, Menedemos didn't mind the innkeeper's wife so much.

"Hail yourself," he said. "How are things here?"

"Tolerable, skipper, tolerable," Diokles answered. "You're out and about earlier than usual, aren't you?"

"Work doesn't wait," Menedemos said. He didn't always take that attitude. But he would have needed a much more enjoyable distraction than the innkeeper's wife to make work wait. He went on, "One of the Hellenes from Antigonos' garrison gave me the name of a merchant here who deals in fine cloth. I'm going to take some of our Koan silk over to him, see what it'll bring in this part of the world."

"Sounds good to me, skipper," the keleustes said. "We're a long ways from Kos, that's for sure, so silk won't come here every day, especially when it's not going through fourteen middlemen. You ought to get a good price."

"I hope so." Menedemos hid a smile. On a Rhodian ship, everybody could speak knowledgeably of trade.

"Does this Sidonian fellow know any Greek?" Diokles asked—another relevant consideration, with Sostratos on his way to Engedi.

"That soldier said he did," Menedemos answered. "Said he does a fair amount of business with Hellenes, so he's had to learn."

"All right." The oarmaster dipped his head. "Good fortune go with you, then."

"Thanks." Menedemos poked through the cargo, wishing he'd made Sostratos leave him a more complete manifest. After a little while, though, he found the oiled-leather sacks that protected bolts of silk from seawater. They weren't heavy, of course. He slung three of them over his shoulder and set off for the cloth merchant's house.

The Hellene in Macedonian service had given him what sounded like good directions: the street opposite the entrance to the temple of Ashtart (Aphrodite's Phoenician counterpart), third house on the left. But Menedemos took a wrong turn somewhere. In a town built by Hellenes, he would have had an easy time spotting a temple, for it would have stood out above the roofs of houses and shops. But the Sidonians built tall. *How am I supposed to find this polluted temple if they go and hide it?* he thought irritably.

He tried asking people on the streets, but they started at him in blank incomprehension and gave back streams of gibberish. Not for the first time since coming here, he wished he'd spent part of the winter learning Aramaic, too. At last, he found a couple of Antigonos' soldiers lurching out of a wineshop.

They were drunk, but they understood Greek. "The temple of Ashtart, is it?" one of them said. "You want a go at the temple prostitutes? Most of 'em are ugly."

"No, not the prostitutes." Menedemos tossed his head, thinking, *Maybe another time.* "I'm trying to find a house near the temple."

"Ugly girls," the soldier repeated. His pal told Menedemos

how to find the temple and even declined the tip the Rhodian tried to give him. That, to a Hellene, was a minor miracle. Menedemos followed his directions and found they worked. That wasn't a minor miracle, but came close.

"Third house on the left, street opposite the entrance," Menedemos muttered when he got to the temple. The street seemed more of an alley, narrow and cramped. Menedemos planted his bare feet with care. When he knocked on the door to the third house on the left, a dog inside began to bark. It sounded like a big, fierce dog. After a minute, somebody on the other side of the door said something in Aramaic.

In Greek, Menedemos answered, "Is this the house of Zakerbaal son of Tenes, the cloth merchant?"

A pause inside. The dog kept barking. Then, very suddenly, it stopped with a yelp, as if someone had kicked it. One word came through the door, in heavily accented Greek: "Wait."

Menedemos waited. After what seemed to him much too long, the door opened. A short, wide-shouldered, muscular man looked out at him. "I am Zakerbaal. Who are you, and what do you want?" he asked. His Greek was considerably better than his slave's.

"I'm Menedemos son of Philodemos, of Rhodes," Menedemos began.

"Ah. The fellow from the merchant galley." Zakerbaal nodded. His heavy features brightened into a smile. "You're at Sedek-yathon's inn these days, aren't you? Tell me, has his wife tried pulling you into bed yet?"

"Zeus!" Menedemos muttered, gaping at the cloth merchant. A moment later, he realized he would have done better to swear by wing-footed Hermes, messenger of the gods and god of rumor. He pulled himself together enough to dip his head in agreement and say, "Yes, that's right, best one. Er— how did you know?"

"Merchants hear about merchants, my master," the Phoenician answered. "I wondered if you might call on me. Or did you mean about the innkeeper's wife? She is no secret in

Sidon, believe me. But come in. Drink wine with me. Eat dates and raisins. Show me your wares. What have you there?"

"Silk from Kos, the finest fabric in the world," Menedemos said proudly.

"I know of it. I will gladly look at it," Zakerbaal said. The reaction was polite, interested, but less than Menedemos had hoped for. Was Zakerbaal so formidable a bargainer? Or was it that, never having seen silk, he didn't know how splendid a cloth it was? Menedemos hoped for the latter.

He followed the Phoenician into the courtyard of his house: a courtyard rather bare by Hellenic standards, for it had no garden. The dog growled and lunged at Menedemos, but a chain brought it up short. Zakerbaal spoke in his own guttural language. Servants brought stools and took the dog away. They fetched a basin of water, in which Zakerbaal ceremoniously washed his hands. Menedemos followed his host's lead. Refreshments followed. The wine was quite good. "Where does this come from?" Menedemos asked.

"Byblos, my master," Zakerbaal replied.

As was the Phoenician way, he served the wine neat. That concentrated its bouquet, which measured up against that of any Menedemos had ever known, even the finest Khian and Thasian vintages. "Very good," he repeated. Its flavor didn't quite match that marvelous, flowery bouquet, but it was more than worth drinking: good enough, in fact, to make Menedemos wonder whether he could get some and bring it back to Rhodes.

With the wine, Zakerbaal's slave brought out figs and dates and raisins and balls of dried chickpeas fried in olive oil and dusted with cumin. Menedemos found those very tasty, but spicy enough to raise his thirst. He drank more wine to put it down.

Zakerbaal chatted affably about matters of little importance while his guest ate and drank. Presently, the cloth merchant said, "Perhaps you would be so good, my master, as to show me some of this famous Koan silk you have. Your servant has heard of it, and would be glad to learn its quality."

"I'd be happy to, most noble one," Menedemos answered. His hands were steady as he undid the rawhide lashing that held one of his leather sacks closed. His wits were steady, too, or he thought they were. He hadn't been silly enough to pour down a lot of unmixed wine, not with a dicker ahead of him. He took out a bolt of the finest, filmiest silk he had and held it up against the sun so Zakerbaal could see how nearly transparent it was. "Imagine a beautiful woman wearing—or almost wearing—robes of this," he told the Phoenician.

Zakerbaal smiled. Whatever he was imagining, he liked it. He reached for the silk but politely stopped before touching it. "May I feel of it?" he asked.

"Of course." Menedemos handed him the fine, fine cloth. "There's nothing like it in all the world."

"Perhaps," was all Zakerbaal said. His fingers traveled the fabric as delicately, as knowingly, as if exploring that imaginary woman's body. He held the silk up to his face so he could peer through it, even breathe through it. When he lowered it, he nodded to Menedemos. "This is good. This is very good. I must tell you, though, my master, and I mean no offense: I have seen better."

"What? Where?" Menedemos yelped. "There *is* no better fabric than Koan silk." He'd heard plenty of ploys for lowering prices. This had to be another one. "If you've got better, O marvelous one"—a bit of sarcasm Zakerbaal might or might not notice—"please show it to me."

He confidently expected the Phoenician to say he'd just sold it, or that he'd seen it year before last in another town, or to give some other excuse for not producing it. Instead, Zakerbaal called out to the slave again, rattling off a string of Aramaic gutturals and hisses. The slave bowed and hurried away. Zakerbaal turned back to Menedemos. "Be so kind as to wait but one moment, my master. Tubalu will fetch it."

"All right." Cautiously, Menedemos sipped more wine. Did

Zakerbaal really believe he had cloth finer than Koan silk? Menedemos tossed his head. The barbarian couldn't possibly. Or, if he did, he had to be wrong.

Tubalu took considerably longer than the promised moment. Menedemos began to wonder if he would come back at all. But he did, carrying in his arms a good-sized bolt of cloth. He bore it as tenderly as if it were a baby. Even so, Menedemos turned to Zakerbaal in perplexity and annoyance. "I mean no disrespect, best one, but that is only linen, and not the finest linen, either."

The Phoenician nodded. "Yes, that is only linen. But it is also only a cover for what lies within, just as your leather sacks cover your Koan silk and keep it safe." He took the bolt of linen from Tubalu as carefully as the slave had carried it. Unfolding it, he drew from it the fabric it concealed and held that out to Menedemos. "Here. Behold with your own eyes, with your own fingers."

"Ohhh." Menedemos' soft exclamation was altogether involuntary. For the first time, he understood exactly how Sostratos had felt the moment he set eyes on the gryphon's skull. Here, too, something completely unexpected and at the same time completely marvelous came before a Hellene for the first time.

Menedemos hadn't cared so much about the gryphon's skull. One had to love wisdom for its own sake more than he did to get excited about ancient bones, no matter how unusual they were. This . . . This was different.

He'd shown Zakerbaal the finest Koan silk he had. Next to the fabric the Phoenician merchant showed him, that cloth might almost have been coarse wool by comparison. Here, it was as if someone at a loom had managed to weave strands of air into cloth. The delicate blue of the dye only made the resemblance stronger, for it put him in mind of the color of the sky on a perfect spring day.

Then, ever so gently, Menedemos touched the cloth. "Ohhh," he said again, even more softly than before. Under his hand, the fabric was as soft, as smooth, as the fanciest courtesan's skin to a lover's fingers.

Zakerbaal didn't even gloat. He only nodded again, as if he'd expected nothing else. "You see, my friend," he said.

"I see." Menedemos didn't want to stop stroking the . . . silk? He supposed it had to be silk, though it was far finer, far smoother, far more transparent than anything the Koan weavers made. He forced himself to stop staring at it and looked up to Zakerbaal. "I see, O marvelous one"—for once, he meant that literally—"I see, yes, but I don't understand. I know cloth—well, I thought I knew cloth—but I never dreamt there could be anything like this. Where does it come from?"

"I know cloth, too—well, I thought I knew cloth," the Phoenician answered. He eyed the blue silk with as much wonder as Menedemos showed, and he'd seen it before. "Your Koan fabric comes here now and again. When I first saw—that—I thought it more of the same. Then I got a better look, and I knew I had to have it." He might have been a rich Hellene speaking of a beautiful hetaira.

And Menedemos could only dip his head in agreement. "Where does it come from?" he asked again. "The Koans would kill to be able to make cloth like this. They never imagined anything so fine, and neither did I." As a trader, he should have stayed blasé, uninterested. He knew that. Here, in the presence of what might as well have been a miracle, he couldn't make himself do it.

Zakerbaal's slow smile said he understood. It even said he might not take advantage, which surely proved how miraculous that silk was. "It comes from out of the east," he said.

"Where?" Menedemos asked for the third time. "The east, you say? India?"

"No, not India." The cloth merchant shook his head. "Somewhere beyond India—maybe farther east, maybe farther north, maybe both. The man from whom I bought it could tell me no more than that. He did not know himself. He had not brought it all the way, you understand—he had bought it from another trader who had got it from another, with who knows how many more since it left the land where it was made?"

Menedemos stroked the astonishing silk once more. As his fingers slid across its amazing smoothness, the gryphon's skull came to mind again. It too had entered the world Hellenes knew from out of the trackless east. Alexander had conquered so much, people—especially people who still dwelt by the Inner Sea—often thought he'd taken all there was to take. Things like this were a reminder that the world was larger and stranger than even Alexander had imagined.

Like a man slowly emerging from a trance, Menedemos looked up from the silk to Zakerbaal. "How much of this do you have?" the Rhodian asked. "What price do you want?"

Zakerbaal sighed, as if he too didn't much care to return to the mundane world of commerce. "I have twelve bolts in all, each much like this in size, some in different colors," he answered. "I would have bought more, but that was all the trader had. Price?" He smiled a sad smile. "I would say it is worth its weight in gold. And now I have made you want to flee, I doubt not."

"No, best one." Menedemos tossed his head. "If I'd heard about this without seeing it, I would have laughed in your face. Now . . . Now I understand why you say what you say." He did laugh then. "Telling you something like that makes me a terrible trader, one who deserves to be overcharged. But here, for this, I can't help it. It's the truth."

"You respect the cloth," Zakerbaal said seriously. "I respect you because of it. With stuffs like this, we throw out the ordinary rules." He mimed tossing the contents of a chamber pot out the window and into the street below.

"Worth its weight in gold, you say?" Menedemos asked, and the Phoenician nodded. Menedemos didn't even try to argue with him. Considering how far the silk had come, considering how fine it was, that seemed fair. But he didn't want to give up gold or silver for the silk, not directly. "What would you say if I offered you half again its weight in my Koan silk here?"

"I would say, that is not enough," Zakerbaal replied at once. "Koan silk is all very well. I mean no insult, Rhodian, but I say this is far better. I say it is so much better, if ever it comes here often and in large quantities, the Koans will go out of business, for they cannot compete with it."

Half an hour before, Menedemos would have laughed at him. With the silk from the distant east in his lap, under his fingers, he suspected Zakerbaal might be right. Even so, he said, "All right. Koan silk is not so splendid. How can I deny it? But Koan silk is still very fine cloth. Koan silk is still no common thing itself in Phoenicia. So—one and a half times the weight is not enough, you say. What would be enough?"

The Phoenician looked up toward the sky. His lips moved silently. Sostratos got the same faraway expression when he was calculating. At last, Zakerbaal said, "Three and a half times."

"No. That's too much." Menedemos tossed his head once more. Zakerbaal had indeed dealt with a good many Hellenes, for he showed he understood the gesture by a small nod of his own. Menedemos, for his part, knew that nod wasn't one of agreement, only of acknowledgment. He went on, "Here in Sidon, you'll be able to get just about as much for Koan silk as you will for this cloth from out of the east, because they're both foreign and exotic in Phoenicia."

"There is, perhaps, some truth in what you say, best one, but only some," the cloth merchant replied. "What I have is better than what you are trying to trade for it, though."

"And I'm offering you more Koan silk than the eastern silk I'd get in return," Menedemos said. In Hellas, Koan silk wasn't exotic, but it was expensive. Just how much he might get for twelve bolts of these new stuffs . . . He didn't know just how much, but he was ever so eager to find out. "Three and a half times by weight leaves me no profit." He doubted even that, but Zakerbaal didn't need to know his doubts.

"Three times, then," the Phoenician said. "Bolt for bolt,

Koan silk is heavier than the fabric I have, because yours is so much coarser and thicker."

They haggled for the next hour, each calling the other a liar and a thief. Menedemos sometimes enjoyed taking on a skilled opponent, even if that meant ending up with a little less than he would have otherwise. By Zakerbaal's small smile, he felt the same. The closer they came to a bargain, the harder they dickered over tiny fractions. At last, they settled on Koan silk for two and seventeen thirty-seconds the weight of the eastern silk.

"My master, you should have been born a Phoenician, for you are wasted as a Hellene," Zakerbaal said when they clasped hands.

"You're a formidable fellow yourself, most noble one," Menedemos replied truthfully. He resolved to make sure that Zakerbaal weighed both kinds of silk on the same pan of his scales. So skillful a bargainer would surely find a way to make everything possible work for him. But the cloth merchant didn't even try setting one kind in one pan and the other in the other. Maybe that was a compliment to Menedemos. Maybe it meant Zakerbaal had some other way to cheat. If so, Menedemos didn't spot it.

The Rhodian's burden on the way back to the *Aphrodite* was lighter than what he'd taken from the ship, but he didn't mind. In fact, he felt like kicking up his heels. No, he didn't mind at all.

I SHOULDN'T BE doing this, Sostratos told himself. *It's wrong. If Menedemos knew, how he would laugh. . . .*

Then he laughed at himself. He was enjoying himself too much to care whether his cousin would mock him.

"Keep going," he said, panting a little. "Don't stop there."

"I don't intend to, my dear," Hekataios of Abdera answered. "I was only getting a pebble out of my sandal. The temple of the Ioudaioi is just around this next corner here."

I should be in the market square, selling whatever I can, Sostratos thought. *But Menedemos does know I aimed to learn about the Ioudaioi, too.* Of one thing he was certain: his cousin wouldn't have minded if he'd stayed away from the market square to bed the innkeeper's pretty wife. That was how Menedemos would have entertained himself in Jerusalem. *If I find my amusement in different places, Menedemos will just have to make the best of it.*

Along with Hekataios, Sostratos rounded that last corner. Having done so, he stopped in his tracks and pointed. *"That's* a temple?" he said, unable to hide his disappointment.

"I'm afraid so," Hekataios told him. "Not very impressive, is it?"

"In a word, no," Sostratos said. He was used to the colonnades, the entablatures, and carved and painted friezes that marked out a sacred place throughout the Hellenic world. Where poleis were rich, the shrines would be built of gleaming marble. Where they were not so rich, or where no more suitable stone was close by, limestone would serve. He'd even heard of temples where tree trunks did duty for columns.

The Phoenicians worshiped their gods with rites different from the ones Hellenes used. And yet, as Sostratos had seen in Sidon, they'd come under the influence of Hellenic architecture, so that from the front their shrines looked much like those to be found anywhere in the Hellenic world from Syracuse to Rhodes. The same held true for other barbarians like the Samnites and Karians and Lykians.

Not here. Seeing this temple in the northern corner of Jerusalem was almost like a blow in the face: it reminded Sostratos just how far from home he was. A stone wall defended the perimeter of the temple precinct. It wasn't the strongest work Sostratos had ever seen, but it was a long way from the weakest. Laughing, he said, "I thought this was part of the citadel."

"Oh, no, best one." Hekataios of Abdera tossed his head and pointed northwest, up toward higher ground. *"There's* the citadel, surrounding the governor's palace."

Sostratos craned his neck. "I see. It's well sited. In any fight that breaks out between the governor and the Ioudaioi, the governor and his garrison here have the advantage of the ground."

"Er—yes." Hekataios dipped his head. "I hadn't thought of it in quite those terms, but you're perfectly correct. The palace, of course, dates back to Persian days, so the Great Kings must have been nervous about trouble from the Ioudaioi even then. An interesting point."

"It is, isn't it?" Sostratos said. "How old is the temple?"

"It was built in Persian times, too," Hekataios answered. "But it's supposed to lie on the spot where an older temple stood before Jerusalem was sacked." He shrugged regretfully. "History in these parts is pretty much a blur before the days of the Persians, unless you want to believe all the mad fables about Queen Semiramis and the rest of those absurdities."

"They are hard to swallow, aren't they?" Sostratos agreed. "Hard to make any real sense of history when you're trying to investigate times too distant to let you question the people who shaped events."

"Just so. Just so," Hekataios said. "You *do* understand how these things work, don't you?"

"I try." Sostratos realized the older man took him for a merchant and nothing more. With some asperity, he said, "I may have to buy and sell for a living, O marvelous one, but I'm not an ignorant man on account of that. I studied at the Lykeion in Athens under the great Theophrastos. I may not be lucky enough to study full time"—the look he sent his companion was frankly jealous—"but I do what I can in the time I have."

Hekataios of Abdera coughed a couple of times and turned as red as a modest youth hearing praise from his suitors for the first time. "I beg your pardon, my dear. Please believe me when I tell you I meant no offense."

"Oh, I believe you." That wasn't the problem. The problem was all the assumptions Hekataios had been making. Sostratos didn't know what to do about those. He doubted he could do anything about them. Hekataios was obviously a gentleman from a privileged family. Like anyone who didn't have to get his hands dirty, he looked down his nose at men who did. He was polite about it; Sostratos had met plenty of *kaloi k'agathoi* who weren't. But the bias remained. With a sigh, Sostratos said, "Let's go on toward the temple, shall we?"

"Certainly. That's a good idea." Hekataios sounded relieved. By talking about the curious customs of the Ioudaioi, he could escape talking—and thinking—about the curious customs of the Hellenes. "We can go into the lower court here—anyone's allowed to do that. But we can't go into the upper, inner, courtyard, the one surrounding the temple itself. Only Ioudaioi are allowed to do that."

"What would happen if we tried?" Sostratos asked—he wanted to get as close a look at the temple as he could. Unlike the shrines in Sidon, this one, he could see even from a distance of several plethra, had been built by men who knew nothing of Hellenic architecture. It was a plain, rather dumpy rectangle of a building, oriented east-west, its face adorned with sparkling gold ornaments, a curtain over the entrance. In front of the temple stood a large altar—ten cubits high and twenty broad, Sostratos guessed—of unhewn white stones.

But Hekataios of Abdera was tossing his head in dismay. "What would happen if we tried? First off, they wouldn't let us. The priests of the Ioudaioi run things here—Antigonos' men don't. Second, if we did manage to sneak into the inner court, they would say we polluted it just by being there. They take ritual cleanliness *very* seriously. Didn't you see that in your travels through Ioudaia coming here?"

"Well, yes," Sostratos said. "But even so—"

"But me no buts," the other Hellene said. "What would happen after we tried to go into the inner court is that Jerusalem would see rioting of a kind you wouldn't believe. Even if the Ioudaioi didn't murder us—and they probably would—Antigonos' men would want to, for causing so much trouble. You have to be a dangerous madman to want to try to go up there. Do you understand me?"

"I suppose so," Sostratos said sulkily. Hekataios waited.

Sostratos realized something more was expected of him. The guard at the gate had warned him about the temple of the Ioudaioi, too, so it really was a problem for Hellenes. More sulkily still, he gave his word: "I promise."

"Good. Thank you. You worried me there for a moment," Hekataios said. "Now we can go on."

"Thank you so much," Sostratos said. Hekataios of Abdera ignored his sarcasm. They entered the outer courtyard. Looking around, Sostratos remarked, "It's all cobblestones. Where are the bushes and saplings that mark off a holy precinct?"

"They don't use them," Hekataios said. "They think this is enough."

"Strange," Sostratos said. "Very strange."

"They're strange people. Hadn't you noticed that?"

"Oh, you might say so." Sostratos' voice was dry. "What I think is especially peculiar is the day of rest they take every seven."

"They say their god created the world in six days and rested on the seventh, and so they think they should imitate him."

"I understand *that*," Sostratos said. "It's not what bothers me. I don't believe their god did what they say he did, but never mind that. If they spent that seventh day relaxing, well and good. But it's more than that. They won't light fires or cook or do anything much at all. If soldiers attacked them, I don't think they would fight back or try to save their own lives. And that's crazy, you know."

"As a matter of fact, yes. I agree with you completely," Hekataios of Abdera told him. "One thing quickly becomes plain when you start looking at the way the Ioudaioi live their lives: they have no sense of proportion whatsoever."

"Sense of proportion," Sostratos echoed. He dipped his head. "Yes, that's exactly what they're missing. Nicely put, noble one."

"Why, thank you, my dear. You're very kind." Hekataios looked suitably modest.

"I was talking with my cousin—he's back in Sidon now—on the way here," Sostratos said. "One of the proverbs from the Seven Sages came up: 'Nothing too much.' I don't believe that one would appeal to the Ioudaioi." He didn't think it appealed to Menedemos, either, but he didn't care to discuss that with a near stranger.

Laughing, Hekataios dipped his head, too. "You're right. The Ioudaioi, I think, do everything to excess."

"Or sometimes, as with their day of rest, they even do nothing to excess," Sostratos said.

Hekataios laughed again. "Oh, that's very nice. I *do* like that." He made as if to clap his hands.

Sostratos went up as close to the terraced stairway leading up to the inner courtyard as he could—close enough to make Hekataios look nervous. He stared at the temple. "*How* old is it?" he asked.

"It was built, I believe, in the reign of the first Dareios," Hekataios replied. "But, as I said before, this isn't the first temple. There was another one before it, but that one was destroyed when Jerusalem was sacked."

"I wish we could figure out exactly when that was," Sostratos said.

"Before the days of the Persian Empire, as I said before—that's all I can tell you," the other Hellene said with a shrug. Then he snapped his fingers. "Come to think of it, though, the Ioudaioi do have a sort of a history that talks about such things, but who knows what's in it? It's not in Greek."

"A history? A written one?" Sostratos asked. Hekataios dipped his head. Sostratos said, "I read Aramaic—a little, anyhow."

"*Do* you? How strange." Hekataios raised an eyebrow. "But that won't help, I'm afraid."

"What? Why not?"

"Because this book the Ioudaioi have isn't in Aramaic," Hekataios answered.

"What? Well, by the dog, what language is it in? Egyptian?"

"I don't think so." Hekataios pondered, then tossed his head. "No, it can't be. I know what Egyptian looks like—all those little pictures of people and animals and plants running riot all over everywhere. No, I've seen this book, and it looks as if it ought to be in Aramaic, more or less, but it isn't. It's written in the language the Ioudaioi used to speak before Aramaic spread all over the countryside, the language the priests use when they pray." He pointed toward the men in fringed robes and fringed, striped shawls who were sacrificing a sheep at the altar.

"Is that what it is?" Sostratos said in relief. "I was listening to them before we started talking just now, and I couldn't make heads or tails of what they were saying. I thought it was just me. Whatever language that is, it sounds a lot like Aramaic—it has the same set of noises at the back of the throat—but the words are different."

"That sort of thing happens with us, too," Hekataios observed. "Ever try to make sense out of what Macedonians say when they start talking among themselves? You can't do it, no matter how much the language sounds as though it ought to be proper Greek."

"Some Hellenes can—the ones from the northwest, whose own dialect isn't too far away from what the Macedonians speak," Sostratos said. "So it's not quite the same."

"Maybe not. I certainly don't care to have to try to figure out Macedonian, and I have to do it in Alexandria every now and again." Hekataios made a wry face. "The men with the money and the power too often aren't the ones with the culture."

"No doubt, O best one," Sostratos said politely. He wanted to scream in Hekataios' face instead, something like, *You stupid, self-centered twit, you don't know when you're well off. You've got patrons in Alexandria, and what do you do? You complain about them! And yet you have the leisure to travel around doing research, and you'll be able to sit down and write your book and have scribes make copies of it, so that it has a chance to live forever. How would you like to deal in perfume and beeswax and balsam and linen and silk instead? Do you think you would find the time to touch pen to papyrus then? Good luck!*

He hoped none of that showed on his face. If it did, it was liable to look uncommonly like murder. He hadn't known this sort of savage envy since he'd had to go home from the Lykeion. For him, a spell in Athens had been the capstone on his education. For others there, it had been the first step toward a life lived loving wisdom. He went back to the world of trade. They went on to the world of knowledge. As his ship sailed out of Peiraieus, bound for Rhodes, he'd wanted to kill them, simply because they got to do what he so desperately wanted to do.

Over the years, his resentment of scholars had faded. It had . . . till he met Hekataios, who complained of problems Sostratos would have been delighted to have.

"Shall we go back?" Sostratos said. "I don't think I want to see any more." What he really didn't want to do was think about Hekataios' good fortune.

"Well, why not?" Hekataios spoke with obvious relief. Now Sostratos hid a smile, though it was a bitter one. Hekataios must have feared he would try to go up the terraced stairs to the second courtyard, the one forbidden to all but the Ioudaioi. From everything he'd seen of the locals, though, he knew how foolish that would have been. No matter how curious he was, he didn't want to touch off an insurrection or get himself killed.

He sent a last glance up to the governor's residence above the temple of the Ioudaioi. That residence was a fortress in its own right. A Hellenic or Macedonian soldier up on the walls peered out and recognized more Hellenes in the lower courtyard below, doubtless by the short chitons they wore and by Hekataios' clean-shaven face. The sentry waved and called out, "Hail."

"Hail," Sostratos replied. Hekataios waved back to the soldier. To Hekataios, Sostratos remarked, "Always good to hear Greek."

"Oh, my dear, I should say so," Hekataios replied. "And you, at least, speak some of this ghastly local language. For me, it might as well be the grunting of animals. I shall be so *very* glad to return to Alexandria, where Greek prevails— though there are Ioudaioi settling there, too, if you can believe it." He rolled his eyes, but then resumed: "I shall also be glad to have the spare time to gather all my notes and memories together, and then to sit down and write."

Sostratos did not bend down, pry a cobblestone out of the ground, and brain Hekataios with it. Why he didn't, he never knew, then or afterwards. The scholar walked on, still breathing, still talking intelligently, still unaware of how much he took for granted and Sostratos craved with a deep, hopeless, desperate yearning.

One of these days. One of these years, Sostratos thought. *I'll do as Thales did, and get so rich I can afford to do as I please. I can gather all my notes and memories together, and then sit down and write. I can. And I will.*

Back at the inn, they found chaos. Teleutas, for once, hadn't caused it: he was off at a brothel down the block. The innkeeper was shouting at Moskhion in bad Greek, and the former sponge diver was shouting right back.

Moskhion turned to Sostratos in obvious relief. "Gods be praised you're here, young sir. This fellow reckons I've done something really dreadful, and I never meant no harm, not to nobody."

"Outrage! Insult!" Ithran shouted. "He profanes the one god!"

"Calm, O best one. Calm, please," Sostratos said in Greek. He switched to Aramaic: "Peace be unto you. Peace be unto us all. Tell your slave. I will make it right, if I can."

"He profanes the one god," the innkeeper repeated, this time in Aramaic. But he didn't seem quite so ready to burst into flames as he had a moment before.

"What happened?" Sostratos asked Moskhion, trying to take advantage of the relative peace and quiet.

"I got hungry, young sir," Moskhion answered. "I craved a bit of meat—haven't had any for a long time. Wanted some pork, but I couldn't make this silly barbarian here understand the word for it."

"Oh, dear." Now Sostratos knew what sort of trouble he was in. "What did you do then?"

"I asked the abandoned rogue for a potsherd, sir, so I could draw him a picture," Moskhion said. "He understood 'potsherd' well enough, Furies take him. Why couldn't he understand 'pork'? He gave me the sherd, and I drew—this."

He showed Sostratos the piece of broken pot. On it he'd scraped with the tip of a sharp knife a commendable picture of a pig. Sostratos had had no idea he could draw so well. Maybe Moskhion himself hadn't even known. But the gift, plainly, was there. Sostratos said, "What happened next?"

"I gave it to him, and he pitched a fit," the sailor replied. "That's where we were when you walked in just now, young sir."

"They don't eat pork, you know," Sostratos said. "They think a pig's a polluted animal. We haven't seen any more pigs than statues in Ioudaia, remember? That's why he got angry. He thought you were outraging him and his god both."

"Well, calm the silly fool down," Moskhion said. "I didn't want any trouble. All I wanted was some spare ribs, or something like that."

"I'll try." Sostratos turned toward the innkeeper and switched to Aramaic: "My master, your slave's man meant no offense. He does not know your laws. He only wanted food. *We* eat pork. It is not against our laws."

"It's against ours," Ithran fumed. "Pigs make everything ritually unclean. That is why no pigs and no swine's flesh are allowed in Jerusalem. Even that image of a pig is liable to be a pollution."

The Ioudaioi forbade graven images of men because men were made in the image of their god, whose image was forbidden them. By such reasoning, Sostratos could see how the picture of a beast reckoned unclean might itself be unclean. But he said, "It is only an image. And you fought for Antigonos. You know Ionians eat pork. Moskhion meant no offense. He will apologize." In Greek, he hissed, "Tell him you're sorry."

"I'm *hungry,* is what I am," the sailor grumbled. But he

dipped his head to Ithran. "Sorry, buddy. I didn't mean to get you all upset. Zeus knows that's so."

"All right." Ithran took a deep breath. "All right. Let it go. No. Wait. Give me that image, one of you." Sostratos handed him the potsherd. He set it on the floor, then stomped it with all his strength. Under his sandal, it shattered into tiny pieces. "There. Gone for good."

Sostratos hated to see such a fine sketch destroyed. For the sake of peace, though, he kept quiet. Hekataios of Abdera hadn't wanted him to cause a riot, and he didn't want Moskhion to cause one. "What was all that?" Hekataios asked now. "Parts of it were in Aramaic, so I couldn't follow." Sostratos explained. When he was done, Hekataios said, "*Euge!* You were lucky there—lucky and clever. The Ioudaioi can go mad when it comes to pigs."

"Yes, I figured as much," Sostratos said. "But it was just a misunderstanding."

"Most of the time, misunderstandings here don't get straightened out," Hekataios said. "They end up in blood. A good thing Master Ithran knows at least something of Hellenic customs, or it would have been worse."

Zilpah had come in while Hekataios was talking. As Hekataios and Sostratos went back and forth in Greek, Ithran explained to his wife in Aramaic what had been going on. Sostratos listened to them with perhaps a quarter of an ear. The mere sound of Aramaic reminded him of the truth of what Hekataios had said. This was not his country. These were not his people. Disaster could so easily overwhelm him, disaster springing from something as trivial as a sailor getting a yen for meat after going a long time without. And if disaster did overwhelm him here, on whom could he call for help?

No one. No one at all.

"We did get through it," he told Hekataios. "In the end, that's all that really matters."

The other Hellene said something in reply. Now Sostratos hardly heard him. He was watching Zilpah listening to her husband's account of the affair—which was, for all Sostratos

knew, quite different from the way it had looked to Moskhion
and him and Hekataios of Abdera.

She's as foreign as any of the other Ioudaioi, Sostratos told
himself: another undoubted truth. But she was, to his eyes, a
great deal more decorative than any of the others. That
shouldn't have made so much difference. It shouldn't have,
but it did.

She happened to look his way at the same time as he was
looking at her. He knew he should have turned his gaze in a
different direction. Staring at another man's wife could easily
bring trouble down on his head. If he hadn't been able to see
that for himself, traveling with Menedemos should have
pounded it home.

And yet . . . He looked, and could not look away. The longer
he stayed in Jerusalem, the more he understood Menedemos'
madness, the madness that had only infuriated him before. The
line of Zilpah's jaw, the way her lips opened just a little when
she breathed, the shine of her eyes, her wavy midnight hair . . .

He knew what he was thinking as he looked at her. But what
was going through her mind while she looked back at him? He
was sure she could read his face as readily as he would have
read an inscription in the agora at Rhodes. And if she could,
she had but to say a word to scarred and dangerous Ithran
there, and hovering danger would hover no longer, but strike.

She did not say the word. Sostratos wondered why.
Moskhion stalked out of the inn, muttering about getting mut-
ton if he couldn't have pork. Hekataios of Abdera said, "I am
going to write up what I saw today, so that I don't forget it.
Hail." Off he went.

Sostratos perched himself on a stool. "Wine, please," he
said in Aramaic.

"Here." Ithran dipped it out of a jar. He also poured a cup
for himself. Before drinking from it, he murmured a brief
prayer. He watched Sostratos pour out a few drops onto the
floor as a libation for the gods and let out a sigh. Had that sigh
held words, it would have meant something like, *You are only
a Hellene. You know no better.*

"Peace be unto you," Sostratos said—not as the usual greeting, but a real request. "We do not aim to offend you. We have our own customs."

"Yes, I know that," Ithran answered. "You cannot help being what you are. And to you also peace." Would he have said that had he noticed Sostratos eyeing Zilpah? Not likely.

The next day was the sabbath of the Ioudaioi. No one lit the fire that morning: that would have been reckoned work. Hekataios went up to the fortress overlooking the temple to talk with one of Antigonos' officers whose acquaintance he had made. Sostratos had intended to see what he might find in the market square, but he knew the square would be quiet and empty on the day of rest. He still thought the local custom a colossal waste of time, but the Ioudaioi cared for his opinion not at all.

With nothing useful to do, he stayed at the inn. Oil and yesterday's bread and wine made a tolerable breakfast. Aristeidas and Moskhion went off to the brothel to find out if the women there were also taking a day of rest. When the two sailors didn't come back right away, Teleutas began fidgeting on his stool. After a bit, he asked Sostratos, "You're not gong anywhere much today, are you?"

"Who, me?" Sostratos said. "I intended to be in Macedonia this morning and Carthage this afternoon. Why?"

"Heh," Teleutas said—almost but not quite a laugh. "Well, if you aren't going anywhere, I suppose I can head on over to the girls myself. I mean to say, you're not likely to get in trouble just hanging around here at the inn, are you?"

"That depends," Sostratos answered gravely. "If the Stymphalian birds and the Hydra come by, I may have to fight them, because I haven't seen Herakles anywhere in these parts."

"Heh," Teleutas said again. He hurried out of the inn, perhaps as much to get away from Sostratos as to choose a woman for himself.

Sostratos hid a smile. He no more wanted Teleutas' company than the sailor wanted his. He held up a hand. Zilpah nodded to him and asked, "Yes? What is it?"

"May your slave have another cup of wine, please?" he said in Aramaic.

"Yes, of course, I'll get it for you." She hesitated, then added, "You need not be so formal for such a small request."

"Better too formal than not enough," Sostratos answered. She set the cup of wine on the little table in front of him. He said, "Thank you very much."

"You're welcome," Zilpah said. "You speak more of our language than any other Ionian I have known. That was good yesterday. You managed to show your man meant no harm with his picture of the unclean beast. That could have caused trouble, bad trouble." Her face clouded. "Some Ionians laugh at us because of what we believe. We do not laugh at other folk for what they believe. It is not for us, but we do not laugh at it."

"I know what I believe," Sostratos said, sipping at the wine.

"What is that?" Zilpah asked gravely.

"I believe you are beautiful." Sostratos hadn't known he was going to say that till the words were out of his mouth.

Zilpah had started to turn away from him. She turned back, suddenly and sharply. If she was angry, Sostratos knew he'd found himself more trouble than he'd helped Moskhion escape. But her voice was quiet, even amused, as she answered, "And I believe you have been away from your home too long. Maybe you should go down the block with your friends."

Sostratos tossed his head. He needed a heartbeat to remember to shake it instead. "I do not want that. The body of a woman . . ." He shrugged. Trying to tell Zilpah how he felt in a language he didn't speak at all well was one more problem, one more frustration. He wondered if even Menedemos would have had any luck under such circumstances. He did his best, continuing, "The body of a woman matters not so much. A woman I care about, that matters."

If Zilpah squawked and ran for her husband, he'd already said enough to get himself in deep trouble. But she didn't. She said, "I have had this happen before. A traveling man happens to be kind enough to think I am pretty, and then he thinks he is in love with me because of that. It is only foolishness, though.

How can you think you care about me when you do not even know me, not in any way that matters?"

That was the sort of question Sostratos often asked his cousin when Menedemos imagined he'd fallen in love with some girl who'd caught his eye. Having it come back at him would have been funny if he'd looked at it the right way. Just then, he was in no mood for that.

"I know ways that matter," Sostratos said. Zilpah giggled. He realized he'd used the feminine verb form, as she had. "I know," he said again, this time correctly. "I know you are kind. I know you are patient. I know you are generous. I know these are good things for a woman to be." He managed a wry grin. "I know my Aramaic is bad."

She smiled at that, but quickly became serious once more. "The other Ionian here tried to give me money so I would give him my body," she said. "I have had that happen before, with us and with foreigners."

"If I want a woman I can buy, I will go down the block," Sostratos said.

"Yes, I believe you. You are a strange man, do you know that? You pay me these compliments—they make me want to blush. I am an innkeeper's wife. I do not blush very often. I have seen too much, heard too much. But I think you mean what you say. I do not think you say it to lure me into bed."

"Of course I mean it," Sostratos said. Menedemos might not have, but he was a practiced seducer. Telling anything but what he saw as the truth hadn't occurred to Sostratos.

Zilpah smiled again. "How old are you, Ionian?"

"Twenty-seven," he answered.

"I would have guessed you younger," she told him. He wondered if that was praise or something else. Maybe she didn't know, either; she went on, "I have not had anyone say such things to me."

"Not even your husband?" Sostratos asked. "He should."

"No." Zilpah's voice was troubled. "When no one says these things, you do not miss them. But when someone does . . . I am not going to take you into my bed here, Sostratos son of Lysistratos, but I think you have made my marriage a colder place even so."

"I did not mean to do that," Sostratos said.

"No. You meant to lay me. That would have been simpler than making me wonder why I have had no praise since I stood under the wedding canopy with my husband."

"Oimoi!" Sostratos said. That was Greek, but Zilpah took the meaning from the sound, as he'd thought she could. In Aramaic, he went on, "I did not mean to make you unhappy. I am sorry I did."

"I don't think you made me unhappy," Zilpah said. "I think I was unhappy. I think I have been unhappy for years without even knowing it. You made me see that. I ought to thank you."

"I am surprised you are not angry," Sostratos said. When someone pointed out to him something he hadn't seen before, he was—usually, when he remembered to be—grateful. Most people, from everything he'd seen, got angry when anyone made them change their view of the way the world worked. If anything did, that marked the difference between those who aspired to philosophy and ordinary men.

"Angry? No." The innkeeper's wife shook her head. "It is not your fault. It is Ithran's fault for taking me as much for granted as the bed he sleeps in, and my fault for letting him do it, for not even noticing he was doing it." Sudden tears glinted in her eyes. "Maybe it would have been different if either of our children had lived."

"I'm sorry," Sostratos said. So many families had a lament like Zilpah's. Infants died so readily, burying them inside city walls brought no religious pollution, as it did with the bodies of older people.

"Everything is as the one god wills," Zilpah said. "The priests say this, and I believe them, but I cannot understand why he willed that my babies died."

"We Ionians wonder about these same things," Sostratos said. "We do not know. I do not think we can know." He finished his wine and held out the cup to her. "May I have more, please?" He was usually very moderate with the unmixed stuff, knowing how strong it was, but nerves made him want a refill.

"Of course. You hardly drink at all," Zilpah said. It didn't seem that way to Sostratos, but he let it go. She poured his cup full and her own as well. He spilled out a little libation onto the floor, while she murmured the blessing the Ioudaioi used over wine. They both drank. Zilpah managed a small laugh. "Here we are, pouring down wine to drown our sorrow because neither of us got what we wanted."

"That is funny, is it not? Or it could be," Sostratos said. The wine, sweet and thick, went down very smoothly. Sostratos hooked another stool with his ankle and slid it over to the table where he sat. "Here. No need to stand. If you do nothing else, you can sit by me."

"I suppose so." When Zilpah did sit, she perched on the edge of the stool like a nervous bird. She gulped her wine, got up to pour herself another cup, and sat again. "I don't know why I drink," she remarked, looking down into the purple wine. "After I am done, everything will still be the same."

"Yes," said Sostratos, who felt the same way himself. "But while you drink . . ." He usually spoke as she did. Today, he found himself praising wine.

"For a little while, yes," Zilpah said. "For a little while, even things you know are foolish seem . . . not so bad."

In Greek, Sostratos would have answered, *That's why people use wine as an excuse for doing things they would never dream of doing sober.* He knew he couldn't say anything so complex—and so far removed from the world of trade and bargaining—in Aramaic. But a nod, once he remembered to use the local gesture and not the one he was used to, seemed to get his meaning across well enough.

"More wine?" Zilpah asked him. Her cup was already empty again.

His was still half full. He took another sip from it and nodded again. He would never have drunk so much neat wine in the morning back in Rhodes, but he wasn't in Rhodes any more. If he had a thick head later in the day, then he did, that was all.

Zilpah got up and filled a pitcher with wine. She stood beside Sostratos to pour more into his cup. *People use wine as an excuse for doing things they would never dream of doing sober,* Sostratos thought again. Before he could tell it not to, his right arm slipped around Zilpah's waist.

She could have screamed. She could have broken the pitcher over his head. She could have done any number of things that would have led to quick irrevocable catastrophe for him. She didn't. She didn't even try to twist free or to knock his hand away. She just shook her head a little and murmured, "Wine."

"Wine," Sostratos agreed. "Wine, and you. You are lovely. I would make you happy, if I could. If you let me."

"Foolishness," Zilpah said. But was she talking to him or to herself? Sostratos couldn't tell, not till she set the pitcher on the table and sat down on his lap.

His arms went round her in glad surprise. He lifted his face as she lowered hers. Their lips met. Her mouth tasted of wine and of her own sweetness. She sighed, back deep in his throat.

The kiss went on and on. Sostratos had thought the wine was making him drunk. This . . . Next to this, the wine was as nothing. He slipped one hand under her robes. It slid up past her knee, up the smooth flesh of her inner thigh, toward the joining of her legs.

But that hand, hurrying toward her secret place, must have reminded her just what game they'd started playing. With a little, frightened moan, she jerked away and sprang to her feet again. "No," she said. "I told you, I would not take you to my bed."

Had she been a slave, he might have pulled her down to the floor and had her by force. Such things even happened to free Hellenic women of good family every now and again, as when they were coming back at night from a religious procession. Comic poets wrote plays about the complications that rose from mischances like that. But Sostratos had never been one to think of force first. And using it on a foreign woman in a town full of barbarians . . . He tossed his head.

He couldn't help letting out a long, angry breath. "If you did not mean to finish, I wish you had not started," he said. The throbbing in his own crotch told him how much he wished that.

"I am sorry," Zilpah replied. "I wanted a little sweetness— not too much, but a little. I didn't think you . . ." She let that trail away. "I didn't think."

"No. You did not. Neither did I." Sostratos sighed. He gulped down the rest of the wine in the cup. "Maybe I should go down the block after all."

"Maybe you should," Zilpah said. "But now, Ionian, now what am *I* supposed to do?" And for that, no matter how much Sostratos prided himself on his cleverness, he had no answer at all.

MENEDEMOS HAD TAKEN his time going over to the dyeworks on the outskirts of Sidon. He kept finding excuses for staying away. The real reason was simple: the dyeworks that made the Phoenician cities famous stank too badly for him to want to get close to them.

That stench came into the city when the wind blew the wrong way. But Sidon, like any town around the Inner Sea, had plenty of other foul odors to dilute that one. Out by the dyeworks, the smell of rotting shellfish was both overpowering and unalloyed.

How did anyone ever find out that murexes, once crushed, yielded a liquor which, after it was properly treated, became the marvelous Phoenician crimson dye? he wondered. Some inventions seemed natural to him. Anyone could see that sticks floated, and all sorts of things caught the wind and were pushed along by it. From there to rafts and boats could only be a small step. But purple dye? Menedemos tossed his head. It struck him as very unlikely.

He wished he had Sostratos along. Seeing a Phoenician

smashing shells with a mallet, he called out, "Hail! Do you speak Greek?"

The fellow shook his head. But he knew what Menedemos was trying to ask, for he said something in Aramaic in which the Rhodian caught the word *Ionian.* The Phoenician pointed to a shack not far away. He gave forth with another sentence full of coughing and hissing noises. Again, Menedemos heard the local word for a Hellene. Maybe that meant someone who spoke his language was in there. He hoped so, anyhow.

"Thanks," he said. The Phoenician waved and went back to smashing seashells. After a moment, he paused, picked up a morsel of meat, and popped it into his mouth. *Can't get your opson any fresher than that,* Menedemos thought.

When he opened the door to the shack, a couple of Phoenicians, one stout, the other lean, looked up at him. The stout one began to speak before he could say a word: "You must be the Rhodian. Wondered when you were going to show up around here." His Greek was fluent, colloquial, and sounded as if he'd learned it from someone right on the edge of the law.

"Yes, that's right. I'm Menedemos son of Philodemos," Menedemos said. "Hail. And you gentlemen are . . . ?"

"I'm Tenashtart son of Metena," the stout Phoenician answered. "This is my brother, Ithobaal. Miserable son of a whore doesn't speak any Greek. Pleased to meet you. You want to buy some dye, right?"

"Yes," Menedemos said. "Uh—where did you learn Greek so . . . well?"

"Here and there, pal, here and there," Tenashtart answered. "I've done some knocking around in my time, you bet I have. There are towns in Hellas . . . But you didn't come here to listen to me bang my gums."

"It's all right," Menedemos told him, more fascinated than anything else. "Do you mind if I ask you a question?"

"Sure," Tenashtart said expansively. "Go right ahead."

"In the name of the gods, O best one, how do you stand the stink?" Menedemos blurted.

Before answering, Tenashtart said something in Aramaic to Ithobaal. Both brothers laughed. Tenashtart went back to Greek: "Everybody asks us that. Doesn't matter who: Phoenicians, Hellenes—even Persians, back when I was a kid. They all say the same thing."

"And do you give them the same answer?" Menedemos asked. Tenashtart *had* spent a lot of time among Hellenes; he dipped his head instead of nodding, as almost all barbarians would have done. Menedemos said, "Well, what *is* the answer?"

"You want to know the truth?" the dyemaker said. "The truth is, we both spend so much time with the shells, we don't even notice it any more. Only time I know it's there is when I've been away for a bit. Then I smell it for a while when I get back. But except for that, it's not even there for me, any more than air is there for me, you know what I mean?"

"I suppose so," Menedemos answered. "It seems hard to believe, though."

Tenashtart said something else in Aramaic. His brother nodded. Ithobaal pointed out toward the workman crushing murexes, touched his formidable nose, and shrugged. He might have been saying he didn't notice the reek of rotting shellfish, either.

Even to Menedemos, it didn't seem quite so appalling as it had when he first got to the dyeworks. All the same, he remained a long way from not noticing it. He wished he were as oblivious as the two Phoenician brothers.

Tenashtart said, "You come all this way to talk about nasty smells, or do you want to do some business?"

"Let's do business," Menedemos said agreeably. "What do you charge for a jar of your best dye?" When the Sidonian told him, he let out a yip. "That's outrageous!"

Tenashtart spread his hands. "That's the way it goes, buddy. I've got to make a living, same as everybody else."

But Menedemos wagged a finger at him. "Oh, no, you don't, my dear. You're not going to get away with that, not for a minute you won't, and I'll tell you why not. I've seen Phoenicians over in Hellas selling crimson dye for the very same price, and that's after their middleman's markup. What do they pay you?"

"You must be talking about men from Byblos or from Arados," Tenashtart said easily. "They've got lower quality dye, so naturally they can charge less."

Menedemos tossed his head. "Oh, no, you don't," he said again. "For one thing, they'd say Byblian or Aradian dye's as good as Sidonian. With Tyre wrecked, nobody has a sure best any more. And, for another, I've seen Sidonians selling for the very same price."

Tenashtart's engagingly ugly grin showed a missing bottom front tooth. "I like you, Rhodian, to the crows with me if I don't. You've got balls. But tell me this—why should I give a Hellene the same rate I give my own people?" He translated his words for Ithobaal, who nodded again.

"Why?" Menedemos said. "I'll tell you why. Because silver is silver, that's why. Now kindly tell your brother *that* in Aramaic, too."

"You've got your nerve," Tenashtart said, but he sounded more admiring than otherwise. He and Ithobaal did go back and forth in their own language, a crackle of sounds strange to Greek ears. When they finished, Tenashtart named another price, this one only a little more than half as high as what he'd suggested before.

"Well, that's better," Menedemos said. "I don't know that it's good—I still think you charge your own folk less than that—but it's better. We'll talk more later. First, though, do you want silver, or are we working a trade?"

"You came here in an akatos," Tenashtart said. "That means you're bound to have goodies tucked away under the rowers' benches. What have you got, and what do *you* want for it?"

"My cousin took perfume into the country of the Ioudaioi, but I've still got plenty left," Menedemos answered. "A merchant galley can carry a lot more than a pack donkey's able to."

"You talking about the rose essence you Rhodians make?" Tenashtart asked. Menedemos dipped his head. The Sidonian said, "That's good stuff, and it doesn't get over here all that often. You sell it in those little tiny jars, though, don't you?"

"Yes. It's concentrated, so a little goes a long way," Menedemos said.

"What do *you* want for one of those jars? No. Wait." Tenashtart held up a dye-stained hand. "Let's settle on how many jars of perfume go into one jar of dye. As long as we're talking about jars, and not sigloi or drakhmai, it seems friendlier, whether it really is or not."

It didn't seem friendly to Menedemos for very long. Tenashtart mocked his initial offer. He scorned Tenashtart's. Each accused the other of being a brigand descended from a long line of pirates and thieves. Each claimed the other was thinking of his own profit at the expense of the deal as a whole. Each was undoubtedly right.

Half a digit's breadth at a time, they got closer together. The closer they got, the more they railed at each other. After a while, Menedemos grinned at Tenashtart and said, "This is fun, isn't it?"

Tenashtart got up from his stool and folded Menedemos into a bear hug. "Ah, Hellene, if you'd only stay in Sidon for a year, I'd make a Phoenician out of you, to the crows with me if I wouldn't." Then he made an offer hardly more reasonable than his previous one.

Menedemos didn't want to be a Phoenician. Coming out and saying so struck him as impolitic. He made another offer of his own. Tenashtart rained curses down on him in Greek and Aramaic. They both started laughing, which didn't mean they stopped yelling at each other or trying to best each other in the bargain.

When at last they clasped hands, they were both sweating. "Whew!" Menedemos said. "Now we're both going to say we got cheated, and then we're both going to make a pile of money on what we just did. But if we see each other again in a couple of years, neither one of us will admit it."

"That's how it goes," Tenashtart agreed. "You're pretty good, Hellene, Furies take me if you're not."

"You're pretty good yourself," Menedemos replied. *I skinned you,* he thought. Tenashtart, no doubt, thought the same. It was a good bargain all the way around.

AS SOSTRATOS AND THE SAILORS FROM THE *Aphrodite* left Jerusalem, Teleutas heaved a sigh. "That wasn't such a bad town, even if I couldn't speak the language," he said. "The wine was pretty good—"

"And plenty strong," Moskhion broke in. "Drinking it unmixed isn't so bad, once you get used to it."

"No, not half bad," Teleutas agreed. "The girls were friendly, too, or they acted friendly enough once you gave 'em silver." He eyed Sostratos. "You ever get yourself laid while we were there, young sir?"

"Yes, once or twice," Sostratos answered truthfully. "The girls in the brothel I went to were just girls in a brothel, as far as I'm concerned. They didn't seem special one way or another."

He couldn't say the same about Zilpah, but he didn't care to talk about the innkeeper's wife with his escorts. For one thing, he hadn't actually done anything with her. For another, even if he had . . . He tossed his head. Menedemos bragged about his adulteries. Sostratos sometimes thought his cousin committed them not least so he could brag about them. *If I ever seduce another man's wife, I hope I'll have the sense to keep my mouth shut about it.*

Aristeidas asked, "How long before we get to this Engedi place?"

"Shouldn't be more than a couple of days," Sostratos answered. "It's supposed to lie by the edge of what they call the Lake of Asphalt, or something like that. They say all sorts of funny things about that lake. They say it holds so much salt, nothing can live in it. And they say that if you walk out into it, you can't even sink—it's so salty, you just float in it, the way an egg will float in water if you put enough salt into it."

"People say all sorts of silly things," Aristeidas observed. "Do you believe any of that nonsense?"

"Right now, I don't know whether to believe or disbelieve," Sostratos said. "Some strange things turn out to be true: look at peafowl. And look at the gryphon's skull we had last year. Who would have thought gryphons were anything but legendary beasts till we came across that? But I'm not going to worry about it now, not when I'll see for myself in a day or two."

"All right. I guess that's fair," Aristeidas said. "This place we're going to, though—it can't be as big as Jerusalem, can it?"

Sostratos tossed his head. "I wouldn't think so, anyhow. By the way the Ioudaioi talk, Jerusalem is the biggest city in their land."

"It's not much," Teleutas said.

He spoke slightingly as a matter of course. Even if things did impress him, he didn't let on. Here, though, Sostratos had to agree with him. Next to Athens or Rhodes or Syracuse, Jerusalem *wasn't* much. Sidon, with its tall buildings, outdid this little local center, too. One day before too long, he supposed, people would forget all about it. Even the temple of the Ioudaioi would probably lose its importance as people hereabouts took on more and more Hellenic ways.

Eventually, he thought, *they'll sacrifice a pig on that altar and no one will care. The world belongs to us Hellenes nowadays.*

The road from Jerusalem toward Engedi first ran south through the hilly country in which the main town of the Ioudaioi sat and then east toward the Lake of Asphalt. Sostratos had asked several different people in Jerusalem how far Engedi was and had got several different answers. No one had ever properly measured distances in this country, as Alexander's surveyors had done during his campaigns of conquest. Eventually, too, Sostratos supposed, whichever of Antigonos or Ptolemaios held on to Ioudaia would do the job. Till then, each man's opinion seemed as good as that of the next—and was certainly maintained with every bit as much passion. Though the precise distance remained loudly in doubt, Sostratos did think Engedi lay about two days' journey from Jerusalem, as he'd told Aristeidas.

He and his men paused to rest in the heat of the day at the little town of Bethlehem. They bought wine from a tavern-keeper and used it to wash down the loaves they'd brought from Jerusalem. The taverner's daughter, who was about ten, stared and stared at them as she carried the wine to their table. Sostratos would have bet she'd never seen a Hellene before.

"Peace be unto you," he said in Aramaic.

She blinked. "And to you also peace," she answered. If it hadn't been a set phrase, she might have been too startled to bring it out. Her dark eyes were enormous in a skinny, none too clean face that still promised considerable beauty as she got older.

"What's your name?" he asked.

"Maryam," she whispered. Then, obviously gathering her courage, she asked, "What's yours?"

"I'm Sostratos son of Lysistratos," he answered. The funny-sounding foreign syllables made her giggle. She skipped away. Sostratos asked the taverner, "Why did you give her a name that means 'bitter'? She seems a happy child."

"Yes, so she does now," the man answered, "but bearing her almost killed my wife. For weeks, I thought it would. That's why, stranger."

"Oh. Thank you," Sostratos said, curiosity satisfied. And then, remembering his manners, he added, "I am glad your wife did not die."

"Thank you again." But the taverner's face did not lighten. "She lived another three years, then perished of—" The word was meaningless to Sostratos. He spread his hands to show as much. The Ioudaian arched his back, threw back his head, and clenched his jaw. He was a good mime, good enough to make Sostratos shiver.

"Oh. Tetanus, we call that in Greek," the Rhodian said. "I am very sorry, my friend. That is a hard way to die. I have seen it, too."

With a shrug, the tavernkeeper said, "Our god willed it so, and so it came to pass. Magnified and sanctified be the name of our god throughout the world he created according to his will." The way he rattled off the words, they had the sound of a prayer he knew by heart. Sostratos would have liked to ask him about that, too, but Moskhion distracted him by asking what he was talking about, so he didn't.

He didn't even think of it again till he and the sailors had already left Bethlehem. When he did, he muttered to himself in annoyance. Then he rode the mule to the top of a little hill and, peering east, got a good look at the Lake of Asphalt.

What first struck him was how far *down* the water looked. These hills weren't very high, but the lake seemed far below him. Teleutas looked in that direction, too. "In the name of the gods," he said, "that's some of the ugliest-looking country I've seen in all my days."

Though Teleutas liked to disparage everything he saw, that didn't mean he was always wrong. He wasn't wrong here; Sostratos thought it far and away the ugliest-looking country he'd seen in his life, too. The hills through which he and his fellow Rhodians were traveling descended to the Lake of Asphalt through a series of cliffs of reddish flint on which hardly anything grew. Below those cliffs were bluffs of buff limestone, every bit as barren.

The plains between the high ground and the lake were dazzlingly white. "You know what that reminds me of?" Moskhion said. "When they set out pans full of seawater to dry up, and they do, and there's all the salt left in the bottom, to the crows with me if that's not what it looks like."

"You're right," Sostratos said. But salt pans weren't very

big. These salt flats, if that was what they were, went on for stadion after stadion. "Looks as though half the salt in the world is down there."

"Too bad it's not worth bringing a donkeyload back with us," Aristeidas said. "It's just lying there waiting for somebody to scoop it up. You wouldn't have to bother with pans."

"If so many Hellenic poleis didn't lie by the sea, we might make a profit on it," Sostratos said. "As things are—" He tossed his head.

Under the sun, the Lake of Asphalt itself shone golden. Beyond it, to the east, lay more hills, these of a harsh, purplish stone. Sostratos had hardly noticed them in the morning, when he'd set out from Jerusalem, but they grew ever more visible as the day wore along and the angle of the sunshine falling on them changed. He saw no trees or even bushes on them, either. The Lake of Asphalt and almost everything surrounding it might as well have been dead.

Pointing east across the lake to the rugged purple hills, Aristeidas asked, "Are those still a part of Ioudaia, too, or do they belong to some other country full of different barbarians?"

"I don't know, though I'm sure a Ioudaian would," Sostratos answered. "By the look of them, though, I'd say they aren't likely to be *full* of anything, except maybe scorpions."

"The scorpions here are bigger and nastier than anything we've got back in Hellas," Teleutas said. "Back in Jerusalem a couple of days ago, I smashed one *this* big." He stuck up his thumb and shuddered. "Almost makes me wish I'd got into the habit of wearing shoes."

For the next quarter of an hour, he and Moskhion and Aristeidas were skittish on the road, shying away from rocks that might hide scorpions and from shadows or sticks they feared *were* the stinging vermin. Even Sostratos, who was on muleback and whose feet didn't touch the ground, kept looking around nervously. Then a scorpion *did* skitter across the dirt, and it vanished into a crevice in the rocks before anyone could kill it. Teleutas' curses should have been plenty to do it in all by themselves.

After a while, the track leading down to the salt flats got so steep, Sostratos dismounted and walked beside the mule. The animal placed each foot with the greatest of care. So did the pack donkey, which Aristeidas led. Slowly, the Rhodians and their beasts descended from the hills.

Not quite halfway down, Teleutas stopped and pointed southeast. "Look there. Furies take me if that isn't green, down there right by the edge of the Lake of Asphalt. I thought this whole place was just—nothing."

"It can't *all* be nothing, or nobody would live there," Sostratos said. "That must be Engedi."

"How do they make things grow, if the lake is salty and if there's all this salt around?" Teleutas demanded.

"I don't know yet. Finding out will be interesting, I think," Sostratos said. "Maybe they have freshwater springs. We'll see." Teleutas still looked dissatisfied, but he held his peace.

Down on the salt flat, the sun beat down on Sostratos with a force he'd never known before. He had to squint to escape the dazzle of Helios' rays off the salt. The very air felt uncommonly thick and heavy. It had the salt tang he associated with the sea and hadn't expected to smell so far inland. Here, in fact, that salt tang was stronger than he'd ever known it before.

A raven flew past overhead. Moskhion said, "In this part of the world, I bet even the birds have to carry water bottles."

Sostratos laughed, but not for long. A traveler who ran out of things to drink in these parts wouldn't last long. Sun and salt might do as good a job of embalming him as natron did for the corpses Egyptian undertakers treated. Heading on toward Engedi, Sostratos wished he hadn't had that thought.

MENEDEMOS TOOK THE bolt of the eastern silk he'd got from Zakerbaal son of Tenes out of the oiled-leather sack where it was stowed and held it up to the sun. Diokles dipped his head in approval. "That's mighty pretty stuff, skipper," he said. "We'll get a good price for it, too, when we go back to Hellas."

"Yes, I think so, too," Menedemos answered. "But I'm not

just thinking about the silver. Look at the cloth! Look how thin it is! The finest Koan silk might as well be wool next to this."

"Wonder how they do it," the keleustes said.

"So do I." Menedemos dipped his head. "And I wonder who *they* are. People beyond India, Zakerbaal said."

"Not even Alexander found out what's beyond India," Diokles said.

"Alexander decided there wasn't anything beyond India," Menedemos agreed. "That way, he could head back toward Hellas saying he'd conquered the whole world." He looked at the silk again. "He was wrong. He was a godlike man—even a hero, a demigod, if you like—but he was wrong."

"I wonder if any more of this stuff will ever come out of the east," Diokles said.

Menedemos shrugged. "Who can guess? I'd bet we never see another gryphon's skull, because nobody in his right mind would pay anything for one. But this? This is different. It's beautiful. Anybody who sees it would pay for it, and pay plenty. So maybe more'll come from wherever it comes from, but who knows when? Next year? Ten years from now? Fifty? A hundred? Who can say?"

He imagined strange barbarians sitting at their looms, turning out bolt after bolt of this wonderful silk. What would they be like? Beyond India, they might look like anything at all. The folk of India itself were said to be black, like Ethiopians. Did that mean everyone beyond India was black, too?

This is only imagination, Menedemos told himself, and tossed his head. *I can make these distant barbarians any color I please. Why, I can make them yellow if I want to.* He laughed at that.

"What's funny, skipper?" the oarmaster asked. When Menedemos told him, he laughed, too. "That's pretty good. It sure is. You think they'd have yellow hair, too, the way the Kelts do?"

"Who knows?" Menedemos said. "In my mind, they had

black hair, but you can make them look however you want. What I want to imagine now is selling this silk and the dye as we go back to Rhodes."

"It'll do even better in the Aegean," Diokles remarked. "The farther from Phoenicia we go, the better the prices we'll get."

"That's probably true," Menedemos said. "Maybe we can make for Athens next sailing season." He laughed again. "That would break my cousin's heart, wouldn't it?"

"Oh, yes, he'd be ever so disappointed." Diokles snorted. Finding the snort not strong enough, he laughed out loud.

"I wouldn't mind getting up there myself," Menedemos allowed. "You can have a good time all kinds of different ways in Athens. If we make port early in the season, we can go to the theater for the tragedies and comedies they put on during the Greater Dionysia. Nothing tops theater in Athens."

"Yes, theater's a nice way to pass a day every so often," the keleustes agreed. "And they've got all kinds of wineshops there, and pretty girls in the brothels—pretty boys, too, if you'd rather do that for a change. It's a good town."

"A boy's all right every once in a while," Menedemos said. "I've never been one to chase every youth in bloom through the streets, though."

"No—you chase wives instead." But Diokles said it indulgently. He didn't sound reproving, as Sostratos always did.

"I think wives are more fun—most wives, anyway." Menedemos made a sour face. "The innkeeper's wife is chasing me. I don't intend to let her catch me, either. Sour old crone."

"No wonder you don't stay there much."

"No wonder at all. If it weren't for the bed . . ." Menedemos sighed. "I didn't feel like sleeping on planks all the time we were here."

"Never bothered me," Diokles said.

"I know. But then, you're comfortable sleeping sitting up. I couldn't do that if my life depended on it."

The oarmaster shrugged. "All what you're used to. That's

what I got in the habit of doing when I pulled an oar—lean up against the gunwale, close my eyes, and doze off. After you do it for a while, it seems as natural as stretching out flat."

"Maybe to you." Menedemos glanced down toward the base of the pier. "If that's not a Hellene coming this way, I'm a yellow barbarian myself." He raised his voice: "Hail, friend! How are you today?"

"Not bad," the other man answered, his Doric drawl not much different from the one that Menedemos spoke. "How's yourself?"

"I've been worse," Menedemos allowed. "What can I do for you?"

"Are you the fellow who was selling books at the barracks a while ago?"

Menedemos dipped his head. "That's me, O best one. I haven't got many left. Why didn't you decide to buy sooner?"

"I couldn't, that's why," the stranger said. "I'm a horseman, and I just got back in from a sweep through the hills after bandits." He had a horseman's scars, sure enough—on his legs and on his left arm. A hoplite's large round shield protected that arm, but a horseman couldn't bear anything so big and heavy.

"I hope the sweep went well," Menedemos said. "You won't find a merchant with a good thing to say about bandits."

"We smoked out a couple of nests," the other Hellene said. "But it's more a matter of keeping them down and making them cautious than it is of getting rid of them. Those hills will spawn robber bands for the next thousand years. Too many hiding places for 'em to use, too many towns and roads close to 'em. Can't be helped." He changed the subject back toward what interested him: "Have you still got any books left?"

"A couple," Menedemos answered. "One's the book of the *Iliad* where godlike Akhilleus and glorious Hektor fight it out; the other's from the *Odyssey,* the book where resourceful Odysseus meets Polyphemos the Cyclops."

"I'd like 'em both," the cavalryman said wistfully. "Nothing like a book to make the time pass by. But you're going to put some great whacking price on 'em, because where else can I buy if I don't get 'em from you?"

"You can't make me feel guilty, most noble one," Menedemos said. "I'm not in business to lose money any more than soldiers are in busi-ness to lose battles. You can have 'em both for thirty-five drakhmai. No haggling, no cheating—that's the same price the garrison soldiers were paying."

"*Papai!*" the cavalryman said. "That's a lot of money, just the same." Menedemos didn't answer. He just stood and waited. The other Hellene frowned. Menedemos thought he knew the expression: that of a man who was talking himself into something. And, sure enough, the fellow said, "All right. All right! I'll take 'em. You count two drakhmai for one Sidonian siglos?"

"Yes," Menedemos answered. That gave the other man a very slight break on the rate of exchange. Maybe Sostratos would have worked it out to the last obolos, but Menedemos didn't feel like bothering. He took the silver, got the last two books in his store out of their sack, and gave them to the horseman.

"Thanks," the man said. "I'll carry these till they fall to pieces. I'd pay even more for the books from Herodotos where the Persians and Hellenes go at it. You don't happen to have those, do you?"

"Sorry, no." Menedemos hoped he hid his bemusement. Not even Sostratos had thought he could sell history books in Phoenicia. Customers never failed to be surprising. This one went on down the pier. Menedemos called after him: "Lykian ham? Fine oil?"

"No, thanks," the soldier answered. "I've spent all the silver I'm going to. Some men would rather eat fancy. Me, I'd rather read." He kept on walking.

To Diokles, Menedemos said, "A pity Sostratos is off in the back of beyond. He would have made himself a friend for life."

"That's the truth," the keleustes agreed. "I know my alpha-beta, but I've never had much cause to use it. Most of the time, you can find out whatever you need to know just by talking with people."

"I enjoy Homer, and I think I do like him better because I can read him for myself," Menedemos said. "Same with Aristophanes—maybe even more so, because you don't hear him read in the agora all the time, the way you do Homer. But I don't dive into a roll of papyrus headfirst like Sostratos."

"He knows all sorts of funny things, I will say," Diokles remarked. "And what's really strange is, every once in a while they come in handy."

"I know." Menedemos drummed the fingers of his right hand on the outside of his thigh. "It happens just often enough to keep me from teasing him too hard about everything he reads." His fingers went up and down, up and down. "Too bad."

Before he went back to Sedek-yathon's inn that evening, Menedemos bought a sausage half a cubit long; the gut-wrapped length of chopped meat smelled strongly of garlic and cumin. He also got himself a small loaf with olives baked into it: sitos to go with his opson. He chuckled when that thought crossed his mind. Could Sostratos have known of it, he would have chided Menedemos for a self-confessed opsophagos: a man who put the relish ahead of the staple. The sausage was supposed to go with the bread, not the other way round.

Sedek-yathon's wife dropped the sausage into hot oil for Menedemos. The oil was the same cheap stuff the innkeeper always used. Not only that, but it had done a lot of cooking before that sausage went into it. The smell filled the taproom at the front of the inn. It wasn't precisely unpleasant, but it was strong.

Emashtart fished the sausage out of the oil with a pair of wooden tongs. She set it on a plate and carried it over to Menedemos. Putting it on the table in front of him, she smirked and said, "*Phallos.*"

"That's not how you say 'sausage' in Greek," Menedemos answered. The word for sausage, *physkê,* was close enough that she might have used the other one in honest error. She might have. Menedemos hoped she had.

The way her smirk got wider—and, to his eyes, less lovely—argued she hadn't. *"Phallos,"* she repeated, and then went on in her horrible Greek: "You to have biggerest *phallos* already, eh?" Her eyes went to Menedemos' crotch.

His went to the formidable length of grayish-brown meat on the table in front of him. "By the gods, I hope not!" he exclaimed. "What do you take me for, a donkey?" He thought Emashtart a perfect donkey, but for different reasons.

She shook her head. "No, just *man.*" She put a slavering emphasis on the word. Her gaze still hadn't risen to Menedemos' face.

A couple of other men were eating in the taproom. They were Phoenicians, though, and gave no sign of understanding Greek. Emashtart could be shameless in front of them without their knowing. Hoping to quell her, Menedemos asked, "Where's your husband?"

She gave him a scornful look. He'd seen that expression on the faces of more than a few women who'd been interested in him and hadn't cared about their husbands at all. It was the last one he wanted to see on Emashtart's. She said, "He drinking." She mimed lifting a cup with both hands, bringing it to her mouth, and then staggering around, as if with too much wine. Menedemos chuckled. It was involuntary, but he couldn't help himself; she made a fine mimic. She added, "Not to coming home at alls."

"Oh," Menedemos said tonelessly. "How nice." He drank some of his own wine, then yawned. "I'm going to go to bed early tonight, I am. I'm very, *very* tired." He yawned again, theatrically.

Emashtart watched him. She didn't say a word. Menedemos didn't like that. He wanted her to believe him. That way, she wouldn't come scratching at his door some time in the middle of the night. He'd been glad to have women scratch at his door before. He expected he would be again, once he could forget about this annoying oath he'd sworn to Sostratos. He couldn't imagine being glad if Emashtart did, not even if she stood in the courtyard naked—maybe especially not if she stood in the courtyard naked.

Finally, despite looking back over her shoulder as she went, she left him alone. He had to eat in a hurry, yawning every so often, so she wouldn't think he'd been lying about how tired he was—which he had. The sausage, though not quite like any he'd eaten back in Hellas, proved tasty. As he brought it up to his mouth, Emashtart ran her tongue over her lips in a silent obscenity that struck him as far grosser and more disgusting than anything the cheerfully bawdy Aristophanes had ever come up with.

As soon as Menedemos finished eating, he hurried out of the taproom and into the cramped, stuffy little chamber where he'd sleep tonight. He didn't even bother lighting the lamp. He just took off his chiton, made sure the door was barred from the inside, and lay down naked on the narrow bed. To his surprise, he quickly fell asleep.

Not very much to his surprise, he was awakened some unknown stretch of time later by someone softly tapping on the door. *Maybe she'll go away if I lie here quietly and pretend to stay asleep,* he thought.

He tried it. Emashtart didn't go away. She kept right on tapping, louder and louder. At last, he doubted whether a dead man could have ignored her. Muttering to himself, he got out of bed and went to the door. "Who is it?" he asked, there being one chance in a myriad it was somebody besides the innkeeper's wife.

But she answered, "I are it."

"What do you want?" Menedemos asked. "And what hour is it, anyway?"

"Not knowing hours," Emashtart said. "Want *binein.*"

Menedemos coughed. He gave back a pace. He supposed he shouldn't have been surprised she knew the nastiest, lewdest verb in the Greek language, but he was. The word had implications of taking by force that usually made it implausible when used by a woman to a man; with her speaking, though, it somehow seemed anything but.

"In the name of the gods, go away," he said. "I'm too tired."

"Want *binein*," she said again. "Want *binein*!" She was almost shouting, careless of what the other luckless lodgers at the inn might think. Had she spent all this time pouring down wine and thinking of assaulting Menedemos?

"No," he said. "Not now. Go away."

"To let in," the Phoenician woman said. "Want *binein!* To be happies."

Was this what women felt when some obnoxious man wouldn't leave them alone? Menedemos had had some idea of what that was like; as a youth in Rhodes, he'd had plenty of suitors sniffing after him. But what he'd known then was chiefly scorn for the silly men who chased him. Now he felt real annoyance—and fear, too, for, in a city of her own people, Emashtart might be able to cause him a lot of trouble. He didn't dare let her in now, lest she claim he'd tried to rape her instead of the other way round.

She started to say something else. Before she could, a man in a nearby room yelled in Aramaic. Menedemos didn't understand a word of it, but he would have bet the other man was telling her to shut up and let him get some sleep. In the other fellow's place, that was what Menedemos would have said.

Emashtart shouted back, anger in her voice. The man in the other room gave as good as he got. He and the innkeeper's wife went back and forth at the top of their lungs. Menedemos couldn't follow their argument, but it sounded spectacular. Aramaic, with its gutturals and hisses, was made for quarreling.

The racket Emashtart and the first man made disturbed others at the inn. Before long, six or eight people were shouting at one another. They all sounded furious. For the next quarter of an hour, Menedemos hadn't the slightest hope of sleeping, but he was entertained.

At last, the bickering died away. Menedemos wondered whether Emashtart would start scratching at his door again. To his vast relief, she didn't. He twisted and turned on the narrow, lumpy bed, and finally went back to sleep.

When he came out the next morning, he found Sedek-yathon sitting on a stool in the taproom drinking a cup of wine. The innkeeper looked somewhat the worse for wear. Menedemos wondered how much he'd drunk the night before. But that didn't matter. Sedek-yathon spoke more Greek than his wife. That did. Menedemos said, "I'm sorry, best one, but I have to move back to my ship today."

"You say you stay till new moon," the innkeeper said. "You already pay to stay to new moon. Not get silver back."

Normally, that would have infuriated the Rhodian. Here, he only shrugged. "Fine," he said. He would have paid more than a few drakhmai to escape the inn. He gathered up his belongings and headed back to the *Aphrodite*. In some ways, he wouldn't be so comfortable. In others . . . In others, he couldn't wait to return to the merchant galley.

GROWING UP IN Rhodes, Sostratos had never seen snow fall till he went to Athens to study at the Lykeion. Even in Athens, snow had been rare. He'd thought he knew everything there was to know about heat. Engedi, on the shore of the Lake of Asphalt, proved he hadn't known so much as he thought.

Whenever he went out of doors, the sun beat down on him with almost physical force. He wore his broad-brimmed hat every moment of the day and imagined he felt the weight of the sunlight pressing it down onto his head. Even the air seemed heavy and thick and suffused with sunshine.

And yet, despite that suffocating heat, despite the poisonously salty lake and the wasteland all around, Engedi lay in the midst of a patch of some of the most fertile soil he'd ever seen. As he'd guessed, springs bubbling up from underground let life not only survive but flourish here.

Outside the walls of Engedi, persimmon trees and henna

plants grew among other crops. Sostratos knew the balsam-makers turned their sap into the medicinal, sweet-smelling product for which the town was famous. Just how they did it, he didn't know. No one outside of Engedi did. He tossed his head. Since coming to Ioudaia, he'd learned that wasn't *quite* true. One other place, a town called Jericho, also produced the balsam.

He shrugged. The stuff was always called balsam of Engedi. If he bought it here, he could truthfully say he had the authentic product.

More persimmon trees grew in front of the house of Eliphaz son of Gatam, the leading balsam-maker in Engedi. In the savage weather the land here by the Lake of Asphalt knew, their shade was doubly welcome.

A skinny, black-bearded slave opened the door when Sostratos knocked. "Peace be unto you, my master," he said in Aramaic with an accent slightly different from that which the Ioudaioi used.

"And to you also peace, Mesha," Sostratos replied. Mesha was a Moabite, one of the nomads who, Sostratos had learned since coming to Engedi, dwelt in the desert east of the Lake of Asphalt. Sostratos didn't know by what misfortune he'd ended up a slave. Getting captured on a raid struck the Rhodian as likely; Mesha had the look of a man who would rob for the sport of it.

"May Khemosh favor you, Ionian," Mesha said. Khemosh was a Moabite god. Sostratos would have liked to find out more about him, but Mesha named him only furtively; Eliphaz didn't approve of anyone's calling on any god in his house save the invisible one the Ioudaioi worshiped. In a lower voice yet, the Moabite added, "May you swindle the beard off my master's chin." He might be a slave, but he wasn't resigned to serving the balsam-maker.

Another persimmon tree and a pale-barked fig spread shade over Eliphaz's courtyard. The Ioudaian waited in that shade. He was tall and solidly made, and within a few years of forty: Sostratos could see the first few white threads in his dark beard. Inclining his head to Sostratos, he said, "Peace be unto you, Ionian."

"And to you also peace, my master," Sostratos said politely.

"My thanks." Eliphaz son of Gatam clapped his hands. "Fetch us wine, Mesha." Nodding, the slave hurried away. Eliphaz muttered something under his breath. It sounded like *lizard-eating savage.* Maybe he had no more love for Mesha than the Moabite did for him.

The wine was good enough without being anything special. Sostratos, unaccustomed to wine without water, drank carefully. After polite chitchat, he said, "Here is a jar of the fine Rhodian perfume I mentioned when we met yesterday." With use, his own Aramaic got more fluent by the day.

"Let me smell of it," Eliphaz said gravely. Sostratos handed him the small jar. He pulled out the stopper, sniffed, touched the rim of the jar, and rubbed his thumb and index finger together. "It is made with grease, I see. What is the grease?"

"Olive oil, my master, nothing else," Sostratos replied.

"Ah." A smile appeared on the balsam-maker's face. "We may freely use olive oil, you understand. If it were animal fat—especially if it were pig fat—I could not think of trading for it no matter how sweet it smells."

"I understand that it is so, yes," Sostratos said. "I do not understand why it is so. If you could make this plain, I would be in your debt."

"It is so because the one god commands us to shun the pig and all other beasts that do not chew their cud and divide their hooves," Eliphaz said.

Even that was more than Sostratos had known before. But it was not enough more to satisfy him. "Why does your one god command you so?" he asked.

"Why?" Now Eliphaz son of Gatam stared at him in amazement. "Who are we, to ask why the one god orders this or forbids that? It is his will. We can only obey, and obey we do." He sounded proud of such obedience.

That struck Sostratos as very strange. It was as if a man de-

clared he was proud to be a slave and had no desire for freedom. Since he saw no diplomatic way to say that to the
balsam-maker, he let it go. He did say, "You can travel all over
the world, my master, and you will find no sweeter, no
stronger, no longer-lasting perfume than what we make on the
island of Rhodes."

"It could be. It is good perfume," Eliphaz said. "But you,
Ionian, you will find no finer balsam than what we make here
by the Dead Sea."

"Is that what you name the water?" Sostratos said. Eliphaz
nodded. Sostratos said, "I have also heard it called the Lake of
Asphalt."

"Call it whatever you please," the Ioudaian said. "But we
trade our balsam for silver, weight for weight. How do we
make the scales balance with perfume?"

All around the Inner Sea, Phoenician merchants traded balsam of Engedi for twice its weight in silver. Sostratos wanted
some of that profit for himself. He said, "I do not sell perfume
by weight, but by the jar. For each jar, I would hope to get
twenty Sidonian sigloi."

Eliphaz laughed. "You might hope to get so much, but how
likely is it? If you think I will give you twenty shekels' weight
of balsam for one of those paltry little jars, I must ask you to
think again."

"Perfume jars are small because what they hold is boiled
many times to make it stronger," Sostratos said. "All this
takes much labor. So does gathering the roses to make the
perfume."

"Do you think there is no labor in making balsam?" Eliphaz
demanded. "Not only is there labor, there is the secret. No one
but we of Engedi knows how to do what needs doing."

"What of the men of Jericho?" Sostratos asked.

"Frauds! Fakes! Phonies, the lot of them!" Eliphaz said.
"*Our* balsam, the balsam of Engedi, is far finer than theirs."

"Well, my master, all trades have secrets," Sostratos said.
"You grow roses here. Do you make perfume? I think not."

"Our secret is harder and more important," the Ioudaian insisted.

"You would say so, of course," Sostratos answered politely.

Eliphaz muttered in Aramaic. "You are worse than a Phoenician," he told Sostratos, who smiled as if what was meant for an insult were a compliment. That smile made Eliphaz mutter some more. He said, "Even if I were to give you ten shekels of balsam for one jar, it would be too much."

"My master, it grieves me to tell a man so obviously wise that he is wrong," Sostratos said. "But you must know you are speaking nonsense. If you truly believed a jar of perfume was worth less than ten sigloi"—he still had trouble pronouncing the *sh* sound that began *shekels,* a sound Greek didn't use—"you would throw me out, and that would be the end of our dicker."

"Not necessarily," Eliphaz said. "I might simply want something to amuse me. And I tell you straight out, it has been a long time since I heard anything so funny as the idea of paying twenty shekels of balsam for a jar of your perfume. You must think that because you come from far away and I stay in Engedi I have no notion of what anything is worth."

"Certainly not," said Sostratos, who had hoped for something exactly like that. "But think, my master. How often does Rhodian perfume come here to your town?"

"None has ever come here before," Eliphaz told him. "And if the price you want for it is any indication, I can understand why not."

Patiently, Sostratos said, "But when you have the only fine perfume in these parts, for how much will you sell it? Do not think only of prices. Remember, think also of profit after you buy."

Eliphaz's smile bared strong yellowish teeth. "I am not a child, Ionian. I am not a blushing virgin brought to the marriage bed. I know about buying, *and* I know about selling. And suppose I said, all right, I will give you ten shekels' weight of balsam for a jar. Yes, suppose I said that. You would only scorn me. You would say, 'It is not enough. You are a thief.'"

Sostratos smiled, too. He thought he recognized an opening gambit there. "Ten sigloi are *not* enough," he agreed, and he let the smile get broader. "You *are* a thief, my master."

In Greek, he would have been sure he sounded like a man playacting. In Aramaic, he only hoped he did. When Eliphaz son of Gatam laughed out loud, he grinned with relief: he'd done it right. "You are a dangerous man, Sostratos son of Lysistratos," the Ioudaian said.

"I do not want to be dangerous," Sostratos said. "I only want to trade."

"Ha! So you say. So you say." Eliphaz shook his head. "Even if I said ten shekels and a half for one of those nasty little jars, still would you laugh. You would not come down at all, not even by one of those tiny coins the governors issue."

That *was* an opening gambit. Sostratos realized he would have to move, that he would lose any chance of a deal if he didn't. "I will come as far as you have come. If you pay me nineteen and a half sigloi of balsam the jar, the perfume is yours."

"Mesha!" Eliphaz shouted. When the Moabite slave came up, the balsam-maker said, "Fetch more wine. Fetch it at once. We have work to do here, and wine will grease the way."

Muttering, the slave went off to get the wine. He was still muttering when he came back with it. When he was a free man, had he had Ioudaioi serving him? Raids across a long-established border could produce ironies like that.

Eliphaz haggled as if he had all the time in the world. Plainly, dickering was among his favorite sports. Sostratos knew Hellenes who took the same pleasure in the act of making the deal. He wasn't among them, though he wanted the best price he could get.

The best price he could get turned out to be fourteen and a half sigloi of balsam per jar of perfume. Eliphaz son of Gatam stubbornly refused to go to fifteen. "I do not need perfume so badly as that," the Ioudaian said. "It is too much. I will not pay it."

That left Sostratos muttering to himself. He knew what he could get for the balsam once he took it back to Hellas, and he knew what he could get for the perfume in ports around the Inner Sea. He would make more for the balsam, yes. Would he make enough more to justify this long, dangerous trip to Engedi? Maybe. On the other hand, maybe not.

But, having come so far, could he justify turning around and going back to Sidon without balsam? He doubted he'd get a better price from any of the other balsam-makers; like any other group of artisans, they would talk among themselves. And he was sure he wouldn't get a *much* better price.

Did you think this would be easy? he asked himself. *Did you think Eli-phaz would say, "Oh, twenty sigloi of balsam the jar isn't enough—let me give you thirty"?* He knew perfectly well he'd thought nothing of the sort. Whether he had or not, though, it would have been nice.

"Fourteen and a half shekels," Eliphaz said again. "Is it yes, my master, or is it no? If yes, we have a bargain. If no, I am pleased to have met you. Some Ionian soldiers have come here before, but never till now a trader."

"Fourteen and a half," Sostratos agreed unhappily, far from sure he was doing the right thing. "It is a bargain."

"Whew!" the Ioudaian said. If that wasn't a sigh of relief, it certainly sounded like one. "You are a formidable foe. I am glad most of your people stay far from Engedi. I'd much sooner dicker with Phoenicians."

Was that true? Or was he just saying it to make Sostratos feel better? It did the job, no doubt of that. "You are a hard bargainer yourself," Sostratos said, and meant every word of it. He held out his hand.

Eliphaz took it. His grip was hard and firm. "A good bargain," he declared. "Neither one of us is happy—it must be a good bargain."

"Yes," Sostratos said, and then, "A different question: may

I bathe in the Lake of Asphalt? Does it hold up a bather so he cannot sink?"

"It does," Eliphaz answered. "And of course you may. It is there." He pointed east, toward the water. "How could anyone stop you?"

"May I bathe naked?" Sostratos persisted. "This is the custom of my people, but you Ioudaioi have different rules."

"You may bathe naked," Eliphaz said. "You would be polite to bathe well away from women and to dress as soon as you come out of the water. And do not get any of it in your eyes or in your mouth. It burns. It burns very much."

"Thank you. I will do as you say," Sostratos told him.

He got Aristeidas to come with him to make sure no light-fingered Ioudaian lifted his tunic after he doffed it. When he walked into the water, he exclaimed in astonishment; it was as warm as blood, as if it were a heated bath. The oceanic smell overwhelmed him. He walked out till the water covered his privates, to satisfy Ioudaian notions of modesty. Then he lifted his feet and leaned back to float.

He exclaimed all over again. Eliphaz had been right, and more than right. He could keep his head and shoulders and feet out of the supremely salty water with the greatest of ease. Indeed, when he tried to force more of his torso down into the Lake of Asphalt, other parts of him rose out of it. So long as that included only more of his long legs, he didn't worry about it. When his groin bobbed up out of the water, though, he set a hand over it, lest he offend any Ioudaioi who happened to be keeping an eye on what a foreigner did.

"What's it like?" Aristeidas called to him.

"I think it may be the strangest thing I've ever felt," Sostratos answered. "It's like reclining on a couch at a supper or a symposion, only there is no couch, and it doesn't resist me if I lean back more. And it's wonderfully warm, too. Do you want to try after I come out?"

"Maybe I will," the sailor said. "I wasn't going to, but coming all this way and then *not* going in would be pretty silly, wouldn't it?"

"I certainly think so," Sostratos said. "Others may think otherwise."

After perhaps a quarter of an hour, Sostratos emerged from the Lake of Asphalt. He put on his chiton as fast as he could, to keep from scandalizing the locals. Half a plethron down the shore, a Ioudaian dawdled much more than he did over re-donning clothes. He found that amusing.

The Ioudaian, he saw before the fellow dressed, was circumcised. He wished the man had been closer; he would have liked a better look at the mutilation. Why anyone would subject himself to anything so painful and ugly was beyond him. The Ioudaian himself would probably say it was at the command of his god; that seemed to be the locals' explanation for everything. But why would a god want such a mark on his people? It was a puzzlement.

Aristeidas did strip off his tunic and walk out into the Lake of Asphalt. As Sostratos had, he exclaimed in surprise at the way the water bore him up. "You can push yourself around with one finger!" he said. "You won't ever drown, either."

"No, but you might turn into a salt fish if you stay in there too long," Sostratos answered. The fierce sun had quickly dried the water on his arms and legs. But a crust of salt crystals remained. His skin itched, far more than it would have after bathing in the Inner Sea. When he scratched, the salt stung. He said, "We'll have to rinse off with fresh water when we get back to the inn."

"No doubt you're right," Aristeidas said. "Then what?"

"Then we go back to Jerusalem," Sostratos said. "And from there, we go back to Sidon. And from *there*—"

He and Aristeidas both said the same word at the same time: "Rhodes."

FOR THE FIRST time in his travels, Menedemos found himself bored. He'd done everything he'd set out to do in Sidon. Most summers, that would mean the *Aphrodite* could go on to some other port and give him something new to do. Not here, though, not now. He couldn't very well leave before Sostratos and his escorts got back.

And he couldn't do what he would have done in most ports to hold off boredom: he'd given his cousin his oath not to go looking for a love affair with some other man's wife this sailing season. He'd known nothing but dismay when Emashtart came looking for a love affair with him.

A visit to a brothel proved not to be the answer he was looking for. It wasn't that he didn't have a good time; he did. But he'd spent some silver and he'd spent some time, and he had nothing but the memory to show for them. Considering how often he'd done the same thing, and in how many cities all around the Inner Sea, he doubted whether in a few years—or even in a few days—that memory would mean much to him.

It was harder to amuse himself in Sidon than it would have been in a polis full of Hellenes. The Phoenician town boasted no theater. He couldn't even go to the market square to pass the time, as he would have in a polis. Among Hellenes, everyone went to the agora. People met and gossiped and hashed out things of more consequence than mere gossip. He couldn't imagine a Hellenic town without its agora.

Things weren't the same in Sidon. He'd seen that shortly after arriving here. The market square among Phoenicians was a place of business, nothing more. Even if it hadn't been, his ignorance of Aramaic would have shut him out of city life here.

And, of course, he couldn't exercise in the gymnasion, for Sidon had no more gymnasion than theater. Sostratos had been right about that. A gymnasion was a place to exercise naked—and how else would a man exercise? But Phoenicians didn't go naked. As far as Menedemos could tell, they didn't exercise, either, not for the sake of having bodies worth admiring. The ones who did physical labor seemed fit enough. More prosperous, more sedentary men ran to fat. Menedemos supposed they would have been even less attractive if they hadn't covered themselves from neck to ankles.

Eventually, Menedemos found the taverns where Antigonos' Macedonians and Hellenes drank. There, at least, he could speak—and, as important, hear—his own language. That did help, but only so much.

"They're funny people," he said to Diokles one morning back at the *Aphrodite*. "I never realized how funny they were till I spent so much time listening to them talk."

"What, soldiers?" The oarmaster snorted. "I could've told you that, skipper."

"I suppose it's just shoptalk when one of them explains how to twist the sword after you've thrust it into somebody's belly, so you make sure the wound kills," Menedemos said. "Killing the enemy is part of your job. But when they start going on about how best to torture a prisoner so he tells you where his silver is . . ." He shivered in spite of the building heat.

"That's part of their job, too," Diokles observed. "Half the time, their pay is in arrears. Only reason they get paid at all, sometimes, is that they'd desert if they didn't, and their officers know it."

"I understand that," Menedemos said. "It was just the *way* they talked about it that gave me the horrors. They might have been potters talking about the best way to join handles to the body of a cup."

"They're bastards," Diokles said flatly. "Who'd want to be a soldier to begin with if he wasn't a bastard?"

He wasn't wrong. He was seldom wrong; he had good sense and was far from stupid. Nevertheless, Menedemos thought, *By the gods, I miss Sostratos.* He couldn't talk things over with Diokles the way he could with his cousin.

Even though the soldiers made him wish they were barbarians (not that Macedonians didn't come close), he kept going back to the taverns they frequented. The chance to speak Greek was too tempting to let him stay away.

Once, he happened to walk in right behind Antigonos' quartermaster. "Oh, hail, Rhodian," Andronikos said coolly. "Did you ever unload that ridiculously overpriced olive oil of yours?"

"Yes, by Zeus," Menedemos answered with a savage grin.

"Almost all of it, as a matter of fact. And I got a better price than you were willing to pay. Some people *do* care about what they eat."

Andronikos only sneered. "My job is to keep the soldiers well fed for as little silver as I can. I have to do both parts of it."

"You certainly do it for as little silver as you can, O marvelous one," Menedemos replied. "But if you kept the men *well* fed, they wouldn't need to buy from me, would they? I've sold all my hams and smoked eels, too."

A soldier said, "Ham? Smoked eels? We wouldn't see those from Andronikos, not if we waited the next hundred years."

The quartermaster was unmoved. "No, you wouldn't," he said. "They're needless luxuries. If a soldier wants them, he can spend his own money to get them. Barley and salt fish and oil are what he needs to stay in fighting trim."

"No wonder we're losing soldiers to desertion," somebody said: probably an officer, by his educated Attic accent. "If we give them only what they need and Ptolemaios gives them what they want, which would they rather have? Which would any man with an obolos' weight of brains in his head rather have?"

"A soldier who has to have luxuries to fight isn't a soldier worth keeping," Andronikos insisted.

"What soldier doesn't want a little comfort now and then?" the other officer returned.

"Antigonos doesn't care to see his money thrown away," the quartermaster said. From everything Menedemos had heard, that was true.

"Antigonos doesn't care to see his men tempted to desertion, either," the other officer answered. "A soldier who's unhappy isn't a soldier who'll fight well."

Menedemos finished his wine and waved to the man behind the bar for another cup. Another soldier, this one plainly a Macedonian by his speech, started laying into Andronikos, and then another, and then another. Before long, half the men in the tavern were shouting at the quartermaster.

Andronikos got angrier and angrier. "You people don't know what you're talking about!" he shouted. His pinched features turned red.

"We know we get the leavings that nobody else would want to eat," a soldier said. "How much money do you salt away buying us cheap garbage and sending out receipts that say we eat better than we really do?"

"Not a hemiobolos, by Zeus! That's a lie!" Andronikos said.

"Furies take me if it is," the soldier answered. "Who ever heard of a quartermaster who didn't feather his own nest every chance he got?"

"How much silver would Andronikos cough up if we held him upside down and shook him?" somebody else said. "Plenty, I bet."

"Don't you try that!" Antigonos' quartermaster said shrilly. "Don't you dare try that! If you fool with me, I'll have you crucified upside down, by the gods! Do you think I won't? Do you think I can't? You'd better not think anything like that, or it's the worst mistake you'll ever make in all your days."

Menedemos raised his cup to his mouth. He quickly drained it. Then he slid off his stool and slipped out of the wineshop. He knew a brewing fight when he saw one. Sostratos might consider him imperfectly civilized, but at least he'd never made tavern brawling one of his favorite amusements, as so many sailors from the *Aphrodite* did.

He hadn't got ten paces from the door before a crescendo of shouts, the thuds of breaking furniture, and the higher crashes of shattering pottery announced the start of the brawl. Whistling gleefully at his narrow escape, he strolled back to the harbor and the merchant galley. He did hope Andronikos got everything that was coming to him, and a little more besides.

THIS TIME, SOSTRATOS and his traveling companions approached Jerusalem from the south. "Are we going back to Ithran's inn, young sir?" Moskhion asked.

"I'd intended to stay there for a day or two, yes," Sostratos answered. "Having an innkeeper who speaks some Greek is very handy, for me and especially for you men, since you haven't learned any Aramaic."

"Who hasn't?" Moskhion said, and let loose with a guttural obscenity that sounded much fouler than anything a man might say in Greek.

Sostratos winced. "If that's all you can say in the local language, you'd do better to keep your mouth shut," he said. Moskhion guffawed at the effect he'd had.

"I can ask for bread. I can ask for wine. I can ask for a woman," Aristeidas said. "Past that, what more do I need?" His attitude was practical if limited. He'd learned a few phrases that came in handy and didn't worry about anything more.

"How about you, Teleutas?" Sostratos asked. "Have you picked up any Aramaic at all?"

"Not me. I'm not going to sound like I'm choking to death," Teleutas said. Then he asked a question of his own: "When we get back to old Ithran's inn, you going to try laying Zilpah again? Think you'll get it in this time?"

Sostratos tried to stand on his dignity, saying, "I don't know what you're talking about." He hoped he wasn't turning red, or, if he was, that his beard would hide his flush. How had the sailors known?

Teleutas' laugh was so raucous, so lewd, as to make Moskhion's Aramaic obscenity seem clean beside it. "No offense, but sure you don't. You think we didn't see you mooning over her? Come on! I think you'll do it this time, too. She likes you plenty, you bet. Sometimes they're shy, that's all. You've just got to push a little—and then you'll push all you want." He rocked his hips forward and back.

Moskhion and Aristeidas solemnly dipped their heads. Sostratos wondered if that meant his chances were pretty good, or simply that all three sailors were misreading the signs the same way.

I'm going to find out, he thought. *I have to find out.* The game seemed worth the risk. All of a sudden, he understood Menedemos much better than he'd ever wanted to. *How can I rail at him when I know why he does it?* he wondered unhappily.

He did his best to tell himself that, unlike his cousin, he wasn't risking anything or anyone by trying to learn whether Zilpah would go to bed with him. But, also unlike Menedemos, he'd been to the Lykeion. He'd learned how to root out self-deception. He knew perfectly well that he was telling himself lies. They were soothing lies, pleasant lies, but lies nonetheless.

What if, for instance, Zilpah had gone to Ithran and told him Sostratos had tried to seduce her? What would the innkeeper do when the Rhodian showed up at his door again? Wouldn't he be likely to try to smash in Sostratos' skull with a jar of wine or perhaps to stab him or spear him with whatever weapons he kept around the inn? Suppose things were reversed. Suppose Ithran, in Rhodes, had paid undue attention to Sostratos' wife (*assuming I had a wife,* Sostratos thought). *What would I have done if he fell into my hands after that? Something he would remember to the end of his days, whether that was near at hand or far away.*

And yet, knowing what Ithran might do on setting eyes on him, Sostratos led the sailors from the *Aphrodite* back toward the inn they'd quitted only a few days before. *This is madness,* he told himself, picking his way through the narrow, winding, rocky streets of Jerusalem. Every so often, he had to spend a few tiny silver coins on a passerby to get steered in the right direction. No one grabbed him by the front of the tunic and exclaimed, "Don't go back there! You must be the woman-mad Ionian Ithran swore he'd kill!" Sostratos chose to take that as a good sign, though he recognized he might be deceiving himself again.

"This is the street," Aristeidas said when they turned on to it. "We just passed the brothel—and there's Ithran's inn up ahead."

"So it is," Sostratos said in a hollow voice. Now that he was here, his heart pounded and his bowels felt loose. He was sure he'd made a dreadful mistake in returning. He started to say they ought to go somewhere else after all.

Too late for that—Ithran himself came out the front door of the inn with a basket full of rubbish, which he dumped in the street not far from the entrance. He started to go back inside, but then he caught sight of the four Rhodians heading his way. Sostratos tensed. He wondered if he should reach for Menedemos' bow, not that he could have strung it, let alone shot, before Ithran charged.

But then the innkeeper . . . waved. "Hail, friends," he called in his bad Greek. "You does good by Lake of Asphalt?"

"Pretty well, thanks," Sostratos answered, breathing a silent sigh of relief. Whatever else had happened, Zilpah hadn't said anything.

"You to stay a few day?" Ithran asked hopefully. "I have my old rooms back." Sostratos realized he was trying to say, *You have your old rooms back.* "Thank you," he said, and nodded, as people did in this part of the world. Switching from Greek to Aramaic, he added, "I thank you very much indeed, my master."

"I am your slave," Ithran said, also in Aramaic. "Name any boon, and it shall be yours." Aramaic was made for flowery promises no one would or intended to keep.

I wonder what would happen if I said, "Give me your wife to keep my bed warm till I go back to Sidon," Sostratos thought, and then, *No, I don't wonder.* That would show the differences between polite promises and real ones, and show it in a hurry.

While such musings filled the Rhodian's head, Ithran turned and shouted into the inn: "Zilpah! Pour wine! The Ionians have returned from the Lake of Asphalt."

"Have they?" The Ioudaian woman's voice, a mellow contralto, floated out into the street. "They are very welcome, then."

"Yes." Ithran nodded vigorously. He returned to Greek so all the men from the *Aphrodite* could understand: "You is all very welcome. Go in, drink wine. Slave will see to your beasts."

Teleutas, Aristeidas, and Moskhion looked eager to do just what he'd said. In a dry voice, Sostratos told the sailors, "Get the goods off the donkey before we start drinking. We've come a long way to get what we've got. If we let somebody steal it, we might as well have stayed in Rhodes."

A little sulkily, the men obeyed. It was only a few minutes before they did sit down in the taproom to drink the wine Zilpah had poured. The room was dark and shadowed, light sneaking in only through the doorway and a couple of narrow windows. That gloom and the inn's thick walls of mud brick left the taproom much cooler than the bake-oven air outside.

"Is Hekataios still here?" Sostratos asked Zilpah when she refilled his cup.

She shook her head. "No. He left the day after you did, bound for his home in Egypt." Her shrug was dismissive. "He is a clever man, but not so clever as he thinks he is."

"I think you are right," Sostratos said. He wondered if she would say the same thing about him after he left for Sidon. He hoped not, anyhow. Because the sailors from the akatos had learned so little Aramaic, he could speak to her as freely as if they weren't there. He took advantage of that, adding, "I think you are beautiful."

"I think you should not say these things," Zilpah answered quietly. Out in the courtyard, Ithran started hammering away at something—perhaps at a door for one of the rooms. A burst of guttural curses in Aramaic proclaimed that he might have hammered his own thumb, too.

Aristeidas gulped down his wine. "What do you say we pay a visit to the girls down the street?" he said in Greek. Moskhion and Teleutas both dipped their heads. All three men hurried out of the inn.

"Where are they going?" Zilpah asked.

"To the brothel," Sostratos said. Ithran kept pounding in the courtyard. As long as he did that, no one could have any doubts of where he was. Sostratos went on, "I was sorry to go. I am glad to be back."

"And soon you will go again," Zilpah said.

Sostratos shrugged and nodded; the gesture was almost starting to feel natural to him. "Yes, that is so. I wish it were different, but it is so." He reached out and touched her hand, just for a moment. "We have little time. Should we not use it?"

She turned away from him. "You should not say such things to me. You make me think things I am not supposed to think."

"Do you think that I think you are beautiful? Do you think that I think you are sweet?" Sostratos said. "Do you think that I want to love you? You should think that, because it is true."

Still not looking at him, Zilpah spoke in a very small voice: "These are things I should not hear from you. I have never heard these things before." She laughed. "I have heard from men who want to sleep with me. What innkeeper's wife has not? But you . . . you mean what you say. You are not telling lies to get me to lie down with you."

"Yes, I mean them. No, I am not lying," Sostratos said.

"People who mean these things should not say them," Zilpah insisted. "I have never heard things like these from someone who means them."

"Never?" Sostratos raised an eyebrow. "You spoke of this before. These are things your husband"—who kept on hammering out in the courtyard—"should say."

"Ithran is a good man," Zilpah said, as if the Rhodian had denied it.

Sostratos said nothing at all. He let her words hang in the air, let her listen to them again and again in her own mind. She brought her hands up to her face. Her shoulders shook. Sostratos knew a moment of raw fear. If she started crying loud enough for Ithran to notice, what would the Ioudaian do to him? He didn't know, not in detail. Whatever it was, though, it wasn't likely to be pretty.

"I think," Zilpah said, "I think you had better go to your room now."

"I would rather sit here and drink wine and talk with you

and look at you so I can see how beautiful you are," Sostratos said.

The Ioudaian woman swung back toward him. Her black
eyes flashed. "I said, I think you had better go to your room,"
she snapped. "Do you understand me when I tell you something?"

"I understand what you say. I do not understand why you
say it," Sostratos replied. Once again, a *why* question seemed
all-important.

Here, though, it got no answer. "Go!" Zilpah said, and he
could hardly tell her no, not when this was her inn, this was
her city, this was her country—and that was her husband out
there in the courtyard. He gulped his wine and hurried out of
the taproom. Ithran waved to him as he hurried back toward
his room. He waved back. The innkeeper might have suspected something if he hadn't. Part of him felt ashamed at
treating the Ioudaian in a friendly way when he wanted to
make love to the man's wife. The rest of him, though . . .
When he saw a good-sized stone in the courtyard, that other
part of him wanted to pick it up and bash in Ithran's head.

Still seething, he went into his room and closed the door
behind him. It didn't drown out the noise of Ithran's hammering. He paced back and forth in the cramped little chamber, feeling trapped. What could he do in here? Nothing
except lie down and go to sleep, which he didn't want to do,
or pace and brood. He didn't want to do that, either, but did
it even so.

After what seemed forever, the hammering stopped. Sostratos kept right on pacing. He wished he'd gone to the brothel
with the sailors. But if he went there now, they'd know he'd
failed with Zilpah. He didn't feel like humiliating himself
right this minute. Later would do.

Someone tapped at the door. When Sostratos noticed the
tapping, he had the feeling it had been going on for some little
while. He wondered what the sailors were doing back from
the brothel so soon. But when he opened the door, no sated
Hellenes stood there. Instead, it was Zilpah.

"Oh," Sostratos said foolishly. "You."

"Yes, me." She ducked inside, past Sostratos, who stood frozen, as if seeing a Gorgon had turned him to stone. "Are you daft?" she said. "Shut the door. Quick, now."

"Oh," he said again. "Yes." He did as she said. He found he could move after all, if only jerkily.

"Ithran is gone for a while. The slave is gone for a while. And so . . ." Zilpah didn't go on for a moment. In the gloom inside the little chamber, her eyes were enormous. With a gesture that seemed more angry than anything else, she threw off her mantling robe and then the shift she wore under it. "Tell me you love me," she said. "Tell me you think I'm beautiful. Make me believe you, at least for a little while." Her laugh was harsh and rough as dry branches breaking. "It shouldn't be hard. No one else is going to tell me anything like that."

"No?" Sostratos said. Zilpah shook her head. He sighed. "You spoke of that before. It is too bad, for someone misses a perfect chance. You are very beautiful, and I will love you as best I know how."

"Talk to me, too," she said. "Tell me these things. I need to *hear* them."

Most women wanted Sostratos to keep quiet while he was making love to them. Talk before or after might be all right. During? Never before had anyone asked him to talk during. He only wished he could do it in Greek. In Aramaic, he couldn't say a tenth part of what he wanted to tell her.

But he did his best. In between kisses and caresses, he assured her that she was the loveliest and the sweetest woman he'd ever met, and that anyone who'd missed the chance to tell her the same thing was surely an ass, an idiot, a blockhead. While he said it, he believed it. That his tongue teased her earlobe, the side of her neck, the dark tips of her breasts, that his fingers stroked between her legs and that she arched her back and breathed hard while they did—that might have had something to do with his belief.

She hissed when he went into her. He'd never known a sound like that from a woman. She took her pleasure almost at once and twisted her head so that his pillow muffled most of her moan of joy. He kept on, and kept on, and she heated again, and the second time she gasped and wailed she forgot all about trying to keep quiet. He might have warned her, but his own ecstasy burst over him then, irresistible as an avalanche.

"I love you," he said again, as soon as pleasure didn't quite blind him.

Zilpah started to cry. She pushed him away from her. "I have sinned," she said. "I have sinned, and I am a fool." She dressed as fast as she could. As she did, she went on, "You will leave tomorrow. If you don't leave tomorrow, I will tell Ithran what we have done. I have sinned. Oh, how I have sinned."

"I don't understand," Sostratos said.

"What do you need to understand?" Zilpah said. "I was angry at my husband for not speaking sweetly to me, and I made a mistake. I sinned, so the one god will punish me for it."

Sostratos had heard Ioudaioi talk of sin before. It was something like religious pollution among Hellenes, but stronger. He got the feeling Zilpah thought her bad-tempered god was angry at her. "I will do as you say," he told her with a sigh.

"You had better." She hurried out the door. She didn't slam it, but only, he judged, so she wouldn't make a scene. He sighed again. He'd had her, and pleased her, and she still wasn't happy. *Am I?* he wondered. Part of him was, anyhow. The rest? He wasn't at all sure about the rest.

10

"I KNOW PEOPLE SAY PHOENICIANS BURN THEIR babies when things are going badly for them," Menedemos told a soldier with whom he was drinking wine. "But is that really true? Do they really offer them to their gods that way?"

"Yea, verily," the mercenary answered. His name was Apollodoros; he came from Paphos, on Cyprus, and used the old-fashioned island dialect. "In sooth, Rhodian, they do nothing less, reckoning it an act of devotion; any who'd refuse or hide his babes'd be torn in pieces, did word of's iniquity seep forth."

"Madness," Menedemos muttered.

"Aye, belike," Apollodoros agreed. "But then, could we look for civilized behavior 'mongst the barbarians, they'd be barbarians no more, but rather Hellenes."

"I suppose so." By then, Menedemos had drunk enough to make his wits a little fuzzy, or maybe more than a little. "When my cousin gets back from Ioudaia, I won't be sorry to say farewell to this place."

"And you'll hie you homeward?" the Paphian said. Menedemos dipped his head. Apollodoros waved to the Phoenician tavernkeeper for a refill. The fellow nodded and waved back to show he'd understood, then came over with a jar of wine. The mercenary turned back to Menedemos: "Have you thought of staying here instead?"

"Only in my nightmares," Menedemos answered. Most of those, these days, revolved around Emashtart. He feared the innkeeper's wife would haunt his nights for years to come, screeching, *Binein! Binein!* He'd never known a woman with whom the prospect of physical congress seemed less appealing.

"I meant not as a trader, O best one, not as a merchant," Apollodoros said, "but as a soldier, a warrior, a fighting man."

"For Antigonos?"

"Certes, for Antigonos," the mercenary answered. "A great man, the greatest of this sorry age. For whom would you liefer swing a sword?"

"I'd gladly fight for Rhodes, as any man with ballocks under his prong would fight for his polis," Menedemos said. "But I never thought to hire myself out." That would do till a bigger understatement came along.

"Ah, my dear, there's no life like unto it," Apollodoros said. "Food and shelter when not on campaign—and pay, too, mind—and all those chances for loot when the drum beats and you fare forth to war."

"No, thanks," Menedemos said. "I'm a peaceable sort. I don't want any trouble with anybody, and I don't get into fights for the fun of it."

"By my troth, the more fool you!" Apollodoros exclaimed. "How better to show the world you make a better man than your foe?"

"By taking home silver he should have kept," Menedemos replied. "By knowing you've made him into a fool."

"A fool?" The mercenary gestured scornfully. "Make him into a slave, or a corpse. An you seek silver, take it by selling the wretch you've beaten."

"This life suits you," Menedemos said. "That's plain. I couldn't live as you do, though. It's not what I want to do."

"A pity. You could make a soldier. I see you're strong and quick. Those count for more than size, nor never let any wight say otherwise."

"Whether they do or not, I don't want to carry a spear and a sword and a shield," Menedemos said.

"Here, drink you more wine," Apollodoros said, and waved to the taverner to fill Menedemos' cup again, even though it was still a quarter full.

Menedemos had already drunk enough to grow a little muzzy, yes, but his wits still worked. *He's trying to get me very drunk, very drunk indeed,* he thought. *Why is he trying to do that?* The grinning tapman came up with the winejar. "Wait," Menedemos said, and put a hand over the mouth of his cup. He turned to the mercenary. "Do you think you can get me blind drunk and turn me into a soldier before I come to and figure out what's happened to me?"

Apollodoros affected shock and dismay. In the course of many, many dickers, Menedemos had often seen it better done. "Wherefore should I essay so wicked a deed as that, most noble one?" the fellow asked, voice dripping innocence.

"I don't know why, but I can make some guesses," Menedemos answered. "How big a bonus do you get for each new recruit you bring in?"

He kept a close eye on the soldier from Paphos. Sure enough, Apollodoros flinched, though he said, "I know not what you mean, my friend, for in sooth I thought but to make symposiasts of us both, that we might revel the whole day through. I'd not bethought me to come upon so fine a boon companion in such a low dive as this."

"That sounds very pretty," Menedemos said, "but I don't believe a word of it." He drained his cup, then set it back on the table. "I don't want any more wine," he told the taverner in Greek. Then, for good measure, he trotted out two words of Aramaic: "Wine? No!" *Sostratos would be proud of me,* he thought as he got up to go.

"Wait, friend." Apollodoros set a hand on his arm. "By my troth, you do mistake me, and in the mistaking do me wrong."

"I don't want to wait for anything," Menedemos said. "Farewell."

But when Menedemos started to leave, Apollodoros hung on tight. "Stay," the mercenary urged. "Stay and drink." He didn't sound so friendly any more,

"Let go of me," Menedemos said. The soldier still clung to him. He used a wrestling move to try to twist free. Apollodoros made the most obvious counter. Menedemos had thought he would—Apollodoros had little in the way of subtlety in him. Another twist, a sudden jerk, a grab . . .

"*Oê!*" Apollodoros yowled as his wrist bent back and back. Menedemos needed only a very little more pressure to break it, and they both knew as much. Apollodoros spoke very fast: "You do but misperceive my intentions, friend, and—"

"I think I perceive them just fine, thanks." Menedemos bent the mercenary's wrist a tiny bit more. Something in there gave under his grip—not a bone but a tendon or something of the sort. Apollodoros gasped and went fishbelly pale. Menedemos said, "I can use a knife, too. If you come after me, you'll be very, very sorry. Do you believe me? Eh?" Yet more pressure.

"Yes!" Apollodoros whispered. "Furies take you, yes!"

"Good." Menedemos let go. He didn't turn his back on the soldier, but Apollodoros only sank down onto a stool, cradling the injured wrist. "Farewell," Menedemos said again, and left the tavern.

This place didn't explode in a brawl behind him. He looked back over his shoulder after he walked out, to make sure Apollodoros hadn't changed his mind and decided to come after him, and that the Paphian didn't have any friends in the place who might want to do the job for him. No one emerged from the wineshop. Menedemos grinned. *My bet is, Apollodoros hasn't got any friends,* he thought.

Around the corner from the tavern, he passed a wineshop of a different sort, one that sold wine by the amphora rather than by the cup. Remembering the fine wine Zakerbaal the cloth merchant had served him, he stuck his head into the place and called, "Does anybody here speak Greek?"

The proprietor was a man of about his father's age, with a bushy white beard, even bushier black eyebrows, and an enormous hooked nose. "Speak little bit," he said, and held his thumb and forefinger close together to show how little that was.

For what Menedemos had in mind, the man didn't need to know much of his language. He asked, "Have you got wine from Byblos here? Good wine from Byblos?"

"From Byblos? Wine?" The Phoenician seemed to want to make sure he'd heard correctly. Menedemos dipped his head. Then, remembering he was in foreign parts, he nodded instead. The Phoenician smiled at him. "Wine from Byblos. Yes. I having. You—?" He didn't seem able to remember how to say *taste* or *try*. Instead, he mimed drinking from a cup.

"Yes. Thank you." Menedemos nodded again.

"Good. I give. I Mattan son of Mago," the wine merchant said. Menedemos gave his name and that of his father. He watched as Mattan opened an amphora, and noted its shape:

each city had its own distinctive style of jar, some round, others elongated. When the Phoenician handed him the cup, he sniffed. Sure enough, the wine had the rich floral bouquet that had struck him at Zakerbaal's home.

He drank. As before, the wine's flavor wasn't quite so fine as its aroma, but it wasn't bad, either. He asked, "How much for an amphora?"

When Mattan said, "Six shekels—sigloi, you say," Menedemos had to fight to keep his jaw from dropping. Twelve Rhodian drakhmai the jar for a wine of that quality was a bargain even without haggling.

Menedemos didn't intend to let Mattan know that was what he thought. He put on the most severe expression he could and said, "I'll give you three and a half."

Mattan said something pungent in Aramaic. Menedemos bowed to him. That made the Phoenician laugh. They haggled for a while, as much for the sake of the game as because either of them was very worried about the final price. At last, they settled on five sigloi the jar.

After they clasped hands to seal the bargain, Mattan son of Mago said, "You not tell. How much of jars you want?"

"How many have you got?" Menedemos asked.

"I look." Mattan counted the amphorai of Byblian resting in their places on the wooden shelves that lined the walls of his shop. Then he went into a back room behind the counter. When he came out, he said, "Forty-six." To make sure he had the number right, he opened and closed his hands four times, and showed one open hand and the upthrust index finger of the other.

"Have you got a counting board?" Menedemos asked. He had to eke out the question with gestures before Mattan nodded and took it out from under the counter. Menedemos flicked pebbles back and forth in the grooves. After a little while, he looked up at the Phoenician and said, "I owe you two hundred thirty sigloi, then."

Mattan son of Mago had watched as he worked out the answer. The Phoenician nodded. "Yes, that right," he said.

"Good, then," Menedemos said. "I'll bring you the money, and I'll bring sailors from my ship to take away the wine."

"Is good. I here," Mattan said.

Had the full crew been aboard the *Aphrodite,* they could have done the job in one trip. With so many of them off roistering in Sidon, it took three. By the time they finished hauling the heavy amphorai to the merchant galley, the men were sweaty and exhausted. A couple of the ones who could swim jumped naked off the ship into the water of the harbor to cool down. Menedemos gave all the sailors who'd hauled wine jars an extra day's pay—that wasn't part of their regular work.

"Smart, skipper," Diokles said approvingly. "They'll like you better for it."

"They earned it," Menedemos replied. "They worked like slaves there."

"We've got a good cargo for the trip home, though," the keleustes said. "That fancy silk you found, the crimson dye, now this good wine—"

"We're only missing one thing," Menedemos said.

Diokles frowned. "What's that? With all we've picked up here, I can't think of anything."

Menedemos answered in one word: "Sostratos."

SOSTRATOS PEERED BACK at Jerusalem from the ridge to the north from which he'd first got a good look at the chief town of the Ioudaioi. He sighed. Next to him, Teleutas laughed. "Was she as good in bed as all that?" he asked. Aristeidas and Moskhion both chuckled. They also crowded closer to hear Sostratos' reply.

"I don't know," he said after a bit of thought. He didn't see how he could keep quiet, not when the sailors already knew so much more than he might have wished. "I really don't know. But it's . . . different when you're not buying it, isn't it?"

Aristeidas dipped his head. "It's sweetest when they give it to you for love."

Menedemos had always felt that way, which was why he liked to chase other men's wives instead of—or in addition to—going to brothels. Now, after bedding Zilpah, Sostratos understood. He sighed again. He wouldn't forget her. But he feared she would spend the rest of her days trying to forget him. That wasn't what he'd had in mind, but it was how things seemed to have worked out.

Teleutas laughed again, a coarse, altogether masculine laugh. "You ask me, it's just fine whenever you manage to stick it in there." The other two sailors laughed, too. Moskhion dipped his head in agreement.

In one sense, Sostratos supposed Teleutas had a point. The pleasure of the act itself wasn't much different for a man regardless of whether he bedded a whore or his own wife or someone else's. But what it meant, what he felt about himself and his partner afterwards—those could, and indeed almost had to, vary widely.

Had Menedemos been there, Sostratos would have taken the argument further. With Teleutas, he let it drop. The less he had to talk to the sailor, the better he liked it. He said, "Let's keep moving, that's all. The faster we go, the sooner we'll get back to Sidon and the *Aphrodite*."

Aristeidas, Moskhion, and Teleutas all murmured approvingly at that. Moskhion said, "By the gods, it'll be nice to speak Greek again with more people than just us."

"That's right." Aristeidas dipped his head. "By now, we're all sick of listening to each other, anyhow." He glanced over at Sostratos, then hastily added, "Uh, meaning no offense, young sir."

"Don't worry about it," Sostratos said. "I know you're sick of me."

He didn't mention the obvious corollary. Aristeidas did it for him: "You're sick of us, too, eh?"

Once again, Sostratos faced the dilemma of choosing between an unpalatable truth and an obvious lie. In the end, he chose neither. With a wry smile, he asked, "How on earth could you dream of such a thing?" That made the sailors laugh, which was better than offending them or treating them like fools.

They tramped on. After a while, Teleutas said, "I think we ought to look to our weapons. We've come this far without any trouble. It'd be a shame if we got robbed when we were so close to getting back to Sidon."

Sostratos wanted to tell him he was worrying over nothing. He wanted to, but knew he couldn't. What he did say, regretfully, was, "That's a good idea."

He'd never let Menedemos' bow get far from him while he was on the road. Now he took it out of its case and strung it. The case itself, which also held his arrows, he wore at his left side, slung over his right shoulder with a leather strap. "You look like a Skythian nomad," Aristeidas said.

"The case looks like a Skythian nomad's," Sostratos said, tossing his head, "for we use the same style they do—I suppose we borrowed it from them. But tell me, my dear, when have you ever imagined a Skythian nomad aboard a plodding mule?" That made the sailors laugh again. Sostratos, a thoroughly indifferent rider even on a mule, thought it was pretty funny, too.

Toward noon, half a dozen Ioudaioi came down the road toward the Hellenes. The strangers were all young men, all on the ragged side, and all armed with spears or swords. They gave Sostratos and his companions long, thoughtful looks as the two parties drew near. The Rhodians looked back, not in a way suggesting they wanted a fight, but as if to say they could put up a good one if they had to.

Both little bands got halfway off the road as they edged past each other. Neither seemed to want to give the other any excuse for starting trouble. "Peace be unto you," Sostratos called to the Ioudaioi in Aramaic.

"And to you also peace," a man from the other band replied.

One of the other Ioudaioi muttered something else, something Sostratos was even gladder to hear: "More trouble than they're worth." A couple of the young man's friends nodded.

Despite that, Sostratos looked back over his shoulder several times to make sure the Ioudaioi weren't turning around to come after his companions and him. Once, he saw a Ioudaian looking back over his shoulder at him and the sailors. "We made them respect us," he told the other Rhodians.

"A good thing, too," Moskhion said, "for I always respect bastards who outnumber me—you'd best believe I do."

"If we run into six bandits, or eight, or even ten, we're probably fine," Sostratos said, "because a little band like that can see we have teeth. They might beat us, but we'd cost them half their men. One of those fellows called us more trouble than we're worth. That's how most bands would feel about us."

"What about a band with forty or fifty men in it, though?" Aristeidas asked worriedly. "A bandit troop that big could roll right over us and hardly even know we were there."

"The thing is, there aren't very many bandit troops with forty or fifty men in them." Teleutas spoke before Sostratos could answer. "A troop like that is more like an army than your usual pack of robbers. It needs a village of its own, pretty much, on account of keeping that many men fed isn't easy. And it's the big bands that soldiers move against, too. Most bandits turn back into farmers when soldiers come sniffing after 'em. A big troop can't do that, or not easily, anyhow—too many people know who they are and where they roost. It either splits up into a bunch of little bands or else it stands and fights."

Aristeidas thought it over, then dipped his head. "Makes sense," he said.

It did indeed make sense. It made so much sense, Sostratos sent Teleutas a very thoughtful look. How had the sailor acquired such intimate knowledge of the way robber bands worked? Had he been part of one, or more than one, himself? That wouldn't have surprised Sostratos, not a bit. There were technical treatises on things like cookery and how to build catapults, but he'd never heard of, never imagined, a technical treatise on how to become a successful bandit. Even if such a monster of a book existed, he didn't think Teleutas could read.

Moskhion must have been thinking along with him. "I got out of sponge diving because pulling an oar was a better job," he said. "What did you get out of to turn sailor, Teleutas?"

"Oh, this and that," Teleutas answered, and gave no details.

The Hellenes took a more westerly route up to Sidon than they had on their way down to Jerusalem. They spent the night in a village called Gamzo. The place was so small it didn't even have an inn. Having got permission from the locals, Sostratos built a fire in the middle of the market square. He bought bread and oil and wine and, feeling extravagant, a duck. He and the other men from the *Aphrodite* roasted the meat over the fire and feasted.

Children—and more than a few adults—came out of their houses to stare at the Rhodians. As elsewhere in Ioudaia, Sostratos wondered if these people had ever seen a Hellene before. He got to his feet, bowed in all directions, and spoke in Aramaic: "Peace be unto you all."

Even though he'd already dickered with them for food, some of them seemed surprised he spoke their language. By their expressions, some seemed surprised he spoke any human language. But three or four men answered, "And to you also peace." That was the right response.

Even though it was, it didn't feel hearty enough to satisfy Sostratos. He bowed again. This time, he said, "May your one god bless Gamzo and all its people."

That did the trick. Broad smiles gleamed on the faces of the Ioudaioi. All the men bowed to Sostratos. "May the one god bless you as well, stranger, and your friends," a graybeard said. The rest of the villagers nodded.

"Stand up," Sostratos hissed in Greek to the other Rhodians. "Bow to them. Be friendly."

One after another, the sailors did. Aristeidas even proved able to say, "Peace be unto you," in Aramaic. That made the people of Gamzo smile. Moskhion refrained from trotting out his frightful Aramaic obscenity. That made Sostratos smile.

Another gray-bearded man, this one wearing a robe of fine wool, said, "You are Ionians, not so?" Sostratos remembered to nod. The Ioudaian said, "We have heard evil things of Ionians, but you seem to be good enough men, even if you are foreigners. May the one god bless you and keep you. May he lift up his countenance unto you and give you peace."

"Thank you," Sostratos said, and bowed once more. A little more slowly than they should have, the sailors bowed again, too. Sostratos added, "And we thank you for your generous hospitality."

"You are welcome in Gamzo," the Ioudaian—plainly a village leader—declared. He strode up, clasped Sostratos' hand, and kissed him on both cheeks. Then he did the same with the rest of the Rhodians. The men in the crowd came up after him. They greeted Sostratos and his companions the same way. Even the women drew near, though the Hellenes got no handclasps or kisses from them. Remembering the kisses he'd had from Zilpah in Jerusalem, Sostratos sighed. Somehow he'd pleased her and made her desperately unhappy all at the same time.

Deciding the Rhodians were safe enough, the folk of Gamzo withdrew back into their homes. Even so, Sostratos said, "We'll divide the night into four watches. Everybody will take one. You never know." The sailors didn't argue with him. He'd half expected that they, or at least Teleutas, would, on the grounds that one sentry couldn't keep the locals from doing whatever they were going to do. *Maybe they're starting to take me seriously,* Sostratos thought with no small pride.

When morning came, Teleutas was all for an early departure. Sostratos' pride only grew. Even the sometimes difficult sailor was acting responsible. Sostratos wondered if Teleutas was following his example.

It was about the third hour of the day when Sostratos noticed Teleutas was wearing a golden bracelet he didn't recall seeing before. "Where did you get that?" he asked.

The sailor grinned a sly grin. "Back in that miserable little dump where we stayed last night."

That was likely to mean only one thing. Sostratos clapped a hand to his forehead. "*Papai!* You stole it?" So much for responsibility!

"Nothing to get upset about," Teleutas said soothingly. "We'll never see that place again in all our days."

"They made us guest-friends, and that's how you paid them back?" Sostratos said. Teleutas only shrugged; the ritual duties of guest-friends plainly meant nothing to him. Sostratos tried another tack: "What if all the men in Gamzo come after us and want to cut our livers out?"

Teleutas looked back toward the south and shrugged again. "I've been watching. No sign of a dust cloud or anything like that. We're far enough ahead of 'em by now that they can't catch us. By Hermes, the fool I lifted it from probably still hasn't figured out it's gone missing."

"No wonder you swear by the god of thieves," Sostratos said. Teleutas grinned again, singularly unrepentant. Sostratos might have said a good deal more, but decided the road in a foreign land was no place to do it. He also decided that if the men of Gamzo came after the bracelet and Teleutas he would hand them the ornament and the sailor without a qualm.

He kept that to himself. He didn't know how Aristeidas and Moskhion would react, and he didn't want to risk destroying his ability to lead unless he had to. But he vowed he would talk with Menedemos about leaving Teleutas behind when he got back to Sidon. A man who would steal from barbarians he was unlikely to see again might not try stealing from his own shipmates. Then again, he might.

For the rest of the day, Sostratos kept looking back over his shoulder. He saw no sign of the villagers. In a way, that relieved him. In another way, it disappointed him. He might have used them as an excuse to be rid of Teleutas.

Farmers tended vineyards and olive groves. Shepherds and goatherds followed their flocks through the hills. Hawks circled overhead, looking for the mice and other small animals frightened out of cover when the flocks went by. Sostratos saw one swoop down and rise with something struggling in its talons. The struggle didn't last long.

As the sun sank toward the Inner Sea, another band of young Ioudaioi came toward the Rhodians. There were eight of them. Sostratos saw they were all armed. He didn't like the way their heads came up when they spotted his comrades and him: it put him in mind of a pack of dogs spotting a sick sheep they hoped to be able to pull down.

"Let's get off the road and let them go by," he said. "Look—there's a clump of boulders where we can make a stand if we have to."

He hoped the sailors would laugh at him and tell him he was starting at shadows. Instead, they all dipped their heads. Teleutas said, "Good idea. They look like a nasty bunch, and I'll be glad to see their backs." If *he* thought the Ioudaioi looked dangerous, they were only too likely to mean trouble.

By the time they came up to the Hellenes, Sostratos and the other men from the *Aphrodite* had already taken cover among the boulders by the side of the road. The sailors and Sostratos got their helmets from the pack donkey and jammed them down onto their heads. The Ioudaioi kept on toward the south, some of them trailing the butts of their spears in the dirt. They did not seem to own any body armor.

One of them waved to the Hellenes as he went past. "Peace be unto you," he called. A couple of his pals laughed. Sostratos didn't like the sound of that baying, mocking laughter. He didn't answer.

"Maybe they'll decide we're a tough nut to crack, and they'll go on by," Moskhion said. "That's what you said they do most of the time."

"Maybe. I hope so." Sostratos watched the young men head on down the track in the direction of Gamzo. "All the same, though, I don't think we ought to leave this place for a while yet. They may try doubling back to catch us out in the open." He thought about the hawk and about the little animal that had writhed—for a bit—in its claws.

Aristeidas peered out from a south-facing crevice between two good-sized stones. After perhaps a quarter of an hour had passed, he stiffened. "Here they come!"

"Oh, a pestilence!" Sostratos exclaimed. He'd been cautious, yes, but he hadn't really believed the Ioudaioi would come back and try to rob his companions and him. But when he peered south himself, he saw that Aristeidas was right. The Ioudaioi were loping across the fields toward the boulders among which the Rhodians sheltered.

"Shoot the gods-detested catamites!" Moskhion said.

Sostratos put an arrow in the bow and drew a bead on the closest Ioudaian. The fellow wasn't quite in range yet, but he would be soon. Sostratos drew the arrow back to his breast and then, in Persian fashion, back to his ear. The would-be robber ran straight at him—probably hadn't seen him there among the rocks.

Well, too bad for him, Sostratos thought, and let fly. The bowstring lashed his wrist. Real archers wore leather guards. Sostratos knew as much but didn't have one. But he felt very much like a real archer a moment later, for his arrow caught the Ioudaian square in the chest.

The man ran on for another couple of paces, clawing at the shaft. Then his legs might suddenly have gone from bone and flesh to wet clay. They gave way beneath him. He crumpled to the ground. The Ioudaioi shouted in surprise and dismay.

"*Euge!* Well shot!" The Rhodians were shouting, too. "Give 'em another one!"

"I'll try." Sostratos nocked a second arrow. The onrushing foes weren't trying to dodge. The only way they could have given him easier marks would have been by standing still. He drew the bow and loosed in one smooth motion.

A second Ioudaian toppled, this one with an arrow through the thigh. He let out a horrible scream of pain. Sostratos didn't think that wound would be mortal, but it would take the man out of the fight. He couldn't ask for anything better, not now he couldn't.

"Knock 'em all down!" Teleutas said.

"I'll do my best," Sostratos answered. Already he'd cut the odds against his side from two-to-one to three-to-two. But the Ioudaioi he hadn't shot were getting dreadfully close.

He let fly at another man, a shot he should have made in his sleep—and missed. Now he scrabbled for an arrow with desperate haste. He'd have time for only one more shot before the fighting went hand-to-hand. He loosed again, at the same bandit, and hit him just above the bridge of the nose. The Ioudaian fell, dead before he hit the ground.

No one cheered this time. The surviving Ioudaioi were scrambling toward the Rhodians. A couple of them flung rocks to make Sostratos and his comrades keep their heads down. "Curses upon them," one of the robbers said. "Already they've cost us too much."

"We have to pay them back," another Ioudaian said. "Come on! Be brave!"

They couldn't know that Sostratos understood Aramaic. He hadn't hailed them when they went by before. It didn't matter, not yet, but it might.

A rock banged off a boulder just above his head, then hit him in the back on the rebound. He yelped. A Ioudaian with a sword came toward him. The fellow's face wore a furious snarl.

Sostratos had only an eating knife on his belt. He stooped and picked up the rock the robber had flung at him. He hurled it back with all his strength. It caught the Ioudaian on the shoulder. He howled out an obscenity. Sostratos had to fight to keep from giggling like an idiot—the curse was the same as the one Moskhion had brought out on the road a few days earlier. The Rhodian grabbed another rock and threw it. It thudded into the robber's ribs. With that, the Ioudaian decided he'd had enough. He turned around and ran away, one hand clutched to his chest. Sostratos hoped the rock had broken something.

He whirled to help his comrades. Moskhion and Teleutas were both fighting hard. Sostratos didn't see Aristeidas among the rocks and didn't have time to look for him. *"Eleleu! Eleleu!"* he shouted, dashing toward the pair of Ioudaioi besetting Teleutas.

Either the war cry or the sound of running feet was enough to discourage them. They ran like their companion. "I never thought we'd pay so dear," one of them cried as he fled.

"We must have angered the one god," his friend said.

Robbing travelers who've caused you no harm might do that, Sostratos thought. He and Teleutas turned on the pair Moskhion was holding off with his pike. Suddenly, Hellenes outnumbered Ioudaioi. The last robbers ran off, too. One of them also loudly wondered why their god had forsaken them. Sostratos understood him, but knowing Aramaic hadn't mattered at all in the fight.

As quickly as that, it was over. "Aristei—" Sostratos began.

He heard the groan before he finished the sailor's name. Most likely, Aristeidas had been moaning behind a boulder a few cubits away ever since he went down, but in the heat of the fight Sostratos hadn't paid any attention. Now, with his own life not immediately in danger, he gave more heed to things around him.

So did the other Rhodians. "That doesn't sound good," Teleutas said. He was bleeding from a cut on one arm and a scraped knee but didn't seem to notice his hurts.

"No," Sostratos said, and scrambled over the rocks till he came upon the *Aphrodite*'s lookout. His breath hissed from him in dismay. "Oh, by the gods," he whispered.

Aristeidas lay on his side, still clutching with both hands the shaft of the spear that pierced his belly. His blood ran down the smooth wood and pooled on the stony ground under him. It also poured from his mouth and from his nose. Every breath brought another groan. He was dying, but not fast enough.

From behind Sostratos, Teleutas said, "Pull out the spear, and that'll be the end of it. Either that or cut his throat. One way or the other, get it over with."

"But—" Sostratos gulped. Killing enemies from a distance with a bow was one thing. Ending the life of a shipmate, the bright, sharp-eyed sailor who'd been on the way toward turning into a friend, was something else again.

"He can't live," Teleutas said patiently. "If you haven't got the stomach for it, young sir, move aside, and I'll take care of it. It's nothing I haven't done before."

Though Teleutas was obviously right, Sostratos might have argued further. But Aristeidas, through his pain, managed to bring out a recognizable word: "Please."

"Do you want to do it, or shall I?" Teleutas asked again.

"I will," Sostratos said. "It's my fault he came here. I'll tend to it." Despite his words, he gulped again. He knelt by Aristeidas and tried to get the dying sailor's hands away from the spear that had drunk his life. But Aristeidas wouldn't let go. Sostratos realized a death grip was something real, not a cliché of bad tragedy.

"Pull it out," Teleutas urged again. "He can't last more than another couple of minutes after you do."

"No." Sostratos tossed his head. He knelt beside Aristeidas, lifted the sailor's chin with his left hand, and cut his throat with the knife in his right. Some of the blood that spurted from the wound splashed his fingers. It was hot and wet and sticky. Sostratos jerked his hand away with a moan of disgust.

Aristeidas thrashed for a little while, but not long. His hands fell away from the spear. He lay still. Sostratos turned away and threw up on the dirt.

"No blood-guilt to you, young sir," Moskhion said. "You were only putting him out of his torment. He asked you to do it. Teleutas and I both heard him along with you."

"That's right," Teleutas said. "That's just right. You did what you had to do, and you did it proper. You put paid to three of the robbers, too, all by yourself, and I guess you drove the fourth bastard away. That's pretty good work for somebody who's not supposed to be much of a fighter."

"Sure is," Moskhion agreed. "You'll never have trouble from *me* any more."

Sostratos hardly heard him. He spat again and again, trying to get the nasty taste out of his mouth. He knew he would, before too long. Whether he ever got the blackness out of his spirit—that was a different question. He looked at Aristeidas' body, then quickly looked away. His guts wanted to heave up again.

But he wasn't done, and he knew it. "We can't bring him

back to Sidon," he said, "and we can't get enough wood for a proper pyre. We'll have to bury him here."

"Cover him with stones, you mean," Teleutas said. "I wouldn't want to try digging in this miserable, rocky dirt, especially without the proper tools."

He was right, as he had been with putting Aristeidas out of his pain. Before beginning the work, Sostratos cut off a lock of his hair and tossed it down on the sailor's corpse as a token of mourning. Moskhion and Teleutas did the same. Teleutas yanked the spear out of Aristeidas' belly and flung it far away. Then the three surviving Rhodians piled boulders and smaller stones on the body, covering it well enough to keep dogs and foxes and carrion birds from feasting on it.

By the time they finished, their hands were battered and scraped and bloody. Sostratos hardly noticed, let alone cared. He stood by the makeshift grave and murmured, "Sleep well, Aristeidas. I'm sorry we leave you on foreign soil. May your shade find peace."

Moskhion let a couple of oboloi fall through the gaps between the stones toward the corpse. "There's the ferryman's fee, to pay your way over the Styx," he said.

"Good." Sostratos looked west. The sun stood only a little way above the horizon. "Let's get moving, and keep moving till it gets too dark to travel or till we find a campsite that's easy to defend. And then . . . tomorrow we'll push on toward Sidon."

MENEDEMOS BUSIED HIMSELF about the *Aphrodite,* fussing over where the jars of crimson dye he'd bought from Tenashtart were stowed. He moved them farther aft, then farther forward. He knew they wouldn't affect the akatos' trim very much, but he fussed over them anyhow.

The amphorai of Byblian wine posed a more interesting problem. He had fewer of them, but each was far heavier than a jar of dye. And he couldn't properly test the merchant galley's trim till he got out onto the open sea any which way.

Diokles said, "Seems to me, skipper, you've got too much time on your hands. You're looking around for things to do."

"Well, what if I am?" Menedemos said, admitting what he could hardly deny. "I don't feel like going out and getting drunk today. As long as I'm messing around here, I may get something useful done." *Or I may change things again tomorrow,* he thought. If he did, it wouldn't be the first time.

The oarmaster tactfully didn't point that out. Maybe Diokles assumed Menedemos could see it for himself. He did say, "Time kind of wears when you stay in one port all summer long."

"It does, doesn't it?" Menedemos dipped his head. "I had the same thought not so long ago."

One of the sailors pointed toward the base of the pier. "Look! Isn't that—?"

"By the dog of Egypt, it *is*!" Menedemos exclaimed. "There's Sostratos, and Moskhion and Teleutas with him. *Papai!* Where's Aristeidas, though?"

"Don't care for the look of that," Diokles said.

"Neither do I." Menedemos ran along the gangplank from the *Aphrodite* to the quay, then down the planks to his cousin and the sailors. "Hail, O best one! Wonderful to see you again at last, after you've tramped the wilds of Ioudaia. But where's Aristeidas?"

"Dead," Sostratos said shortly. He'd lost weight on his travels. His skin stretched tight over the bones of his face. He looked older, harder, than he had before setting out for Engedi. "Robbers. Day before yesterday. Spear in the belly. I had to put him out of his pain." He slashed a thumb across his throat.

"Oh, by the gods!" Menedemos said, thinking, *No wonder he looks older.* He put an arm around his cousin's shoulder. "That's a hard thing to do, my dear, none harder. I'm very sorry. Aristeidas was a good man."

"Yes. It would have been hard with anyone." Sostratos' eye slid toward Teleutas, who fortunately didn't notice. "With the lookout, it was doubly so. But with the wound he had, all I did was save him hours of pain."

"See what would have happened if you'd gone alone?" Menedemos said.

"Who knows?" Sostratos answered wearily. "Maybe I would have taken a different road back to Sidon traveling alone. Maybe I would have been earlier or later on the same road and not run into the bandits at all. There's no way to tell, not for certain. Why don't you just let that be?"

He sounded older, too, as impatient with Menedemos as a grown man might be with a child who'd asked him to pull the moon down from the sky. "All right. Excuse me for breathing," Menedemos said, stung. "How did the business go? Did you get to Engedi? Have you got the balsam?"

"Yes, and some other things besides," Sostratos said. "Beeswax, embroidered cloth . . . I'll show you everything, if you'll let us get on down to the ship. Your inn will have a stable for the mule and donkey, won't it?"

"I'm not staying there any more," Menedemos said. "The innkeeper's wife tried to seduce me, so I came back to the ship." He held up a hand to forestall Sostratos. "The oath had nothing to do with that, though I've kept it. I wouldn't want her on a bet."

"We'll find somewhere else to put the beasts, then," Sostratos said. "It doesn't matter. After everything I've been through the past couple of days, I have trouble seeing what does matter, aside from getting home safe. To the crows with everything else."

Menedemos started to ask him about profit. He started to, but then checked himself. Here, for once, he saw no point in making Sostratos say something he would regret later. That was all very well for a joke, but not just after a good man died. Regardless of whether Sostratos did, Aristeidas' shade deserved more respect than that.

His cousin said, "When we got back here, I was going to surprise you: I was going to quote from the *Odyssey*."

"Were you?" Menedemos said. "What, the bit where

Odysseus has slain the suitors and made love to Penelope who's stayed home all those years, and then he tells her of his adventures in about thirty lines?"

"Yes, that's the very passage I had in mind, as a matter of fact," Sostratos answered. "I don't suppose I ought to be surprised you could guess."

"I hope you shouldn't, my dear," Menedemos said. "And I don't thank you for putting me in the woman's role. I wasn't idle here in Sidon, you know."

"I never said you were—not that Penelope was idle in Odysseus' palace." Sostratos scowled. "After what happened to poor Aristeidas, though, I haven't the heart for any sort of playfulness."

Moskhion said, "Skipper, he's a host in himself, your cousin is. Eight thieving Ioudaioi set upon us—eight! Sostratos shot two of 'em dead before they could close, he wounded a third, and he went and drove off another one with rocks. If he didn't show himself a second Teukros there, we all would've died amongst those boulders."

"That's the truth," Teleutas agreed.

"Euge!" Menedemos stared at Sostratos as if he'd never seen him before. He'd known his cousin could shoot pretty well, but to hear him described in such terms was . . . startling. Sostratos was among the mildest and most inoffensive of men. Or, at least, he was most of the time. With his freedom and his life in the balance, that might be a different story. That evidently *was* a different story.

"I wish I'd done better," he said now. "If I'd shot the bastard who speared Aristeidas, he'd still be with us now."

"You can't blame yourself," Menedemos said.

"We've been telling him the same thing," Teleutas said. "He doesn't want to listen."

"Well, he should." Menedemos looked straight at Sostratos. "You should. For four to drive off eight—that's no mean feat, my dear, all by itself. You can't expect everything to have gone perfectly."

"Everything had, near enough, till we ran into those polluted robbers on the way back here," Sostratos said. "Were another couple of days of luck too much to ask of the gods?"

"You can't ask such things of *me*—I'll tell you that," Menedemos said. "Let's get the goods off your donkey and onto the akatos. Balsam and beeswax and what all else did you tell me?"

"Embroidered cloth," Sostratos answered. Business seemed to recall him to himself. "How did you do here?"

"Could have been worse. Could have been a lot worse, in fact," Menedemos said. "I got rid of almost all your brother-in-law's olive oil, and at a good price, too."

Worn and sorrowful as Sostratos was, he sat up and took notice of that. "*Did* you? And what escaped madman came along to buy it?"

"Some went to the soldiers of Antigonos' garrison here, after their gods-detested quartermaster wouldn't pay a decent price," Menedemos replied. "A Phoenician dealer bought the rest for the luxury trade. The books are all gone—you had a good idea there. And the Koan silk—and I got something better for it." Just thinking of the silk he'd got from Zakerbaal set excitement bubbling inside him.

"What? More cloth?" Sostratos asked. When Menedemos dipped his head, his cousin looked dismayed. Sostratos, in fact, looked downright disgusted. He said, "What were you drinking, my dear, when the wily Phoenician convinced you of that? There *is* no finer cloth than Koan silk."

"We do have some jars of Byblian wine aboard, and crimson dye, too," Menedemos said. "But you're wrong about the Koan silk. Before we got here, I would have said you were right, but I know better now."

"This I have to see for myself," Sostratos declared.

"Come aboard, then, O best one, and see you shall." Menedemos steered Sostratos back toward the *Aphrodite*. He went on, "By what you and the sailors say, you *were* the best one with the bow. No one could have done better than you did."

"It wasn't good enough," Sostratos said bleakly. "Otherwise, we all would have come back from Engedi." As always,

Sostratos looked for perfection from himself. Being only human, he didn't always get it. And, when he didn't, he blamed himself more fiercely than he should have for falling short.

Menedemos almost said so to his face. But then, knowing his cousin as well as he did, he thought better of it. Instead, he simply guided Sostratos down into the merchant galley, guided him along to the leather sacks storing the silk, and opened one of them to draw out a bolt.

Sostratos' eyes widened. Menedemos had known they would. Sostratos stared at the fine, fine fabric, then reached out to feel it. He dipped his head decisively. "Well, when you're right, you're right. The Koans never dreamt of anything like this. Where does it come from? How is it made?" Curiosity came close to bringing him back to his usual self.

"I don't know how it's made," Menedemos replied. "It's from out of the east, Zakerbaal said—he's the Phoenician I got it from. From somewhere beyond India, maybe north, maybe east, maybe both."

"Like the gryphon's skull," Sostratos said.

"Yes, that occurred to me, too," Menedemos agreed. "But I think we'll see more of this silk coming west into the lands around the Inner Sea, where the gods only know if another skull like that will ever turn up."

Plainly, Sostratos wanted to argue with him. Just as plainly, he couldn't. He asked, "What did you pay for this, and how much did you get?" When Menedemos told him, he muttered to himself, then dipped his head again. "That's not bad."

"Thanks. I think we're going to squeeze a pretty fair profit out of this run, though we'll take a while to do it because so much of what we earn will depend on selling things we've got here back in Hellas," Menedemos said.

"Yes, I'm pretty sure you're right," Sostratos said. "I know where we can get a good price for some of this silk, or maybe all of it: in Salamis."

"Do you really think so?" Menedemos asked. "Don't you want to take it farther from Phoenicia?"

"Normally, I'd say yes," Sostratos replied. "But remember,

my dear, Menelaos is in Salamis. And if Ptolemaios' brother can't pay top price for something strange from far away, who can?"

Now it was Menedemos' turn to say, "When you're right, you're right. I'd thought you meant we'd sell it to some rich Salaminian. But Menelaos is a special case, sure enough. Yes, we'll definitely have to call on him when we get back to Cyprus."

"How soon can we leave?" Sostratos asked.

"Now, or as soon as Diokles pulls all the men out of the wineshops and brothels," Menedemos answered. "I've been waiting for you to get back—that's all that's been keeping me here. You'll want to sell the mule and the donkey, too, I suppose, but that won't take long. Diokles has always been good at getting the crew out of their dives, so we should be ready to go in a couple of days. I won't be sorry to head home, believe me."

"I don't look forward to calling on Aristeidas' family," Sostratos said.

Menedemos grunted. "There is that, isn't there? No, you're right. I don't look forward to it, either. But we've got to do it. How did he and the others do while you were wandering through Ioudaia?"

Sostratos looked around to see where Moskhion and Teleutas were before he answered. Once he'd made sure they couldn't hear him, he said, "I haven't got a bad word to say about poor Aristeidas, or about Moskhion, either. Teleutas . . . Teleutas did everything he was supposed to do as far as helping me went. He fought bravely against the robbers, too—of course, it was fight or die—but he stole from the Ioudaioi on the way back here from Jerusalem."

"Did he?" Menedemos eyed Teleutas, who was talking to some of the other sailors, probably telling them of his adventures. "Why am I not surprised?"

"I don't know. Why aren't you?" Sostratos said. "I wasn't all that surprised, either. I was just glad the Ioudaioi didn't come after us with murder in their hearts. We could have had a lot worse trouble than just robbers. We didn't, but we could have."

"Yes, I see that," Menedemos agreed. "But it's not the biggest question, not now. The biggest question is, will Teleutas steal from his own shipmates?"

"I know. I wondered about the same thing." Sostratos looked very unhappy. "I don't know what the answer is. This is the third year he's sailed with us, and no one's complained about theft on the *Aphrodite,* I will say that. Even so, I don't like what happened. I don't like it at all."

"And I don't blame you a bit." Menedemos studied Teleutas again. "He always tries to find out how close to the edge of the cliff he can walk, doesn't he? When somebody acts like that, he *will* fall off one of these days, won't he?"

"Who can say for certain?" Sostratos sounded as unhappy as he looked. "That seems to be the way to bet, though, doesn't it?"

"Yes. What shall we do about it? Do you want to leave him behind here in Sidon?"

Regretfully, Sostratos tossed his head. "No, I suppose not. He hasn't done anything to a Hellene that I can prove— though the way he offered to cut Aristeidas' throat for me chilled my blood. He said he'd had practice, and I believe him. But I think we should take him back to Rhodes. Whether I want him sailing with us next spring . . . That's liable to be a different question."

"All right. I suppose you have a point," Menedemos said. "If he gives us trouble on the way home, we can always put him ashore in Pamphylia or Lykia."

"Yes, and do you know what will happen if we do?" Sostratos said. "He'll turn pirate, sure as we're standing here talking. One of these days, we'll sail east again, and there he'll be, swarming out of a hemiolia with a knife clamped between his teeth."

"I'd like to go east in a trihemiolia," Menedemos said. "Let's see the Lykians come after one of *those* in their miserable, polluted pirate ships, by the gods."

"That would be pretty fine," Sostratos agreed. "It could happen, you know. They're building one now—probably have built it by this time."

"I know," Menedemos said. "But even so, even if it was my idea, they probably won't name me skipper. How can they, when I have to sail away every spring to make a living? No, it'll be some *kalos k'agathos* who can afford to spend his time serving the polis like that."

"Not fair," Sostratos said.

"In one sense of the word, no, for I do deserve it," Menedemos replied. "In another sense, though . . . Well, who can say? A rich man is able to give his time in a way that I'm not, so why shouldn't he have the chance?" He muttered under his breath, not wanting to think about whether it was fair or not. To keep from having to ponder it, he called, "Diokles!"

"What do you need, skipper?" asked the keleustes, who'd hung back to let Menedemos and Sostratos talk by themselves.

Menedemos grinned at him. "What do I need? I need the whole crew back aboard as fast as we can get 'em here. Now that Sostratos is back, we've got no reason to stay in Sidon any more."

"Ah," Diokles dipped his head. "I thought you were going to say that. I hoped you were going to say that, as a matter of fact. Time for me to go hunting—is that what you're telling me?"

"That's just what I'm telling you," Menedemos said. "The sailors know they can't hide from you—or if they don't by now, they'd better."

Now the oarmaster grinned, too. "That's right, skipper. I'll bring 'em in, never you fear. Shouldn't even be that hard. It's not like this was a Hellenic polis—they can't just disappear in amongst the people."

He was, as usual, as good as his word. A lot of sailors came back to the *Aphrodite* of their own accord once they heard the merchant galley would head back to Rhodes. "Be nice to find more than a handful of people who speak Greek," was a comment Menedemos heard several times.

A few others were less eager to go home. One man they

didn't get back; he'd taken service with Antigonos. "Many goodbyes to him," Menedemos remarked when he found out about that. "Anyone who wants to eat the food Andronikos' cooks serve up . . ." He tossed his head.

Another sailor had taken up with a courtesan. Diokles came back to Menedemos empty-handed. "Philon says he'd sooner stay here, skipper," the oarmaster reported. "Says he's in love, and he doesn't want to leave the woman."

"Oh, he does, does he?" Menedemos said. "Does the woman speak any Greek?"

"Some. I don't know how much," Diokles answered.

"All right. Go back there. Make sure you find 'em both together," Menedemos said. "Then tell him his pay's cut off, as of now. Tell him he gets not another obolos from me. If the woman doesn't throw him out on his ear after that, maybe they really are in love. In that case, you ask me, they deserve each other."

Philon came back aboard the *Aphrodite* the next day. He looked ashamed of himself. No one chaffed him very hard, though. How many sailors kept from falling in love, or imagining they were in love, at some port or another around the Inner Sea? Not many.

The day after that, Menedemos had his crew back again but for the one fool who thought Antigonos a better paymaster. A good many men looked wan, having thrown away their silver on a last carouse, but they were there. Sostratos grumbled about the price he'd got for the two animals he'd taken to Engedi, but the difference between that and what he'd paid was still less than what hiring them for the journey would have cost.

Menedemos, steering-oar tillers in his hands once more, grinned at the sailors and called, "Well, boys, are you about ready to see your home polis again?" They dipped their heads as they looked back at him from the rowers' benches. "Good," he told them. "Do you think you still remember what to do with your oars?" They dipped their heads again. Some of them managed smiles of their own. He waved to Diokles. "Then I'll give you to the keleustes, and he'll find out if you're right."

"First thing is, we'd better cast off," Diokles said. "We'd look like proper fools if we tried to row away while we're still tied up." Lines snaked back aboard the *Aphrodite*. Sailors came back aboard down the gangplank, then stowed it at the stern. Diokles raised his voice: "At my order . . . *back oars!* Rhyppa*pai*! Rhyppa*pai*!" The merchant galley slid away from the pier.

"How does she feel?" Sostratos asked quietly.

"Heavy," Menedemos answered as Diokles smote his little bronze square with his mallet to set the stroke. "It's to be expected, when she's been sitting here soaking up seawater for so long." He pushed one tiller away and pulled the other one in. The *Aphrodite* spun in the sea till her bow faced west-northwest.

"At my order . . . ," Diokles said again, and the rowers, knowing what was coming, held their oars out of the water till he called, "Normal stroke!" They reversed the rhythm of what they'd been doing. Now when their oars dug in, they pushed the akatos forward instead of pulling her back.

Little by little, Sidon and the promontory on which the Phoenician city sat began to recede behind her. Menedemos adjusted her course, ever so slightly. He laughed at himself, knowing how inexact navigation was. "Cyprus," he told Sostratos. He was confident he'd bring the *Aphrodite* to the island. Whereabouts on its east or south coast? That was a different question, and much harder to answer.

"Cyprus," his cousin agreed.

Sostratos stood on the foredeck, feeling out of place and all too conscious of his own inadequacies as lookout. Aristeidas should have been here, he of the lynxlike eyes. Sostratos knew his own vision was average at best. But he still lived, while Aristeidas lay forever beneath boulders in Ioudaia. He had to do the best he could.

He peered ahead, looking for land rising up above the infinite smooth horizon of the Inner Sea. He knew Cyprus should come into sight any time, and he wanted to be the first to spy the island. Aristeidas surely would have been. If Sostratos was doing the dead man's job, he wanted to do it as well as he could. Having some sailor spy Cyprus ahead of him would be a humiliation.

Above and behind him, the sail made strange sighing noises, now bellying full, now falling flat and limp in the fitful breeze from the northeast. The yard stretched back from the starboard bow to take best advantage of what wind there was. To keep the merchant galley going regardless of whether that wind blew hard or failed altogether, Menedemos kept eight men rowing on either side. He changed rowers fairly often so they would stay as fresh as they could if he needed them to flee from or fight pirates.

"Pirates," Sostratos muttered. He had to keep watch for sails and hulls, too, not just for the jut of land out of the sea. Sailing west toward Cyprus, the *Aphrodite* had met a couple of ships bound for Sidon or the other Phoenician towns from Salamis. Everyone had been nervous till they passed each other by. Any stranger on the sea was too likely to prove a predator waiting only for his chance to strike.

He peered ahead again, then stiffened. Was that . . . ? If he sang out and it wasn't, he would feel a fool. If he didn't sing out and somebody beat him to it, he would feel a worse fool. He took another, longer look.

"Land ho!" he shouted. "Land off the port bow!"

"I see it," a sailor echoed. "I was going to sing out myself, but the young sir went and beat me to it." That made Sostratos feel very fine indeed.

From his station at the stern, Menedemos said, "That's got to be Cyprus. Now the only question is, where along the coast are we? See if you can spy a fishing boat, Sostratos. Fishermen will know."

But they proved to need no fishermen. As they came closer to the shore, Sostratos said, "To the crows with me if this isn't the very landscape we saw when we sailed out of Salamis for Sidon. You couldn't have placed us any better if you'd been able to look across every stadion of sea. *Euge,* O best one!"

"Euge!" the sailors echoed.

Menedemos shuffled his feet on the poop deck like a shy schoolboy who had to recite. "Thank you, friends. I'd thank you more if we didn't all know it was just luck that put us here and not two or three hundred stadia up or down the coast."

"Modesty?" Sostratos asked. "Are you well, my dear?"

"I'll gladly take credit where credit's mine—or even when I can get away with claiming it," his cousin answered. "Not here, though. If I say I can navigate from Sidon to Salamis every time straight as an arrow flies, you'll expect me to do it again, and you'll laugh at me when I don't. I'm not fool enough to say anything of the sort, because I'd likely make myself a liar the next time we had to sail out of sight of land."

Before long, a five flying Ptolemaios' eagle pendant roared out of Salamis harbor's narrow mouth and raced toward the *Aphrodite.* An officer cupped his hands in front of his mouth and shouted, "What ship are you?" across the water.

"The *Aphrodite,* out of Sidon, bound for Rhodes and home," Sostratos yelled back, resigning himself to another long, suspicious interrogation.

But no. The officer on the war galley waved and said, "So you're the Rhodians, are you? Pass on. We remember you from when you came here out of the west."

"Thank you, most noble one!" Sostratos exclaimed in glad surprise. "Tell me, if you'd be so kind: is Menelaos still here in Salamis?"

"Yes, he is," Ptolemaios' officer replied. "Why do you want to know?"

"We found something at Sidon we hope he might be interested in buying," Sostratos said.

"Ah. Well, I can't say anything about that—you'll have to

find out for yourselves." The naval officer waved once more. "Good fortune go with you."

"Thanks again," Sostratos said. As the *Aphrodite* made for the harbor mouth, he went back to the poop deck. "That was easier than I expected," he told Menedemos.

His cousin dipped his head. "It was, wasn't it? Nice to have something go right for us, by the gods. And if Menelaos likes this fancy silk of ours . . ."

"Here's hoping," Sostratos said. "How can we even be sure he'll look at it?"

"We'll show some to his servants, to the highest-ranking steward they'll let us see," Menedemos answered. "If that's not enough to get us brought before him, I don't know what would be."

Sostratos admired his confidence. A merchant needed it in full measure, and Sostratos knew he had less than his own fair share. "Here's hoping you're right," he said.

With a shrug, Menedemos said, "If I'm not, we just don't sell here, that's all. I hope Menelaos will want what we've got. He's someone who can afford to buy it. But if he doesn't, well, I expect someone else will." Yes, he had confidence and to spare.

And he and Sostratos also had that marvelous silk from the land beyond India. When they presented themselves at what had been the palace of the kings of Salamis and was now Menelaos' residence, a supercilious servant declared, "The governor does not see tradesmen."

"No?" Sostratos said. "Not even when we've got—this?" He waved to Menedemos. Like a conjurer, his cousin pulled a bolt of that transparent silk from the sack in which he carried it and displayed it for the servant.

That worthy immediately lost some of his hauteur. He reached out as if to touch the silk. Menedemos jerked it away. The servant asked, "Is that . . . Koan cloth? It can't be—it's too fine. But it can't be anything else, either."

"No, it's not Koan silk," Sostratos answered. "What it is isn't any of *your* business, but it is Menelaos'." To soften the sting of that, he slipped the servant a drakhma. In a lot of households, he would have overpaid; here, if anything, the bribe was barely enough.

It didn't suffice to get the Rhodians an audience with Ptolemaios' brother. But it did get them to his chief steward, who blinked when he saw the silk they displayed. "Yes, the master had better have a look at this himself," the steward murmured. A few minutes later, Sostratos and Menedemos stood before Menelaos son of Lagos.

"Hail, Rhodians," Menelaos said. He not only looked like his older brother, he sounded like him, too, which was, in Sostratos' experience, much more unusual. "Simias says you've got something interesting for me to see, so let's have a look, eh?"

Ptolemaios also had that way of coming straight to the point. Sostratos said, "Certainly, sir," and showed him the silk as he and Menedemos had shown it to Simias.

Menelaos whistled. "By the dog, that's something!" he said, and dipped his head. "Yes, indeed, that's really something. It's not Koan. It can't be Koan. The Koans couldn't match this if their lives depended on it. Where's it come from? You got it in Sidon, but you can't tell me the Phoenicians made it."

"No, sir." This was Menedemos' story, and he told it: "Zakerbaal, the cloth merchant who sold it to me, says it comes from a country beyond India—he doesn't know whether to the east or to the north. He knows Koan silk, too, and said the same thing you did."

"Next question is, how much do you want for it?" Yes, Menelaos did cut to the chase.

"Zakerbaal said it was worth its weight in gold," Menedemos answered. "But it's worth more than that, just because it's so very light and filmy. I paid him in Koan silk, at five times its weight for the weight of each bolt of this." Sostratos sent him a sharp look; he'd really paid only about half that. Of course, how would Menelaos know?

And Menedemos knew what he was doing, too, for Ptolemaios' brother said, "So you're telling me each bolt of this is worth five times as much as a bolt of Koan silk? That seems fair enough, I think."

Sostratos and Menedemos both tossed their heads at the same time, an almost identical motion that looked odd because Sostratos was so much taller than his cousin. Sostratos said, "Not quite, O most noble one. We're telling you that's what we paid."

"Ah." Menelaos' grin displayed strong yellow teeth. "And you're telling me you want a profit, are you?"

Some Hellenes—usually those who didn't have to worry about it—looked down their noses at the mere idea of profit. Menelaos didn't sound as if he was one of those. Sostratos hoped he wasn't, anyhow. Menedemos said, "Sir, that silk didn't swim across the sea to Salamis by itself. We have to pay our crew. We have to take care of our ship. We have to live, too."

"And you're thinking, *Besides, Menelaos has all the money in the world,* aren't you?" Menelaos rolled his eyes. "That's because you don't know what a skinflint my brother is."

"As a matter of fact, we do," Sostratos said. "We dealt with him last year on Kos."

"If you were to give him some of this silk, he might not worry so much about what you spend on it," Menedemos said, his voice sly.

"How much have you got?" Menelaos asked.

"A dozen bolts, all of size and quality like this, dyed several different colors," Menedemos replied.

Menelaos rubbed his chin. "You're a sneaky one, aren't you, Rhodian? Yes, that might do the trick." He raised his voice: "Simias!"

The steward appeared on the instant. "Yes, your Excellency?"

"What would a bolt of good Koan silk cost?"

"About a mina, sir."

Menelaos looked to Sostratos and Menedemos. "Is he right?"

They glanced at each other. Sostratos answered, "I'd say it might cost a little more, but he's not far wrong, though."

"So you paid five minai, more or less, for each bolt of this eastern silk?"

The Rhodians looked at each other again. "Probably be closer to six, best one," Menedemos said.

"And how much more than that would it take to make it worth your while to sell the silk to me?" Menelaos asked.

"Twice as much," Sostratos said.

"What? You'd want a dozen minai, by your reckoning, per bolt? By Zeus, Rhodian, that's too much! I'll give you half again as much, not a drakhma more."

Counting on his fingers, Sostratos worked out how much that would be. "Nine minai the bolt. We have twelve bolts in all, so you'd pay"—he muttered to himself as he did the arithmetic—"one hundred eight minai all told?" Almost two talents of silver—10,800 drakhmai. That was, by anybody's standards, a lot of money.

Menelaos turned to his steward. "Is that what it would come to, Simias? My head turns to mush when I try to figure things without a counting board."

"Yes, sir. He calculated it correctly," Simias answered. "Whether you want to pay the price is a different question, of course."

"Isn't it just?" Menelaos agreed. "Still, if I share the silk with Ptolemaios, he can't very well complain about it." He dipped his head in sudden decision. "All right, Rhodians—a bargain. Your fancy eastern silk, all twelve bolts, for one hundred eight minai of silver—or would you rather have it in gold? Gold would be a lot easier for you to carry."

Egypt was a land rich in gold, where most Hellenes used silver as their main monetary metal. "What rate of exchange would you give?" Sostratos asked. "That makes a difference, you know."

"Ten to one, no more," Menelaos said. "This isn't Philip of Macedon's day, when a gold drakhma would buy you twelve silver ones."

He wasn't wrong; ten to one was the most common exchange rate nowadays. A century before, the ratio had been thirteen or even fourteen to one. "If you'll wait till we can bring a couple of men here, I think I'd sooner have it in sil-

ver," Sostratos answered. "As you say, gold's fallen over this
past generation, and it may fall further."

"However you please," Ptolemaios' brother said with a
shrug. "I've got the silver." Sostratos was sure he had it. How
big was his army on Cyprus? He probably spent more than a
couple of talents every day on his soldiers' pay.

Menedemos said, "I'll go over to the *Aphrodite* to get the
sailors. Can you give us some guards when we're taking the
money back to the ship, most noble one?"

"Certainly," Menelaos answered. "Worried about getting
knocked over the head between here and the harbor, are you?
Don't blame you a bit. Salamis can be a tough town."

"Thank you, sir," Menedemos said. "If you'd told me no,
I'd've come back with a lot more than just two men, I'll tell
you that." He waved and hurried away.

That left Sostratos alone with Menelaos and Simias. He
usually hated such situations, as he was a man of little small
talk. Now, though, he asked, "Sir, did you hunt tigers in distant India, as Ptolemaios did?"

"Did I? I should say I did!" Menelaos exclaimed, and he
was off on a hunting story that not only fascinated Sostratos
and told him two or three things about tigers that he hadn't
known but also relieved him of the obligation to say much
more till his cousin got back with the sailors. *Not bad,* he
thought, *for a double handful of words.*

MENEDEMOS PULLED IN ON ONE STEERING-OAR
tiller and pushed the other one out. The *Aphrodite* rounded
Cape Pedalion, the highland that marked the southeastern corner of Cyprus. Diokles said, "That headland is supposed to be

sacred to Aphrodite, so there's a good omen for our ship, if you like."

"I like good omens just fine, thanks very much," Menedemos answered. "I'll take 'em wherever I can find 'em, too."

"Why is this part of Cyprus sacred to the love goddess?" Sostratos asked. "Didn't she rise from the sea at Paphos? Paphos isn't near here, is it?"

"No, young sir, Paphos is way off to the west," the oarmaster said. "I don't know why Cape Pedalion's sacred to her. I just know that it is."

Sostratos still looked discontented. Menedemos shot him a glance that said, *Shut up*. For a wonder, his cousin got the message. Menedemos wanted the sailors to think the omens were good. The happier they were, the better they'd work. If Diokles hadn't given him a real one, he might have invented a good omen to keep them cheerful.

The beaches west of Cape Pedalion were of fine white sand, the soil inland from them a red that promised great fertility, though fields lay fallow under the hot sun, waiting for fall and the rains that would bring them back to life. But the promontory did strange things to the wind, which went fitful and shifting, now with the merchant galley, now dead against her.

"By the gods, I'm glad I'm in an akatos," Menedemos said. "I wouldn't care to sail this coast in a round ship. You could spend days going nowhere at all. And if the wind did blow in one direction, like as not it'd drive you aground instead of taking you where you wanted to go."

"You don't want that," Sostratos said. "You don't want that anywhere. You especially don't want it on a shore where nobody knows you."

Diokles dipped his head. "No, indeed. And you really especially don't want it on this shore, where most of the people are Phoenicians, not Hellenes at all. Kition, the next city up ahead, is a Phoenician town."

"From what we saw in Sidon, Phoenicians aren't any worse than Hellenes," Sostratos said.

"I'm not saying they're worse. I'm saying they're foreign," the keleustes replied. "If I were a Phoenician skipper, I'd sooner go aground here than up by Salamis, where the people are mostly Hellenes."

"I'd sooner not go aground anywhere," Menedemos said. "I'd sooner not, and I don't intend to."

He did put in at Kition the next day to buy fresh bread. It looked like a Phoenician town, with tall buildings crowding close together and with men in caps and long robes. The gutturals of Aramaic dominated over Greek's smooth rising and falling cadences.

"I can understand what they're saying," Sostratos exclaimed. "When we first set out, I wouldn't have followed even half of it, but I can understand almost all of it now."

"You've been speaking the language yourself," Menedemos said. "That's why. I can even understand a little myself. But I expect I'll forget it as soon as we get back to Rhodes. I won't need to know it any more."

"I don't want to forget!" Sostratos said. "I never want to forget anything."

"I can think of a few things I'd just as soon forget," Menedemos said, "starting with Emashtart." He laughed and tossed his head. "I didn't have any trouble keeping my oath on account of her. How about you, O best one? Outrage any husbands in Ioudaia? You never swore you wouldn't."

To his surprise—indeed, to his amazement—his cousin coughed and shuffled his feet and generally acted flustered. "How did you know?" Sostratos asked. "Were you talking with Moskhion or Teleutas? Did they blab?"

"They never said a word, my dear, and I never thought to ask them about that," Menedemos answered. "But now I'm asking you. Who was she? Was she pretty? You wouldn't have done it if you hadn't thought she was pretty, would you?"

"Her husband ran the inn where we stayed in Jerusalem," Sostratos said slowly. "Her name was Zilpah." He bared his teeth in what wasn't quite, or wasn't just, a smile. "While I was going after her, I thought she was the most wonderful thing in the world."

Menedemos laughed out loud. "Oh, yes. I know all about that. I kept trying to tell you, but you didn't want to listen."

"I understand better now." By the way Sostratos said it, he wished he didn't.

Laughing still, Menedemos said, "So you finally got her, did you?"

"Yes, on the way back from Engedi." Sostratos didn't sound particularly proud of himself. "If she hadn't been angry at her husband, I never would have."

"They all say that," Menedemos told him. "Maybe they even believe it. It gives them an excuse for doing what they want to do anyhow. Well? How was it?"

"Better than with a whore, certainly—you're right about that," Sostratos admitted.

"Told you so," Menedemos said.

"You tell me all sorts of things," Sostratos said. "Some of them turn out to be true, and some of them don't. She started crying afterwards, though, and wished she'd never done it. Everything was fine—better than fine—up till then. As soon as we'd finished, though . . ." He tossed his head.

"Oh. One of those. Just your luck to run into one like that the first time you play the game," Menedemos said sympathetically, and put his hand on his cousin's shoulder. "It happens, I'm afraid."

"Obviously, since it happened to me," Sostratos said. "And it *did* feel like a game. I didn't like that."

"Why not? What else is it?" Menedemos asked in honest puzzlement. "Best game in the world, if you ask me, but still, only a game."

Sostratos groped for an answer: "It shouldn't be only a game. It's too important to be only a game. For a little while there, I was . . . in love, I suppose. I don't know what else to call it."

"That can happen," Menedemos agreed. Sostratos hadn't sounded happy about it. Menedemos didn't blame him. Love was as dangerous a passion as the gods had inflicted on mankind. Menedemos went on, "I don't suppose you can do anything halfway, can you?"

"Doesn't seem that way, does it?" Sostratos spread his hands. "There's my story, such as it is. I'm sure it's nothing you haven't done before."

"That's not the point. The point is, it's something *you* haven't done before."

"I know." No, Menedemos' cousin didn't seem happy at all. "Now I understand the fascination of your game. I wish I didn't."

"Why?" Menedemos asked. "Because now you have a harder time looking down your nose at me?"

Relentlessly honest, Sostratos dipped his head. "Yes, that's the main reason why, and I won't tell you any different. And because I don't know if I'll be able to keep from doing something like that again one of these days. I hope so, but how can I know for certain?"

"Don't worry about it so much," Menedemos told him. "You got away. You'll never see the woman or her husband again. Nobody got hurt. Why are you in such an uproar? You don't need to be."

Sostratos was relentlessly precise as well as relentlessly honest. "I wouldn't say nobody got hurt. If you'd seen Zilpah afterwards . . ." His mouth tightened. He was looking back on a memory that didn't please him at all.

But Menedemos repeated, "Don't worry about it. Women get funny sometimes, that's all. The day after you left the inn, she'd probably forgotten all about you."

"I don't think so," Sostratos said. "I think she thought she loved me, the same way I thought I loved her. Then we lay with each other, and that made her decide her husband was really the important one. I think she—how do I put it?—blamed me for not being who, or maybe what, she thought I was." He sighed.

"Well, what if she did?" Menedemos asked. "How is that your fault? It isn't, my dear, and that's all there is to it."

"'That's all there is to it,'" Sostratos echoed in a hollow

voice. "Easy enough for you to say, O best one. Not so easy for me to persuade myself."

Menedemos started to tell him not to be a fool. Considering how many times Sostratos had told him the same thing, he looked forward to getting some of his own back. But before the words could pass the barrier of his teeth, a sailor called out a warning from the bow: "Skipper, a soldier's coming up the pier to look us over."

"Thanks, Damagetos," Menedemos answered with a sigh. Kition might have been a Phoenician town, but, like the rest of Cyprus, it lay under Ptolemaios' rule these days. The garrison here had to prove itself alert. The *Aphrodite* wasn't likely to be part of an invasion fleet ordered out by Antigonos, but at first glance she easily might have seemed a pirate. Scorching Sostratos would have to wait.

"What ship are you?" The inevitable question floated through the air as soon as the officer got within hailing distance.

"We're the *Aphrodite,* out of Rhodes," Menedemos answered, resisting the impulse to yell back, *Whose man are* you? He'd asked it before and discovered what he should have known anyhow: cracking wise with a fellow who could cause you trouble wasn't a good idea. Even so, the temptation remained.

"Where have you been, and what's your cargo?" Ptolemaios' officer asked.

"Sidon, and lately Salamis," Menedemos answered. "We've got Byblian wine, crimson dye, balsam of Engedi, and a few jars of Rhodian perfume and olive oil."

"Olive oil?" the soldier said. "You must have been daft, to carry olive oil in a scrawny little ship like that."

Everyone who heard about that part of the cargo said the same thing. For a long time, hearing it had made Menedemos grind his teeth. Now he could smile. "You might think so, best one, but we unloaded almost all of it," he said. "Would you care to try one of the jars we have left?"

"No, thanks," the officer replied with a laugh. "But you're

traders, all right. Welcome to Kition." He turned and walked back into the city.

A sharp, metallic clicking in the sky made Menedemos and a good many others look up. He stared. "What in the world are those?" he said.

"Bats," Sostratos answered calmly.

"But I've seen bats before—everybody has," Menedemos protested. "They're little things, like dormice with wings. These aren't little. They've got bodies like puppies and wings like a crow's."

"They're still bats," Sostratos said. "They've got noses, not beaks. They've got ears. They've got bare wings and fur, not feathers. What else would they be?"

"They're too big to be bats," Menedemos insisted. "If they were any bigger, they'd be like vultures, by the gods."

"So you say big bats are impossible?" Sostratos asked. "Fine. Have it your way, my dear. They're big birds that happen to look exactly like bats."

Menedemos' ears burned. To make matters worse, Sostratos spoke in Aramaic to a Phoenician longshoreman. The fellow answered volubly, pointing back into the long, rolling hills behind Kition. Sostratos bowed his thanks, exactly as a Phoenician might have done.

He turned back to Menedemos. "They *are* bats," he said. "They live in caves, and they eat fruit. That's what the fellow said, anyhow. I always thought bats ate bugs. I wish we could stay and learn more about them. May we?"

"No," Menedemos said. "You would be the one to care more for learning about bats than for learning about women, wouldn't you?"

Sostratos winced. "I didn't say *that*."

And so he hadn't, but Menedemos, having been embarrassed over the bats, was delighted to take a little revenge. If he ruffled his cousin's feathers (or, seeing that those creatures *were* bats, his fur), too bad.

* * *

THE TROUBLE WITH being angry at someone aboard an akatos, as Sostratos had long since discovered, was that you couldn't get away from him. The ship wasn't big enough. And so, even though he thought the crack Menedemos had made was grossly unfair, he couldn't go off by himself and sulk. The only possible place for him to go off by himself was up on the tiny foredeck, but he didn't have the luxury of sulking there. If he stood on the foredeck, he had to do look-out duty.

That he did, staring out at the water of the Inner Sea in lieu of looking back at his cousin. But the first thing that crossed his mind then was how, had everything gone well, Aristeidas would have stood here instead. He blamed himself because the sharp-eyed sailor wasn't. Blaming himself, he forgot all about blaming Menedemos.

More big bats flew overhead the next evening, as the *Aphrodite* neared the town of Kourion. Sostratos pretended not to notice them. Menedemos didn't say anything about them, either: a strange sort of truce, but a truce even so.

Menedemos even made an effort to be friendly, asking, "What do you know about Kourion? You know *something* about almost every place where we stop."

"Not much about this one, I'm afraid," Sostratos answered. "King Stasanor of Kourion went over to the Persians during the Cypriot rebellion almost two hundred years ago. Thanks to his treachery, the Persians won the battle on the plains near Salamis, and the rebellion failed."

"Sounds like something a town'd rather *not* be remembered for," Menedemos remarked. "What else do you know?"

Sostratos frowned, trying to flog more bits from his memory. "Kourion is a colony sent out from Argos," he said, "and they worship an odd Apollo here."

Diokles dipped his head. "That's right, young sir: Apollo Hylates."

"Apollo of the Wood—yes! Thanks," Sostratos said. "I

couldn't recall the details. You know more than I do here, Diokles. Go on, if you would."

"I don't know *much* more," the oarmaster said, suddenly shy. "I've only been here a couple of times myself. But I do know the god has strange rites, and anyone who dares touch his altar gets thrown off those cliffs yonder." He pointed to bluffs west of the town. As cliffs went, they weren't very impressive; Sostratos had seen far higher and steeper ones in Lykia and in Ioudaia. Still, a man flung from the top was bound to die when he hit the bottom, which made them high enough to punish sacrilege.

Menedemos asked what struck Sostratos as a couple of eminently reasonable questions: "Why would anybody want to touch that altar, if people know what happens to those who do? And how often is anybody going to be mad enough to do it?"

"I couldn't begin to tell you, skipper," Diokles replied. "All I know is what I remember—or what I think I remember—from when I did put in here. That was years ago now, so I may have it wrong."

No war galleys patrolled outside Kourion, or none Sostratos saw. He hadn't spied any around Kition, either. Ptolemaios seemed to be keeping his whole fleet at Salamis, that being the port closest to the Phoenician coastline from which Antigonos might launch an attack against Cyprus. And if the ruler of Egypt had garrisoned Kourion, as Sostratos assumed he had, the local commander was most incurious. No one asked any questions of the *Aphrodite*'s crew except the longshoremen who moored the merchant galley to a quay.

"Whence come ye?" a naked man inquired in the old-fashioned Cypriot dialect as he made a line fast. "Whither be ye bound?"

As usual, Menedemos told him, "We're the *Aphrodite,* out of Rhodes. We're heading home from Sidon." The Doric drawl Sostratos' cousin spoke seemed all the stronger after the longshoreman's archaic speech.

"Rhodes, say you, good sir? And Sidon? In sooth, you've traveled far, and seen many things passing strange. What think you the most curious amongst 'em?"

"I'll answer that, if I may," Sostratos said, and Menedemos waved for him to go on. He did: "In Ioudaia, inland from the Phoenician coast, there's a lake full of water so salty, a man can't drown in it. He'll float on the surface with head and shoulders and feet sticking out into the air."

"Tush! Go to!" the Cypriot exclaimed. "Think you to gull me so? You rank cozener! Why, water's water, be it salt or fresh. An you throw a man in't, if he swim not, he'll sink down and drown. 'Tis but natural that it be so. Who told you such lies?"

"No one told me," Sostratos said. "I saw this with my own eyes, felt it with my own body. I went into this lake, I tell you, and it bore me up from the great amount of salt in it."

Try as he would, though, he couldn't make the longshoreman believe him. "By Apollo Hylates, I've met folk like you aforetimes," the fellow said. "Always ready with a tall tale, the which no man hereabouts may check. Go to, I say again! You'll not catch me crediting such nonsense and moonshine."

Sostratos wanted to insist he was telling the truth. He wanted to, but he didn't bother. He knew he would only waste his time and end up out of temper. People who often clung to the most absurd local superstitions wouldn't trust a foreigner to tell them the truth about a distant land. The Cypriot had asked him for a strange story and then refused to believe it once he got it.

Moskhion came up onto the poop deck. "Don't worry about it, young sir," he said. "Some people are just natural-born fools, and you can't do a thing about it."

"I know," Sostratos said. "Arguing with somebody like that is nothing but a waste of breath. He wouldn't have believed you and Teleutas, either."

"That's why I kept quiet," Moskhion said, dipping his head. "I didn't see any point in quarreling, that's all. It wasn't on account of I wouldn't back you."

"Of course not," Sostratos said. "I'd never think such a

thing, not when we fought side by side there in the rocks north of Gamzo. We owe each other our lives. We're not going to split apart over a foolish argument with somebody who's probably never gone fifty stadia from Kourion in his life."

Menedemos said, "We still have a little while before sunset. Shall we go into the agora and see what they're selling there?"

"Well, why not?" Sostratos answered. "You never can tell. I wouldn't bet on finding anything worth buying, but I might be wrong. And walking around in any market square will remind me I'm back among Hellenes."

His cousin dipped his head. "Yes, I had the same thought." He ran the gangplank from the poop deck to the quay. "Let's go."

Kourion wasn't a big city, but it was an old one. Even its larger streets meandered in every direction. One of these days, Sostratos supposed, someone might rebuild the place with a neat Hippodamian grid of avenues, such as Rhodes and Kos and other newer foundations enjoyed. Meanwhile, the locals knew their way around, while strangers had to do their best. Eventually, he and Menedemos did find the agora.

Men wandered from stall to stall, examining produce and pots and leather goods and nets and carved wood and cloth and a hundred other things. Sellers praised their goods; buyers sneered. Men with trays ambled through the square, selling figs and wine and fried prawns and pastries sweetened with honey. Knots of men gathered here and there, arguing and gesticulating. It was the most ordinary scene imaginable, in any town full of Hellenes along the Inner Sea.

Tears stung Sostratos' eyes. "By the gods, I never dreamt I could miss this so much."

"Neither did I," Menedemos agreed. "Let's see what they've got, eh?"

"Of course, my dear," Sostratos said. "You never know what we might find." They strolled the agora together. Sostratos knew what he hoped to find: another gryphon's skull. That one was most unlikely to turn up in this out-of-the way little polis bothered him not at all. He had his hopes, and would keep on having them as long as he lived.

He saw no sign of any such wonder in Kourion, though. He saw no sign of any wonders in the market square. The agora was almost staggeringly dull, at least for someone looking for cargo for a merchant galley. A local miller or farmer would surely have found it delightful.

As soon as he realized he wouldn't see anything much he wanted to buy, he started listening to the talk in the agora. Talk, after all, was the other main reason men came to the market square. Thanks to the Cypriot dialect, he had to listen harder than he would have back in Rhodes. The more he listened, though, the more easily he followed it.

People kept talking about a gamble or a risk. They all knew what it was, and they wisely discussed this fellow's chance of bringing it off, or that one's, or someone else's. They also talked about the price of failure, without saying what that was, either.

Finally, Sostratos' curiosity got the better of him. He walked up to a local and said, "Excuse me, O best one, but may I ask you a question?"

The man from Kourion dipped his head. "Certes, stranger. Say on."

"Thank you kindly." As had happened before on Cyprus, the accent here made Sostratos acutely conscious of his own Doric dialect, which came out more than usual. He persisted even so: "What is this gamble I hear you all talking about?"

"Why, to touch the altar of Apollo Hylates unbeknownst to the priests serving the god, of course," the man from Kourion replied.

Sostratos stared. "But isn't it death to touch that altar? Don't they throw you off the cliffs?" He pointed westward.

"In good sooth, sir, 'tis indeed. An a man be caught, he suffereth infallibly that very fate. 'Tis the price of failure," the local said.

Menedemos said, "In that case, why on earth would anybody be crazy enough to want to do it?"

Shrugging, the man from Kourion replied, "It hath of late become amongst the youth of this our city a passion, a sport, to make their way to yon temple by twos and threes—the odd young men being witness to him who dareth—to lay hold of the altar, and then to get hence with all the haste in 'em."

"Why?" Sostratos asked, as Menedemos had before him. Again, the local only shrugged. When he saw the Rhodians had no more questions for him, he politely dipped his head again and went on his way.

Sostratos kept scratching his own head and worrying at the question like a man with a bit of squid tentacle stuck between his teeth. At last, he said, "I think I understand."

"More than I can say," Menedemos replied.

"Look at Athens more than a hundred years ago, when Alkibiades and some of his friends profaned the mysteries of Eleusis and mutilated the Herms in front of people's houses," Sostratos said. "They probably didn't mean any real harm. They were drunk and having a good time and playing foolish games. That's what the young men are doing here, I suppose."

"It's not a foolish game if the priests catch you," Menedemos pointed out.

"I wonder what sort of watch they keep," Sostratos said. "If it is only a game, they might look the other way most of the time . . . though Alkibiades came to grief when people who should have kept their mouths shut didn't."

"We'll be out of here tomorrow," Menedemos said. "We'll never know."

"I wish you hadn't put it like that," Sostratos said. "Now it will keep on bothering me for the rest of my days."

"Not if you don't let it," Menedemos said. "What bothers me are the goods in this agora. I can't see a single thing I'd want to take away from here." He snapped his fingers. "No, I take that back—there was one very pretty boy."

"Oh, go howl!" Sostratos told him. Boys' beauty drew his eyes, but in the same way as a fine horse's beauty might have. He admired without wanting to possess. When he thought about such things, he wondered if that was because he'd been so completely ignored while he was a youth. Maybe the sting of that humiliation remained with him yet.

Menedemos, by contrast, had had his name and the usual epithets—MENEDEMOS IS BEAUTIFUL or MENEDEMOS IS BEST or THE BOY MENEDEMOS IS MOST LOVELY—scrawled on walls all over Rhodes. He knew Sostratos hadn't—he hardly could help knowing. Most of the time, as now, he was tactful: "Well, my dear, I did happen to notice him. But he's probably got no honor—just another little wretch with a wide arsehole."

Perversely, that made Sostratos want to defend the boy. "You don't know the first thing about him," he said.

"No, but I know the type," Menedemos answered. "Some people go through their beauty like *that*"—he snapped his fingers again—"because they've nothing else to spend."

"Heh," Sostratos said.

"What? Do you think I'm joking?" Menedemos asked.

"No, my dear, not at all," Sostratos answered. When they were both youths, when Menedemos was swimming in attention while he had none, Sostratos had told himself his cousin had only beauty to go through and would be worthless by the time he grew up. He'd been wrong, but that didn't mean he hadn't consoled himself so.

They walked back to the *Aphrodite*. One of those enormous bats flew overhead. Menedemos said, "It's got a pointy nose, just like the pretty boy I saw. Do you suppose bats call one another beautiful?"

Sostratos contemplated that, then tossed his head. "What I suppose is, you're very peculiar, to come up with a question like that."

"Why, thank you!" Menedemos said, as if Sostratos had praised him. They both laughed.

Some of the sailors went into Kourion to get drunk. Diokles had no trouble rounding them up, though. "I didn't figure I would," he said when the job was done. "Nobody wants to get stuck in a miserable little place like this."

That perfectly summarized Sostratos' view of Kourion. He was glad when the merchant galley left the town early the next morning. Of course, she would stop for the night at some other small Cypriot city, perhaps one even less prepossessing than Kourion, but he chose not to dwell on that.

Diokles was clanging out a slow, lazy stroke for the men at the oars—there was no breeze to speak of—when a sailor pointed toward the shore a few plethra away and said, "What are they doing there?"

Sostratos looked in the direction of the bluffs west of Kourion. A procession marched along the heights. No—not everybody marched, for one man, bound, went stiffly and unwillingly, dragged toward the cliff-edge. Ice ran through Sostratos. His voice shook when he called, "Do you see, Menedemos?"

His cousin dipped his head. "I see." He sounded thoroughly grim, continuing, "Well, now we know how seriously the priests of Apollo Hylates take the game of touching their altar."

"Yes. Don't we?" Sostratos watched—couldn't stop watching, much as he wanted to turn away—the procession reach the place where land gave way to air. The akatos lay far enough out to sea that everything on the shore happened not only in miniature but also in eerie silence. Only the sound of waves slapping against the ship's hull and the regular splash of oars going into and out of the water came to Sostratos' ears.

What were they saying, there at the top of the bluffs? Were they cursing the bound man for profaning the god's altar? Or were they—worse—commiserating with him, saying it was too bad he'd got caught, but now he had to pay the price? As with Thoukydides, who'd written down speeches he hadn't heard, Sostratos had to decide what was most plausible, most appropriate to the occasion.

Then, suddenly, without Sostratos' quite seeing how it happened, the bound man went over the cliff. For a heartbeat, the scene there ashore wasn't silent any more. The man's shriek of terror and despair reached the *Aphrodite* across a stadion of seawater. It cut off with horrid abruptness. At the foot of the cliffs, his broken body lay as still as if it had never held life. Pleased with a job well done, the men of Kourion who'd put him to death went back toward the temple to attend to whatever other important business they had that day.

Sailors muttered among themselves. Even if some of them thought the man had brought it on himself by profaning the god's altar, watching him die wasn't easy and couldn't possibly have been a good omen. Diokles fingered the amulet of Herakles Alexikakos he wore to turn aside evil.

Sostratos walked back to the stern and up onto the poop deck. In a low voice, he said, "I'm glad we didn't buy anything in the agora at Kourion,"

Menedemos had to look back over his shoulder now to see the corpse lying there under the bluffs, close by the sea. After a moment, his gaze swung toward Sostratos once more. He slowly dipped his head. "Yes," he said. "So am I."

AHEAD OF THE *Aphrodite*, the Anatolian mainland slowly rose above the horizon. Behind her, Cyprus sank into the sea. Between the one and the other, she was alone in the midst of immensity. Menedemos had sailed for the mainland from Paphos, on the west coast of the island. That made for a longer journey over the open sea than if he'd crawled up to the north coast of Cyprus, but it also shaved several days off the journey back to Rhodes.

"Euge," Sostratos told him. "Everything seems to be going well."

"Yes, it does, doesn't it?" Menedemos said. "But I can already hear my father complaining I took a chance going this way." He sighed. Now that they were well on the way to Rhodes, the things of home crowded forward in his mind once more. He didn't look forward to dealing with his father. Part of him didn't look forward to dealing with his father's second wife, either. But part of him was eager, ever so eager, to see Baukis again. And he knew exactly which part that was, too.

Sostratos came up onto the poop deck. He pointed dead

ahead. "Nicely sailed," he said. "With the headland of Lykia there, you've skipped a lot of the waters that pirates haunt."

"I wish I could have skipped them all," Menedemos answered. "If I thought I could have got away with sailing straight across the sea from Cyprus to Rhodes, I'd have done it. Then we wouldn't have had to worry about pirates at all."

"Maybe not," Sostratos said. "But if you were able to cross the open sea like that, easy as you please, don't you think pirates would be, too?"

Menedemos hadn't thought of that. He wished his cousin hadn't thought of it, either. "There are times, my dear, when you make seeing both sides of the picture seem a vice, not a virtue."

"What is the world coming to, when I can't even tell a plain truth without getting carping criticism back?" Sostratos looked up to the heavens, as if expecting Zeus or Athena to descend and declare that he was right.

Neither Zeus nor Athena did any such thing. Maybe that proved Sostratos was wrong. Maybe it proved the gods were busy elsewhere, on some business more important than Sostratos'. Or maybe it proved nothing at . . . Menedemos shied away from that speculation before it fully formed. Still, he wished that just once he would see a god, any god, manifest himself on earth or openly answer a prayer. That would make his own piety, which while sincere didn't run especially deep, much easier to maintain.

Still not quite letting that question take shape in his mind, Menedemos asked, "What was the name of the wicked fellow who said priests invented the gods to frighten people into behaving the way they should?"

"Kritias," Sostratos answered at once. "He's ninety years dead now, but you're right—he was as wicked as they come, and not just on account of that."

"He was one of Sokrates' little pals, wasn't he?" Menedemos said.

His cousin flinched. "He did study with Sokrates for a

while, yes," he admitted. "But they broke when he did something shameless and Sokrates called him on it in public."

"Oh." Menedemos hadn't known that. He enjoyed teasing Sostratos about Sokrates, but the answer he'd just got killed his chances for the time being. He watched Sostratos eyeing him, too. His cousin knew the games he played, which meant he would be wiser not to play this one right now. Half the sport disappeared when the other fellow knew the barbs were coming.

Menedemos concentrated on sailing the *Aphrodite* instead. He took his hand off a steering-oar tiller to point, as Sostratos had, at the Lykian highlands that rose so steeply from the sea. "They make a lovely landmark, but I wish they weren't there."

"I should hope so, my dear," Sostratos replied, understanding him perfectly. "If they weren't, the Lykians wouldn't be half so much trouble. Those heights hide bandits the way river mouths and little capes and promontories hide pirate ships." His face clouded. "I'd never had trouble with bandits before this trip."

"That's because you never did a lot of traveling on land," Menedemos replied. "Who does, if he can help it?"

"Travel by sea's not safe, either," Sostratos said. "We found that out last year, when the pirates stole the gryphon's skull."

"They didn't intend to steal the skull. It just happened to be something they got away with," Menedemos pointed out. "I know the loss pains you, but it wasn't what they had in mind. Let me remind you what they did have in mind—stealing our money and our valuables, and killing us or selling us into slavery or holding us for ransom. Losing the gryphon's skull is a fleabite next to what might have been."

His cousin had the grace to look shamefaced. "Yes, that's true, of course," he said. "I don't believe I've ever claimed otherwise; if I have, I'm sorry for it. But I will say it's a fleabite that rankles."

"I know you will—you will at any excuse, or none,"

Menedemos said. "After a while, hearing about it over and over rankles, too."

He wondered if that was *too* blunt. Sostratos could be sensitive and could also sulk for days after having his feathers ruffled. Now he said, "I'm so sorry, my dear. I won't bore you with my presence any more," and stalked off the poop deck like an indignant Egyptian cat. Menedemos sighed. Sure enough, he'd hit too hard. Now he'd have to figure out a way to jolly Sostratos back into a good mood.

Meanwhile, he had the ship and the sea and the approaching Lykian coast to worry about, which meant his cousin got short shrift for a while. Sostratos had been right about one thing: just as no army had ever cleared brigands from the Lykian hills, no navy had ever cleared pirates from the coastline. Menedemos wished the *Aphrodite* were a trihemiolia. Let the Lykians beware then!

In a merchant galley, though, he was the one who went with caution. By the end of the day, the highlands had bulked their way out of the sea, tall and dark with forest. He might have tried to make a town. He might have, but he didn't. He had enough food. He'd taken on as much water as the *Aphrodite* would carry in Paphos. He could afford to spend one more night at sea. He could afford to, and he did.

Not a sailor grumbled, not off this coast. Maybe the men would have put up with striking straight across from Cyprus to Rhodes after all. If the other choice was running the gauntlet of Lykian pirates . . . He wondered whether the akatos could have carried enough bread and cheese and olives and wine and water for so long a journey. Maybe. But maybe not. There would be risks. He chuckled under his breath. At sea, there were always risks.

As the sun went down, anchors splashed into the Inner Sea. Sailors ate their suppers and washed them down with watered wine. A waxing gibbous moon glowed in the southeastern sky. As twilight deepened, the stars came out. Zeus' wandering star hung low in the southwest. A little to the east of it shone Ares' wandering star, now entering the Scorpion and thus close to its ruddy rival, Antares. Kronos' wandering star, yellow as olive oil, beamed down from the south, a little west of the moon.

Snores began to rise in the quiet darkness. Sostratos came back from the poop deck to wrap himself in his himation and stretch out beside Menedemos. He wasn't quite ready for sleep, though. Pointing up toward Ares' wandering star, he spoke in a low voice: "I wonder why it's so much dimmer now than it was this spring. Then it would have easily outshone Antares. Now . . ." He tossed his head.

Menedemos *was* sleepy. "How can we know why?" he asked, his voice grumpy. "It does what it does, that's all. Do you expect to go up into the heavens and look?"

"If I could, I'd like to," Sostratos said.

"Yes. If. But since you can't, won't you settle for going to sleep instead?"

"Oh, all right. Good night."

"Good night," Menedemos said.

When he woke the next morning, twilight streaked the eastern sky behind the *Aphrodite*. "Rosy-fingered dawn," he murmured, and smiled. He yawned, stretched, and got to his feet. Shivering a little, he picked up the crumpled chiton he'd used for a pillow and put it back on. The day would soon warm up, but the night had been on the chilly side. He walked to the rail and pissed into the Inner Sea.

Sostratos still snored. He hardly seemed to have moved from where he'd lain down the night before. Diokles was awake; he looked back from the rower's bench where he'd curled up for the night and dipped his head at Menedemos. As the day brightened, more and more sailors woke. Finally, just before the sun came up over the horizon, Menedemos waved to the men who'd already roused, and they set about waking the rest.

He woke Sostratos himself, stirring him with his foot. His cousin muttered something, then jerked in alarm. His eyes flew open. For a moment, they held nothing but animal fear. Then reason returned, and anger with it. "Why didn't you just stick a spear in me?" Sostratos demanded indignantly.

"Maybe next time, my dear." Menedemos made his voice as sunny as he could, the better to annoy his cousin. By Sostratos' scowl, it worked.

Barley cakes and oil and more watered wine served for breakfast. Grunting with effort, sailors hauled on the capstans to bring up the anchors. They hauled them out of the sea and stowed them near the bow. Menedemos gauged the wind. It was easy to gauge: there was none to speak of. He sighed. The rowers would earn their pay today.

At his orders, Diokles put eight men a side on the oars: plenty to keep the merchant galley going, yet few enough to keep the crew fresh in case they needed everyone rowing to escape pirates or fight them off. Menedemos spat into the bosom of his tunic to avert the unwelcome omen.

As often happened, fishing boats fled from the *Aphrodite*. They took one look at a galley centipede-striding across the waters of the Inner Sea and assumed they saw a pirate ship. That always saddened Menedemos. Still, had he skippered one of those little boats, he would have run from the *Aphrodite*, too. Anyone who took chances with his crew's freedom and lives was a fool.

The wind did blow up, fitfully, as the morning wore along. Menedemos ordered the sail lowered from the yard. He wondered why he'd bothered. Now it would fill and shove the akatos forward, and then a moment later, when the breeze died again, it would hang as loose and empty as the skin on a formerly fat man's belly after his polis was besieged and starved into surrender.

"A pestilence!" he muttered when the wind failed for the fourth time in half an hour. "Might as well be a girl who teases but doesn't intend to put out."

Sostratos stood close enough to hear him. "Trust you to come up with that figure of speech," he said.

"I wouldn't dream of disappointing you," Menedemos said.

He would have gone on in that vein, but Moskhion, who was taking a turn as lookout, shouted from the foredeck:

"Ship coming out from behind that headland! No, two ships, by the gods! Two ships off the starboard bow!" He pointed.

Menedemos' eyes swung in the direction Moskhion gave. Even so, he needed several heartbeats to spy the ships. They were galleys, their masts down, their hulls and even their oars painted a greenish blue that made them hard to spot against sea and sky. No honest skipper painted his ship a color like that.

Sostratos saw the same thing at the same time. "Pirates," he said, as if remarking on the weather.

"I'm afraid you're right, my dear." Menedemos dipped his head. He gauged the speed at which those long, lean galleys were approaching, gauged it and didn't like it a bit. "I'm afraid we can't very well run, either, not with the hull as soaked as it is. They'd catch us quick, and this polluted fitful breeze won't let us sail away, either."

"We have to fight, then," Sostratos said.

"Yes." Menedemos dipped his head again. "I'm afraid we do." He shouted orders: "Raise the sail to the yard! Serve out weapons to everyone! Man all oars! Diokles, as soon as we have a rower on every bench, I'll want you to up the stroke. We can't outrun 'em, but we'll need as much speed as we can get."

"Right you are, skipper." The oarmaster pointed toward the approaching pirate ships, which stayed a couple of plethra apart. "They're a little overeager, you ask me. If they'd waited a little longer before they came out of cover, we'd've had less time to get ready."

"We're a good ways out to sea; maybe they wanted to make sure we didn't get away," Menedemos said. "If they did make a mistake, it's up to us to prove it."

"They're triakonters," Sostratos said. "Only thirty rowers in each one, but look how many extra men they've packed in for boarding."

"Bastards," Menedemos said. "Grab my bowcase, O best one. Your archery will help us."

"I hope so," his cousin answered. "I can't shoot all of them, though, however much I wish I could."

"I know. I wish you could, too," Menedemos said. "But the more you hit, the fewer we'll have to worry about if they do manage to board us." *If they board us, we're ruined,* he thought. As Sostratos had, he saw how full of men the pirate ships were. The *Aphrodite*'s crew might well have been able to fight off one. Both together? Not a chance. He knew as much, but he wouldn't say so out loud. By the expression on his cousin's face, Sostratos knew as much, too.

Up went the sail. Rowers hurried to their places. Sailors who weren't rowing served out swords and pikes and axes and cudgels. Men stowed them where they could grab them in a hurry. Everyone's eyes were on the pair of triakonters speeding toward the merchant galley. The men also had to know they couldn't beat back that many boarders. But they'd been through sea fights with Menedemos before. He'd always managed to do something to keep them free and safe.

What are you going to do this time? he asked himself. He found only one answer: *The best I can.* Aloud, he said, "Sostratos, loose the boat from the sternpost. Then go forward to shoot. If we win, maybe we'll come back for the boat. If we don't . . ." He shrugged and turned to Diokles as his cousin obeyed. "Up the stroke some more. Don't show them quite everything we can do, though, not yet. Let them think we're a little slower and deeper laden than we really are."

"I understand, skipper." The keleustes raised his voice so even the men at the forwardmost oars could hear: "Put your backs into it, you lugs! If you want to pay the whores on Rhodes again, you do what the captain and I tell you. Come on, now! Rhyppa*pai*! Rhyppa*pai*! Rhyppa*pai*!" He beat out the rhythm with mallet and brass square, too.

The *Aphrodite* seemed to gather herself, then to spring across the water toward the two pirates. The akatos' rowers couldn't see the foe, of course; they looked back at Menedemos and Diokles. Diokles had been wise to remind them to obey orders. They relied on the oarmaster and the skipper to be their eyes and brains. They staked their freedom, maybe their lives, on that reliance. By the anxious expressions some of them wore, they were well aware of it, too.

Then Menedemos had no more time to spare for his own rowers. He steered the merchant galley at the two triakonters as they made for the *Aphrodite*. The eyes at the bows of the pirate ships stared balefully across the water at the merchant galley. Their rams, and the *Aphrodite*'s, too, gnawed through the sea, churning it to white foam. Their oars rose and fell, rose and fell, not quite so smoothly as the *Aphrodite*'s but at a remarkably quick stroke. Both ships were faster than the akatos. *But not by so much as you think,* Menedemos told himself. *I hope.*

"I'll give you something nice, Father Poseidon," he murmured, "if you let me come home to do it. I promise I will." He bargained with men almost every day. Why not with the gods as well?

Things on the sea didn't always happen swiftly. Even though the *Aphrodite* and the pirates were closing faster than a horse could trot, they had twenty or twenty-five stadia to cover before they met: close to half an hour. Menedemos had plenty of time to think. So did the pirate captains, no doubt. He suspected he knew what they would do: keep their distance from each other, ply the *Aphrodite* with arrows for a while, and then close and board from port and starboard at the same time. With numbers thus on their side, they could hardly fail.

As for what he could do to counter that . . . There, his thoughts remained murkier than he would have liked.

Those pirate ships swelled. Suddenly, Menedemos could hear shouts from the men aboard them, see sunlight spark from swords and spearheads. He didn't think the shouts were Greek, not that it mattered. There had been plenty of Hellenes aboard the pirate ship that attacked the merchant galley the year before in the Aegean. They counted as pirates first.

He steered the *Aphrodite* straight for the nearer triakonter here: the left-hand one of the pair. No matter how she altered course—and her fellow with her, in some nice seamanship—

he swung the steering-oar tillers so his bow and hers pointed at each other.

"You going to try ramming her, skipper?" Diokles asked. "You want the extra from the rowers now? I think they can still give it to you, though they've been working pretty hard."

"I'll watch what the pirates do, and that'll tell me what I can do," Menedemos answered. "Don't up the stroke till I yell, no matter what."

"All right." The oarmaster didn't sound doubtful, no matter what he was thinking. That left Menedemos grateful. If Diokles let worry show, it would surely infect the rowers, and that would make a bad situation even worse.

Archers aboard the closer pirate ship started shooting. Their arrows splashed into the Inner Sea well short of the *Aphrodite.* Menedemos dipped his head in wry amusement. Bowmen were always overeager. Before long, though, the shafts would start to bite. More arrows arched through the air. These fell short, too, but not by nearly so far.

Where time hadn't mattered much before, suddenly now heartbeats were of the essence. Menedemos swung the *Aphrodite* hard to port, aiming her ram straight for the side of the second triakonter, the one he'd ignored up till now. "Everything they've got, Diokles!" he called.

"Right," the oarmaster said without hesitation. He upped the stroke: "Come on, boys! You can do it! Rhyppa*pai*! Rhyppa*pai*! Rhyppa*pai*!" Not even Talos the bronze man could have held that sprint for long. Gasping, thrusting, faces gleaming with sweat and oil, the rowers gave him everything they had in them. The akatos suddenly seemed to bound forward over the sea.

Menedemos' only advantage was that he knew what he was doing and neither of the pirate captains did. Had the skipper of the closer ship been more alert, more ready for something unexpected from the *Aphrodite,* he might have rammed her as she turned toward his comrade. He tried, in fact, but he waited a couple of heartbeats too long before starting his own turn—

and the merchant galley's sudden burst of speed also caught him by surprise. His triakonter passed a few cubits astern of the *Aphrodite.*

Two arrows hissed past Menedemos from behind. He couldn't even look back. If he got hit, he hoped Diokles would shove him out of the way and drive home the attack on the other pirate ship. He aimed the merchant galley at a point halfway between the triakonter's ram and where her mast would go when it was up.

The man at the steering oars on the pirate ship should have started to turn toward the *Aphrodite* or away from her, to make sure the akatos' ram didn't hit squarely. The black-bearded ruffian should have. Maybe he even would have; though taken by surprise, he probably had time to do it. But Sostratos shot three arrows at him in quick succession. Two of them missed. The other one hit him in the neck. He shrieked and clawed at himself and forgot all about steering the triakonter.

"Euge!" Menedemos roared exultantly.

Another pirate pushed the wounded helmsman aside and seized the steering oars. Too late. Much too late. Heartbeats counted now, and the men in the second ship had none to spare. Menedemos heard their screams, saw their mouths— and their eyes—open wide, wide, *wide* as the ram slammed home. One of them tried to use an oar to fend off the merchant galley, which did him no more good than a straw would have in fending off an angry dog.

Crunch! The impact staggered Menedemos. The ram's three horizontal flukes stove in the triakonter's timbers, breaking tenons, tearing mortises open, and letting the sea flood in between planks formerly watertight.

"Back oars!" Diokles shouted. The rowers, who'd known the command was coming, obeyed at once. Menedemos' heart thudded. If the ram stuck, the pirates could swarm aboard the *Aphrodite* from their mortally wounded vessel and perhaps yet carry the day. But then he breathed again, for it came away cleanly. He turned the akatos toward the other pirate ship.

A rower howled as an arrow from the stricken triakonter bit. Another sailor took his place. Menedemos thanked the gods that hadn't happened during the ramming run, or it might have thrown off his timing and made him deliver a less effective blow. He noticed yet another sailor, not a man who'd been pulling an oar, down and clutching at a shaft through his calf. That fellow must have been wounded in the attack, but Menedemos, his attention aimed wholly at his target, hadn't noticed till now.

Archers aboard the surviving triakonter kept shooting at the *Aphrodite,* too. Sostratos answered as best he could. One of his shafts hissed just in front of the face of the pirate ship's helmsman. He jerked back with a startled cry Menedemos could hear across the couple of plethra of water between the two galleys.

He also heard cries for help coming from the ship he'd rammed as she settled ever lower in the water. She wouldn't sink to the bottom of the sea—she was, after all, made of wood. But already the oars were of little use; when her hull filled completely, they would be altogether worthless. And she was a good many stadia out to sea. Menedemos, a strong swimmer, wouldn't have cared to try to get to shore from here by himself. And not so many men could swim at all.

The other pirate ship might take her crew off her, but that triakonter was already crowded. Besides, if she came up alongside her stricken sister, she would lie dead in the water, waiting for another ramming run from the *Aphrodite.*

A nice problem for her skipper, Menedemos thought. He and the other pirate captain maneuvered warily. Neither of the ships was at its best any more; the rowers on both were worn. Still, the triakonter remained faster. Menedemos couldn't catch up to her. After a little while, he stopped trying, for fear he would altogether exhaust his men and leave them at the pirates' mercy.

As they sparred, the rammed ship continued to settle. Before long, pirates were bobbing in the sea clinging to oars and to anything else that would float. Their cries grew ever more pitiful—not that they would have known any pity themselves, had they rammed the merchant galley rather than the other way round.

The breeze began to rise. It made the sea rougher. The pirate ship filled faster yet. The men who'd abandoned her rose on wavecrests and slid down into troughs. Menedemos tested the wind with a wet thumb. "What do you think?" he asked Diokles. "Will it hold for a while?"

"Hope so." The oarmaster leaned into the wind. He smacked his lips, as if tasting it, then dipped his head. "Yes, skipper, I think it will."

"So do I." Menedemos raised his voice: "Let down the sail from the yard. I think these polluted temple robbers have had all they want of us. If they come after us with the ship they've got left, we'll make 'em sorry all over again."

Cheers rang out, weary but heartfelt. Diokles eased back on the stroke; now the wind was playing a larger role in pushing the merchant galley across the sea. Menedemos looked over his shoulder. Sure enough, the one triakonter hurried over to the other, taking men off her. No one aboard the sound pirate ship seemed to be paying the *Aphrodite* any mind. And even if the pirates were still thinking about her, a stern chase was a long chase. The extra weight of the several dozen men would make the surviving triakonter slower, too.

Sostratos came back toward the stern to help the sailor who'd been shot through the leg. He knew something about doctoring—Menedemos suspected he knew less than he thought he did, but even the best physicians could do only so much. He drew the arrow and bandaged the wound. The sailor seemed grateful for the attention, so Menedemos supposed his cousin was doing no harm.

And Sostratos had done very well indeed from the foredeck. *"Euge!"* Menedemos called once more. "You shot the pirate at the steering oars at just the right time there."

"I would have shot the abandoned wretch sooner if I hadn't missed him twice," Sostratos said. "I could practically have spit across the sea and hit him, but the arrows went past." He looked disgusted with himself.

"Don't fret about it," Menedemos said. "You did hit him, and that's what counts. They lost enough time so they couldn't turn into our stroke or turn away from it, either, and we hit 'em good and square. The ram does a lot more damage that way."

"Do you think the other one will come after us?" Sostratos asked.

"I don't know for certain. We'll just have to find out. I hope not," Menedemos replied. "I promised Poseidon something nice if he brought us through. I'll have to make good on that when we get back to Rhodes."

"Fair enough, my dear," his cousin said. "The god earned it. And you earned praise, too, for your seamanship." He called out to the sailors: "Another cheer for the skipper, boys!"

"*Euge!*" they shouted.

Menedemos grinned and raised one hand from a steering-oar tiller to wave. Then he looked over his shoulder again. Still no sign of the other pirate ship. Not only was the triakonter not pursuing, she'd disappeared below the horizon. Menedemos didn't say anything, though, not yet. Though he couldn't see her from his place on the poop deck, her crew might still be able to make out the *Aphrodite*'s mast and sail. He was content to sail on and see what happened.

The breeze continued to freshen. At last, he took his men off the oars and went on under sail alone. He thought the pirates would have to do the same: either that or wear out their men altogether. He kept looking back in the direction from which the merchant galley had come. Still no sign of a sail.

At last, he allowed himself the luxury of a sigh of relief. "I truly don't think they're coming after us," he said.

"*Euge!*" the sailors yelled again.

"HOW DOES YOUR leg feel, Kallianax?" Sostratos asked anxiously.

"It's still sore as can be, young sir," the sailor answered.

"It'll stay sore a while longer, too, I reckon." His Doric drawl was thicker than most. "You don't get shot without having it hurt. By the gods, I wish you did."

"I understand that," Sostratos said. "But is it hot? Is it inflamed? Is there any pus in it?"

"No, none of that there stuff," Kallianax said. "It just hurts."

"As long as it doesn't swell or turn red or start oozing pus, though, it's healing the way it should," Sostratos told him. "You keep pouring wine on it, too."

Kallianax made a face. "That's easy for you to say. It's not your leg. Wine makes it burn like fire."

"Yes, I know," Sostratos said. "But it does help make you better. Do you want to lose a long-term advantage because of some pain now? If a wound goes bad, it can kill. You've seen that—I know you have."

"Well, yes, but I don't figure this here one would," Kallianax said.

"Please don't take the chance," Sostratos said. With obvious reluctance, the sailor dipped his head. Sostratos resolved to keep an eye on him to make sure he did as he was told. Some people did habitually place the short term ahead of the long. He knew that, knew it as a fact without altogether understanding it.

Menedemos laughed when he said as much. "I can think of a couple of reasons why it's so," his cousin said.

"Enlighten me, O best one," Sostratos said.

That only made Menedemos laugh more. "I know you, my dear. You can't fool me. Whenever you get too polite for your own good, that means you don't think I *can* enlighten you. Some people are fools, plain and simple. They wouldn't care about month after next if you whacked them over the head with it."

"But are they fools by nature or only because they haven't been educated to be anything else?" Sostratos asked.

He expected a neat either-or answer. That was how *he'd*

been educated. But Menedemos said, "Probably some of each. Some people *are* fools, like I said. They'll act like idiots whether they're educated or not. Others—who knows? Maybe you can show some people that folly is folly."

Sostratos grunted. His cousin's reply wasn't neat, but it made a good deal of sense. "Fair enough," he said, and started to turn away.

But Menedemos said, "Hold on. I wasn't done."

"No?" Sostratos said. "Go on, then."

"Thank you so much." An ironical Menedemos was a dangerous creature indeed. Go on he did: "If the reward you get *now* is big enough, you won't care about trouble later on, either. After Alexandros chose Aphrodite above Hera and Athene, he got Helen to keep his bed warm. Do you think he worried about what might happen to Troy later on account of that? Not likely!"

"There you go, making comparisons about women again," Sostratos said. Menedemos didn't let go of the steering-oar tillers, but he made as if to bow even so. But Sostratos, after a little thought, had to admit, "Yes, that's probably true, too."

"Are you enlightened, then?" Menedemos asked.

"I suppose I am."

"Good." Menedemos grinned. "You have any more of these little problems, just bring them to me. I'll set you straight."

"Go howl," Sostratos said, which only made Menedemos laugh more.

The *Aphrodite* put in at several towns along the Lykian coast, not so much to do business as because the coastal cities, held by Ptolemaios' garrisons, were the only safe halting places in that stretch of the world. If none was near when the sun went down, the merchant galley spent the night well offshore.

Another reason the Rhodians didn't do much business in the Lykian towns was the hope they would get higher prices for their goods in the Aegean the following spring than they could hereabouts. Phoenician merchants sometimes brought their own goods this far west; few of them got to the poleis of Hellas proper.

One of Ptolemaios' officers in Myra bought a couple of amphorai of Byblian for a symposion he was planning to put on. "This will give the boys something to drink they haven't had before," he said.

"I'd think so, yes," Sostratos agreed. "How do you like being stationed here?"

"How do I like it?" The soldier made a horrible face. "My dear sir, if the world needed an enema, they'd stick the syringe in right here." That jerked a laugh from Sostratos and Menedemos both. The officer went on, "The Lykians are jackals, nothing else but. And if you killed every single one of them, you wouldn't do yourself any good, because these mountains would just fill up with other human jackals in no time flat. This kind of country is made for bandits."

"And pirates," Sostratos said, and he and Menedemos took turns telling of their fight out on the Inner Sea.

"You were lucky," Ptolemaios' officer said when they finished. "Oh, I don't doubt you're good sailors and you have a good crew, but you were lucky all the same."

"I prefer to think we were skillful." Menedemos had his share of faults, but modesty had never been among them.

Dryly, Sostratos said, "I prefer to think we were skillful, too, but there's no denying we were lucky—and we caught the pirates by surprise."

"We're Rhodians," Menedemos said. "If we can't outdo a rabble like that, we hardly deserve our freedom. Our friend here"—he dipped his head to the soldier—"wishes he could scour the mountains clean. I wish we could do the same to the shore and burn every triakonter and pentekonter and hemiolia we find."

"That would be good," Sostratos said.

"That would be wonderful," the officer said. "Don't hold your breath."

Menedemos puffed out his cheeks like a frog inflating its throat sac in springtime. Sostratos chuckled. So did the soldier who served Ptolemaios. Menedemos said, "Sadly, though, it's no wonder most of this town is set back fifteen or twenty stadia from the sea. Everyone in these parts expects pirates, takes them for granted, and even plans cities taking them into account. And that's wrong, don't you see?" He spoke with unwonted earnestness.

"No, it's right, if you want to keep your city from getting sacked," Ptolemaios' officer said.

"I understand what my cousin is saying," Sostratos told him. "He means people should fight pirates instead of accepting them as part of life. I agree with him. I hate pirates."

"Oh, I agree with him, too, about what people *should* do," the officer said. "What they *will* do, though—that's liable to be another story."

Much as Sostratos would have liked to argue with him, he couldn't.

The rest of the trip along the Lykian coast went smoothly. One triakonter came dashing out from the mouth of a stream when the *Aphrodite* sailed past, but thought better of tangling with her: a single pirate ship, even if she carried a large boarding party along with her rowers, was anything but certain of seizing the merchant galley.

"Cowards!" the sailors from the *Aphrodite* yelled as the triakonter turned about and headed back toward shore. "White-livered dogs! Spineless, stoneless eunuchs!"

To Sostratos' enormous relief, those shouts didn't infuriate the pirates enough to make them turn back. Later, he asked Menedemos, "Why do they yell things like that? Do they really want a fight with the polluted Lykians?"

"I don't think so," his cousin answered. "I certainly hope not, anyway. But wouldn't you yell your scorn if a foe decided he didn't care to have anything to do with you? Are you going to tell me you've never done anything like that in your life?"

Thinking about it, Sostratos had to toss his head. "No, I can't do that. But I can tell you I'll try not to do it again. It just isn't sensible."

"Well, maybe it isn't," Menedemos said. "But so what?

People aren't always sensible. They don't always want to be sensible. You have trouble understanding that sometimes, if you want to know what I think."

"People should want to be sensible," Sostratos said.

"Ptolemaios' officer had it straight, my dear: what people should want and what they do want are two different beasts."

Rhodes lay only a day's sail—or a bit more, if the winds were bad—west of Patara. Sostratos and Menedemos picked up a few more hams there to sell at home. Menedemos said, "I was thinking of going up to Kaunos for a last stop, but to the crows with it. I want to get back to my own polis again."

"I won't quarrel with you, my dear," Sostratos answered. "We'll have a nice profit to show, and it'll get better still once we sell everything we're bringing back from Phoenicia. No one can complain about what we did in the east."

"Ha!" Menedemos said darkly. "That only shows you don't know my father as well as you think you do."

Sostratos had always thought Menedemos' troubles with his father were partly his own fault. But he knew telling his cousin as much would do no good at all and would make Menedemos angry at him. So he sighed and shrugged and dipped his head, murmuring, "Maybe you're right."

The sailors cheered when they learned Menedemos intended to sail straight for Rhodes. They wanted to go home, too. When the northerly breeze went fitful, they clamored to take a turn at the oars. Breeze or no, the *Aphrodite* cut through the waters of the Inner Sea like a knife through meat boiled tender.

With his wounded leg, Kallianax still found rowing painful. Using a spearshaft as a stick, he'd taken his place on the foredeck as lookout. The merchant galley was only a couple of hours out of Patara when he called, "Sail ho! Sail ho, dead ahead!"

"Better not be another gods-cursed pirate, not so close to Rhodes," Menedemos growled. His hands tightened on the tillers till his knuckles whitened.

That same thought had just crossed Sostratos' mind. He

stood on the poop deck, not far from Menedemos and Diokles. Like both of them, he peered toward the new ship. Having the sun at their backs helped. And . . . "She's really closing the distance hand over fist, isn't she?" Sostratos murmured a few minutes later.

"She sure is." His cousin sounded worried. "I've never seen anything honest move so fast." He shouted, "Serve out the weapons, by the gods! Whoever she is, she won't have an easy time with us."

But then, from the bow, Kallianax called, "She's got a foresail, skipper!"

"Belay the weapons!" Menedemos called. Any galley big enough to carry foresail as well as mainsail was also big enough to carry a crew that could overwhelm the *Aphrodite*'s without breathing hard: was, in fact, almost surely a war galley, not a pirate ship.

Shading his eyes with the palm of his hand, Sostratos said, "What's that emblem painted on her sails? Isn't it . . . isn't it the Rhodian rose?" He hesitated for fear of being wrong.

But Menedemos, whose eyes were probably sharper than his, dipped his head. "It *is*, by the gods!" He shouted again, this time in joyous relief: "She's one of our own, boys!" The sailors whooped and clapped their hands. But after a moment, in more nearly normal tones, he went on, "But *which* one of our own is she? She's not a regular trireme, or you'd see marines stomping around up on her decking, and her oarbox would be fully timbered to keep arrows and catapult bolts from tearing up the rowers. But she's too big and too fast for anything else. What in the name of the gods could she be?"

A lamp went on inside Sostratos' head. "My dear, to the crows with me if she's not your trihemiolia."

"Do you think so?" Menedemos rarely sounded awed, but this, Sostratos thought, was one of those times. "Do you really think so?"

"What else could she be?" Sostratos asked. "She's very new. Look how pale and unweathered her planking is."

Whatever she was, she was curious about the *Aphrodite*. As

she drew near, Sostratos saw she did indeed have three banks of oars. Her crew had stowed the rear benches of the upper, thalamite, bank so she could lower mast, yard, and mainsail in a hurry, but those hadn't come down yet. An officer at the bow called the inevitable challenge: "What ship are you?"

"We're the *Aphrodite,* out of Rhodes and bound for home from Phoenicia," Menedemos yelled back. "And what ship are you? You're a trihemiolia, aren't you?"

"You must be a Rhodian, or you wouldn't know the name," the officer answered. "Yes, we're the *Dikaiosyne.*"

"'Justice,'" Sostratos murmured. "A good name for a pirate hunter."

The officer on the *Dikaiosyne* went on, "The *Aphrodite,* you say? Who's your skipper there? Is that Menedemos son of Philodemos?"

"That's me," Menedemos said proudly.

"You're the chap who had the idea for a ship like this, aren't you? I heard Admiral Eudemos say so."

"That's me," Menedemos repeated, even more proudly than before. He grinned at Sostratos. "And now I know how it feels to look at my baby, and I didn't even get a slave girl pregnant." Sostratos snorted and grinned back.

12

MENEDEMOS WALKED WITH SOSTRATOS THROUGH a poor quarter of Rhodes: the southwestern part of the polis, not far from the wall and not far from the cemetery south of it. With a sigh, Menedemos said, "This is the sort of duty I wish we didn't have."

"I know," Sostratos answered. "I feel the same way. But that only makes it more important we do a good job."

"I suppose so." Menedemos sighed again.

Skinny naked children played in the street. Even skinnier dogs squabbled over garbage. They eyed the children warily. Maybe they were afraid the children would throw rocks at them. Maybe they were afraid they would get caught and killed and thrown into a pot. In this part of town, they probably had reason to worry. A drunk staggered out of a wineshop. He stared at Menedemos and Sostratos, then turned his back on them, hiked up his tunic, and pissed against a wall.

"O pai!" Menedemos called, pointing to one of the children. He would have said, *Boy!* to a slave just the same way.

"What do you want?" the boy, who was about eight, asked suspiciously.

"Where is the house of Aristaion son of Aristeas?"

The boy assumed a look of congenital imbecility. Not knowing whether to sigh one more time or burst out laughing, Menedemos took an obolos from between his cheek and his teeth and held out the small, wet silver coin in the palm of his hand. The boy rushed up and snatched it. He popped it into his own mouth. His friends howled with rage and jealousy. "Me! Me!" they clamored. "You should have asked me!"

"You've got your money now," Menedemos said in a friendly voice. "Tell me what I want to know, or I'll wallop the stuffing out of you."

There was language the youngster understood. "Go over two blocks, then turn right. It'll be on the left-hand side of the street, next door to the dyer's place."

"Good. Thanks." Menedemos turned to Sostratos. "Come on, my dear. And mind the dog turd there. We don't want to step in it barefoot."

"No, indeed," Sostratos agreed.

They had no trouble identifying the dyer's: the reek of stale urine gave it away. Next to it stood a small, neat house that, like a lot of homes in a neighborhood such as this, doubled as a shop. Several pots, nothing especially fancy but all sturdy and well shaped, stood on a counter. Menedemos wondered how much the stink from the dyeworks hurt the potter's trade. It couldn't help.

"Help you gents?" the potter asked. He was a man of about fifty, balding, with what was left of his hair and his beard quite gray. Except for the beard, he looked like an older version of Aristeidas.

To be sure, Menedemos asked, "Are you Aristaion son of Aristeas?"

"That's me," the man replied. "I'm afraid you've got the edge on me, though, best one, for I don't know you or your friend." Menedemos and Sostratos introduced themselves. Aristaion's work-worn face lit up. "Oh, of course! Aristeidas' captain and toikharkhos! By the gods, my boy tells me more stories about the two of you and your doings! I didn't know the *Aphrodite*'d got home this year, for you've beaten him back here."

Menedemos winced. This was going to be even harder than he'd feared. He said, "I'm afraid that's why we've come now, most noble one." Sostratos dipped his head.

"I don't understand," Aristaion said. But then, suddenly, his eyes filled with fear. He flinched, as if Menedemos had threatened him with a weapon. "Or are you going to tell me something's happened to Aristeidas?"

"I'm sorry," Menedemos said miserably. "He was killed by robbers in Ioudaia. My cousin was with him when it happened. He'll tell you more."

Sostratos told the story of the fight with the Ioudaian bandits. For the benefit of Aristeidas' father, he changed it a little, saying the sailor had taken a spear in the chest, not the belly, and died at once: "I'm sure he felt no pain." He said not a word about cutting Aristeidas' throat, but finished, "We all miss him very much, both for his keen eyes—he was the man who spotted the bandits coming after us—and for the fine man he was. I wish with all my heart it could have been otherwise. He fought bravely, and his wound was at the front." That was undoubtedly true.

Aristaion listened without a word. He blinked a couple of

times. He heard what Sostratos said, but as yet it meant nothing. Menedemos set a leather sack on the counter. "Here is his
pay, sir, for the whole journey he took with us. I know it can
never replace Aristeidas, but it is what we can do."

Like a man still half in a dream, Aristaion tossed his head.
"No, that's not right," he said. "You must take out whatever
silver he'd already drawn—otherwise you unjustly deprive
yourselves."

"Don't worry about that," Menedemos said. "For one thing,
he drew very little—as you'll know, he saved his silver. And,
for another, this is the least we can do to show what we
thought of your son."

"When he died, everyone on the *Aphrodite* was heartbro-
ken," Sostratos added, and that was nothing but the truth, too.

When he died. Aristaion finally seemed not only to hear but
to believe. He let out a low-voiced moan, then reached under
the counter and brought out a knife. Grunting with effort and
with pain, he used it to haggle off a mourning lock. The gray
hair lay on the counter. Menedemos took the knife and added
a lock of his own hair. So did Sostratos; the lock he'd cut off
in Ioudaia was beginning to grow out again. He sacrificed another without hesitation.

"He was my only boy that lived," Aristaion said in a faraway voice. "I had two others, but they both died young. I
hoped he'd take this place after me. Maybe he would have in
the end, but he always wanted to go to sea. What am I going to
do now? By the gods, O best ones, what am I going to do
now?"

Menedemos had no answer for that. He looked to Sostratos.
His cousin stood there biting his lip, not far from tears.
Plainly, he had no answer, either. For some things, there *were*
no answers.

"I mourned my father," Aristaion said. "That was hard, but
it's part of the natural order of things when a son mourns a father. When a father has to mourn a son, though . . . I would
rather have died myself, you know." The sun glinted off the
tears sliding down his cheeks.

"I'm sorry," Menedemos whispered, and Sostratos dipped his head. No, for some things there were no answers at all.

"Thank you, gentlemen, for bringing me the news," Aristaion said with haggard dignity. "Will you drink wine with me?"

"Of course," said Menedemos, who wanted nothing more than to get away. Again, Sostratos dipped his head without speaking. If anything, he probably wanted to escape even more than Menedemos did. But this was part of what needed doing.

"Wait, then," Aristaion said, and ducked back into the part of the building where he lived. He came out a moment later with a tray with water, wine, a mixing bowl, and three cups. He must have made the bowl and the cups himself, for they looked very much like the pots he was selling. After mixing the wine, he poured for Menedemos and Sostratos, then poured a small libation onto the ground at his feet. The two cousins imitated him. Aristaion lifted his cup. "For Aristeidas," he said.

"For Aristeidas," Menedemos echoed.

"For Aristeidas," Sostratos said. "If he hadn't spotted the bandits coming, we all might have died there in Ioudaia—and other times before that, out on the sea. He was a good man to have on our ship, and I'll miss him. Everyone who sailed with him will miss him."

"Thank you kindly, young sir. You're generous, to say such a thing." Aristaion raised the cup to his lips and drank. Menedemos and Sostratos also drank to their shipmate's memory. The wine was better than Menedemos would have expected it to be. Like the ware Aristaion made, it suggested the best taste not a great deal of money could buy.

"I wonder why these things happen," Sostratos said, "why good men die young while those who are not so good live on and on." Menedemos knew he was thinking about Teleutas. His cousin took another sip of wine, then continued, "Men who love wisdom have always wondered such things."

"It was the will of the gods," Aristaion said. "In front of Troy, Akhilleus had a short life, too, but people still sing about him even now." He murmured the opening of the *Iliad*: "'Rage!—Sing, goddess, of Akhilleus'. . . .'"

Sostratos had often wrangled with Menedemos about whether the *Iliad* and *Odyssey* deserved to hold their central place in Hellenic life. He wasn't always the most tactful of men; there were times, especially in what he saw as pursuit of the truth, when he was among the least tactful. Menedemos got ready to kick him in the ankle if he wanted to argue philosophy today. But he only dipped his head once more and murmured, "Just so, most noble one. Nor will Aristeidas be forgotten, so long as any one of us who knew him still lives."

Menedemos took a long pull at his own wine. He silently mouthed, *"Euge,"* at Sostratos. His cousin only shrugged a tiny shrug, as if to say he hadn't done anything worth praise. He'd remembered the occasion. To Menedemos, that was plenty. Only later did he wonder whether that was unfair to Sostratos.

The two of them let Aristaion fill their cups again. Then they made their farewells. "Thank you both again, young sirs, for coming and telling me . . . telling me what had to be told," Aristeidas' father said.

"It was the least we could do," Menedemos said. "We wish we didn't have to do it, that's all."

"Yes," Sostratos said softly. By the distant look in his eyes, he was back among those Ioudaian boulders again. "Oh, yes."

They gave Aristaion their sympathies one last time and left the potter's shop. They hadn't gone far before a woman started to shriek behind them. Wincing, Menedemos said, "Aristaion must have told his wife."

"Yes," Sostratos agreed. They walked on for a few more paces before he went on, "Let's go back to your house or mine and get drunk, shall we? There's nothing more we really have to do today, is there?"

"Nothing that won't keep." Menedemos put an arm around Sostratos' shoulder. "That's a good idea—the best one you've had all day, I'm sure."

"Will we think so in the morning?" Sostratos asked.

Menedemos shrugged. "That will be in the morning. We'll worry about it then."

SOSTRATOS OPENED HIS eyes and wished he hadn't. The early-morning sunlight leaking in through the shutters pained him. His head hurt. His bladder seemed about to burst. He reached under the bed and found the chamber pot. After easing himself, he went to the window, opened the shutters, called, "Coming out!" to warn anyone walking by below, and flung the contents of the pot into the street.

Then, still moving slowly, he went downstairs and sat down in the cool, shadowed courtyard. A few minutes later, Threissa, the family's redheaded Thracian slave girl, poked her snub nose into the courtyard. Sostratos waved to her. He saw her wondering if she could get away with pretending not to see and deciding she couldn't. She came over to him. "What do you want, young master?" she asked in accented Greek.

Every so often, he took her to bed. She put up with that rather than enjoying it, one reason he didn't do it more. It wasn't what he had in mind now. He said, "Fetch me a cup of well-watered wine and a chunk of bread to go with it."

Relief flowered on her face. "I do that," she said, and hurried away. Some requests she minded much less than others. Sostratos didn't even eye her backside as she went off to the kitchen, proof he'd drunk too much the day before. She soon returned with the wine and a barley roll. "Here you is. Roll just baked."

Sure enough, it was still warm from the oven. "Thanks," Sostratos said. He made as if to push her away. "Go on. I'm sure you've got plenty to do." She nodded and left him by himself. He took a bite from the roll. It was nice and bland, just what his stomach needed. He sipped the wine, a little at a time. Bit by bit, his headache eased.

He'd almost finished breakfast when his father came downstairs. "Hail," Lysistratos called. "How are you?"

"Better now than when I first got up," Sostratos answered. "The wine helped."

"Pity it's not springtime," Lysistratos said. "Raw cabbage is good for a thick head, but this is the wrong season." He walked over and sat down beside his son. "I understand why you and Menedemos did what you did. Losing a man is hard. Sometimes telling his family he's gone is even harder."

"Yes." Sostratos dipped his head. "His father was such a gentleman—and then, as we were leaving, his mother began to wail. . . ." He grabbed the winecup and gulped the last couple of swallows.

"A bad business. A very bad business." Lysistratos hesitated, then went on, "I hear you made something of a hero of yourself in the same fight."

With a shrug, Sostratos said, "My archery isn't hopeless. I should have shot more of the bandits, though. If I had, we wouldn't have had to pay a call on Aristaion yesterday." He wished he had more wine. What he'd already drunk had taken the edge off his headache, but another cup might take the edge off his thoughts. He looked around for Threissa, then decided it was just as well he didn't see her. A man who started pouring it down early in the morning wouldn't be worth much as the day wore along.

Lysistratos said, "What do you plan on doing today?"

"I'll go over to see Damonax and settle accounts with him," Sostratos answered. "The olive oil worked out better than I expected, but I'm *not* going to fill the *Aphrodite* up with it if we go to Athens next spring. That would be like taking crimson dye *to* Phoenicia. If he can't see as much for himself, I'll make it as plain as I have to."

"I understand." His father smiled. "I don't think you'll have to beat him about the head and shoulders, or anything of the sort. Uncle Philodemos and I made it plain to him that he pushed his luck this past spring. We let him get away with it once because of his own family's debts, but we're not going to let him be a permanent anchor weighing down *our* family's profits."

"Euge!" Sostratos said. "How did he take that?"

"Pretty well," Lysistratos replied. "He is a charming fellow, no two ways about it."

"Yes, but especially when he's getting his way," Sostratos said, which made his father laugh. He went on, "I hope I see Erinna when I'm there. Is she happy with Damonax?"

"She seems to be," Lysistratos said. "And did you hear last night? She's going to have a baby in a few months."

Sostratos tossed his head. "No, I didn't. That's wonderful news! I know how much she wants a family." He hesitated, then asked, "If it happens to be a girl, will they keep it or expose it?"

"I don't know," his father said. "I hope they'd keep it, but that's Damonax's choice, not mine." He looked troubled. "It would be hard, very hard, for your sister finally to give birth and then to lose the baby."

"I know. That's just what I was thinking," Sostratos said. But his father was right. That wasn't anything where the two of them had a say. He ate the last bit of barley roll, then got to his feet. "I'll head over there now. I've got the figures written down on a scrap of papyrus. With a little luck, I'll catch Damonax before he's gone to the agora or the gymnasion. Farewell, Father."

"Farewell." Lysistratos got up, too, and clapped him on the back. "You did very well in Phoenicia—on the whole voyage, from all I've heard. Don't be too hard on yourself because you weren't perfect. Perfection is for the gods."

Everyone told Sostratos the same thing. He'd told it to himself a good many times, too. That he had to keep telling it to himself showed he still didn't believe it. He wondered if he ever would. Shrugging, he headed for the door.

Damonax's house lay in the western part of Rhodes, not far from the gymnasion. It was far larger and finer than Aristaion's, and presented only a whitewashed wall and doorway to the outside world. Damonax, who made his money from lands outside the polis, didn't need a shop at the front.

Munching on some raisins he'd bought from a street peddler, Sostratos knocked on the door. He remembered coming here during Erinna's wedding celebration and, before that, when he'd shown Damonax the gryphon's skull. He sighed. If he'd taken six minai of silver from the man who would become his brother-in-law, the pirates in the strait between Euboia and Andros wouldn't have had the chance to steal the skull.

He knocked again. "I'm coming!" a slave shouted in good Greek. A moment later, the fellow opened a little barred shutter set into the door at eye level and peered out. "Oh, hail, Master Sostratos," he said, and opened the door itself. "Come in, sir. The master will be glad to see you."

"Thank you," Sostratos said. "I hope Damonax is well? And my sister, too? I hear from my father she's expecting a baby?"

"Yes, that's right," the slave answered. "They're both as well as anyone could hope. Here, sir, it's a nice day. Why don't you sit down on this bench in the courtyard? I'll let Damonàx know you're here." He raised his voice to a shout: "Master! Erinna's brother is back from overseas!"

Erinna's brother, Sostratos thought with wry amusement. That was probably how he'd be known here for the rest of his life. Well, fair enough. He perched on the bench the slave had suggested and looked around. The first things his eye lit upon were the flowerbed and herb garden in the courtyard. He smiled. They looked much more like those back at his family's house than they had the last time he was here. Erinna was an enthusiastic gardener and was making her mark felt.

The slave came back to him. "He'll be here in just a bit. Would you like some wine, sir, and some almonds or olives?"

"Almonds, please," Sostratos answered. "Thanks very much."

Damonax and the slave returning with the snack came into the courtyard at the same time. Sostratos rose and clasped his brother-in-law's hand. "Hail," Damonax said with a smile that showed off his white teeth. He was as handsome and well groomed as ever; he'd rubbed a scented oil into his skin so that he smelled sweet. Had it been a little stronger, it would have been annoying. As things were, it just marked him as a man who enjoyed fine things.

"Hail," Sostratos echoed. "And congratulations."

"I thank you very much." Damonax's smile got broader. He sounded pleased and reasonably contented with life and with his marriage. Sostratos hoped he was. That would be likely to mean Erinna was contented, too. "Do sit down again, best one. Make yourself at home."

"Kind of you," Sostratos said. The slave served the two of them and withdrew. Sostratos ate an almond. He inclined his head to Damonax. "Roasted with garlic. Tasty."

"I'm fond of them that way. Glad you like them, too," his brother-in-law replied. He made polite small talk; his manners had always been almost too perfect. Only after a quarter hour of chitchat and gossip about what had gone on in Rhodes while Sostratos was away did Damonax begin to come to the point: "I hope your voyage was successful and profitable?"

"We'll end up doing quite well for ourselves, I think," Sostratos said, "though much of what we bought—balsam and crimson dye and the Byblian, especially—we'll have to resell before we can realize the profit I'm sure we'll make."

"I understand," Damonax said. "I trust my oil was well received?" He was tense but trying hard not to show it. Here was the meat of the business, sure enough.

"The quality was good," Sostratos answered. "We sold most of it in Sidon. Here is what we made for it." He took out the scrap of papyrus on which he'd worked out just how much silver the olive oil had earned.

When Damonax saw the number at the bottom, his face lit up. "But this is wonderful!" he exclaimed. "It's quite a bit more than I expected. I'll be able to pay off a good many debts."

"I'm glad to hear it, best one," Sostratos said. "Even so, though, as I hear my father and uncle told you, I don't expect we'll want another cargo of olive oil when we go out next spring. I'm letting you know now, so you can't say we're pulling a surprise on you then."

"But why not, when you did so well?" his brother-in-law said. "You made money with it."

"Yes, but not so much money as with other goods that have more value and less bulk," Sostratos replied. "And I must say I think we were lucky to do as well as we did this past sailing season. I doubt we could come close to matching what we made if we go to Athens, as looks likely. Athens exports oil; you don't bring it there."

Damonax whistled, a low, unhappy note. "You're very frank, aren't you?"

"I have to be, wouldn't you say?" Sostratos replied. "You're part of my family now. I did business for you, and I'm glad it went so well. You need to understand why I don't believe it would go that well again. I have nothing against you or your oil. In bulk, on a round ship without the great cost of paying an akatos' crew every day, it would do splendidly. But the *Aphrodite* truly isn't the right ship to carry it. Menedemos feels the same, even more strongly than I do."

"Does he?" Damonax said. Sostratos dipped his head. Damonax grunted. "And he's the captain, and he's not married to your sister."

"Both those things are also true," Sostratos agreed. Trying to soften the disagreement, he went on, "This isn't malice, most noble one—only business. Silver doesn't spring from the ground like soldiers after Kadmos sowed the dragon's teeth."

"Oh, yes. I do understand that." His brother-in-law managed a wry grin. "My own reverses these past couple of years have made me all too painfully aware of it."

How angry was he? Not too, or he would have shown it more openly. Hellenes looked down their noses at men who felt one thing but feigned another. How could you trust anyone like that? Simple—you couldn't. Sostratos said, "May I see my sister for a few minutes? I'd like to congratulate her myself."

As Erinna's husband, Damonax could say yes or no as he chose. "Certainly nothing scandalous about it, not when you're her brother," he murmured. "Well, why not?" He called for a slave woman to bring her down from the women's quarters.

By the haste with which Erinna appeared in the courtyard, she must have hoped Sostratos would ask after her. "Hail," she said, taking his hands in his. "It's good to see you."

"Good to see you, my dear," he answered. "You look well. I'm glad. And I'm very glad you're going to have a child. I was happier than I can say when Father told me."

Her eyes glowed when she smiled. She freed her right hand, setting it on her belly. When she did that, Sostratos could see the beginning of a bulge there under her long chiton. "So far, everything seems to be well," she said. "You'll have a nephew before you sail next spring." She didn't even mention the possibility of a girl.

"That'll be fine," Sostratos said, and then stuck fast as he cast about, wondering what to say next. He and Erinna couldn't talk the way they had back at his family's house, not with Damonax standing there listening to every word. He'd been foolish to imagine they could. By his sister's expression, she was realizing the same thing. He sighed. "I'd better be going. It's wonderful you're going to have a baby. I'll help spoil him for the two of you."

Damonax chuckled at that in an indulgent, husbandly way. Erinna smiled but looked disappointed as Sostratos turned and headed for the doorway. For a moment, he wondered why. He could tell she too knew they couldn't talk the way they had in the old days. What point to pretending they could?

Then he thought, *You can go out that door. You can do what you please in the city. Erinna's a respectable wife. That means she has to stay here.* Such restrictions had chafed at her back when she was living in her father's house. They were even stronger, even harsher, for a married woman.

"Take care of yourself," Erinna called after him.

"And you, my dear," Sostratos answered. "And you." He hurried away then, not wanting to look back.

PHILODEMOS SAT IN the andron, drinking wine and eating olives. When Menedemos started out of the house, he wanted to pretend he didn't see his father's wave. He wanted to, yes, but he didn't have the nerve. He stopped and waved back. "Hail, Father," he said. "What can I do for you?"

"Come here." Philodemos sounded as peremptory as usual. "You don't need to go drinking or whoring right this minute, do you?"

Menedemos' hackles rose. His father always assumed he was in the wrong. Sometimes he was, of course, but not always. "I'm coming," he replied with what dignity he could. "As a matter of fact, though, I was going to the agora, not out drinking or whoring."

"That's easy enough for you to say." Philodemos rolled his eyes up to the heavens. "I can't prove you're wrong." By his tone, the matter of proof was just a detail.

After helping himself to an olive from the bowl on the table in front of his father, Menedemos tried a thrust of his own: "You're the one with the wine cup here."

"Yes, and it's properly watered, too," his father snapped. "Do you want a taste, so you can tell for yourself?"

"No, never mind," Menedemos said. "Why did you call me?" *Except to carp at me,* he added, but only to himself. That would have made things worse.

"Why did I call you?" Philodemos echoed. He took a pull from the cup himself, perhaps to disguise his confusion. Menedemos wondered if he'd called for any real reason at all, or just for the sake of exasperating him. At last, Philodemos said, "About the eastern route. Yes, that's it— about the eastern route. Do you think we can use it every year?"

That was a legitimate question; Menedemos could hardly deny as much. He said, "We *can,* sir, but I don't think we'd be wise. It's not just pirates. The war between Antigonos and Ptolemaios looks to be heating up. Any ship at all heading for Phoenicia is taking a chance these days."

Philodemos grunted. "If *you* talk that way, we never should have sent the *Aphrodite.*"

"Perhaps we shouldn't have," Menedemos agreed.

His father didn't just grunt this time. He blinked in astonishment. "You really do say that? You, the fellow who took the ship through a Carthaginian siege into Syracuse a couple of years ago?"

Ears heating, Menedemos dipped his head. "Yes, Father, I do say that. Taking the *Aphrodite* to Syracuse was *one* risk. As soon as we got past the Carthaginian fleet, we were fine. But there's risk every digit of the way between here and Phoenicia, from pirates and from the Macedonian marshals. We got into trouble, and I think almost any ship heading that way would. We came out the other side all right. Whether another ship would . . . Well, who knows?"

"Maybe you really are starting to grow up a little," Philodemos muttered, more to himself than to Menedemos. "Who would have believed *that*?"

"Father—" Menedemos broke off. He didn't want to quarrel if he could help it. That being so, he kept talking about the struggle between the marshals: "Did Alexander the Great's sister ever get out of Sardis? When we headed east, there was talk she wanted to get away from Antigonos and go over to Ptolemaios. Did old One-Eye let Kleopatra get away with it? We never heard anything after that, going to Sidon or coming back."

"Kleopatra's dead. Does that answer your question?" Philodemos replied.

"*Oimoi!*" Menedemos exclaimed, though he wasn't really much surprised. "So Antigonos did her in?"

"He *says* not," Philodemos answered. "But when she tried to leave Sardis, his governor there wouldn't let her go. Later on, some of her serving women murdered her. They wouldn't have done it if the governor hadn't told them to, and he wouldn't have told them to if Antigonos hadn't told him to. He made a show of putting them to death afterwards, but then, he would."

"Yes." Menedemos clicked his tongue between his teeth. "Sostratos called that one when we first heard Kleopatra wanted to get away from Antigonos. She wouldn't marry him, and she was too valuable a prize for him to let any of the other marshals have her." He sighed. "So now none of Alexander's kin is left alive. These Macedonians are bloodthirsty bastards, aren't they?"

"That they are." Philodemos dipped his head. "And your cousin is a clever fellow." *Which means you aren't.* Menedemos heard the addition even though his father didn't say it. It stung. It always did. And then Philodemos quivered, like a dog taking a scent. "Or are you telling me we shouldn't go back to Sidon because you made it impossible for any ship from our family to go back to Sidon? Whose wife did you debauch while you were there? The garrison commander's, maybe?"

"Nobody's, by the gods," Menedemos said.

"Is that the truth?" But Philodemos checked himself before Menedemos became really angry. "You don't lie about your adulteries; I will say that. If anything, you revel in them. All right, then. That's good news."

"I didn't have any adulteries to revel in, as I say," Menedemos replied. "Sostratos did—an innkeeper's wife down in Ioudaia—but not me."

"Sostratos . . . your cousin . . . seduced another man's wife?" his father said. Menedemos dipped his head. Philodemos clapped a hand to his forehead. "*Papai!* What is the younger generation coming to?"

"Probably about the same as yours did, and the one before yours, and the one before that, and the one before *that,*" Menedemos said with a cheerful grin. "Aristophanes complained about the younger generation a hundred years ago."

"Well, what if he did?" Philodemos retorted. "He was an Athenian, and everybody knows about *them.* You and your cousin are Rhodians. Good people. Sensible people."

"What about Nestor, in the *Iliad*?" Menedemos said. "He complained about the younger generation, too."

That gave Philodemos pause. He loved Homer no less than Menedemos did; Menedemos had got his fondness for the *Iliad* and *Odyssey* from his father. Philodemos returned the best answer he could: "You can't tell me we Hellenes haven't gone downhill since the days of the heroes."

"Maybe," Menedemos said. "Speaking of going downhill, how many speeches did Xanthos give in the Assembly while I was away?"

His father sent him a sour stare. Xanthos was a man of Philodemos' generation: was, in fact, a friend of Philodemos'. He was also a great and crashing bore. Philodemos could hardly deny that. To his credit, he didn't try. "Probably too many," he answered. Then, to forestall Menedemos, he added, "And yes, he gave them all over again, first chance he got, whenever he saw me."

"And how's Sikon?" Menedemos asked. "I've hardly had the chance to say good day to him, but those were some very nice eels last night, don't you think?"

"I've always liked eels," Philodemos said. "And Sikon is as well as a cook can be." He rolled his eyes again. Cooks had— and deserved—a reputation for tyrannizing the households in which they lived.

"Is he still quarreling with your wife?" Menedemos asked cautiously. The less he spoke about Baukis around his father, the better. He was sure of that. But he couldn't ignore her feud with Sikon. The way the two of them stormed at each other, the whole neighborhood had trouble ignoring it.

"They . . . still don't get along as well as they might," Philodemos said.

"You really ought to do something about that, Father." Menedemos again seized the chance to take the offensive.

"Wait till you have a wife. Wait till you're running a household with a temperamental cook—and there's no other kind," Philodemos said. "Better they should yell at each other than that they should both yell at me."

To Menedemos, that seemed a coward's counsel. He said, "Better they shouldn't yell. You ought to put your foot down."

"Ha!" his father said. "How many times have I put my foot down with *you*? How much good has it done me?"

"I wasn't the one who chased women this summer," Menedemos said. His father snorted at the qualification, but he pressed on: "And I wasn't the one who loaded so much olive oil onto the *Aphrodite*, either. No—I was the one who not only sold it but got a cursed good price for it, too."

"I told you before—we won't have to worry about that again," Philodemos said. "Damonax and his family needed the silver that oil brought. Sometimes there's no help for something. Sometimes there's no help for the kinsfolk one has."

By the way he looked at Menedemos, he wasn't thinking of Damonax alone. "If you'll excuse me, Father . . . ," Menedemos said, and left the andron before he found out whether Philodemos would excuse him. He stormed out of the house, too. If Philodemos tried to call him back, he made himself not hear.

Why do I bother? he wondered. *Whatever I do, it will never satisfy him. And, knowing it will never satisfy him, why do I get so angry when it doesn't?* But the answer to that was all too obvious. *He's my father. If a man can't please his own father, what sort of man is he?*

Sparrows hopped around, pecking in the dirt for whatever they could find. Menedemos pointed at one of them, which fluttered off for a few cubits but then lit again and went back to pecking. *Is your father angry at you because you don't gather enough seeds to suit him?* The bird bounced this way and that. Whatever worries it had—kestrels, snakes, ferrets— its father wasn't among them. *Ah, little bird, you don't know when you're well off.*

The day was warm and bright. The shutters to the upstairs windows were open, to let in air and light. They let out music: Baukis was softly singing to herself as she spun wool into thread. The song was one any girl might have sung to help make time go by while she did a job that needed doing but wasn't very interesting. Her voice, though true enough, was nothing out of the ordinary.

Listening to her, though, made Menedemos wish his ears were plugged with wax, as Odysseus' had been when he sailed past the sweetly singing Sirens. He clenched his fists till his nails bit into his palms. *It's always worse when I'm angry at Father . . . and I'm angry at him so much of the time.* He fled his own house as if the Furies pursued him. And so, maybe, they did.

SOSTRATOS BOWED TO Himilkon in the Phoenician's crowded harborside warehouse. "Peace be unto you, my master," he said in Aramaic.

"And to you also peace," the merchant replied in the same language, returning his bow. "Your slave hopes the poor teaching he gave to you proved of some small use on your journey."

"Indeed." Deliberately, Sostratos nodded instead of dipping his head. "Your servant came here to give his thanks for your generous assistance."

Himilkon raised a thick, dark eyebrow. "You speak better, much better, now than you did when you sailed for Phoenicia. Not only are you more fluent, but your accent has improved."

"I suppose that comes from hearing and speaking the language so much," Sostratos said, still in Aramaic. "I could not have done it, though, if you had not started me down the road."

"You are kind, my master, more kind than you need be." Himilkon's face still wore that measuring expression. He scratched at his curly black beard. "Most men could not have done it at all, I think. This is especially true of Ionians, who expect everyone to know Greek and do not take kindly to the idea of learning a foreign language."

"That is not altogether true," Sostratos said, though he knew it was to a large degree. "Even Menedemos learned a few words while he was in Sidon."

"Truly?" Himilkon raised that eyebrow again. "He must have met a pretty woman there, eh?"

"Well, no, or I don't think so." Sostratos was too honest to lie to the Phoenician. "As a matter of fact, I was the one who met a pretty woman there—in Jerusalem, not Sidon."

"Did you? That surprises me," Himilkon said. "I would not have guessed the Ioudaioi had any pretty women." He didn't bother hiding his scorn. "Did you see how strange and silly their customs are?"

"They are wild for their god, no doubt of that," Sostratos said. "But still, my master, why worry about them? They will never amount to anything, not when they are trapped away from the sea in a small stretch of land no one else wants."

"You can say this—you are an Ionian," Himilkon answered. "Your people have never had much trouble with them. We Phoenicians have."

"Tell me more, my master," Sostratos said.

"There was the time, for instance, when a petty king among the Ioudaioi wed the daughter of the king of Sidon—Iezebel, her name was," Himilkon said. "She wanted to keep on giving reverence to her own gods whilst she lived amongst the Ioudaioi. Did they let her? No! When she kept on trying, they killed her and fed her to their dogs. Her, the daughter of a king and the wife of a king! They fed her to the dogs! Can you imagine such a people?"

"Shocking," Sostratos said. But it didn't much surprise him. He could easily picture the Ioudaioi doing such a thing. He went on, "I think, though, that they will become more civilized as they deal with us Ionians."

"Maybe," Himilkon said: the *maybe* of a man too polite to say, *Nonsense!* to someone he liked. "I for one, though, will believe it when I see it."

Sostratos didn't care to argue, either, not when he'd come to thank the Phoenician for his Aramaic lessons. Bowing again, he said, "Your slave is grateful for your hearkening unto him and now must depart."

"May the gods keep you safe," Himilkon said, bowing back to him. Sostratos made his way out of the warehouse, past shelves piled high with treasures and others piled even higher with trash. Himilkon, no doubt, would be as passionate about selling the trash as he would the treasure. He was a merchant down to the very tips of his toes.

After the gloom inside Himilkon's lair, the bright morning sun sparkling off the water of the Great Harbor made Sostratos blink and rub his eyes till he got used to it. He saw Menedemos talking with a carpenter over at the base of a quay a plethron or so away. Waving, he walked over toward them.

His cousin clapped the carpenter on the back, saying, "I'll see you later, Khremes," and came toward him. "Hail. How are you?"

"Not bad," Sostratos answered. "Yourself?"

"I could be worse," Menedemos said. "I could be better, but I could be worse. Were you making horrible growling and hissing noises with Himilkon?"

"I was speaking Aramaic, yes. You can't say my learning it didn't come in handy."

"No, I don't suppose I can," Menedemos agreed. "After all, you never would have been able to seduce that innkeeper's wife if you hadn't been able to speak her language."

"That isn't what I meant," Sostratos said. "I was talking about the beeswax and the balsam and the embroidered cloth and the help I gave you in Sidon. I think of those things, and what do you talk about? What else but a woman?"

"I'm entitled to talk about her. I didn't go to bed with her," Menedemos said. "I didn't go to bed with anybody this sailing season, unless you count whores—and I wouldn't, believe me. You were the one who had the good time."

"It wasn't that good a time," Sostratos said. "It was strange and sad."

His cousin started to sing a melancholy love song. The object of the lover's affection in the song was a pretty boy, but that didn't stop Menedemos. "Oh, go howl!" Sostratos said. "It wasn't like that, either." The lovemaking itself had been fine. He would have remembered it fondly if Zilpah hadn't changed her mind about him the moment the two of them finished. But she had, and he couldn't do anything about it now.

"Well, what *was* it like?" Menedemos asked with a leer.

To keep from having to answer, Sostratos looked out to sea. He pointed. "Hello!" he said. "What ship is that?"

Such a question would always draw a merchant skipper's attention. Menedemos turned and looked out to sea, too, shading his eyes with the palm of his hand. "To the crows with me if that's not the *Dikaiosyne,* coming back from her cruise," he replied. "Shall we go over to the naval harbor and get a good close look at her?"

"Why not, best one?" Sostratos said, though he couldn't help adding, "We almost got a closer look at her than we wanted while we were coming back to Rhodes."

"Oh, nonsense," Menedemos said. "A trihemiolia's made to hunt pirates—that's the whole point of the type. Of course she's going to come up to any galley she spots and sniff around like a dog at another dog's backside."

"You always did have a gift for the pungent figure of speech," Sostratos said, whereupon his cousin held his nose.

Chuckling, they walked up to the naval harbor, which lay just to the north of the Great Harbor. Like the latter, it had long moles protecting its waters from wind and weather. Ship-sheds lined it, so the Rhodian naval vessels could be hauled up out of the sea, keeping their timbers dry and them light and swift. The narrower sheds sheltered pirate-hunting triremes; the wider ones warded the fives that would fight against any navy presuming to move against Rhodes.

Pointing to the *Dikaiosyne,* which had entered the harbor by way of the north-facing entrance, Menedemos said, "They won't have had to build anything special for her: she'll fit into the same shed as any trireme."

"True." Sostratos dipped his head. The trihemiolia put him in mind of a trireme stripped of everything that added even a drakhma's worth of extra weight. Triremes, these days, had their projecting oarboxes, through which the upper, or thran-ite, oarsmen rowed, covered over with planking to protect them from arrows. Not the *Dikaiosyne:* hers was open. Nor was she fully decked, to let her post a maximum complement of marines. Only a narrow stretch of decking ran down her midline from foredeck to poop.

Backing oars, the *Dikaiosyne*'s crew positioned her just in front of a shipshed. A couple of naked slaves came out of the shed and fitted a stout cable to the ship's sternpost. One of them turned his head and shouted back toward the shed. More slaves inside hauled at an enormous capstan. The line went taut. Little by little, the work gang hauled the trihemiolia out of the sea and up the sloping ramp inside the shipshed. The beech planking of her protective false keel scraped on the timbers of the ramp.

As soon as the ship's stern came out of the water, the slaves at the capstan paused. Sailors and marines began leaving the *Dikaiosyne,* lightening her so the haulers would have an easier time. *Easier,* though, was a relative term; Sostratos wouldn't have cared to bend his back and push against one of the great bars of the capstan.

He and Menedemos waved to the trihemiolia's crew. "Hail, best ones!" Menedemos called. "How was the hunting?"

"Good," answered a sailor who wore only a loincloth. He laughed. "As we were heading away from Rhodes, we scared the piss out of one of our own merchant galleys coming home. She looked like a pirate till we got up close. We were all set to sink her and let her crew try and swim back to Rhodes, but they had the right answers, so we let 'em go." He spoke with a certain rough regret.

Sostratos could laugh about it, too—now. He bowed to the sailor. "At your service, sir. We're the toikharkhos and captain from the *Aphrodite.*"

"Is that so?" The fellow laughed some more as he returned the bow. "Well, I bet you're glad we did stop and ask questions, then."

"Oh, you might say so," Menedemos allowed. "Yes, you just might say so. How did things go once you got to the Lykian coast?"

"Pretty well," the sailor from the *Dikaiosyne* replied. "She's fast as a galloping horse, the *Justice* is. We went after one hemiolia that couldn't have been anything but a pirate. Most of the time, those bastards'll show their heels to anything, even a trireme. But we didn't just keep up—we gained on her. Finally, the fellow in charge beached her. The pirates aboard her ran for the woods and got away, but we sent men ashore and burned the ship."

"*Euge!*" Sostratos said. "To the crows—to the cross—with pirates."

"Pity you couldn't have burned them, too," Menedemos added.

"We sank a couple of others, and many goodbyes to the whipworthy rogues they carried," the sailor said. "Whoever came up with the notion for the *Dikaiosyne* was a pretty clever fellow, let me tell you. And now farewell, friends—I'm off for some wine and a go or two at a boy brothel." With a wave and a smile, he hurried away.

"Well, you pretty clever fellow, what do you think of that?" Sostratos asked.

"I like it," Menedemos said. "Let the pirates beware, by the gods. Here's a ship they can't hope to fight, and one that can hunt them down even when they try to run. I hope we build a fleet of trihemioliai, a big fleet. It'd make things a lot safer for merchant skippers. What do *you* think, my dear?"

"I'm with you," Sostratos answered. "With any luck at all, your name will live forever—and deserve to."

He expected his cousin to strut even more after that. He didn't praise Menedemos every day. When he did, Menedemos had to know he meant it, and to be sure such praise was well deserved. But Menedemos, as it happened, wasn't thinking about him just then. With a sigh, he said, "I could be as famous as Alexander, and it wouldn't be enough to suit my father. He'd stay convinced nobody'd ever heard of me."

"You must exaggerate," Sostratos said. "It can't be so bad as that."

"As a matter of fact, it can be worse than that. It can be—and it is," Menedemos said.

"That's . . . unfortunate," Sostratos said. "And you didn't give him anything to complain about this sailing season. See what a handy thing your oath was?"

"Oh, yes." But that was sarcasm from his cousin, not agreement. "He started railing at the whole younger generation, not just at me."

"Why did he start railing at the—?" Sostratos broke off. "You told him about Zilpah?" he asked in dismay.

"I'm afraid I did, O best one. I'm sorry. Part of me is sorry, anyhow. He was holding you up for a paragon, and I wanted to show him you were made of flesh and blood, too, not cast from bronze or carved in marble. But that wasn't the lesson he drew. I suppose I should have known it wouldn't be."

"Yes, you should have." For a moment, Sostratos was furious. He discovered he couldn't hold on to his anger, though. "Never mind. It can't be helped, and it's not as if you told him about anything I didn't do." He kicked at a pebble with the side of his foot. "I understand the temptation now, where I never did before. To have a woman want you enough to give herself to you regardless of the risk— that's a powerful lure. No wonder you enjoy fishing in those waters."

"No wonder at all," Menedemos agreed. "In fishing, though, you eat what you catch. With women, if you like, what you catch eats you."

Sostratos made a face at him. "I should have known better. Here I was trying to tell you I'd found some sympathy for what you've been doing, and what do I get for it? A lewd pun, that's what. I think all your Aristophanes has gone to your head—or somewhere."

"Why, whatever can you mean, my dear?" Menedemos asked archly. Sostratos made another face. Menedemos went on in a more serious vein: "You're right, though. That's what makes wives more fun than whores—they really want it. Anybody can buy a whore's twat. Wives are different. Some wives are, anyhow."

"True enough. Some wives stay loyal to their husbands."

"Well, yes, but those aren't the ones I meant," Menedemos said. "Some wives'll give it away to just about anybody, too. They aren't worth having. That horrid Harpy of an

Emashtart . . ." He shuddered. "You had the luck with women this trip, believe me."

"Mine wasn't all good," Sostratos said.

"Mine was just about all bad," Menedemos said. "I could make it better, but—" He tossed his head.

"What do you mean?" Sostratos asked.

"Nothing. Nothing at all. Not a thing," Menedemos answered quickly. He was lying. Sostratos had no doubt of that. But, whatever the truth was, his cousin wouldn't give it to him.

A DELICIOUS SMELL came from the kitchen. Menedemos drifted toward it, sniffing like a hunting dog on the trail of a hare. He stuck his nose in the door. "What *is* that?" he asked the cook. "Whatever it is, you've outdone yourself."

"Thanks, young master," Sikon answered. "Nothing fancy— just prawns baked with a little oil and cumin and some leeks."

"'Nothing fancy,' he says." Menedemos came all the way in. "If the gods had you for a cook, they'd be better-natured than they are."

"That's kind of you—mighty kind." Sikon scooped a prawn, still in its shell, off the clay baking dish and handed it to Menedemos. "Here. Why don't you try one? Supper won't be for a little while yet, and I expect you're hungry."

"Starving," Menedemos agreed. As it often did, flattery had its reward. Holding the prawn by the tail, he left the kitchen. He paused just outside to peel off the shell and take a big bite, then sighed ecstatically. It tasted as good as it smelled. He could imagine no higher praise. Another bite got him down to the tail. He took the prawn by the very end, bit gently, and pulled it away from his mouth. The flesh stuck in the tail came free. Savoring the last delicious morsel, he tossed the empty tail to the ground next to the rest of the shell.

"I hope you enjoyed that."

By the way Baukis sounded, she hoped Menedemos would have choked on the prawn. "Oh. Hail," he told his father's young wife. All of a sudden, the treat didn't seem nearly so sweet and succulent. He went on, "I didn't notice you come into the courtyard."

"I'm sure of *that*." She sounded chillier yet. "You had your eyes closed while you slobbered over your seafood."

That stung. "I don't slobber," Menedemos said. "And it *was* good. You'll see for yourself—supper won't be long."

"I'm sure Sikon gave you that prawn from the goodness of his heart."

Menedemos wondered where Baukis, who was very young and who, like any woman of good family, had led a sheltered life, had learned such irony. "Well, why else?" he asked.

"To keep you sweet, that's why!" Baukis flared. "As long as you get little tidbits every now and then, you don't care how much they cost. Your tongue is happy, your tummy's happy, and to the crows with everything else."

"That's not fair," he said uncomfortably. Was Sikon devious enough to do such a thing? Easily. The next question Menedemos asked himself was harder. *Am I foolish enough to fall for a ploy like that?* He sighed. The answer to that looked to be the same as the one before: easily.

"You're right—that's *not* fair, but what can I do about it?" Baukis looked and sounded on the edge of tears. "If the slaves in my own house won't obey me, am I a wife or just a child? And if no one else in the family will back me against a slave, am I even a child, or only a slave myself?"

Her words held a painful amount of truth—certainly painful to her. But Menedemos said, "My dear, you'll find yourself without allies if you pick the wrong fight. I'm afraid that's what's happened here. We really can afford to eat well, so why shouldn't we?"

She stared at him, then did start to cry. "Oh! You hate me! Everyone hates me!" she stormed. She spun away from him and rushed toward the stairs. Up she went. A moment later, the door to the women's quarters slammed.

"Oh, a pestilence," Menedemos muttered. Now he was liable to end up with not only Baukis but also his father angry at him. Philodemos could find any excuse for getting in a temper against him, but Baukis. . . . He muttered some more. Having her dash away from him was the last thing he wanted—*even if it may be the best and safest thing for you,* he told himself.

That slamming door brought his father out into the courtyard. "By the gods, what now?" Philodemos asked, scowling.

Despite that scowl, Menedemos knew a certain amount of relief that he could be the first to tell his father what had happened. If Philodemos listened to Baukis first, he probably wouldn't heed anyone else afterwards. Menedemos summarized what had led to Baukis' abrupt departure. When he finished, he waited for Philodemos to start railing at him.

But all Philodemos did was slowly dip his head. "Well, maybe it's for the best," he said.

"Sir?" Menedemos gaped, hardly believing his ears.

"Maybe it's for the best," Philodemos repeated. "Her quarrel with Sikon's been going on far too long. I didn't want to stick my nose into it; one or the other of them would have bitten it off. But maybe she'll pay attention to you. She takes you seriously, though I'm sure I can't imagine why."

"Thank you so much," Menedemos murmured. His father couldn't possibly praise him without stirring some vinegar in with the honey. Even so, he was glad to learn Baukis *did* take him seriously.

She didn't come downstairs for supper. Sikon sent some of the prawns up to her, along with fine white barley rolls for sitos and a cup of wine. When the slave woman brought back the dish without a prawn left on it, the cook looked almost unbearably smug. Menedemos was tempted to smack him. Even Philodemos noticed, and said, "Gloating isn't a good idea."

However harsh he was with his own son, he was usually mild to the cook. Sikon got the point. "All right, master—I'll remember," he promised.

"See that you do," Philodemos said.

Clouds drifting down from the north not only warned of the beginning of the autumn rains but also brought darkness sooner than it would have come with good weather.

Menedemos was just as glad to be back in Rhodes. He wouldn't have wanted to try steering the *Aphrodite* through rain and fog and light murky at best. He tossed his head. No, he wouldn't have wanted that at all. Too easy to end up aground before you even knew you were in trouble.

Yawning, he went upstairs to bed. These longer nights made him want to curl up like a dormouse and sleep and sleep. But he hadn't drifted off when his father came upstairs, too. Philodemos went into the women's quarters. A few minutes later, the bed there started creaking rhythmically.

Menedemos pulled his himation up over his head to smother the noise. No good. After a while, it stopped. After a much longer while, he slept.

He woke before sunrise the next morning and tiptoed down to the kitchen for some barley rolls, olive oil, and wine to break his fast, then sat down on a bench in the courtyard to eat. He managed a wry chuckle when his gaze went to the stairs. After the exertions of the night before, how late would his father sleep?

That thought had hardly occurred to him when he heard footsteps on the stairs. But it wasn't his father coming down; it was Baukis. She paused in the doorway when she saw Menedemos up before her. For a moment, he thought she would withdraw. After a brief pause, though, she came out. "Hail," she said, and, after gathering herself, "Good day."

"Good day," he answered gravely. "How are you?"

"Well." Baukis thought about that, then made a slight correction: "Well enough."

"I'm glad," Menedemos said, as if he hadn't heard the correction. He didn't want to keep up a fight with her. "The rolls from yesterday's baking are still very good," he offered. No matter what she thought about Sikon's choices for opson, she couldn't very well complain about the sitos . . . could she?

She came close. "Are they?" she said tonelessly. Menedemos dipped his head. She let out a small sigh. "All right," she murmured, and went into the kitchen to get her own breakfast.

When she came out again, Menedemos shifted on the bench to give her more room to sit down. She hesitated but did. She poured out a small libation from her cup of wine before tearing off a chunk from a barley roll, dipping it in oil, and eating it.

Sikon came out of his little downstairs room just then. "Good day, young master," he said, "Good day, mistress." Whatever he thought about Baukis, he remembered Philodemos' warning and kept it to himself.

"Hail," Menedemos said. He wondered if Baukis would scold the cook for not being up before her and hard at work. She seldom missed a chance to fuel their feud.

But all she said this morning was, "Good day, Sikon." Looking both surprised and relieved—he'd evidently expected a snarl from her, too—Sikon hurried into the kitchen. Pots clattered. Firewood thumped. Baukis let out what was unmistakably a snort of laughter. "He's showing off how busy he is."

"Well, yes," Menedemos agreed. The cook didn't have to make half that much noise.

Baukis thought the same thing. "He really is an old fraud, you know."

"Well—yes," Menedemos said again. "But he really is a good cook, too, you know."

"I suppose so," Baukis said grudgingly. She sipped from her wine. "I don't like quarreling with you."

"I've never like quarreling with you," Menedemos said, which was nothing but the truth.

"Good." Baukis ate some more of her barley roll. "This is good, too," she admitted, licking crumbs and a smear of oil from her fingertips with a couple of quick strokes from the tip of her tongue.

Menedemos watched, entranced. "Yes, it is, isn't it?" he said, a heartbeat slower than he should have. He might have been talking about the barley roll. On the other hand, he might not have been.

Baukis, to his relief, chose to answer as if he was: "Sikon is almost as good with sitos as he is with opson."

"You shouldn't tell me that," Menedemos said. She raised

an eyebrow in surprise. "By the gods, Baukis, you shouldn't," he insisted. "You should go right into the kitchen and tell Sikon to his face."

She didn't have to think about that, but dipped her head at once. "You're right—I should. I should, and I will." She got to her feet and strode into the kitchen as a hoplite might have gone into battle. Menedemos, though, wouldn't have watched a hoplite striding into battle in anything like the same way.

He had trouble reading her expression when she came out again. "Well?" he asked.

"He asked me how much wine I'd had, and if I'd bothered putting any water in it at all. That man!" Baukis looked as if she didn't know whether to be furious or to burst out laughing. After a moment, laughter won.

"What's so funny?" Philodemos called from the bottom of the stairs.

Menedemos got to his feet. "Hail, Father."

"Good day, sir," Baukis added, prim as a young wife should have been.

"What's so funny?" Menedemos' father asked again. Baukis explained. Philodemos listened, then chuckled. "Let me understand you, my dear," he said after a moment. "*You* went in to Sikon and told him this? And then he said that to you?"

"That's right, sir," Baukis answered. "It was Menedemos' idea."

"*Was* it?" Menedemos' father gave him a long look. "Well, good for you," he said at last. "Good for both of you, in fact. High time everyone remembers we're all living in the same house here." He went into the kitchen to get his own breakfast.

"Thank you, Menedemos," Baukis said quietly.

"Why?" he said. "I didn't do anything—you did." He smiled at her. She smiled back, looking as happy as he'd seen her since she came into the household.

Philodemos walked out munching on a roll, a cup of wine in his other hand. "Did I tell you, son, I'm going to a symposion at Xanthos' tonight?" he said. "You're invited, too, if you care to come along."

"No, thanks," Menedemos said at once, miming an enormous yawn.

Philodemos chuckled again. "I told his slave I was pretty sure you had another engagement," he said, "but I did think I'd let you know about it. The wine and the food and the entertainers *will* be good."

"No doubt, sir, but the price is listening to one of Xanthos' windy speeches, or maybe more than one," Menedemos replied. "That's more than I care to pay, thank you very much. And with Sikon in the kitchen, the food here will be good, too."

"So it will," Baukis agreed, sounding as if she really was working hard to give the cook proper credit. Menedemos wondered how long that would last, but was willing, even eager, to enjoy it while it did.

Philodemos looked pleased, too. He'd seemed cheerful ever since he got up, unusually so. Menedemos recalled the creaking bed the night before. "All right, then," his father said. "I've done my duty—I've told you about the symposion. Past that, it's up to you."

"Thank you for giving me so much sea room." Menedemos meant it; his father more often preferred to bark orders than to let him make his own choices. Ordering him to Xanthos' would have gone a bit far, even for Philodemos, but it wouldn't have been out of the question. Knowing as much, Menedemos tried to be thoughtful, too: "I wish it were the season for cabbage, to help you with your headache tomorrow."

"The only thing that really helps one of those headaches is a little more wine, if your stomach can stand it," his father said. But then, as he seldom did, he realized he was turning down kind words from Menedemos, and checked himself. "Thanks," he added gruffly. "Raw cabbage is better than nothing; I will say that."

Dressed in his best chiton (but still barefoot, as befit a man who'd spent a good many years at sea himself), Philodemos went off to Xanthos' house late that afternoon. Menedemos knew he'd come reeling home some time in the middle of the night, a beribboned wreath on his hand, songs on his lips, and a torchbearer or two lighting his way through the dark streets of Rhodes.

And here I am staying home, Menedemos thought. *Which of us is the old man and which the young?* Then he reminded himself where his father was going. He'd used the right word in describing those speeches. More winds lurked in Xanthos' house than in the oxhide sack King Aiolos had given to Odysseus to help him make his way homeward—and they would all come out tonight, too. Menedemos laughed. Sure enough, he liked his choice better than his father's.

He was pretty sure he had a better supper than his father's, too, no matter what Xanthos' cook turned out. Sikon brought a fine stingray back from the market. He baked it Sicilian style, with cheese and silphium from Kyrene. He'd also baked some light, fluffy bread of wheat flour for sitos. Replete, Menedemos said, "This is luxury the Great Kings of Persia couldn't top."

The cook leaned toward him and said, "And your father's wife didn't grumble about the fish, either. You ask me, that's the best luxury of all."

After supper, with night already fallen, Menedemos went up to his bedroom. But a full belly didn't make him sleepy, as it often did. He tossed and turned for a while, then put on his chiton again and went back downstairs to the courtyard to wait for his father. He could tease him about how drunk he was and boast of the lovely ray Philodemos had missed.

Everything was dark and cool and quiet. Sikon and the other slaves had long since gone to sleep. Blowing clouds drifted past the moon, hiding it more often than not, though the rain still held off. A nightjar flew past overhead; its croaking call put Menedemos in mind of a frog. An owl hooted in the distance. Even farther off, a dog barked, and then another.

Menedemos yawned. Now that he was out of bed, he felt like getting back into it. Laughing at himself, he started toward the stairs. Then he stopped in surprise, for someone else was coming down to the courtyard.

Seeing his motion, Baukis stopped in surprise, too, right at the foot of the stairway. "Who's there?" she called quietly, and then, as the moon came out from behind one of those clouds, "Oh. Is that you, Menedemos? I was going to wait for your father."

"So was I," he answered. "We can wait together, if you like. We'll keep each other awake—I was getting sleepy out here by myself."

"All right." Baukis walked over to the bench in the court-yard. "Aren't you cold in just your chiton?" she asked. "I'm chilly, and I've got a mantle on."

"Not me," he said, sitting down beside her. "You can always spot a sailor in a crowd. He'll be the barefoot fellow who never bothers with a himation. The only reason I take a man-tle aboard the *Aphrodite* is to use it for a blanket when I sleep aboard ship."

"Oh," she said. That owl hooted again. Another cloud slid in front of the moon. She looked toward the entrance. "I won-der how long it will be before Philodemos comes home."

"Probably a good while yet," said Menedemos, who had considerable experience of symposia. "Xanthos isn't the type to order a strong mix to the wine, so people will have to do a lot of drinking before they get properly drunk."

"And before he brings out the flute-girls and the dancing girls and the acrobats or whoever else he's hired from the brothelkeeper." Baukis' voice stayed quiet, but she couldn't keep a snarl from it.

"Well, yes." Menedemos knew he sounded uncomfortable. "That's what men do at symposia."

"I know." Baukis packed the two words with devastating scorn.

Any answer would have been worse than none. Menedemos didn't even shrug. The moon came out again. Its pale light showed Baukis angrily staring down at the ground between her feet. Something small skittered, over by the an-dron. Her head swung toward it. So did Menedemos'. "Just a mouse," he said.

"I suppose so," she said, and then, hunching her shoulders a little, "I *am* cold."

Before he thought, he slipped an arm around her. She sighed and slid closer to him. The next moment, they were kissing, his hands stroking her hair, her hand caressing his cheek, the soft, firm flesh of her breasts pressed maddeningly against him.

And, the moment after that, they flew apart as if each found the other red-hot. "We can't," Baukis gasped.

"We don't dare," Menedemos agreed. His heart thudded hard in his chest. "But oh, darling, how I want to!"

"So do—" Baukis tossed her head. She wasn't going to admit that, perhaps not even to herself. She changed course: "I know you do, dear Mene—" She tossed her head again. "I know you do. But we can't. We mustn't. The scandal! I'm trying to be—I *want* to be—a proper wife to your father. And if anyone sees us . . . If anyone saw us . . ." She looked around in alarm.

"I know," Menedemos said grimly. "Oh, by the gods, how I know. And I know it isn't right, and I know—" He sprang to his feet and ran up the stairs, taking them two and three at a time even in the dark, careless of a stumble. He shut the door to his room and barred it, as if to lock temptation away. But it was there inside with him, inside him, and now that he knew it dwelt in his father's wife, too. . . .

He lay down again, but he didn't sleep. Quite a while later, Philodemos came home. Baukis greeted him as if nothing at all were wrong. Menedemos knew he would have to do the same in the morning. It wouldn't be easy. He also knew that, knew it all too well. From now on, nothing in the world would be easy.

HISTORICAL NOTE

THE SACRED LAND is set in 308 B.C. Menedemos himself is a historical figure. Sostratos and the other members of their families are fictional. Other real people who appear in the novel are Ptolemaios' brother Menelaos, Areios the kitharist, and Hekataios of Abdera. Historical figures mentioned in the novel but not actually on stage include Ptolemaios; Antigonos; Lysimakhos; Kassandros; Philip of Macedon's daughter, Kleopatra; King Nikokreon of Salamis; and his victims, Stratonikos the kitharist and Anaxarkhos of Abdera.

Hekataios of Abdera's account of the Jews survives, though just barely. Diodorus Siculus quoted him fairly extensively in his universal history, written in the first century B.C. That part of Diodorus' work does not itself exist in the original, but was in turn excerpted by the Byzantine scholar-patriarch Photios in the ninth century A.D. How closely Photios' excerpt of Diodorus' excerpt of Hekataios' work resembles the latter remains a subject of scholarly debate, and it obviously will never be answered in full without a miraculously fortunate papyrus find. Hekataios worked in Egypt. He probably did not in fact go up into Palestine itself, but a novelist is entitled to bend history a bit now and again.

As usual in this series, I've spelled most names of places and people as a Greek would have: thus Lykia, not Lycia; Kassandros, not Cassander. I've broken this rule for toponyms that have well-established English spellings: Rhodes, Cyprus, and so on. I've also broken it for Alexander the Great and Philip of Macedon. The two great Macedonians dominate this period even though Alexander was about fifteen years dead when *The Sacred Land* begins. Also as usual, translations from the Greek are, for better or worse, my own.